MW01225312

THE SERAPH'S PATH

Neil Dykstra

Book 1 of *The Seraph*

Copyright © 2019 Neil Dykstra
All Rights Reserved
Version 1.3
ISBN: 9781670157140

To My Daughters.
So that you will never be without one of my stories.

TABLE OF CONTENTS

ACKNOWLEDGMENTS

Thanks to Julia VanDelft, Martin VanWoudenberg, and Matt Dykstra for editing; Kassidy VanOene for cover art; Clayton Tait for map art.

PROLOGUE

N 2 Taephin, 1348[1]

I am leaving this note in my makeshift study in the event that I perish on my journey.

My name is Avareon, house Atlan. I am a young man, an aspiring scholar, of the kingdom of Tauril. That kingdom is no more. I have seen its destruction with my own eyes.

Its kings have long been faithless, though the same could not be said for all its people. The rulers made alliances with godless nations, defiled themselves in worship to foreign emperors, and sullied their hands with the blood of innocents. They had been warned by many prophecies of their impending destruction. Yet they persisted in their wickedness.

The empire of Kardumagund devoured the tribute that Tauril sent it, while secretly building a massive army to conquer it. At the head of these armies, four captains were set: men who gave themselves up to the dominion of evil Seraphs who granted them unnatural power, invincibility in combat, and a will to prevail over beasts and men.

Oh, if Arren would only see fit in his infinite wisdom to appoint one of his own, a deliverer who would lead his people to victory over the forces of darkness. Many, including my uncle, who was a prominent noble in the kingdom, hoped that they could fight the invaders until such a thing came to pass. But it was for nought. Arren did provide one to deliver them, but not in the fashion they expected.

---

[1] Saturday, September 7, 1348 (see the appendices for the calendar and dating system).

Eldorin was his name. He was of the ruling house of Teren. He was blessed by the Servants, those good Seraphs who helped the men of old. He was granted the sword that flamed, the Crillslayer, though he did not openly wear it or use it. His task was difficult. He was to prepare a fleet of ships to escape this land and go into exile. All who were faithful to Arren were called to depart with him, to abandon their homeland. My cousin was one of the few who listened to him.

Eldorin was branded a traitor by the king. Before he could depart on his ships, he was imprisoned within the capital as the war waged on. But my uncle, who was sympathetic to Eldorin's cause, devised a ruse. He and I came to visit Eldorin in prison, and in the privacy of his cell we exchanged our clothes. Eldorin escaped, took command of his fleet, and left these lands with a remnant. I remained behind, content to know that my short life was, at the very least, used for the service of Arren.

In the following days, Tauril was utterly defeated and crushed. I was ripped from my cell and forced to assist the invaders in cataloguing the deaths of the entire royal family. That is how they found out that Eldorin had escaped. In a baffling act of mercy, one of their captains, who called himself Kharon, permitted me to retrieve what I wanted from the Royal Library, and set me free.

As a scholar, I wept when I beheld all of the knowledge within the library that would soon be put to the torch. I had a singular focus in my salvage: the writings of Melandar, the man who sinned and repented, who recorded history, issued prophecy, and laid down laws. Long ago, he led the people over the great river to safety when threatened with destruction. He is the father of the ruling House of Teren. He is my own ancestor as well, through adoption. I retrieved as many of his writings as my arms and satchel could carry.

Then the floor caved in under my feet. Great rumblings were heard outside. Explosions ripped through the city. I crawled through an opening to find a ghastly sight. The entire city, indeed, the entire land, was aflame. Molten rock flowed hither and thither. Pools and ponds turned into geysers of mud. The mighty river was now a bubbling cauldron. The sun was blotted by ash. I do not know how

I survived. Perhaps I would have died if it had not been for my companion, a stranger who accompanied me through days of hardship. He is my source of courage, though I still do not know his name.

I was pursued. Though very few survived the conflagration, the Captains of Kardumagund were not so easily overcome. One of them rose from the ashes and came after me. As I arrived at the ruined stronghold of my uncle, my companion engaged him in combat and defeated him while I escaped into the caves beneath.

I did not find the body of my uncle. Yet I found his last words, sealed within these caves. With sufficient supplies, I stayed here in this cave for some time, resting. I decided I could not carry all of Melandar's writings with me if I was to escape this land. For that reason, I sat down in this place to compile them. I arranged them into three volumes. The first, *Of the Events That Shaped Mankind*, is all of his histories. The second, *Of the Nations of Mankind*, concerns law. The third, *Of the Promise for Mankind*, is a collection of prophecy. These I took with me. You will find here, left behind, the original writings of Melandar, and my notes.

I am striking out for the realm of Azenvar. There I hope to find refuge. I have not seen my companion for days. I hope he is all right.

I thank Arren for my companion. I thank the Servants that Melandar's writings have been preserved. I praise the Most High for his deliverance of a remnant of Tauril under the leadership of Eldorin. May His purposes always come about.

Avareon son of Aveter House Atlan

CHAPTER 1:
THE DREAM

Dyrk raised his tawny-haired head and peered into the cave. The familiar murky gloom stared back at him. He unshouldered his backpack and looked behind him.

"Come on, Gavon, you're always lagging," the twelve-year old boy berated his younger brother. "You always get tired so quick."

"That's just because you're bigger than me," Gavon answered with his characteristic lisp, huffing and puffing. The age difference was only two years, but Dyrk was easily the larger of the two.

Dyrk took flint and steel from his belt pouch and began to strike it together. "When I was your age, I could run down here in a half an hour," he derided as he worked.

"Sorry," Gavon said, catching his breath. "I could go faster if I didn't have to carry these heavy rocks." He gestured to his backpack.

"Yeah, well I'm carrying rocks too," Dyrk said, finally getting the torch to light. "And all of the torches, and the provisions, and the weapons."

"Can I have my weapons yet?"

The older boy gave an exaggerated sigh. "I guess so. But don't break your arrows like last time. We may need them." He unstrapped two makeshift bows made from willow branches and twine from the back of his pack. He handed the smaller one to Gavon. He counted the arrows that were in the pack, dividing them up as he did. He gave Gavon four, keeping eight for himself.

"Okay, Gavon, remember what Januz said about the monsters in here," Dyrk began to lecture like he was an experienced adventurer. "Since we're going to be exploring parts we've never been in yet, we've got to be careful. We'll take turns carrying the torch. Whoever isn't carrying it will walk behind and kill anything that moves!"

"I'm ready. Can I hold the torch first?"

Dyrk passed the flaming torch to him. "Don't burn yourself."

The older boy made sure his knife was within easy reach, and then notched his best arrow into his bow. They moved into the cave. A sense of exhilaration overcame Dyrk yet again, like it always did when he explored these caves. He felt he couldn't live without it every once in a while. The feel of danger, of unknown, and of doing something that his parents most seriously expressed that he not do.

The cave was an old mine shaft cut into the side of a hill. It had been boarded up years ago, but that didn't stop the boys. Their father knew about it, and he had told them in no uncertain terms that it was dangerous and not for their amusement. But the town drunk, Januz, had regaled the boys with tales of great riches, and hideous beasts, that could be found in the mine. Their eyes sparkled with every word, and their temptation overcame their good sense.

Dyrk had been in the caves several times before. He had the first few turns memorized. His strategy was to leave a trail of coloured rocks to mark his progress. This would mark the route by which they could find their way back. At first, he armed himself with a wooden sword. Recently, with the help of Nabir the farm's bondservant, he had made a bow out of a stout willow branch and twine. His first creation wasn't very good, so he had passed it on to Gavon and begun a second. The final product still wasn't very effective, but it was a wonderful plaything. They made several arrows by sanding some sticks and sharpening the tops. Dyrk's father had helped them fletch chicken feathers onto the blunt ends. If either Nabir or father knew what they were doing with their makeshift weapons, hunting imaginary monsters in the old mine, the boys would be in big trouble.

Oily smoke irritated Dyrk's eyes as he trailed a step behind and to the left of Gavon. They passed through the tunnels for about a hundred paces before Dyrk asked for a halt.

"Time to start marking our passage," he said. "We're entering a new part we haven't explored yet. I'll hold the torch now."

Gavon handed him the source of light. "Do you want me to make a pile of rocks right here?"

"Always in the passage that we came from," Dyrk said.

Gavon made a small pile of reddish-coloured stones, ones they had gotten from the cliff near the stream. None of the rocks in the caves were coloured red, so they expected their path would be easily distinguishable. When he finished, Gavon took his bow out and put an arrow on the string.

"Let's go," he said.

Dyrk started down the passage he had selected. The roof there dropped until it was only a half a foot above Dyrk's head. The floor was smooth, not covered in rubble like much of the other tunnels were. They had to watch their footing when they found the floor had been moistened by a small rivulet coming from a fissure. Around another corner, the tunnel branched again. After Gavon marked their passage with another pile of rocks, Dyrk chose the passage that sloped down the steepest.

Then Dyrk suddenly stopped. "Did you hear that?"

"What?" Gavon drew the arrow back.

"A low rumbling. Shhh!"

They stood silent for a moment. Dyrk didn't hear the sound again. Maybe he had imagined it.

"Okay, let's keep going, but stay on your guard."

"All right."

They passage ahead twisted and turned even more, reminding him of a cow's intestine. As Gavon walked in front of him with the torch, Dyrk had an idea. He noticed that Gavon could always see things before he could. Maybe it was because he was looking into the torchlight while Gavon's eyes were ahead of it.

"Let's try it the other way around for a change." he said.

"Not so loud," Gavon whispered. "Monsters can hear too."

"Don't tell me what to do, runt."

"You calling me a runt? At least I can shoot."

Dyrk stood up tall. "I'm in command of this quest anyway, so you'll listen to me. Let's try it with the torchbearer behind."

"Why?"

"Are you dense? I can't see because I'm getting blinded by the torch in my eyes."

"If I'm so dense, why didn't you think of this before?"

Dyrk was losing his temper and raising his voice. "Just shut your mouth and let's go before we're ambushed."

The sound of a large rock hitting the ground nearby made them both recoil in fright. Dyrk's bow went off, the arrow just missing Gavon's head as it deflected off the roof. Gavon spun to flee the other way. He tripped over something and fell. The torch hit the wall of the cave and was snuffed out.

A high-pitched scream escaped Dyrk's lips. He didn't care if he sounded like a girl. He was really frightened. Turning to run towards the cave entrance, he could not get his bearings in the dark. His hands in front saved him from serious injury as he collided with the side of the cave.

The pitch blackness was very conducive to panic. He frantically felt around to find any exit, but it was near impossible. He heard something scraping against the rock. Backing up, he tripped over something and pitched backwards onto the cave floor. He fell onto a smooth sloped surface and began to slide. He tried to find a handhold, but there was none. He slid faster and faster, down a narrow crevasse. As he fell, he hit his head on something leaving him dazed. At the end, the crevasse dumped the frantic boy into a shallow pool of cool water.

Dyrk stood up, his head throbbing, and turned back to the way he came. The water only came up to the top of his shins. He immediately tried to get up the same way that he came down, but it was impossible, the sides of the crevasse were much too smooth. He groped his way around the cavern until he came to an edge to the water. Sobbing with fright, he crawled out of the water and sat on dry rock for a few minutes.

He listened carefully as he was resting in the blackness. No other sounds reached his ears. Was that a monster that they had encountered? If it was, he didn't hear it now. Nor did he hear Gavon. He was totally lost, without light, deep in the caves. How would he get out? And, much worse, how would he explain this to his parents?

He slowly got up. He told himself that he had to stay calm, to think with his head and not with his hands and feet. He resolved to move slowly, to avoid other mishaps like the one that had gotten him here. He groped around in the darkness on all fours until he found a wall of the cavern. Keeping one hand on the wall, he made his way to his left. He began to make progress, but to his disappointment that he was sloping downwards, further into the mountain. Just as he was about to turn back to search for an upwards path, he thought he saw the slightest glimmer of light. Drawn towards anything by which he could escape the oppressive darkness, he carefully made his way further down.

He was sure that there was light, now. He could make out the sides of the tunnel which were quite smooth. Quickening his step, he stumbled on some loose rubble. The sounds of the rocks clattering against the floor shattered the silence like an avalanche. He shrunk into a ball against the side of the tunnel, staying very still and listening. He proceeded again only when he was absolutely sure that nothing had heard the noise.

He cautiously peered around the corner. He was shocked when he beheld the source of the radiance.

A man stood there, glowing with a faint light. He was tall and muscular, with shoulder-length black hair and brown skin. He was clean-shaven, but Dyrk had trouble making out the facial features due to the brightness. He wore a long flowing garment of white wrapped around him, his bare feet protruding from the bottom. His eyes, looking straight at the boy, were a shimmering blue, and it felt like they pierced him to his very being.

Strangely, Dyrk felt no urge to run. Instead, he stepped into the light. The eerie gaze held him, and one arm that until now was folded at his chest spread forth. Words were being spoken, but he couldn't understand them. Vaguely it registered on him that the language spoken was Melandarim, a formal and ceremonial language that was taught to students. It was used in writing legal and religious documents, but rarely spoken in conversation. Dyrk didn't focus on the words. His eyes were fixed on the sword that the man held out to him, hilt first.

"Who are you?" he heard himself ask, his own voice sounding

insignificant.

Again words flowed past him, into his ears but not registering in his brain. Only at the end, as the sword was lifted to him, did he comprehend the final statement. "Now take this, as a symbol of your calling."

The apparition held out the sheathed blade. At first Dyrk was hesitant to take it, his traditions dictating that only a soldier may touch a sword. But he felt compelled. He grasped the hilt which was wrapped in red cloth.

At once the man disappeared, and Dyrk was plunged into darkness again. He tightly held the sword in his hands and for the next minute only listened to the sound of his heart thumping in his ears. A sword. Tradition dictated that he was not supposed to touch one, but it had been given to him. By someone. Maybe it was a Servant of Arren. It had to be! That meant that he could have it! The Servants had authority over traditions.

He was startled back to reality by a sound in the distance. It was the sound of rocks striking each other. He felt his panic return, lost in the depths of the earth one again. *I am definitely dreaming*, the thought finally came to him. Relief flooded over him. Of course he was. This was all preposterous. Glowing men with swords in an abandoned mine. Even the thought that he would so rashly disobey his father by coming into the mine in the first place reinforced his conclusion. *I am still in my bed, safe and sound. Mother is going to wake me soon. Another day on the farm will start.*

Another sound came to his ears, this time resembling fingernails scraping across the rock. This may be a dream, but the fear he felt was most definitely real. He put his right hand on the hilt and felt surprisingly comforted. He drew the blade from its sheath. Red, angry light erupted forth, and a blast of heat overcame him. He almost stumbled to the ground but caught himself in time. Holding the sword at arm's length so as not to burn himself, he stared in wonder.

Red flame engulfed the short blade from the crosspiece to the point, tongues of fire leaping and playing. As he swung it through the air, flames trailed behind and crackled in the stillness. The heat on his arms was uncomfortable, but he wasn't burned. At least not yet.

Noise reverberated around him. This time it sounded much closer. Dyrk turned to his left, holding the burning blade to the side to keep its brilliance from blinding him. His blood chilled as he saw two points of red light. Rasping of breath could be heard above the crackling of the sword. It moved into the light, a large, misshapen form that only vaguely resembled a man. It was over eight feet tall, its skin a hideous green with many sores and boils all over it. Its short fingers ended in wicked-looking talons. In one hand it clutched a huge hammer, dragging along the ground behind the creature. Spittle drooled down its jaw, which seemed too wide for its face, filled with jagged teeth. Its eyes were the most frightening of all, swimming with a red glow that was completely unearthly. It stopped about ten paces from him, staring at the frightened boy.

One part of him had to laugh at the absurdity of it all. Wouldn't this be a tall tale? It sounds like Januz, the town drunk, was right after all. There really was a troll in the mine. Januz had seen it with his own delusional eyes. And now a flaming sword to boot! Despite not having drunk a drop of alcohol in his short life, Dyrk could now be numbered with the addled and scrambled. At least this was a dream, while Januz swore the truth of his claims day and night to whoever would waste their time listening to him.

Yet his body was still seized with fear. It would not respond to the pleadings of his mind to treat this all as ludicrous. What if this was real? He was too young to die. Didn't Arren have some sort of plan for him that was meant for greater things than a troll's dinner?

A voice erupted from the creature, with clarity that could not possibly be produced from the monster's misshapen mouth. "Where did you get that weapon, little boy? It is not something for you to be playing with. Give it to me."

Shivering with fright, Dyrk at first couldn't even say a word. Finally his voice came in a pathetic squeak, "It was given to me, and you aren't going to have it."

Time seemed to slow, yet the speed and ferocity of the fight blended into a blur that left no room for coherent thought. The creature ferociously attacked with sledge and talons. Every time Dyrk was about to be struck, the sword jumped in his hands and parried the blow. Fire issued forth from the blade from time to time, scorching the beast. Once the fire flew into its face, and it clutched its head in agony. Dyrk drove the blade into its unprotected abdomen, slicing through as if it were butter. No blood issued from the wound, grievous as it was. Then Dyrk turned and ran. The sword lit the way as he went. He thought he heard sounds behind him as he hurried up the passage. He did not slow until he reached the pool.

There he stopped to catch his breath. He listened for anything that could be coming after him. There was only silence punctuated by the occasional drop of water. He sat on a rock and gathered his wits about him. What was that creature? Had he killed it? What was he to do now?

A low rumbling began to echo through the cavern. He lifted the burning sword again, ready for whatever would come against him. Small pebbles began to rain on him, and dust filled his nostrils. The ground began to shake. What was happening? A boulder crashed to the floor just at the edge of the sword's light, and various other debris was tumbling from the ceiling. Splitting pain suddenly erupted in his head, and he remembered no more.

CHAPTER 2:
DOLETH SARIN

The earth smelled fresh and new after the night rain. It was one rain he could do without, Dyrk thought as he shifted uncomfortably in his saddle. His night had been cold and miserable, and still his clothes were damp and clammy. Only the rising of the midsummer sun brought him some relief, its rays gently warming him even in the early morning.

He wondered what his family was doing at that very moment. Mother probably wasn't even up yet. Father was likely in the circle track, breaking in that yearling that he thought might make the best warhorse he ever produced. Gavon would be on his way to his lessons, continuing his advanced instruction in reading and writing in Melandarim by Arene the scribe. His three young sisters would be combing the coop for eggs, or weeding the garden, or perhaps Mother would just let them play. Elzabi, their foreign Zindori bondservant, was cutting the first hay, wielding that huge scythe with long, powerful strokes. Nabir, their elderly Derrekh bondservant, still had trees to cut and wood to split. Some of the fences needed rebuilding after being washed out when the creek flooded. Nabir's son Hagris was lame and spent most of his time cleaning the stables. Nabir's wife Karam might be taking a break after the early morning baking, playing with her infant granddaughter to free up Gozen, her daughter-in-law, to hang up the washing.

All that, of course, was assuming none had noticed his escape. That was doubtful, since he was supposed to be back last night before sundown. He hoped they did not look too far or wide for him. They would not catch up with him for some time, since he was already a good half-day's ride from Tanvilon.

He was going to the Rhov-Attan, the Midsummer's Feast[1] of the year 2794. Three times had he experienced it in the past, when his father was healthy enough to make the trip all the way to Doleth Sarin to take part in the festivities. But over the past two years, his father's maimed foot had bothered him more than ever, to the point that he would spend entire days doing little more than hobbling around.

But now Dyrk was twenty years old. He had grown much in the past two years, finally exceeding his mother in height. Using the Veranian measure of feet, he was just over six feet tall, the average height for a Karolian male. He had not yet filled out his lanky frame, but his father assured him that it would come in time. Too soon, his father had joked, referring to his own slowly expanding midsection. So far, Dyrk had not been able to grow facial hair. The scraggly stubble that sprouted had to be shaved occasionally in order to keep him presentable.

---

[1] This religious festival falls on Tuesday, June 11, but festivities carry on for the entire week.

The day of Dyrk's passing into manhood had happened last fall. His father's gift on that day was the very horse that he was riding upon. It was a fine young warhorse that was named Tanakh, which was the Melandarim word for Thunder. Dyrk had spent much time helping his father in training the horse. But it was much too fine of a horse for him to buy from his father. Why, the beast would fetch a small sack of gold from a buyer who knew fighting horses well. When his twentieth birthday arrived, his father fulfilled the usual coming-of-age gift by granting his son the beautiful stallion.

Father had forbidden him to attend the Rhov-Attan that year. This had angered Dyrk immensely. Every year, each headman in the province was permitted to select a young man who had just come of age to be his squire at the Rhov-Attan and compete in the Contest of the Squires. Headmen were important local officials that administered local justice, policing, and basic military training of the citizenry. Each ward, or group of about five hundred people, were overseen by one headman. In order to be eligible for appointment as a headman, one had to be trained as an Eratur, at the Eratur's College. The word Eratur was Melandarim for a "kingsman", which referred to a class of elite mounted warriors who were also trained in the matters of leadership and administration. They were held to a high standard of integrity and personal conduct. Most Eraturs took up the position of headman after serving in some royal capacity for twenty or thirty years, often as an officer in the military.

Thur Madwin was the headman overseeing the small town of Tanvilon. He was rather young for the position, around the same age as Dyrk's father. He was every bit the image of an Eratur: tall, broad-shouldered, with a full head of hair and finely trimmed beard. He looked older than he was, given the streaks of grey in his hair. He kept a stiff posture which communicated alertness and aloofness at the same time. His piercing blue eyes were his most potent weapon among the boys he mentored. Dyrk, along with other boys his age, were required to spend a few days per month in his service, starting at age sixteen. Sometimes they trained for battle, in formation or individually. Sometimes they laboured in public works for the village or were assigned to help a needy family. The Eratur would also teach the young men how to sing, a tradition that was no doubt strange to outsiders of the kingdom. Each time the boys were with Thur Madwin, the headman would keep a close eye on each one to find out which showed the most promise to become an Eratur like himself. That took more than just combat prowess. Eraturs were expected to be wise, gracious, and of exemplary character.

Thur Madwin had shown favour to Dyrk over the other boys his age. Madwin had expressed that, if it were not for Dyrk's father's command, it would be Dyrk who would be competing at the Rhov-Attan, not Breven. Dyrk's friend Breven had been excited about the possibility of competing at the Contest for the single yearly appointment to the Eratur's College, granted by Lord Cassius himself. Several more of the entrants would eventually be selected to enter the College, but special honour was given to him who won the Contest.

The world seemed to be passing Dyrk by until the unfortunate accident last week. Breven was thrown from his horse and broke his leg. Left with few choices, Madwin had declared that none would accompany him, rather than make a hasty decision on one of the remaining boys, none of whom showed the promise of Dyrk and Breven. Dyrk was very sympathetic to his friend Breven but saw that his chance had come. He made plans to escape from home and travel to Doleth Sarin in time for the festival, there to find Madwin and hopefully become his squire.

There was still a hurdle to overcome. Dyrk did not know exactly how he was going to convince Thur Madwin, since the Eratur knew of his father's prohibition on his attendance of the festival. That did not concern him at the time, his thoughts were now on the field of battle. He imagined the feel of the warpole in his left hand, and the blunted shortsword in his right. He had never touched a sword before, only in that strange dream he had while he lay unconscious in the mine eight years ago, before he was rescued by Madwin and his father. He had never even seen his father's sword, which stayed locked in the chest in his parent's attic, along with the suit of armour that had never come forth. If it were not for Madwin's confirmation, and his father's war stories, Dyrk might never have believed that his father had once been an Eratur, grievously wounded in the bloody Battle of Rocavion.

His mother Loriah always cringed when his father, Maryk, regaled the heroics of the frantic three-day ride to Rocavion, only to be ambushed by enemy Vekh marines who took them by surprise. After killing a Vekh infantryman, which Maryk relished describing in detail, his warhorse was taken out from under him by a halberdier. A vicious slash to his foot nearly severed it between the ball and heel. After some battlefield surgery, nothing was left of Maryk's foot but a misshapen stump below the ankle.

It always struck Dyrk that an event so traumatic could be recounted without much pain. Perhaps it was the passing of time. After all, it had happened shortly after Maryk and Loriah were married.

The distance passed under Tanakh's hooves with ease, Dyrk's mind being elsewhere. He had taken some of his savings in a small bag on his belt. It had brass and copper coins which were the most common form of money in Karolia. A silver coin for emergencies was sewn to the inside of his tunic so that robbers might not find it. A hunting knife was at his side, a little shorter than the maximum length at which it would be considered a blade and therefore illegal for a non-soldier to carry. A small satchel at his waist held some dried fruit and jerked meat which he partook of occasionally. A change of clothes was packed into his saddlebag, but he didn't want to use them until he reached town. His riding clothes would have to do until then.

He passed many people on the road, most of them heading the same way that he was. Some were driving horse or ox carts loaded with goods, usually covered with a canvas so that Dyrk could not make out their contents. Many of the drivers scowled at him, and armed men who rode with them kept hands near their weapons as he passed. Dyrk forgave their uneasiness, for he probably did look like a young brigand riding an expensive stolen horse.

A few carts even had entire families in it, no doubt heading to the festival. Other travelers were on foot, some with large bundles on their backs. A few like himself rode on horseback. The mounts they rode were a little smaller than Tanakh, looking like old nags in comparison.

Normally a war-horse wouldn't be ridden casually cross-country like Dyrk was doing, but Tanakh was no ordinary war-horse. Cross-bred with Belorin stock, his father had produced a breed that took advantage of the endurance, range, and speed of the steppe breeds. "Show breeds", his father often scoffed at the Karolian war-horses. "They look great in a parade, but give me a raw-boned Belorin mare in a fight."

The forest had thinned out a league-tenth[1] ago, and now the land on both sides of the road was a mixture of pasture and tilled land, with small stands of trees interspersed. The road upon which he rode was made of hard-packed gravel, with occasional patches filled with larger rocks to allow water to drain. Bridges crossed the streams, built generously high to allow for spring floods that would otherwise wash the bridge out. A row of stones on each side marked the edges of the road for when snow fell in the winter. Sometimes these rows turned into stone walls, as nearby farmers cleared stones from their fields and left them at the sides of the road. The road was built wide enough to allow room for two military supply wagons to pass by each other, the wagons being each drawn by two teams of horses. This was the Great East Road, a critical artery of the kingdom.

The closer he came to the city of Doleth Sarin, the more the mood of his surroundings seemed to lift. The traffic increased, making it necessary for carts to use the middle of the road while those on foot and horseback stuck to the dirt and grass shoulder. Nearby residents had hung blue and white banners, flags, and ribbons on their houses and gates to mark the occasion. When he passed through a small village, he could hear flutes and harps playing, and children laughing. Several merchants who did not wish to brave the crowds in the city had set up their stalls there, crowing

---

[1] A league is about a day's easy foot travel, or 16 miles, or 26 kilometers. A league-tenth is an hour's easy travel, 1.6 miles, or 2.6 kilometers.

at the travelers to quickly buy what they could now before they faced inflated prices within the city.

Ignoring them, Dyrk pressed on. He wished to reach the city before nightfall. There likely wouldn't be any lodging in the city for the prices that he could stomach, so he wished to find Thur Madwin as soon as possible to avoid sleeping in the streets. He had only a slight idea of where to look, but that did not worry him. His main concern was what he would say when he finally did find him.

The road topped a large hill, and the view opened up before him. The heartland of Karolia was extensively populated, and very little land was left unclaimed. This was in sharp contrast to the area around Tanvilon, in which the rolling hills were mostly untamed and wild. Men could carve out their fields and dwellings where they saw fit, always with permission of the Headman. The lands back home were not nearly as fertile, though. The soils were rockier and did not hold moisture well. But below him now, on the floodplain of the Elgolin, there grew orchards of fruit trees, fields of wheat, corn, and vegetables, and rows upon rows of berry bushes and grape vines. In the cold months snow only occasionally fell in that part of Karolia, which allowed for winter grain and vegetable crops as well.

Passing through another small village, the gravel road ceased, and the roadway was paved with close-fitting flagstones. Tanakh's metal-shod hooves clattered loudly amidst the cacophony of the other travelers, at times throwing up sparks. Delicious aromas of cooking meat drifted from some of the buildings, mixed in with the smell of fresh strawberries, always abundant at Midsummer. Dyrk's stomach rumbled, and instead of buying some overpriced food from the vendors or inns he munched on some jerky from his satchel. He passed by a group of three Eraturs, resplendent in their dark blue cloaks embroidered with silver threads. He stared unabashed at their horses, assessing them with his father's occupational eye. Fine they were, but they came from the stock of province Thoral. While they were slightly taller and wider at the shoulder than the breed Dyrk's father raised, he knew that Tanakh could run a greater distance than any of these and still be in fighting condition afterwards.

The walls of Doleth Sarin were visible now. While only a fifth of the city was actually inside the walls, they were still maintained out of tradition. No plans for new, larger walls were in the works, defences all but forgotten among the peace and prosperity of that part of Karolia. The setting sun had peeked out from behind the clouds and was now almost directly behind the city, shining into Dyrk's eyes. He could now make out the tent city that arose whenever a festival took place in the city.

A few beggars sat at the side of the road, rags or hats laid before them into which passing travelers could cast a coin. Their faces were to the ground in shame. In Karolia, any man who was honourable enough could sell themselves as bondservants to the Lord of the province for seven years when he was destitute. There the lord would provide for him and his family in exchange for labour. But some did not wish to work for another, perhaps out of fear of the loss of their freedom. Because of the system of bondservitude, beggars were reviled as the lowest of society. They were looked upon as personally responsible for their own plight. They rarely spoke a word to those that passed by, since it was against the law for a beggar to solicit a pittance. Many kept their hands from view, to conceal the evidence that they were runaway bondservants themselves. Marks were inscribed on the back of the hand to designate the owner of a bondservant, which faded over the seven years of the pledge.

At first, Dyrk ignored them as he was told by his father. "Those who do not help themselves, should not in turn receive help," he remembered his father quoting from the Teachings of Melandar. But still he felt a tug of compassion for the impoverished.

After all, I'm disobeying my father already, he said to himself. He picked two small copper coins from his money pouch and tossed it into a cloth spread in front of a dark-skinned Zindori. The man bowed his head further toward the ground in thanks, then scooped the coins up and hid them in his ragged clothing. As Dyrk passed, he saw out of the corner of his eye the face of the man as he raised his head to look at his benefactor. The face was drawn and thin, with hollow cheeks, but he could not have been much older than Dyrk.

Trying to forget the emaciated image, he kept his eyes forward. Tents spread before him on either side of the road, some large and opulent, while others were small and tattered. Most could not afford the high prices of the inns at a festival like that. Dyrk had found that staying a few nights in tents at midsummer was a pleasant experience if one ignored the overcrowding. He hoped that he could find Madwin before nightfall, or he would be forced to sleep outside the city, possibly paying a tent owner a brass or two to let him and his horse stay for the night.

Dyrk knew Madwin well, better than most of his peers. There was a special, but rather unusual, bond between Madwin and Maryk. They regularly sought each other out, at festivals, gatherings, or even random evenings. Yet they didn't drink and joke as most men did with their friends. Instead, they seemed to commiserate, as if they had both shared some great loss. Dyrk had at first guessed that Madwin had also fought at Rocavion, but later he learned that it was not the case: Madwin was still at the College when the skirmish broke out.

As the eldest son, Dyrk received the lion's share of attention that Madwin paid to Maryk's children. Given that Dyrk had never met any of his extended family, he considered Madwin the equivalent of an uncle. Because of the closeness, Dyrk had been mystified when Maryk had forbidden him to come to the festival. His mother had been similarly resolute. Madwin had never explained it, though he had seemed unsurprised.

He was nearing Doleth Sarin. Dyrk's resolve and confidence began to erode as the city sprawled before him. The lanes and roads were choked with people going about their pre-festival business. How could he possibly find Madwin in all that? He put on his cloak again, not for warmth but more for the comfort that the weight gave to his shoulders. The fact that the cloak was well-made would also make him seem less like a farm-boy. Despite being from a remote rural village, Dyrk was from a well-off family. His father was one of the best breeders and trainers of war-horses in the province, if not the kingdom. They lived in a beautiful two-story stone house and could afford fine clothing and imported delicacies. He had no reason to feel inferior to anyone.

The tents gave way to permanent buildings, and soon other

streets criss-crossed the main roads. While only a fifth the size of the nearby capital city of Altyren, Doleth Sarin still amazed Dyrk with its size and grandeur. Twenty taverns it boasted, no doubt all would be full at that hour. When father came to the city to sell some of his horses, he had sometimes taken Dyrk with him. There seemed to be no end to the services that were provided, from cobblers to stonemasons, weaponsmiths to wainwrights, tanners to weavers. Usually father would also buy many supplies there, for the prices and selection were much better than they were in Tanvilon or Rovenhall from the traveling merchants.

Once again, Dyrk was bombarded by the delicious smells coming from the nearby houses. His mouth watered as he thought about a hot meal. He pressed on. Food could wait, finding Madwin couldn't. Pushing his way through the throngs in the street, he kept his cloak tight around him.

The street dipped sharply. Ahead of him, it descended down the side of an embankment. He was passing through the Upper City. Below was the Lower City, and beyond that, up another escarpment, stood ancient walls in which was encased the Old City. At the edge of the Lower City, a place was cleared for great shows and competitions. Clefts cut into the earth of the embankments on either side were used by spectators, which permitted a great many to get a good view of the action below. At the moment, the field was a bustle of activity, with preparations of the coming festival which began tomorrow with a parade.

Dyrk made his way through the busy streets, heading towards the Old City. Coming to one of the gates that permitted access, he passed a few guards that appeared to be more interested in their conversation than the passers-by. But before Dyrk could get past, one held his hand out to him to stop.

Dyrk reined his horse to a halt. The guard stepped down from his guard post. "Only Lords and Eraturs may ride within the walls," he commanded. "You'll have to get off and lead your mount, boy."

Dyrk obeyed without a word, and the guards returned to their idle talk. Inside, the buildings were quite a bit higher and more solidly built than the rest of the city. They often featured four stories.

Some were elaborately decorated and expensively furnished. Everything was cleaner than the rest of the city. Traditionally, the Lord of each province was supposed to be allotted a modest home, roughly equivalent to that of a craft-master. However, in recent years, the Lords of the land tried to outdo each other in building extravagant residences. The stone steps and marble colonnades that formed the front of Lord Cassius's residence were anything but modest.

Several guards stood on duty, looking a great deal more alert than the ones at the gate. Dyrk approached one of them, reins in hand.

"What be your business, young lad?" the guard said, relaxing his grip on his halberd. "If it's something inside, you are going to have to wait until tomorrow, after a bath and change of clothes, I might add."

"Good soldier, I hate to trouble you," Dyrk used his best manners. "I am a messenger from Scribe Arene of Tanvilon. I seek Thur Madwin who is here for the Rhov-Attan. Could you aid me in finding him?"

The guard gave a nearly imperceptible smile. "Messenger? I say, boy, you look more like an outlander who has stolen his master's horse. Let me see your hand."

Confidently, Dyrk held out his right hand, palm down. No mark was visible on the back of his hand.

Unruffled, the guard stroked his beard as he thought. "Your best chance to find him would be to go to the Squire's Tap, but I'm sure they won't let you in, especially looking the way you do right now. It's near the North Gate."

"I thank you, kind soldier," Dyrk said politely. It never paid to needlessly provoke a soldier. The scales of Kemantar always tipped in a soldier's favour.

He turned Tanakh around. The north gate was only two streets away, and he found the tavern without difficulty. Only a few horses were tied up at the side, and Dyrk paid the boy who watched the horses two copper pieces, one more than the usual. "An extra copper is worth a five-crown horse," his father always said.

At the door, he was forced to wait as an armed guard concluded a conversation with an Eratur. Dyrk kept well out of the way as the Eratur exited the building. He tried to enter the tavern, but the guard's hand against his chest stopped him.

"Ho there, young lad, what do you think you're doing? You would be a little out of place here. Blades only." The guard was saying that only soldiers and Eraturs were permitted inside the taphouse. Karolian law stated that no one else was allowed to carry a sword.

"I'm looking for Thur Madwin," Dyrk said. "Could you get him for me? It's an important message."

The guard laughed. "Messages can wait, especially from youngsters. You can't find anyone else to blow your nose?" he chortled. "Anyway, he's not here."

Dyrk felt his cheeks go red. "Can you tell me where I might find him?"

"I'd sooner send you back to Lord Cassius's labour-masters where you belong. Get out of my sight."

A blond, bearded Eratur had approached the door. He wore an ornate breastplate over an embroidered tunic with long sleeves. A gold medallion hung from his neck, denoting him a Headman.

"Of what nature is this message, courier?" the Eratur asked. "Is it of grave importance?"

Dyrk was at loss for words for a second. "It is of a personal nature, and therefore is of minor importance," he said. "The messenger who normally makes the trip to Doleth Sarin had taken ill, and I am not familiar with the city."

"You can likely find Madwin at the fairgrounds," the Eratur said. "Though he expressly told me that he did not wish to be disturbed for quite some time. He is trying to train a squire at last minute." He gave a wry smile. "I suspect he will have quite a difficult time."

With a quick gesture of gratitude, Dyrk took his leave. He began to panic. Another squire? How had Madwin gotten another boy from Tanvilon? He hadn't heard of anyone leaving with him! Who could it be?

Upon turning the corner into an alleyway, his knees ran into something, causing him to trip. He heard an exclamation of surprise.

Dishes and cutlery clattered to the ground.

Dyrk picked himself up immediately. He looked back to see what he had stumbled over. It was an old man, dressed in threadbare clothes and only a few patches of gray hair left on his head. Slowly, the man uncurled himself from the ground, looking pitiful.

"Very sorry, dear friend," Dyrk apologized, then turned to go.

"Sorry?" the man burst at his back. "Sorry doesn't keep my belly from growling, you miserable country imp. You overturned my meager dinner like a chamber pot, and now you saunter away like the Lord's consort? Both my legs could be broken and you let me lie in a pool of my own blood to die like an irritating bug you've squashed with your palm. Worms and maggots, the heartless-"

Dyrk had reached his horse and was untying the reins. He turned and interrupted the tirade. "I've said I'm sorry, old man, and I'm in a hurry. You don't seem hurt to me."

"Vekh could be covering the hillsides and still a good man would be civil. Your mother must have been Zindori, and your father a melon, for you to have such manners."

Dyrk bristled. He felt like knocking the man down again, but he held his hand. "I see no need to scorn my parents. I do believe that you've never met them."

"I don't have to. You stink like an Ogre enough for me. Go on, ride off, and leave a poor old man to his death. You've got much more important things to do, after all."

Dyrk bit his lip. The man was right, and he knew it. Though he wanted so badly to find Madwin, common decency was more important. He stepped away from his horse. The old man had still not gotten up. Dyrk reached out and grabbed the man's arm to help him up.

"Ouch!" he wailed, "What are you trying to do, rip my arm off? I've only got two of those, flea-bitten and boil-ridden as they are."

"Sir, I am only trying to help you up." Dyrk said patiently.

Grumbling endlessly, the man was finally put back onto his feet. Dyrk then offered him two brass coins for him to buy another meal. The man at first refused, but at Dyrk's insistence finally took it.

Only once the old man was satisfied did Dyrk leave, leading his warhorse. Twilight had come by the time he passed through the gate again. He made haste towards the fairgrounds, which now were bare save for a few slowly moving lanterns. He rode past the spectator's boxes that had just been built, festively decorated for more prestigious audiences. Several sawhorses had been moved into the middle of the arena, now arranged to form an oval in the middle. But nobody was there. Dyrk walked Tanakh through the field, looking and listening, but he was alone.

A light rain began to fall, the first drop falling squarely on his nose. The gloom and wet complimented his mood. How was he ever going to find Madwin? Did that blond Eratur send him off with a lie? Were all the sword-bearers in the Squire's Tap swilling their beers and laughing at the stupid country lad who they had so easily fooled? Even the old man was probably howling to himself after humiliating him.

He turned Tanakh to leave, not even spending any effort to think of where to go next. What was he thinking, that he could even find Madwin, much less convince him to take him as his squire?

A lone horse and rider appeared from the darkness between two of the viewing boxes. The horseman had his hood pulled up because of the rain. Dyrk felt a twinge of fear. The hooded man was coming straight for him. *What could he want from me?* he thought. Dyrk turned his horse aside and gave it a nudge to start it walking. But after a few steps, the rider held out a hand, palm outwards.

"Stop there, son of Teren," the voice seemed eerily familiar. He had been called by his house name. House Teren was the royal house, descended from the king of Tauril long ago. Dyrk was, therefore, distantly related to the king. Very distantly.

"What do you want with me?" Dyrk asked. Tanakh had stopped, though not by his command. "I've done nothing wrong."

"Yes you have," the voice said, and a hand came up to remove the cowl. "You've come here against your father's wishes, haven't you?" The face was handsome and finely chiseled, a thin moustache and goatee were black, peppered with gray like his temples. For the first time Dyrk noticed the medallion visible at the man's chest through the open cloak.

"Madwin!" he exclaimed. "Thur Madwin! Forgive me for any disrespect. I did not know it was you."

"Indeed," Madwin said, his face showing a wry grin. "It was not difficult for me to recognize you, a backwoods lad out of place in this city. A place he no doubt does not belong."

"I've been searching for you, my Headman. They said you would be down here."

Madwin's hands rested on his saddlehorn. "Apparently you have an important, but personal message for me. What, pray tell, is so important that you must deliver it in person, rather than send Therv the messenger, who is in good health, no doubt."

Dyrk floundered for words, his carefully prepared speech falling to pieces now that he had found his quarry. "I- I learned that Breven had suffered an injury. I knew you to be without a squire. I know that coming to the Fair without a squire would be, well, it would not look very good." He drew a long breath. "You always told me that I would make the best squire out of the boys my age, so I thought that you might, ah, wish for me to be your squire during the festival."

Madwin's face remained expressionless except for the curl at the corner of his mouth. "Don't you think, Dyrk, that if I wished for you to be my *jadweir*[1], that I would have asked you?"

"N-, no, because my father told you-"

"That you were not to come to Doleth Sarin, correct." Madwin finished the sentence. "Of course I could not ask you, and go against your father's wishes."

"But-" Dyrk cut himself off, thinking better of it.

"But what? Out with it lad, before I send you back to Tanvilon this minute!"

Dyrk gulped. "You see, Thur Madwin, I was thinking that, especially at my age, why should my father be making decrees as to my way of life, that he would shape it for me? Is it not written in the Teachings of Melandar that each man should prove his own way? Sons shall not languish in their father's poverty, nor shall offspring

---

[1] "Jadweir" is Melandarim for apprentice. It was often used to refer to squires at the Rhov-Attan.

live in comfort off the prosperity of their parents. Why should he deny me at least a chance to march in the Parade of Glory, and fall in the Contest of the Squires? I know myself that I am the equal to Breven. I would not prove dishonour to you."

Madwin hesitated. Dyrk was sweating in spite of the chill that the rain brought. He longed for his cloak that was bundled in his saddlebag.

"Well said," Madwin spoke. "Though I am loath to defy your father's wishes, it is true that I have seen in your exceptional horsemanship and courage. Being that Eraturhood, or even squireship, requires more than just skill and strength, I have also seen that you have taken well to your studies under Arene and myself, and can already speak and sing with honour. But being a *jadweir* requires doing what is honourable, a task that you were close to failing."

"What do you mean?" Dyrk asked, surprised.

"He even had to remind you to do what was honourable before it would enter your mind," the Headman answered.

The old man! "But my lord, he was scolding me with childish words, so that I did not see it fit to-"

"A Eratur will help everyone, even if it is his enemy," Madwin cut him off. "No matter how demeaning it may seem. We are here to serve, Dyrk."

The youth bowed his head. "I am sorry. I was not thinking straight." So Madwin was in the Squire's Tap all along! The whole thing had been a test! "How did you know I was coming?"

"I was hardly not expecting you," Madwin gave a sharp laugh. "You are too headstrong to be kept away from the action."

"So you will allow me to be your squire?" Dyrk asked, excited.

Madwin raised his hand. "Not so fast, son of Teren. Like I said, I would not quickly transgress the words of your father." He paused for a moment while Dyrk stood there, nervous and confused. "I will permit you to be my squire under the following conditions."

"Anything, my lord, anything you ask."

"First of all, you will not be entered as Dyrk son of Maryk of House Teren, but rather as Breven son of Wolben of House Teren.

You may keep your house colours. Second, you are not to tell your real name for the duration of the Parade or the competition. Finally, once we return to Tanvilon, you are to tell your father that I did not permit your entry into the festival, but rather I forced you to wait in the tent. Is that clear?"

Dyrk nodded vigorously. "Thank you, Thur Madwin. I won't disappoint you."

CHAPTER 3:
CONTEST OF THE SQUIRES

The Rhov-Attan was one of seven festivals that were spaced out in the Karolian calendar. Their religion was based almost wholly on the Three Books of Melandar and the truths found therein. It spoke of seven Servants, good Seraphs sent by Arren to minister to the people in the early days. Melandar's calendar was built on a system of seven months, each with seven weeks of seven days. The days of the week and the months of the year were named after these Servants. In order, the names were Kemantar, Anakdatar, Harophin, Valeron, Telmanitar, Taephin, and Nedrin. Each Servant had their own realm of influence, and their festivals followed the theme. So did each priestly order that formed beneath each of the Servants except Nedrin. Valeron, for example, was known as the Wandering Servant, and governed the air, the skies, the sun, stars, and moon. His festival, the Rhov-Attan, was close to the summer solstice, the time of greatest sunlight, and celebrated the coming of summer. His priests were cartographers and astronomers. They were responsible for determining the shortest day of the year, which began the new calendar year[1].

The Rhov-Attan was Valeron's festival, occurring during the fourth month of the year. Only the Rhov-Attan and the New Year celebrations were truly provincial affairs, while the other festivals featured smaller local gatherings. During that particular festival, there were many contests, sporting events, and other entertainment. The climax was the final chapter of the Contest of the Squires, in which the winners of the earlier races would battle on horseback to

---

[1] For more on Arren and the Seven Servants, see the appendices.

win the coveted admission to the College.

Dreams of fighting in that glorious battle were brought to a sudden halt when Madwin woke him from his sleep the next day. He had spent the night in Madwin's room at the Squire's Tap, sleeping on the floor in front of the cold fireplace. Exhausted from the day's activities, he had fallen asleep without thought of food. Now his hunger was the first thing he felt as he roused himself.

He smelled fresh baked bread. The room wasn't as large as he would expect in an expensive city inn, but it was comfortably furnished. A bed large enough for two was laid with cotton sheets and a down-stuffed quilt, and looked very comfortable. A small desk and chair were against the wall directly under the large glass window, curtains spread wide to allow the early morning sun. Against the wall near the bed sat a familiar heavy trunk, similar to the one in his father's attic. A stand close to the door had a washbowl and pitcher. Madwin was looking into his reflection from a burnished silver plate hung on the wall above the stand as he shaved his sideburns. Dyrk spied the tray of food on the small table in the corner of the room. He quickly pulled his trousers on and headed for the food.

"Morning petition?" Madwin inquired from where he stood, rinsing the razor in the basin. While unadorned, the Eratur's dark green shirt was made of some exotic fabric that Dyrk had never seen before. Madwin had always dressed well, but not ostentatious. This contrasted with some of the other Headman that Dyrk had seen in the city. "Valeron deserves your thanks. The sun didn't rise on its own," Madwin continued.

Feeling a little ashamed, Dyrk returned to his pallet and took out the bundle of small blank papers that most citizens kept. In his excitement on waking up in a place such as that, with the anticipation of the day to come, he had forgotten his religious duty. With a charcoal pencil, he quickly wrote out the lines of the verse. It was custom every morning to address that day's Servant with a memorized petition. It was thought that Arren was too great, too wonderful, too incomprehensible for simple humans to address him directly. Today was Valeron's Day[1]. The petition thanked the Wandering Spirit for bringing the sun back to where it rose. It then asked for guidance in the lives of the faithful, just as the stars guide a wanderer in the wastes. Dyrk neatly folded the paper four-fold and placed it into the small wire basket just above the flame of the lantern that was on the table. The paper flared, blackened, and crinkled, a tiny curl of smoke rising and taking his petition to heaven. The ashes added to an existing pile at the bottom, evidence of Madwin's past petitions.

When he had finished the fresh bread and a half bowl of strawberries that had been left for him, he returned to his saddlebags and took out his clothes that he had been saving for the festival. A white cotton tunic, worn but twice, with a dark woolen vest with copper buttons to go over top. But before he could put it on, Madwin stopped him.

"You would roast in that, boy." He handed Dyrk another tunic of the strange material, coloured grey. "Try this. And discard the vest. You want as little as possible underneath your hauberk and mail."

Mail! Why hadn't he thought of it? Of course! He would be wearing armour during the parade. And it was a necessity during the Contest, for even with it many a squire was carried off the field with injuries. He gratefully accepted the garment, surprised when he touched it for the first time. It was so incredibly smooth that he could not resist running his hand along it again after he put it on. It felt very thin, yet strong.

"Made from the cocoons of worms in Corsava," Madwin informed him. "It's called silk. It's very expensive, so I expect it back after your few days of distinction."

Once he was ready, the Headman led him from the boarding house into the early morning sun on the street. Though the day had just broken, many people were about already. The festival would start at midday with the March of Glory, to celebrate the longest days of the year. There were still many preparations to be done.

---

[1] Wednesday

They scaled the steps of the government building, entering through the front. Dyrk gaped in amazement at the magnificent statues and beautiful relief carvings upon the walls. Tapestries and hangings covered surfaces not already adorned. The floor was of alternating plates of white and purple marble. But he had little time for sight-seeing, for he was rushed through a side door.

They took a stairwell down to the basement. Unlike the hall above, the surroundings down below were plain and utilitarian. Four guards gave them a nod as they passed by and through a large double door, open wide. Many others were there, obviously for the same purpose. After a short wait, a clerk sitting at a desk greeted Madwin by name, and with a flourish of a pen admitted them in.

The large room that they had entered was covered on all sides with a latticework made of wood. Torchlight was required to supplement the limited daylight that came through high, barred windows, and the flames reflected off hundreds of items of leather and steel. All were carefully cleaned or polished and hung upon the lattice. They were not alone in the room. A handful of Eratur-squire pairs were doing the same task as Madwin and Dyrk.

Madwin selected for Dyrk four small pieces of chain mail, two steel pauldrons, and a layered breastplate made of hardened leather. At first Dyrk lifted the heavy breastplate to put it on, but Madwin stopped him. "Ease off the spurs, young one. We will get dressed back in our room. I would, however, like you to try on one of those for size." He pointed at a broad shelf piled high with light, long-sleeved quilted hauberks. They had leather straps protruding from their shoulders and arms. Dyrk found one that fit him snugly.

Dyrk waited as Madwin also picked out some greaves, made of light leather with steel splints on the outsides of the legs. Two light, blunted swords were chosen, stored in bright blue scabbards to indicate that they were sporting weapons. Finally, a visored helm was fitted with two small red plumes to complete the array. Dyrk looked at the twin plumes with pride. He was to be in the parade bearing the colours of the Royal House of Teren! He was thankful that he could at least keep his house name, even if he was to be entered as Breven son of Wolben, who was actually of house Huric.

"No plate for you yet," the headman mumbled. "You wouldn't be able to move in it." He clapped his hands. "All right, you're done. Back to the inn to get these on."

Dyrk could barely carry all the armour as he stumbled his way up the stairway. Madwin didn't carry anything. He seemed to enjoy making Dyrk struggle with it. Back at their room, the armour was laid out on the floor.

"Remember, you will first assist me in dressing just outside our tent. It's part of the spectacle. After that, you will go inside the tent and dress yourself. At least that's how it's supposed to be. There will be a servant in the tent who will help you get dressed, because we can't have embarrassments." A slight grin played across Madwin's moustache for a moment. "Nevertheless, we should go through both of our kits now for practice."

"The struggle with armour is the balance of protection with comfort and breathability," Madwin spoke without looking at Dyrk. He took off his dressing-robe and stood there in his silk undershirt. Most curious was that it was long-sleeved, had a tall neck, and descended well past the waist. Standing there in nothing but hose and the undershirt, Madwin looked a bit silly, like a cat without its fur.

Madwin gestured towards a stout chest that was sitting against the wall. Its decoration was quite different from the rest of the room, which suggested that it was Madwin's personal belongings. Opening it, Dyrk saw at the top a quilted hauberk that was similar to the one Madwin picked out for him, but far more ornate. There were many attachment points, with leather straps, along the arms and sides upon which the other armour pieces would be secured.

"Do as much as you can while standing behind or beside me," Madwin directed. "If you have to be in front of me, kneel or crouch." Dyrk thought for a moment, then stood at Madwin's left while he held out the left side of the interior of the hauberk. He slipped behind to the other side and lifted the right side for the other arm to enter. Finally, he began to do up the clasps in the back, hands trembling a bit.

"Too tight is worse than too loose," Madwin instructed. "I'd rather have my armour fall off than be pinched part way through the parade."

The hauberk fit Madwin's torso exquisitely. Madwin showed him several pieces of chain mail that would normally come next; one around the waist, one around the neck, and one on each shoulder. "On parade I don't expect to be shot," Madwin stated dryly. "I'd rather have the extra breathing room. No doubt Kur-Ethiakh will be happy to have a few less pounds to carry around." The waist-piece could not be discarded, though. Dyrk struggled with its weight.

The two-piece breastplate came next, front and back. Burnished pauldrons, greaves, gauntlets, and boots completed the attire. The weight of each piece surprised Dyrk, and he couldn't imagine how Madwin could move with all of it on at once.

"Your mount is responsible to move you," Madwin responded to his unasked question. "Your strongest blows, they come not from your own strength, but from the momentum of horse and rider."

Dyrk lifted the helmet out of the chest. It was fitted with plumes of black and dark blue, colours of Madwin's House Ithniar. "At the end, don't put my helmet on," the Eratur instructed. "Hand it to me from my left."

Dyrk helped Madwin undress, and then the roles were switched. First the hauberk, then the waist-piece. Dyrk was also exempt from the chain around his armpits and neck, for now. Despite it being made of leather, the breastplate felt suffocating on Dyrk when it was fastened around his torso. He felt twice his own size. *If only the boys at home could see me now*, he thought. *Thur Madwin is cinching my armour on me.*

Just then Madwin viciously yanked the left pauldron so tightly that it pinched Dyrk's shoulder. He gave a yelp, reaching in vain for the strap that was driving the steel cuff into his flesh. Madwin stood back, watching him writhe in pain, a look on his face similar to a father watching his son learn a hard lesson. Finally, Madwin reached over and uncinched the offending strap.

"That would completely disable you if it were to happen during a fight," he lectured, "or a parade. Remember that when you're dressing me tomorrow."

Dyrk flexed his sore shoulder. Madwin reached out and, without a word of warning, pushed him over onto his back. The floorboards resounded with a great crash as the young man hit the floor and gasped for breath. After a few moments, he tried to get up but couldn't. He felt like a crab that had been placed upside-down, flailing helplessly while his enemies prepared to feast on his soft underbelly.

Madwin patiently showed him how to roll on his side and get up on all fours. Just to be certain he had it figured out, Madwin put his foot to the back of Dyrk's knees and had him repeat the ordeal. Further instructions came on how to wear a sheathed weapon without stabbing oneself or sitting on it.

Dyrk wondered how many more hard lessons the headman had in store for him.

Though many parts of Dyrk's adventure had been much different than his expectations, the parade was not. Three hours of wearing suffocating ceremonial armour and brightly covered overcoats in midsummer's heat was about as exhausting as he had guessed. To top it off, the Eraturs rode on their horses while the pitiable squires walked in front. It was exciting, though, to be part of the exhibition for once instead of a spectator. True, he knew that few were looking at the squires, trudging ahead of their master's mounts. The Eraturs, resplendent in their finest battle-gear, were the star of the show, at least for the ladies. The children preferred to watch the jesters and merry-makers. The men mostly used it as an excuse to start drinking early in the day without the disapproval from their women or their parading headmen.

The next morning started with a whirl of activity. All their gear had been left in their tent at the fairground, guarded carefully during the night by watchmen. As they made their way from the inn to their tent, Dyrk was surprised at the busyness. Everywhere they went there were people, people, people. To a country boy who grew up in a backwater village of a few hundred, he felt like a fish out of water.

Once they arrived at their tent, Dyrk began to sort through the gear to make sure it was all there. He arranged it in the right order to prepare for dressing. He put on the cloth hauberk over his silk undershirt. Then he went out to Tanakh, housed in a temporary stable.

"Good morning, *istran*," Dyrk said, using the Melandarim word for "fellow soldier". "Had a good sleep?" He brushed out the war-horse's mane and continued lightly on the flanks. Tanakh had been given grain, but he had not eaten it until Dyrk arrived, something peculiar to the Belorin instincts in the horse.

"We've got a big day ahead, you and I," Dyrk continued to speak to his horse as a friend. His father had drilled it into him that horses, while they don't understand words, read their master's tone of voice as well or better than an eavesdropping busybody maid. "I may be just a country boy, but I've got the best horse in Saringon," he crooned. "We're going to show them."

Back in the tent, Dyrk tried to quell the butterflies in his stomach. His nervousness was beginning to make his hands shake. He was only hours away from riding with the Contest of Squires. The memories of yesterday's parade were still fresh in his mind. Only now the crowds would be looking at him rather than Madwin. He took up the practice sword that Madwin had given him yesterday. It was quite unlike the one he had dreamed of in the mine. This one was heavy and cold, with no markings on it. He knew that the edges were rounded, for safety's sake. Squires were hurt every year, and sometimes even killed in the Contest, and real edges had been removed many years ago to cut down on the casualties. He was surprised at how much he remembered the feel of the sword hilt in his hand during his childhood vision.

Madwin entered the tent behind him, resplendent in his Eratur's cloak and the breastplate of his armour. His helm was tucked into the crook of his elbow, and his other hand rested on his sword hilt. He was every bit a symbol of the honour and glory that Karolians had bestown upon their gifted men. But Dyrk noticed that a frown was on the Eratur's face. Puzzled, he was about to speak when Madwin cut him off.

"I have bad news, young one."

Dyrk's heart sank. "Am I not to compete? What-"

"No, my squire, of course you are to compete." Dyrk breathed a sigh of relief as the Eratur continued. "Several of the other Eraturs have expressed their concern over your mount. They feel that I gave you that horse and therefore are disqualified. As much as I assure them that it is your own horse, they have insisted that you ride another."

"Tanakh! But he's my mount! I've been-"

Madwin cut him off again with a wave of his hand. "Do not speak against what an Eratur has said," he reprimanded. "I understand you are close to Tanakh, but this is the only way that you will compete. Like most squires, you have been assigned a horse, and it is being brought."

Dyrk was crestfallen. That was his advantage over all the rest, the only way that he saw he could possibly win. Dyrk, after all, had little combat training beyond his occasional sessions with Madwin. He had a bond built with Tanakh that enabled him to pilot the horse with subtle signals from his legs or voice.

But as much as his heart was broken to be without his horse, it would be more crushing to be removed from the competition. His resolve to compete and at least fall on the field in honour was too great. He heaved a disappointed sigh and said resolutely, "So be it, my headman. They cannot take away my spirit, after all."

Madwin smiled. "That's what I like to hear. Show respect to your fellow squires out there, and always do as the Eraturs or even Lord Cassius says. And do remember what I've told you: don't use your name."

Dyrk nodded. Madwin peered out the flap of the tent. "Your horse is here," he said. "It is already saddled. I do suggest you get familiar with it."

The brown gelding that Dyrk was to ride was a far cry from Tanakh. Its height and girth were nothing in comparison. This horse looked more like a lady's riding mount than a combat horse. Dyrk removed his gauntlets. He touched the horse's neck, feeling it shudder under his bare hand. He recognized that the horse was frightened, probably by all the steel that the Eraturs were wearing.

He continued to stroke the neck and head. The horse smelled his other hand.

After getting the horse used to his presence and smell, he turned to Madwin. "I must go for a ride without armour first," he said. He put his leg in the stirrup and vaulted into the saddle in a slow but continuous motion, not wanting to frighten the horse. *A good deal more fright you will receive later*, he thought.

The horse became more responsive and less afraid as he rode. But when it tried to go in a direction that Dyrk didn't, he pulled sharply on the reins and dug a heel into its side. Though he knew that he would never have the time to get the horse comfortable in the time allotted, he knew that he must establish who was the one in charge.

"I will call you Rothai, the Replacement, for you have taken Tanakh's place," Dyrk said quietly. He focused on using what little time he had left as best he could.

The low drones of the battle horns echoed over the field. The sun was at its apex in the sky, making it uncomfortably warm for all the young men in their armour. At the cue from the Eratur at the fore, the column marched on foot into the field. Sixty sets of twin plumes displayed a variance of colour, each denoting the respective house of the squire. Each held their warpole, a lightweight lance, upright. A small piece of cloth was fixed below the point, bearing emblems of the squire's sponsoring Eratur. As the two columns of squires reached the middle of the field, they split apart and gathered according to their respective houses, facing the Lord's seat in neat columns. The trumpets continued their droning in the background as they stood, sweating in the hot sun. Cheers arose in the crowd that remained to watch that portion of the festival, the Contest of the Squires.

The horns abruptly stopped their droning, and as one the squires dropped to their knees as Lord Cassius arose to address them. Before speaking, the nobleman stepped down from his dais and approached the line. He had taken off the lavish robes that had been worn in the parade, and now wore a gold-colored breastplate, emblazoned with a flaming eagle. The rest of his clothing was bordering on gaudy to Dyrk, who was not normally exposed to the rich tastes of aristocrats. The lord's helmet had been left behind, and his bald head shone under the midsummer sun.

"Young men of Saringon," he began with a deep, booming voice that carried far. The entire crowd hushed immediately. The lord said roughly the same thing every year, yet the dramatic oration still electrified the audience. "You are before me here as a representative of all my province. In fact, you also are a likeness of Karolia itself, standing here in the image of Melandar and even as delegates from the Seven Servants."

The crowd cheered, but the young men remained frozen in their kneeling positions.

"Do you know what that means?" Cassius thundered. "Do you realize what is on your shoulders? Do you understand that whatever you do in your life will subject the rest of us here to judgement?" At that Cassius lifted his arms to indicate everyone who was listening. "Our lives will be weighed by what you do! Because you are the strongest, bravest, hardiest, and, above all, kindest of the young men of this province. Therefore, you will travel difficult roads on behalf of all who stand here. The deeds you will accomplish will be shared by all, just as your defeats will be felt by all. And if you should fail, know that the many of whom you bear upon your shoulders will fall as well, with their suffering upon your head.

"If there is any of you who cannot accept this, the time has come to declare it. All those whose knees quiver, whose lips tremble, and whose heart is faint, you will now take a step back, and enter into the safety that the others will provide. But for those who know that it is their calling to serve Karolia, its God and its people, make it known! Declare it before those gathered here as a pledge. And in whatever capacity you may have, may it be lords, headmen, Eraturs, craftsmen, or even tillers of the soil, you shall be Karolia's men, leaders every one of you, and all shall look up to you. Now, declare!"

In unison, the squires stood up from their position, hoisted their warpoles, and took a giant step forward. They all shouted, "We declare before Karolia, before the Seven and the people!"

Cassius drew his sword and bellowed, "May the Contests begin!"

The horn began their fanfare again. As Cassius turned and walked back to his viewing chair, the column of armoured young men turned and marched in a circle, forming a broad ring in the middle of the field.

The Contest of the Squires happened in every province of Karolia, though the nature of the Contest itself varied considerably. In Saringon, the first round of competition was akin to a horse race. An oval track would be set up, marked by bales of spring hay. Just behind the starting line a single fencepost would be pounded into the ground in the middle of the track, on top of which would be tied a loop of ribbon. The winner was the one who could catch the ribbon on his warpole as he thundered past on his horse. The squires were welcome to use their poles and blunted swords to dislodge the others from their mounts. Any who touched the ground would be disqualified. If the first-place squire passed by the pole without catching the ribbon, they would continue around the track for another try. To keep the speed of the competition high, the trailing squire at an unsuccessful pass would be taken out of the competition and disqualified. Many a time the competition was won by attrition, the winner being the one who was left after all else are disqualified. Ten squires would compete at a time, and each would always get at least two races.

After sixteen winners were selected, all that were still physically able to continue would proceed to the final combat on the last day of the festival. The squires would be loosed into a small round field, where they would fight with pole and blunted sword to unsaddle their opponents. The last one mounted would be declared the winner and be granted entry into the College of Eraturs.

Other contests were held at the same time for other ages. Archery competitions, wrestling, sparring, hold-the-line[1], and even foot races would take place in the three days of the festival, though none having

---

[1] "Hold The Line" is a team sport in which players have to dislodge opponents from a narrow beam without falling off themselves.

the same ramifications as the Squire's Contest. The entire three days were also punctuated by dances, feasts, and various entertainments. The most loved events were those that took place under the roofs of the taverns at night. For there, by the light of lanterns and fireplaces, would the Tellers perform. Regular citizens over the course of the year would band together and choose an ancient story to tell at one of the festivals, and they would practice the drama and dialogue in secret. Some of the best had made an occupation out of it, and those would go into the employ of the King. When the King chose to bless a province by sending his Tellers to a festival, the people had a treat indeed. This year would have no King's Tellers. Nevertheless, the local townspeople still had the ability to put on quite a show.

The Lord's Crier stepped into the field from his seat near Cassius. In his deafening shout that qualified him for his position, he announced to the audience in Melandarim, "Behold, ye people of Saringon, the sons of your strength! Behold, ye people of Karolia, the daughters of your beauty!"

Dyrk stood motionless in his place in the circle, waiting for the drums to begin their pounding rhythm. Karolian society had little mastery or appreciation of instrumental music and timbre. Though the Eraturs were all trained as singers, society in general preferred oratory to vocal performances. Dances were typically performed only to the beat of drums and other percussion instruments.

Dyrk had seen the Dance of Maidens twice before, but now it would be happening right in front of him, and with him as part of the group of squires that were the primary benefactor. The drums began, and two long rows of girls dressed in purple and light blue proceeded in haste to surround the young men in an ordered, pulsating circle. Onto the sleeves of the dresses was sewn a large triangle of cloth that extended to the hips, purple on the left and blue on the right. The movement of their arms caused the material to flutter into view. Done in unison, the entire procession treated the crowd to dazzling flashes of opulent colour.

As the deeper, lower-pitched drums began to crash into the rhythm, the dancers swayed up and down, in and out, this and that way, but always in symmetry with their partners, and always in step with the beat. As he was standing stock-still, the entire group of girls passed by Dyrk's vantage point several times during the dance, which was a veritable feast for the eyes to a young man.

With the exception of a few of the leaders, all the girls that took part were eighteen years old. For men, the process for coming of age was quite complex – at seventeen they were eligible to apprentice. At twenty they were eligible to enter the King's Service, as Eraturs-in-training, soldiers, students at one of the colleges, or simply entering the royal labour force. After three years' service, they were eligible to own land and marry. Then, once they had satisfied all four conditions of citizenship – age twenty-five, completed King's service, a land-owner, and married – they became a full citizen of the kingdom with all its rights, privileges, and responsibilities.

Women, on the other hand, had a much simpler route to adulthood in Karolia. At eighteen, they were eligible for courtship. At twenty, they could get married. At thirty, they were officially ineligible for citizens' marriage, and thereafter could only enter into a civil marriage or remain single. The options for single women were limited, as they were barred from most colleges and trades. In general, the way up for them was to marry well. And that started here, at the Midsummer's Festival.

Compared to the teenage girls back at home, these young women seemed more confident, more graceful, and more skilled. Later, Dyrk realized that his first impression was based on a rehearsed, choreographed performance and not at all on real life. Along with the other squires, the girls with unusual hair colour and redder complexion caught his notice more than the dark-haired girls with grey skin.

The squires in their open helms had been instructed to avoid direct eye contact with any of the girls lest they make them stumble. It was clear that the dancers were under a similar rule. Yet Dyrk couldn't help but notice some of the girls stealing furtive glances and brief smiles at the boys. Dyrk's eyes began to dart back and forth among the moving shapes within his field of vision, hoping for some forbidden attention.

He got exactly what he was looking for.

She wasn't difficult to remember, but not because she was especially attractive. In fact, she was shorter than most of the girls, with long braided hair the colour of unpainted pottery. A fine dash of freckles covered her face. Her skin tone was unremarkable, her eyes dark brown. What Dyrk noticed most was a look of intense concentration, of a girl who was giving everything she had to perform a challenging task, and yet she was basking in the exhilaration of having conquered it. He noted that her facial features were generous and full, not thin and fine like those of the most popular girls. Her body was not particularly slim, lithe, or graceful, but in contrast with the rest was more mature and developed.

She caught his eyes looking in her direction, breaking her look of concentration long enough to flash him a smile, accompanied by a lowering of her eyes. Dyrk immediately felt his colour ride; he chose a cloud low on the horizon on which to fix his gaze until the event concluded.

Following the dance, setting up for the Contest took little time. A half-score of men carried sheaves of hay to the middle and arranged it in a long oval. Another man used a stepladder and sledge to pound a tall fencepost into the ground in the middle of the track, until the top of the post was six feet above the ground. On the top the man tied a single loop of bright ribbon, an unassuming little string that would be the goal of all sixty young men. The ten squires selected for the first race were already trotting out onto the field, to the adulation of the crowd. Perhaps as many as five thousand were watching, the sheer number of the audience boggled Dyrk's mind.

Several Eraturs were also on horseback in the ring, and they would serve as judges. Though there were few rules, the stakes were high, and cheating could not be permitted. One raised a white banner as his horse tramped nervously. The squires lined their mounts up with the banner, across the track. The fencepost was only ten feet behind them, so they would have to circle the entire track once before making an attempt at the ribbon.

The white banner fell to the ground. Immediately there was a churning of hooves, clanging of steel, and shouts of young men.

Two were thrown from their mounts almost instantly, and it took some time before any of them could break from the melee to race down the track. A blue-and-white plumed rider led the way, slashing with his blade at a second who was close behind. They rounded the near side of the oval, and the leader lowered his warpole to catch the ribbon. But just before he could do so, the trailing squire leaned far forward, and struck with his sword, cleaving the pole in two. Both galloped past the post, neither able to make an attempt at it. The crowd cheered them on.

Two revolutions later, the squire with the blue and white plumes rode his last opponent into the bales of hay, throwing him from his mount. As the noise of the audience reached his climax, he slowly rode to the side, took an intact warpole that someone handed him, and calmly scooped the ribbon on the end of it. He trotted to the seats from which the maidens watched, lowering the pole to one of the prettiest ones in the front row. Beaming from ear to ear, she undid the ribbon from the pole and tied it in her hair, blowing kisses at the squire as he rode away.

Dyrk had scanned the girls, trying to find the one that had smiled at him during the dance. The more confident girls had made their way to the front row, where they were more likely to be selected by a victorious squire. He found the one he was looking for in the top row, near the side. She was laughing and clapping like the rest of them, but she had made no move to attract the victor's attention. Compared to the other girls, though, she was rather plain, and his eye was drawn to others in the front.

"Nay but a few of us will get to drop them a bow," a voice said from beside him. "And it likely won't be either of us."

A dark-haired young man in armour similar to his own leaned his elbows on the fence just as Dyrk was doing. He was at least three inches shorter than Dyrk, with a mop of brown hair. His thin face and thick eyebrows made him look old, but the sparse stubble on his chin belied his young age.

"Can't say that 'till we try," Dyrk responded. The squire's plumes were grey and blue, colours of House Vaneth. Dyrk had the colours memorized, long days in Scribe Arene's instruction chambers reciting the Sixty Houses of Karolia.

"Which would you give it to?" the boy asked. Not waiting for an answer, he pointed towards the girls. "I'd take the third from the right, on the bottom. She's a beauty. I don't know her. she must be from the northern towns."

Indeed, the blonde girl had beautiful, straight hair, with a single braid wrapped around her crown. But with his mother and sisters being blonde, Dyrk didn't quite have the same attraction to blonde hair as others did. "Do you know the one to the left of her?"

"Junia is her name. Daughter of a cloth merchant here in Doleth Sarin. A nice catch, I must say. She was in the ward next to mine, I've spoken with her a past festival or two."

"What about the second from the left in the top row?"

"The stout one?" Dyrk winced at the ungentlemanly term the boy used to describe her. "Oh, right, I remember. Her father is a cartwright, and not a very good one, I might add. My father's done business with him. She's from Harwaith, just west of Doleth Sarin. She's had weak health ever since she was young. I'm surprised to see her here. I think her name was Meriah, or Neriah, can't recall which."

As the two ogled the girls, the next group of squires lined up. Only the roaring of the crowd brought the boys' gazes back to the action. Clashes of steel arose immediately, and the terrified whinnying of a mount which had lost its footing. Horrified, Dyrk saw the horse fall to the ground, crushing the squire beneath it. The race continued around the squire as he lay prone, the horse struggling to get back onto its feet. Quickly two Eraturs rode up and dismounted. One took the horse's bridle while the other freed the limp youth from the saddle. They cleared the track just before the group of remaining riders charged through the starting line again.

"Do you think he's still alive?" Dyrk was incredulous, his stomach flip-flopping inside him nervously. "That was a nasty fall."

"If he is, he's not going to be walking again for some time," the squire said. "By the way, the name's Kureth. House Vaneth, Fifth Ward in the Upper City. What's yours?"

"Dyrk, house Teren." He didn't mention his ward or hometown.

There was only one ward in Tanvilon, anyway. He had already forgotten about his deal with Madwin to not use his real name.

Kureth smiled. "Ah, from the kingly house. May it cause the face of the Servants to shine upon you, my friend. Otherwise you may end up like our colleague out there. Are you from Doleth Sarin? I don't remember seeing your face in the city before."

Dyrk shook his head. "I'm from out of town."

Both became silent as a third joined them at the fence. While Kureth was slight, the newcomer was built squarely, every inch as tall as Dyrk and thirty pounds heavier. His brown hair was cut short military-style, his chin clean shaven. His armour bore some subtle filigree in bronze and silver, evidence that he wasn't outfitted by the Lord's armoury. He carried his burnished helm in the crook of his elbow, the reflection from the sun almost blinding Dyrk.

"You see what took place?" the larger boy pointed with a condescending look. "That will happen every time some idiot tries to race with a horse he's not familiar with. Kemantar knows he got what he deserved."

"How could you tell?" Dyrk challenged the newcomer. "There's nothing to say that he's known that horse for years."

"His reins were wrapped twice around his hand. What a nervous wreck. Any man worth his weight in dirt would need a little trust in his mount if he was to ride in the Contest. I'm sure you two have prepared more rigorously than that."

The race ended as a squire pulled away from his pursuers and deftly speared the ribbon with his warpole. Dyrk and Kureth gave their applause, all but lost in the roar of the crowd.

"Speed won't help him in the last phase of the competition, the Combat," the bigger boy remarked with a wry grin. "He'll have nowhere to run." He gave a little laugh.

"You stand a pretty good chance out there to win it all, Bayern," Kureth leaned forward to address the other. "You've been training for months."

"Aye that I have," Bayern sighed, none too modest. "The competition will be strong, though. There's many a good man out there. Holy Nedrin will have his pick the day after tomorrow."

"I'm sure you'll be one of the last still standing," Kureth fawned. "Fighting's in your blood, after all."

Dyrk leaned back to take a look at the plumes on Bayern's helmet. Dark blue and red, colours of House Lyrus. Tradition dictated since the days of Teren that the High Captain of the Army would always be appointed from House Lyrus.

"Which race are you two in?" Bayern inquired.

"Fourth," Kureth said. "What about you, Dyrk?"

"Sixth," Dyrk said from the side of his mouth.

Bayern slapped his armoured gauntlet on Dyrk's back. "Looks like we'll be foes, my friend. You look like a strapping lad, though, and might give me some trouble. I'll not be easy on you just because you're from the farms." He smiled at Dyrk's plumes, but there was no kindness in that smile. "May the royal House protect you from serious injury at my hands, son of Teren."

Bayern turned on his heel and left. Kureth turned to watch him go like a lost puppy.

"What's his story?" Dyrk asked.

Kureth sighed. "Son of Thur Daynen, Headman of the second ward of the Old City. He's so much like his father that it doesn't matter if he wins this competition or not, he'll still become an Eratur."

Dyrk felt nothing but indignance. It had been drummed into his head as a child, that a man's destiny should in no way be tied to his father's accomplishments, or lack thereof. It was a central dogma of the religious training he had received. Concerning the Generations of Men, the second chapter of Melandar's ancient tome Of the Nations of Mankind, routinely promoted the separation of father and son, lest the father be idolized in place of Arren. Most in the countryside still practiced the old tradition of Mentorship, in which at the age of twenty a son must leave his father's household and enter into apprenticeship of an occupation entirely different than his father's. He had heard that the old traditions were being left to the wayside in the cities, but he was upset to see it himself for the first time.

Kureth left him to get ready for his race. Dyrk began to feel out of place and alone, homesickness arising in his soul. What was he actually doing here? He was a youth far from home without the blessing of his father. His previous courage began to wane as he watched the next race. Each clash of steel and scream of horse and rider made him wince. He buried his chin into his forearm as he watched, so that his expression would not betray his feelings.

More races whipped by him, and still the sickness in his stomach did not abate. At one point, he felt the bile rise in his throat, and choked it down. It left a repulsive taste in his mouth, adding to his discomfort. He watched, feeling helpless, as Kureth was knocked from his mount by a much larger boy. Dyrk's new acquaintance collided with a fencepost before sprawling on the track. Two Eraturs leapt into the ring and dragged him out of harm's way. Dyrk's stomach gave out on him at that point, as that same wave of hot, feverish sickness overtook him. Embarrassed, he ran behind a tent and retched. An older man carrying warpoles laughed in his direction. He managed to find a bucket of water with a dipper in front of another tent with which to wash out the disgusting taste.

Rothai's ears pricked with recognition as Dyrk approached. He was amazed with the horse's progress in just a few short hours. But as he led the gelding forth, his heart ached with frustration. His source of pride was based almost completely on his horse, and now that had been ripped away from him. He came to the staging area, where many others like him were gathering, checking their equipment for the last time. They wished each other the blessing of Nedrin, while secretly hoping that their opponents would trip and stumble. Dyrk checked the cinch, sliding two fingers easily between the strap and the horse's belly. Like many mounts, Rothai had a habit of holding a deep breath while being saddled, and now the strap was considerably loose. He put his knee against Rothai's side and tightened the strap, ensuring that he didn't pinch the horse's hide. He pulled the reins over Rothai's head and mounted. After walking the horse a few steps, he got off in order to check the strap once more.

As he worked, the fifth race began with plenty of noise, and Rothai visibly jumped and quivered. *I'm going to get myself crushed*, Dyrk said to himself as he looked at the horses around him, unresponsive to the noises of the Contest. Then he saw Bayern, astride a white warhorse that was larger than Tanakh. The mount was equipped with the best of tackle, a noseplate etched in flaming silver filigree. Dyrk recognized the breed: it was a Tevledain war-horse, immense in size and girth but slower and easily tired. Though Bayern was the same height as Dyrk, the son of Thur Daynen sat a head taller than any of those around him.

Dyrk could not believe the unfairness of it all. He had been told by Madwin tales of common farmboys becoming Eraturs by their own virtue, while the indolent sons of princes tilled the land in their place. Why should Dyrk be forced to put aside his own mighty horse and ride a nag with which he had no experience while that long-plumed cocksure city-boy could choose his own Tevledain from a herd? In fact, Dyrk was the son of an Eratur too – why shouldn't that count?

Cheers broke his thoughts again. Two of the remaining squires were bearing down on the red ribbon, jostling for position. Both had lost their swords earlier in the race, and now grappled each other's reins with their free hand. As they thundered past the post, both riders were spilt from their saddles as they collided. One horse stumbled and rolled while the other continued its gallop. The first squire jumped to his feet empty-handed, moving quickly to get out of the way of trailing riders. But the ribbon was no longer on the post; it was on the pole of the motionless squire still on the ground.

A long delay ensued as the injured horse was removed and the winner was revived. With his wounded arm limp at his side, the squire weakly passed the ribbon to a lass who Dyrk figured would have preferred her champion to be in one piece. The post was put back in place and a new, bright red ribbon was gently tied to the nail.

Dyrk nervously triple-checked the tack from his position on the saddle as Rothai was led to the starting gate. He tried his hardest not to think of the grievous injuries that he was witnessing, knowing that coming out of the Contest with a clipped wing was no dishonour whatsoever. He flexed his muscles as he waited for the white flag to drop, if only to feel one last time what it was to be whole. Dulled though he was to the sounds around him, he couldn't help but hear the Eratur with the flag offer his encouragement – to Bayern, and no one else.

As it was the sixth race, the interest of the crowd had waned considerably. Many of the ones who stayed were there more for the spectacle of violence, and therefore cheered as young men were spilled from their saddle or took a blade to the helm. At the drop of the flag, only a few cheers greeted the riders as they sprang from the stocks. Rothai started with a frightened jump, and not with a charge. Once the gelding realized that nine other horses were dashing down the track, its instincts overcame its fear. Dyrk spurred it on, knowing he had to catch up to someone if he was to keep from being disqualified. He crouched low, raising his bottom from the saddle and putting his weight in the stirrups. One hand held the warpole to Rothai's side, the other gripped the reins. His sword stayed in its sheath for now, as Madwin had advised.

He rode past an unfortunate participant who had been knocked from the saddle. Two more were jostling ahead, and Dyrk directed Rothai toward the outside so that he could pass them without them noticing. He succeeded. He hoped as he raced on that at least one of them might stay on their mount and save him from disqualification. As he sprinted into the second curve, he heard hoofbeats close behind him. Not being the leader, he was not allowed to make an attempt at the ribbon this time around. He had expected that Rothai would at least be a little faster than Tanakh, being a smaller horse, but it wasn't so. He noticed the horse's ears were flattened and its shoulders were trembling. He had to continually spur it on, digging heels into the sides and slapping the haft of the warpole against the flanks to remind his mount of the urgency.

The post and ribbon passed him by with a flash. Dyrk was encouraged that it still remained intact. He heard to his relief the shout of an Eratur calling out the disqualification of a squire of House Kromar. He became worried of Rothai, whose eyes were getting larger and head wilder as the race continued. Heading into the first turn, Dyrk let up on the warpole and instead began to firmly spur the horse with his voice. Coming out of the turn, he was back with the other three riders that remained, with Rothai nipping at the tail of Bayern's warhorse. Dyrk switched the pole to his left hand that held the reins, drawing his sword with his right to protect himself.

In the second turn, Rothai began to cut inside on Bayern's horse. Dyrk did not have enough leverage on the reins to prevent his horse from doing so, and his heart leapt into his throat. The gilded and fearsome helm turned toward him. Dyrk had enough warning to duck the wild backhand swing that Bayern sent his way. Dyrk cocked his arm and returned the blow. Though it felt like he put all his strength into the strike, it seemed to harmlessly deflect off of the mail protecting Bayern's back.

Bayern's steed, having been trained for war, abruptly leaned into Rothai's path. The smaller horse was caught unprepared for the force of a massive warhorse bearing down on it. With nowhere to go, the frightened horse reared to leap the barrier of hay on the inside. The sharp, crippling impact of Bayern's sword snapped Dyrk's head back, blinding and deafening him at the same time. Colours played across his eyes, as if the sun had multiplied many times and all the golden spheres were spinning around his head. He felt weightless, floating in the air between heaven and earth. His thoughts drifted to, among all things, the taste of new cheese and fresh bread, his first sip of cool ale. Then the ground rushed toward him. The impact stole his breath from him, as though there were no air to breathe any more. Suddenly his limbs worked again, acting of their own accord. Both hands clawed towards his throat, though he couldn't get at it for all the armour he wore. He barely felt something hit him again. He knew nothing else, only to breathe again, only to take those deep, delicious gulps of air that he once did.

Somehow his helm was removed. He didn't even notice the light hitting his eyes. His fingers dug over the rim of his neckplate, finally reaching his throat where there was little good that they could do. A hand grabbed him. His flailing arms connected with something, and then he heard shouting.

"Easy there, boy! Stop your thrashing!" Dyrk's eyes and ears returned with a rush, overwhelming him such that he sucked several quick breaths without realizing that he had. Feeling began to return slowly, almost completely composed of pain. But through it all, relief flooded into him as breath returned, filling his lungs with life again.

The stern, wrinkled countenance of an older man did not seem to hold much compassion. The brows on his broad face were furrowed together to form one black line across his forehead. One firm hand gripped Dyrk's arm to prevent him from thrashing any further.

"Up with you," he said gruffly from underneath his bushy beard, the voice barely registering in Dyrk's foggy brains. "I'll have you out of here before the next race."

Dyrk slowly began to get up, the pain in his limbs exploding as he moved each one. He now began to feel that parts of his armour had shifted and were causing great pain. A fold of chain mail felt like it was embedded into his back, and he was sure that he was bleeding from where a pauldron dug into his collar. Worst of all, his head would not stop spinning. Once upon his knees, the man forced a dirty rag into his hand.

"You're bleeding," he muttered, directing Dyrk's hand to his face. He then roughly prodded Dyrk until he got up and stumbled across the track. He could hear the jeers of a few onlookers who laughed at his condition. He pushed his way through the row of hay sheaves that ringed the track on the outside. As he ducked under the fence, he winced at the pain that swelled up in his head.

He was standing alone in a muddy horse path. The man who moved him off the track was nowhere to be seen. A row of unfamiliar tents met his squinting eyes. He forced down the panic again. Where was his horse? He had no idea what had happened to Rothai. What if the horse's leg had been broken in the impact? Dyrk should be caring for the horse. And where were his weapons? His scabbard was empty at his side, his warpole nowhere to be found. He had lost his bearings in his fall. He did not know which way to go. Pain again welled in his head, washing over him like the springtime floods. He put one hand on the fence to steady himself, and buried his face in the other, still holding the bloodied scrap of cloth.

The sting of defeat was being overwhelmed by the hollow pain of loneliness. What was he even doing there?

CHAPTER 4:
THE RIBBON

Dyrk felt the steadying hand of Madwin under his shoulder. He knew who it was just by the firmness of the touch, the sound of Madwin's breathing in his ears. He sucked air into his lungs, the tension and confusion seeping away. The rag was forced from his face for a second as Madwin assessed the cut. Then the Eratur bent down and half-whispered to him.

"Dyrk, listen to me. You will not be in the next race if you do not make it to my tent on your own two legs. Do you understand me?"

Dyrk nodded.

"The cut is not bad. Leave the cloth here and do not hold your face."

Dyrk obliged, ignoring the dribble of blood that rolled down the side of his face. Madwin sheathed the practice sword into Dyrk's scabbard and thrust a helmet with two red plumes, one broken off, into his arms. A smear of dirt was visible on the helm's forehead.

Madwin seemed to read his mind. "Your mount was perfectly fine as soon as you left its back. Now let us go!"

Then it was all Dyrk could do to put one foot in front of the other without looking down or clenching his eyes shut in pain. He kept his gaze on Madwin's back, the blue and silver cloak that looked so magnificent on him. They passed other squires, a few boys attending to horses, a servant with buckets of water. But it was the two Eraturs that they encountered that lifted Dyrk's spirits. The one tapped a gauntlet on Dyrk's pauldron, the other said, almost imperceptibly, "plucky effort, lad."

Madwin pulled aside the flap of the tent for Dyrk to enter. The inside was dark; Dyrk's eyes took a few seconds to adjust.

"Undress," Madwin said curtly.

Dyrk obediently tried to remove the hauberk, forgetting to remove the pauldrons first. After a few awkward tugs, he recalled the order in which to remove them.

"Did I – did I do all right?" Dyrk asked sheepishly. "I did you no dishonour out there, did I, Thur Madwin?" Dyrk had a hard time reading Madwin's expression, but all his body language was up until now quite stiff. But when Dyrk asked the question, he could see that Madwin's face relaxed considerably, and he broke out into a mild laugh.

"You most certainly did well," Madwin said as he put his own helm on the post of a chair. "You almost did too well."

Dyrk was a little puzzled by that statement, but let it pass. "Who won the race?"

Madwin stroked the shadow under his chin. "Why, I think it was the very squire who upended you. I believe he is the son of Thur Daynen. You did well just to keep up with him."

Bayern! Dyrk felt his face heat up with jealousy. How could the cocky cabbage-head lose with a horse like that? Now a sweet young girl carried Bayern's ribbon in her hair, earned only because Bayern's father had more gold than he knew what to do with. But instead of showing his resentment, Dyrk knew Madwin would be expecting a more upright attitude from him.

"If I might ask, how is it best to overcome such a situation?" he asked.

"Certainly not forcing your way on the inside of a much larger mount," Madwin began. "You must always keep out of range of a trained warhorse's flanks, for you should know as well as I that their instinct is to use them as weapons."

Dyrk finally was able to crawl out of the cloth hauberk, emerging bare-chested as the sweat-soaked silk clung to the leather. He extracted the tunic and hung it on the back of another chair. "So I should have stayed outside. But then I would not have caught up in time."

"A light cavalry-man carries a bow for a reason," Madwin told him. "They cannot afford to come within range of the Tevledain war-horses. You must strike from a distance or do not bother."

"The Tevledain are slow, plodding beasts," Dyrk said. "Why, if I had Tanakh I could…"

"But you do not have Tanakh," Madwin cut him off sternly. "Though Bayern may win competitions, he must show much more in order to become an Eratur. And so must you. I think you fail to see the competitions for what they are, Dyrk. The crowd comes to see entertainment, a spectacle, and in time, a victor. They see feats of strength and power, as well as grievous tragedy and injury. But most importantly, they come to see the quality of young men when put under a hammer, to be witnesses of their trials. Is the King's service all about victory? Will Arren reward only those whose arms are bestowed with strength? To what end would it serve if you could read and write Melandarim and ten other languages besides? Of what worth is it that you can speak with eloquence and persuasion? Or had the skill to best ten men in combat?"

With that, Madwin waited for an answer. "Why, all those things you say are noble skills," Dyrk ventured. "Why should I not desire and pursue them?"

"There was once a man who possessed all that and more," Madwin said, leaning forward with his elbows on his knees. "He spoke well, showed respect to all, was undefeatable in combat, and was an unparalleled leader of men. You would find no more a champion in a contest such as this one. Do you know of whom I speak?"

"Do you tell of Eldorin, or even of Tawkin?" Dyrk asked, recalling some of his heroes of old.

"Tawkin's tongue was of stone, while Eldorin quailed at the thought of combat," Madwin said. "I speak of Korhal," Madwin enunciated the name the way of the Vekh, eliciting a fright from Dyrk. "A man of unequalled might and valour. But you know his end, and to which he dedicated his purpose."

Korhal was the Vekh general against which Melandar and Tawkin struggled. He was eventually murdered on orders of his brother. "Korhal defeated Melandar himself. Korhal tried to kill Tawkin, the father of Teren. How can you call that man valorous and mighty?"

"And there you see what I am trying to tell you." Madwin looked up as a hand drew back the flap of the tent. The eyes of a Vekh servant woman peered in. Madwin nodded to her but continued his speech. "All the gifts from above will do little, indeed, can even do great harm, if the heart is not wholly devoted to Arren. Korhal made the mistake of placing his loyalty too firmly with his father and brothers."

The woman entered the tent carrying a small bucket, several cloths, and a small satchel. Dyrk had rarely seen Vekh before. He impolitely stared at her for some time. Stories were told in Tanvilon of grotesque, diseased, disfigured people with sickly green skin and putrid smell. But every Vekh Dyrk had ever seen didn't look anything like those stories. Yes, they were smaller than Karolians, and not as sturdily built. But they didn't look much different than the local Derrekh tribespeople, save for their gray-green skin and eyes so dark that they looked larger than most.

This woman was no exception. Though she looked to be as old as Dyrk's mother, her skin was smooth save for a small blemish on her left cheek. She bent close to him with the wet cloth to clean his wound, and the smell that came to his nose was quite pleasant: lavender flowers mixed with a faint body odor. She was dressed in a clean, plain, loose-fitting frock, and wore her black hair braided. As she scrubbed the blood from Dyrk's face, she smiled at him. She had more teeth than the average Karolian working-class woman of her age, but the gums were nearly black, which set off the whiteness of her teeth.

The histories stated that the people of Tauril were struck by a disease once Melandar and his brothers murdered their father the king. This turned their skin a sickly green, and they were known as the Vekh. Melandar repented of his part in the murder some years later, and Arren granted him and his people relief from the disease. Their skin, however, did not return to the healthy bronze colour that all non-Taurilians shared, from Derrekh to Belorin to Zindori to Corsavans. Instead, the skin of Melandar's people remained a lifeless grey, a reminder of the curse that had been lifted.

Most residents of Karolia were descended in part from

Melandar's people, afterward called Taurilians. They had mixed with native peoples of that land, and so in Dyrk's day their skin was a combination of light-brown and grey.

Modern Karolians were questioning the traditional stories. Some regarded the differences in skin tone as chance artifacts of each race's local environment. Others saw a manifestation of some mystical Power. Ultra-traditionalists saw the ashen skin as a badge of racial superiority, which Dyrk found ironic since Melandar himself regarded it as a reminder of a curse lifted, and not a blessing. Indeed, the religious patriarch once said when he met the bronze-skinned Belorin that he once again beheld the appearance of man as Arren had created them.

A strange, acrid smell entered Dyrk's nostrils and his head snapped back involuntarily. The woman had crushed a small dried leaf and waved it under his nose. His head instantly felt clearer, sharper, but his nasal passages hurt. He did not like the feeling.

Her healing tasks complete, the servant woman began to cluck at him. "Less than an hour until your next competition, *jadweir*," she chided, surprising Dyrk by using the Melandarim term for squire.

Competition! Dyrk jumped to his feet and inspected his armour. There were always at least two races for each group, possibly a third if not enough winners were able to continue. He had to check on Rothai to make sure he had not come up lame after their mishap. But first, he needed to dress again. The slave woman seemed to be one step ahead of him, already picking up the stiff leather hauberk for him to get inside.

Dyrk was still sore, but the initial effects of the impact had worn off. A new shot of adrenaline surged through him as he realized he would be competing without Bayern this time – maybe he stood a chance! The armour went back on in the correct order, feeling heavier and clammier than it did before. He tied his weapon belt and did a mental check of all his equipment before rushing from the tent.

The second race did not start so well for Dyrk. Again, Rothai was skittish out of the starting gate and reared almost immediately when another rider cut in front. Dyrk knew how to ride out a panicked horse better than most, but it was still a terrifying ordeal. Eleven hundred pounds of muscle and bone were able to crush the most stalwart rider at any time. Compounded with the fact that thousands were watching, the emotions rolling through Dyrk were the furthest thing from peaceful.

Rothai settled and his instincts re-engaged. He took off after the other disappearing mounts. Dyrk steered him to the outside to avoid one squire who lay on the dust of the track. As long as the ribbon was on the post and he didn't touch the ground, he had a chance. His first task was to avoid disqualification. That meant overtaking at least one mounted rider.

The lead rider had others on his right flank, but still lowered his warpole for an attempt at the ribbon. His aim was low, and by some turn of fate struck the post itself. Not expecting it, the boy's right arm snapped back and put him off balance. The warpole, free of its owner's grip, careened to the right and the butt end caught the next rider in the chest, lifting him off his saddle as his mount continued on. The strange sequence of events continued, with chaos erupting amongst the riders that followed; one mount reared and spilled its rider, another turned to the side and jumped the bales of hay. Dyrk chose the outside path and galloped past them all.

He waited for the horn blast and the name of a house that would disqualify someone from the race for being the last to pass the post. It did not come. The judges had determined that enough riders had been spilled at the post and declined to take out another.

Now he was in the clear. Two horses were ahead of him, but one was riderless and beginning to flag. Dyrk knew that Rothai was strictly a follower. As Dyrk caught up to the riderless mount, he slapped the horse with his warpole and got it running again. He gave further encouragement with shouts and whoops, working the other mount to a frenzied gallop which Rothai followed beautifully. With half a lap to go, he overtook the other rider. A feeble sweep with a blunted sword was all the leader could do as Dyrk raced past, easily out of range. Dyrk realized the rider was either hurt or very tired.

He had imagined a far more glorious victory in the contest. Here he was, using another mount as the necessary encouragement for his own. He had not upended a single rider, and for the most part was the benefactor of some unusual circumstances. As he rounded the last curve, he saw a black-haired Eratur trying to lift the post back into position after the events of the previous lap. Failing that, the Eratur bravely hunched over, supporting the post with his hands and shoulder to give Dyrk an opportunity to snare the ribbon.

Steadying the warpole as he had practiced so many times at home, he followed the undulations of Rothai's gait with the rest of his body. He put the pole dead-center through the loop of ribbon, but it did not close properly around the warpole and snapped off, still lodged into the post.

The crowd nevertheless broke into cheers and applause. A horn sounded three blasts to end the race. The spectators were a bit thinner than that morning, interest in the races having waned somewhat, but Dyrk soaked it in. He turned Rothai around to face the black-haired Eratur walking towards him with the broken ribbon. After he tied it around the end of the warpole, he grinned at Dyrk and said, "Now go get your girl."

There were many who questioned the ritual. Marriage was far more complex than browsing through three rows of potential mates. Few that found matches during the Contest ever ended up marrying. It also placed the choice squarely in the hands of the boys, while the girls were obliged to accept. Many women refused to let their daughters take part in the dance as they found it demeaning, and a movement was afoot to at least separate the dance from the selection ritual that followed. Yet, just like Dyrk, girls would run away from their indignant mothers and take part anyway, chasing the lure of some romantic ideal.

One part of him was steering him towards the lower row, where there were still several attractive girls who had not received the favor of a squire. One in particular had caught his eye, a raven-haired girl with long eyelashes, slim build, and a beautiful smile. Bayern's words, though, echoed in his head. "From the farms," he had said, reminding him that most of these girls were "from the city".

Dyrk extended the pole as high as he could, beyond the reach of the outstretched arms of the bottom two rows. The look on the face of the freckled girl changed from one of passive enjoyment to a dignified surprise. She darted glances at the girls on her left and right, then put two fingers daintily to her collarbone and mouthed towards Dyrk, "me"?

Dyrk nodded.

Her face went redder than a sour-root[1]. She stood up and tried with trembling fingers to untie the ribbon but was unable to do so. At first Dyrk was alarmed when the girls on either side stood, putting their fingers to the task. His arm was getting sore holding the pole up so high. As the ribbon was finally released, he saw that his fears were unfounded. The girls helped tie the ribbon in the hair of the freckled girl, who was shaking with nervousness. Her companion whispered something in her ear. Reminded of the convention, she put her hand to her lips and blew a kiss towards Dyrk.

Rothai was getting an extra-long brush after the work he had put in that day. Some of the other horses were getting similar treatment from the squires, while other mounts of the more well-to-do were being tended to by servants. Kureth had been all over him after the race, content to simply be in the same company as one of the winners. Dyrk had obliged his presence. They had chatted for some time as Dyrk cared for his horse, comparing childhoods, families, and dreams. Finally Kureth stood up to go, leaving Dyrk to give Rothai some extra attention.

But within a minute Kureth was back. "Someone is here to see you," he said, trying to sound matter-of-fact, but the expression on his face betrayed him.

"Show him in then," Dyrk said.

"The stable is no place for a lady," Kureth responded with a rather urgent motion of his head.

Dyrk peeked his head around the corner. Just outside the stable door he could see three figures draped in blue and purple. He looked down at himself. He was wearing only Madwin's silk undershirt. He

---

[1] A "sour-root" is a red beet. Sugar beets, which were the most common source of sweetening in Karolia, were called sweet-root.

grabbed the quilted hauberk and pulled it over his head. Now he had strings and straps sticking out at all angles. What was he to do?

Kureth's head jerked again, his face insistent. "There's three of them, so I'll go with you," he said, clearly in it for his own benefit and not Dyrk's.

As they walked towards the door, Dyrk whispered, "Why are they still in their dresses? Don't they suffocate?"

Kureth shrugged and whispered, "Not sure, but I can tell you I wouldn't take off an Eratur's armour for days once it was put on me."

Kureth took the lead with the introductions, given that he knew the girls better than Dyrk. The freckle-faced one wearing a bright ribbon bashfully stayed behind the other two as they were introduced: Hilla and Vannis. "And the lovely lady with the ribbon," he said expectantly, fishing for help with her name.

"This is Neriah", Vannis said, taking the girl by the arm and thrusting her forward. "Please bear with her, she's a little flustered."

Indeed, Neriah's face hadn't changed much in colour from when Dyrk had given her the ribbon. Dyrk showed the proper courtesy, going to one knee and bowing his head, mumbling "m'lady" as he held out his right hand. The straps on his left arm dangled awkwardly. Without a word, Dyrk felt the soft, tentative touch of Neriah's hand in his. The other two girls stifled a giggle.

Kureth tried to break the ice. "So how long did it take you to practice for that dance, anyway? Looked pretty impressive to me."

"Oh, it was sheer torture," Hilla gushed, her brown curls bobbing with her movements. "Day after day of learning the steps with my mum, only to get to the rehearsal to find they had changed it. Changed it!" she raised her hands in mock indignation. "Who changes traditions like that?"

Whatever the change was, Dyrk hadn't noticed any difference. He also didn't notice that he hadn't let go of Neriah's hand, either, until she pulled it away.

"I tell you, I was stuck with the most horrible partner," Vannis jumped in. "I swear, her father was a goat, because her feet were nothing more than split hoofs." Vannis was lithe and athletic but rather plain in the face, with straight, limp dark hair that was clearly attempting to be grown longer than it should. Her features exaggerated the expression with which she spoke. "I half expected to be flat on my face in front of you boys. Thankfully, we made it through."

"You all looked great out there," Dyrk contributed, trying to say it with appropriate feeling.

Neriah gave a demure smile when he said that. Hilla nodded in acknowledgment, but Vannis put her hands on her hips.

"Great? I found it a bit sloppy. I hope they'll let me be a dance leader next year, because they need some straightening out."

Hilla complained, "Count me out. If you had been in charge, we wouldn't have had a social life at all for the past three months."

Vannis flicked the hair from her shoulder in a look of disdain. "If you can't do something with excellence, then you should be farming," she said, in a badly mangled version of one of Melandar's proverbs. Dyrk winced inwardly with the derogatory reference to an honest occupation.

Neriah finally spoke. "But what about you?" She used the plural form, but she was looking at Dyrk's chest as she spoke it. "Didn't you get hurt in that first race?"

Hilla crowed in mock honour, "That, my friends, was spectacular. You, dear sir, are the first to get up by your own power after being thrashed by Bayern's monstrosity."

"I take it there were others not so fortunate," Dyrk remarked dryly.

Vannis hadn't taken her hands from her hips, elbows splayed and trailing the purple and blue wings. Dyrk guessed that she naturally stood that way whenever she discussed anything. "Dreamy as he may be, I couldn't imagine being with that arrogant *Bru*." She used a Melandarim term for an empty vessel. "Let Kaerin and Junnah fawn over him. He broke their hearts by giving his ribbon to Raell anyway."

Hilla turned to Vannis in surprise. "It wasn't Junnah's fault. She had been given a ribbon earlier."

"Rules don't say that you can't take two," Vannis retorted. "She could have given the first away when Bayern won, if she was so infatuated with him."

Dyrk saw Neriah shake her head in disgust at the latest outburst from Vannis. Part of him longed to spend time with Neriah without the others chattering away, but convention remained that boys and girls could not be alone together without the explicit permission of the girl's parents.

"Let's walk to the stands," Dyrk said, suddenly feeling both his injured tailbone and the crick in his neck. He also wanted to put some distance between the group and the stables, which emanated a smell that must have been off-putting to the rest, despite Dyrk being used to it.

"I've been sitting all day," Vannis finally dropped her arms from her hips. "But it wouldn't hurt to walk over there. Maybe we'll see some of the archery."

The five of them made their way to a bank of empty stands at the end of the track. Sure enough, there were archery targets set up, and some of the contestants were practicing just before the event started. Their vantage point was probably the worst, which was fine with Dyrk because his attention was more on the girls than the event.

Kureth sat down and began chatting with Vannis, who refused to sit, about his schooling. That left Dyrk to converse with Neriah and Hilla. "So as you guessed, I'm not familiar with Doleth Sarin. Tell me about yourselves," he said, hoping to get Neriah talking.

To Dyrk's slight disappointment, Hilla started. She did, in fact, live on a farm just north of Doleth Sarin. Her father ran a successful dairy operation that spanned four *Duoma*, or traditional plots of land that were large enough for a self-sufficient homestead. Owning one *Duoma* of rural land was enough to qualify for citizenship; it was typically forty acres of fertile land.

Hilla's father was known for the butter he produced in a semi-industrial process. Hilla herself had attended school inside Doleth Sarin all the way through her seventeenth year, which was the furthest a girl could go. She was proud to be an accomplished seamstress and hoped one day to live in Doleth Sarin or some other large city where her skills would be in high demand.

Neriah took a little more prodding, but she confirmed Kureth's recollection. She lived in Harwaith, just to the west of Doleth Sarin. She was the eldest of the seven children of a cartwright. She loved flowers, and one of her favorite activities was making floral arrangements for some of the special events in the town. She had stopped going to school at sixteen because of a prolonged illness.

Vannis was telling some tall tale that caught Hilla's attention, and she moved over to argue with her friend. This left Dyrk alone with Neriah for a few precious seconds.

As Dyrk was trying to think of something to say, Neriah took the initiative. "Thank you for the ribbon," she said. It struck Dyrk that the ribbon itself was so insignificant, just a small piece of brightly-coloured cloth that was dwarfed by the beautiful dress that she wore. But it wasn't the material gift that she was thanking him for.

"Do you remember catching my eye during the dance?" Dyrk asked.

"Oh yes," she tumbled over her words. "I almost stepped on Hilla's feet after that. You weren't supposed to be looking at me." She kept her eyes low, only furtively glancing to ensure that Dyrk was listening.

"How could I not?" he questioned rhetorically. "I've watched the dance every year I've been here, and this is the first time I had a front-row seat." His mind hammered with self-criticism, trying to find the right balance between making her feel special without being too forward. Just then he realized he missed an opportunity by turning the focus away from Neriah. "But surely I wasn't the only one looking at you."

"You were the only one who stared for three turns," she pointed out teasingly. "I had to make sure you weren't looking at Hilla, so I had to get some sort of reaction." Then her voice shifted, sounding wistful. "Hilla is so much better at dancing than me. It was difficult to keep up."

Dyrk recalled her look of intense concentration. "You did just fine out there," he assured. "You said you weren't feeling well, though, did that make things more difficult?"

She nodded, the bright red ribbon at the end of her braid

swinging to her other shoulder. "I still get sick a lot. Father says I should live in the country, where the air is cleaner. I think he blames himself that the smoke from his smithy affects me."

Dyrk had a brief flash of living in the countryside of Tanvilon with Neriah, as children scurried about. He shook his head. *Getting way ahead of yourself*, he thought. *Focus on the present.*

"Are you going to take part in the fight tomorrow?" she asked.

How could that even be a question? "Of course," he said. "By Nedrin's grace I have come this far, why stop now?"

She was fidgeting with the purple cloth under her left arm. "You might get hurt," she said, keeping her eyes down. "Those boys are trained to fight and kill. Don't you remember what happened to Esdaric?"

Esdaric House Brevaz was killed two years ago when his helmet was dislodged in a collision with another horse. A swinging practice blade, dull as it was, caught him on the side of the head and fractured his skull. He was carried off and reported to be making a full recovery. Once the event was over, it was revealed that he had died almost immediately. Some had tried to get his parents to lead an effort to tone down the games and make them safer, but the parents had refused to make their son's death political.

"It happens," Dyrk said dismissively. "It's part of the territory. I wouldn't miss this for the world." He looked at the ribbon in her hair. "Besides, you wouldn't get to sit in the place of honour if I wasn't participating." The girls who had received ribbons from the squires taking part in the final combat were allowed to sit in the front row.

Her face fell, and with it Dyrk's heart. "Just think for a second, Dyrk. The girl who received Esdaric's favour, her name was Maesse. Just think for a second of what it cost her."

Dyrk refused. Not only was it improper to put himself in a woman's place, he had enough to think about in his own life. Why did it matter what Maesse felt? The same thing wouldn't happen to him and Neriah.

"Every year a group of girls sits at the front, gasping in sorrow at the beating that a boy takes on her behalf," she continued. "Yet all of them are the ones who urge them to do it in the first place. If they truly cared for the boy, they would put a stop to it before it started." Neriah abruptly stopped talking, biting her lip. She seemed to regret what she had just said.

He was about to ask if he should give the ribbon to someone else. If she couldn't stomach it, there would be others. But he thought twice. Madwin would want him to approach this differently. There was more to life than the competition. If he couldn't do something small, however painful it might be, right here, right now, for a girl like Neriah, how could he ever sacrifice big things for the ones that would mean everything in life?

"You would like me to pull out of the competition, then?" he said slowly, trying his best to avoid sounding crushed.

She looked at him, for the first time not breaking her gaze. "No," she said plainly, but not without emotion. "I don't. You have things you need to do, and so do I. I will sit on the front row and plead with Nedrin for your safety. I…" she faltered, her gaze lowering for a second. "I just need you to know why I'm not looking forward to it. All the other girls seem to be so excited about being in the front row. They haven't paid that price. Yet."

Dyrk wanted some way to reassure her, but any physical touch was improper. Hilla and Vannis were still a short distance away, laughing at some jokes that Kureth was telling. Instead, Dyrk bent a little to capture her eyes with his own. "I understand I'm not going to win," he said. "But most squires who lose, they get up and walk away, better for the experience. I won't be going out there to throw my life away, but rather to be able to wake up every day for the rest of my life knowing that I gave it my best and didn't back down from the danger."

She took a deep breath. "Just promise me," she asked solemnly. "Don't be foolish. Protect yourself. I would rather have my conscience clear that you came out whole, than a thousand times the glory that comes with you winning but getting hurt in the process."

He nodded. "Telmanitar is my witness." He pointed his index finger to the sky as was proper whenever the name of the Servant Telmanitar was invoked to seal a vow.

"Hey you two," Vannis interrupted. "We're about to get some cinnamon cookies. Come along."

Dyrk got up, his tailbone still complaining, and joined them for an afternoon treat. Neriah said she couldn't have any cookies, but she wanted to come anyway.

On the way, there was a question that was still tugging at his mind.

"Do you know Maesse?"

Neriah nodded. "She's the oldest sister of my best friend. She has now entered the Convent of Harophin and pledged never to marry."

CHAPTER 5:
UNWELCOME

The booming voice of the Lord's Crier called out t
of the archery competition as Dyrk emerged from
Last night's stay at the inn had been mostly the sa
Madwin had sat down with him to discuss the competition t(
Dyrk hadn't known better, he would have thought that Madw
trying to talk him out of it. "You are well accomplished
horseman," he had said, "But not as a warrior."

Indeed, that was true. Dyrk was a stranger to physical confl
beyond sports and playful jousting. Once he had gotten into a fist
fight with an older boy; Dyrk had struck just one punch that glanced
off the cheekbone. He got pummeled pretty good before others
came to his aid. Even while hunting, he was uncomfortable with the
fact that an animal was suffering because of some action of his. He
was not at all accustomed to putting his full strength behind a blow
that might injure another human being.

He wasn't unfamiliar with corrective punishment. He grew up on
a farm that reared, broke, and trained horses. Pain was inflicted on
the horses in that process, but it wasn't intended to injure. It was
similar to the whippings he received as discipline from his father
when he was a small boy.

This was different. The boys had to fight and overcome each
other by whatever means necessary to win the competition and the
coveted enrolment at the Eratur's College. There were no holds
barred, and no rules, save for the boundaries of the arena and the
prohibition on violence against any unhorsed participant. There was
a gentleman's agreement that horses should not be deliberately
targeted, but a mounted squire was fair game.

Madwin along the same lines of what he

Dyrk had res⟩ it wasn't his competition to win, that he
told Neriah. H⟩rt of it. He wasn't going out there to put
was happy ju⟩ould help it. And when he hit the ground,
his life on t⟩e as quickly as possible.
he would ⟩ctant but did not protest. By morning, Dyrk
Madw⟩count of the borrowed horse. If something
guessed⟩Madwin would not only be out a few silver
happ⟩so strain relations with the horse's owner.
ring⟩ morning had passed in careful preparations.
⟩he start of the Combat, Dyrk found himself
⟩le in the ready area just outside of the large gates
M⟩he competitors inside. The fighting ring was set up
⟩of barriers: hay bales, temporary wooden walls, even
⟩roughly formed a ring, about fifty paces in diameter.
⟩s were outside the gate with Dyrk, including Bayern,
⟩ir fellow competitors to detect any sort of weaknesses
⟩ be exploited in the coming fight. Not one of them left
⟩ for fear of sabotage.
⟩your horse?" Bayern asked gruffly in Dyrk's direction. He
⟩ding near his own horse, making a show of putting on his
⟩et, flexing his fingers, and taking it off again.

Dyrk bristled. "You accusing me of stealing it?"

Bayern rolled his eyes nonchalantly in his direction. "No, farm
boy. I was about to say I'm impressed at what you can do with a
horse that you barely know."

"I'm impressed at what you can do without a ten-crown
warhorse. Oh, my mistake." Dyrk regretted his biting response as
soon as he said it. That was not gentlemanly of him.

Bayern chuckled, but it wasn't a friendly sound. "I certainly
couldn't ride on it all the way from Tanvilon," he said, giving Dyrk
a bit of a fright. *How much does he know*, he thought. Bayern's
Tevledain war-horse backed up suddenly. Bayern was distracted and
he barked an order at the bondservant holding the bridle.

Dyrk saw Thur Madwin appear from between two tents, and then
his heart fluttered as he saw two girls with him. The first was dressed

in regular city-clothes, but the second was wearing the ceremonial dress of the Dancing Maidens of yesterday. The first was Hilla, the second was Neriah. Just then Dyrk remembered that the girls sitting in front were expected to wear the dancing dresses to set them apart from the rest of the spectators.

Madwin found him quickly. "These two were asking to see you," he said with a twinkle in his eye. "I'll watch your horse." Dyrk took a deep breath and left his horse to walk with them for a bit through the tents.

"We just wanted to wish you Taephin's strength, for health and healing" Hilla said brightly, invoking the blessing of the Sixth Servant. Dyrk knew that Taephin also represented love and fertility.

"And the protective grace of the Servant Nedrin," Neriah said, echoing her sentiments of the day before. "It's so brave just to enter that place. Just remember our promise." Her brown eyes pierced Dyrk's soul just then, and he would have agreed to anything she asked for, even if he couldn't deliver.

After an awkward pause, he agreed. "It won't be long before it's over," he said to reassure her. "Bayern will be on his way to the College and I'll be headed back home."

Hilla gave him a playful slap on his armour. "Don't talk such rubbish", she said gaily. "You'll do great. Bayern will get a concussion from falling so far." Dyrk thought she said it loud enough that Bayern would hear, intentionally.

"Do let me see you before you go home," Neriah pleaded. "I need to see that you're all right. Hilla will come with me, won't you?"

Hilla agreed. "That is, unless you win," she said, her curls framing her childish smile. "Only Neriah will be allowed on the field then."

Dyrk saw a sudden look of fear on Neriah's face at the thought of being on the field with all those spectators, but it quickly passed. He said goodbye and returned to his horse.

"I just need to check the straps," he told Madwin who was holding the bridle.

"No need," Madwin said. "I already did. You're getting tight for time, anyway." He motioned towards Bayern who was being hoisted into his saddle by his servant.

Dyrk gulped. He checked his mobility at all joints in his armour to make sure that nothing was caught. Putting a foot in the stirrup, he hoisted himself up with great effort under the weight of his armour. In total, he was wearing about a third of the weight of a fully-armoured Eratur. *How in the world do they get on their horses?* he thought to himself. Focusing on these questions helped calm the nerves.

Madwin handed him his helmet. It was a classic design, with a generous crosswise slit for vision and a vertical slit for breathing. There was no way to strap it to the rest of his armour without restricting his neck movement. Though it seemed to fit, he dearly hoped it wouldn't slip off at a most inopportune moment. He recalled being upended by Bayern in the first race. If his helmet hadn't popped off during that ordeal, it was as good as being nailed to his head.

Sixteen mounted squires sat nervously as the last awards were given and the final contest was introduced. One by one the riders entered the arena to the announcement of the Crier. Dyrk grimaced when he was announced second as Breven son of Wolben House Teren. He had forgotten all about his alternate persona. Would anyone realize?

Thankfully, he saw that Neriah had not yet reached her seat. Perhaps she hadn't noticed.

After additional fanfare, the competitors were separated to sixteen separate points around a circle. One Eratur was with each one to guide the mounts into position. Dyrk realized that the one accompanying him was the same black-haired Eratur that had bravely held the post in his second race. He was now wearing the chain hauberk and skullcap of a footman.

"Nice to see you again," Dyrk said, his voice muffled through the slits of the helmet.

"Aye, brave son of Teren," the Eratur said, his moustache twitching. "Come out of there on your own two feet, might I ask? I'd rather not have to dive in there after you."

"I'll do my best," Dyrk said, the nerves again fluttering uncontrollably.

The seconds ticked by slowly. Rothai was getting restless, his ears pricking back towards Dyrk as if to ask what exactly was going on. Dyrk tried to assure him with his voice. He looked to his left, where twenty feet away another squire was sizing him up as his first victim. On the right was a similar lad, though on a strong grey horse that usually indicated a Veranian breed. Across the circle he spied Bayern on the Tevledain. Bayern's legs were so wide on the great horse that it almost looked comical from his vantage. *At least my hips won't give out before my thirtieth birthday*, he thought to himself.

The starting trumpet sounded. Half the riders were released, including Dyrk, into the center, followed by the other half three seconds later. This was to encourage the melee to converge on the center and not fragment into separate battles on the perimeter. Within moments, Dyrk knew that his mount would give him trouble. Rothai tentatively cantered a few strides but then broke sideways when it spied an enemy coming at his flank.

Dyrk had planned to be fully defensive, warding off attacks with his practice sword and not getting flanked amidst a charge. He was ready with his blade to meet the first threat from his right. Only, when he turned in his saddle to square himself to his attacker, he felt a sickening feeling in his stomach as he realized his saddle had slid several inches to the right.

He threw himself onto Rothai's withers, both to avoid the attack and to keep himself from going down with the saddle. Rothai lurched to the left, struggling to stay on all fours. Dyrk got his feet from the stirrups just in time, as the entire set of tack slid off Rothai's back to the left. Over the sounds of hoofs beating, steel clashing, and young men shouting, Dyrk could hear laughter was erupting from the spectators closest to him. He was in too much danger to care. *Stay on your mount*, he told himself. *You're only disqualified if you hit the ground.*

But Rothai was not in agreement with being ridden bareback. He tossed his neck, eyes wide with fright, and tried unsuccessfully to rear Dyrk off his back. Still off-balance to one side, Rothai turned that way and drove Dyrk against another rider. The impact released Dyrk's grip on the withers. He let go of the reins and grabbed onto whatever he could hold. His left gauntlet closed on another rider's arm. His right found a saddle horn. His helmet was twisted to the side, blocking his view and stifling his breathing. His chest was across the withers of another horse.

If it weren't for the seriousness of the situation, Dyrk could have laughed along with the crowd. But right now his body was engaged in a fight for his life. All of his survival instincts were engaged, giving him great strength and quickness.

First, he got his leg up onto the horse that he had just commandeered. Blows rained down on his neck as the rider sought to dislodge him. Suffocating in the helmet, but not wanting to release his grip, he smashed his head forward. Once he made contact, he used whatever object he was against to slip his helmet high enough that he could at least breathe again. Another blow from his adversary knocked it clean off.

He was tangled up with Bayern, sitting backwards on the Tevledain's neck. Dyrk's right hand had pinned Bayern's right arm, which neutralized his practice sword. Bayern had released the warpole in his left and was beating on Dyrk with his gauntlet. A strike with the mailed fist landed on the crown of Dyrk's head, sending stars through his vision. Instinctively, he used his left hand, now freed from the saddlehorn, to grapple Bayern's head, wrenching it to the right. A passing strike from another squire landed on Bayern's left shoulder, which started both of them toppling off the side. Bayern grabbed the saddlehorn, while Dyrk put both arms over the horse's back to keep from slipping off.

His sword arm now free, Bayern could not swing it in close quarters. But he raised the hilt and smashed the jagged end of the pommel against Dyrk's face, directly into his right eye.

Dyrk would never forget the horrible sensation of a shard of steel entering his eye and piercing the far side of the eye socket. His face was immediately covered in a wet substance. His body was too much in shock for him to feel pain. His mind could not process normally amongst the fresh trauma that had just been inflicted on him. Flashes of memories past flitted over his eyes. Horrified, he had one conscious thought: is this it? Am I going to die? The memory that came to the fore was the statue he had dreamed about in the cave, who had handed him that flaming sword...

A loud crash of steel on the ground jolted Dyrk back to awareness. He was slumped across the back of the Tevledain's saddle, itself pitching back and forth as it could not figure out for itself what to do. Bayern was gone. Dyrk opened his eyes and grasped the saddlehorn. Could he do it? Turn himself around? He didn't even know if he still had all his limbs. It barely registered that he could, miraculously, see out of both eyes.

With great effort he splayed himself across the back of the pitching warhorse and righted himself into the saddle. Another lurch from the Tevledain to the right jolted him off the side, saved only by his left foot that caught the stirrup and both his hands that gripped the saddlehorn. He now saw that the warhorse had instinctively shoved another rider who came too close. Dyrk couldn't believe it. Here was one of the most powerful warhorses in the land, who didn't know him from anyone, not only consenting to let him ride, but even defending him!

Dyrk scrambled for the reins and fitted his feet in the stirrups. He was weaponless. There was nothing in the Tevledain's equipment that he could use. His field of vision began to expand to the battlefield immediately below the mount. He saw two squires on the ground, desperately trying to avoid the churning hooves of Bayern's warhorse.

Dyrk heaved the reins back and drove his heels into the sides. The horse turned aside from the dismounted squires and stepped away. It was only then that Dyrk heard the crowd. They were not laughing anymore. They were cheering.

Additional movements came in from his left. His right eye was blurred. He was about to spur the Tevledain into the new adversaries when he heard them call out.

"Whoa, whoa there boy! Stand down!" A desperate plea came from an Eratur. Dyrk did his best to stop the horse, which finally complied and stood there, champing and snorting.

Dyrk took off his right gauntlet and raised his hand to his face. It was sticky with a fluid that was coloured red, but it was not thick enough to be blood. He rubbed his right eye and finally cleared his vision. Two Eraturs had come astride him on horses. The rest of the arena was clear, save for one mount who had broken a foreleg and was about to be put down. Dyrk was relieved to see it was not Rothai.

The two Eraturs were arguing across him. "Where does it say you couldn't change mounts?" a blond-moustached one on his left vehemently insisted.

The other, which was the black-haired one that had helped Dyrk before, wasn't so friendly now. "You saw what happened! We can't allow that!"

Others were racing onto the scene. The black-haired Eratur stopped his arguing long enough to look Dyrk in the face. "You all right boy? I thought you took one in the eye!"

Dyrk stammered out a response. His eye socket hurt, and his face was beginning to swell. But he could still see all right when he closed his left. Was it some sort of illusion? A dream? It had felt so real, his eye being punctured by the hilt, the metal cutting the inside of his eye socket. He wiped the bloody substance from his cheek and said, "I think I'm doing all right."

"Let's get you off the horse. The Lord is approaching," said the blond Eratur.

"I can't touch the ground," Dyrk mumbled. "It's against the rules."

Both Eraturs laughed. "Look around you, *jadweir*, the competition is over."

Dyrk could barely believe his eyes. Indeed, he was the last one mounted. He made sure to count the squires that were standing, seated, or prone at the edges of the arena. Fifteen, including Bayern who was without helmet, shouting something incomprehensible and pointing towards him. Only then did Dyrk consent to dismount.

As Dyrk was helped down, Lord Cassius was indeed approaching, with the Crier and another man that Dyrk recognized as a prominent scribe. The black-haired Eratur dismounted and repeated his protest to Cassius. With a wave of his hand, Cassius silenced him, then turned to the scribe.

"The rules state that the winner is the last one to touch the ground," the scribe said dryly. "There is no provision to censure the transfer of mounts."

"Very well," the black-haired Eratur grumbled. "But we should get that fixed next year. The last thing we need is squires willy-nilly leaping from horse to horse. It isn't proper."

The blond Eratur guffawed. "Like you'll see that ever happen again!"

Cassius reached for Dyrk's arm. The crowd was chanting "Teren, Teren, House Teren!"

"Your name, boy?" the balding Lord gruffly asked.

"Dyrk, son of Maryk, House Teren," Dyrk said.

Cassius was about to raise Dyrk's arm to acknowledge the winner when his eyes began to bulge out of his head. A bright red blood vessel suddenly showed on his forehead. He turned back to Dyrk.

"Maryk?" He hissed. "You are Maryk's eldest?"

Dyrk gulped, remembering too late Madwin's admonishments. But honesty was the better part of valour. "That's correct," he said.

Cassius suddenly looked like he wanted to be anywhere but in the middle of ten thousand spectators with some sort of dilemma on his mind. But he quickly came to a decision. Dyrk's arm was raised. "The winner," he boomed, "Dyrk House Teren!"

Dyrk noted that Cassius left out his patronym. He became dimly aware that Neriah had been taken onto the field, and now was at his side. She was saying something to him, pleading with him about something, but he was only listening intently to Cassius. "Call Madwin to my tent immediately," Cassius barked. He named a couple more individuals to accompany him. The scribe followed dutifully, but the two Eraturs stayed at Dyrk's side.

Finally Neriah's hysterical cries entered his consciousness. She seemed very distraught. In violation of many of the rules between young men and women, she was brushing his cheek and running her fingers along his scalp. He now noticed that blood was staining the ends of her sleeves.

"Dyrk, you've got to tell me where else it hurts," she insisted, then became more plaintive. "You've got to say something to me, anything at all!"

Dyrk turned his eyes towards her but didn't move his head, as it was still in her hands. "I'm here," he said softly. "Not really in any pain."

Neriah put her hand to her mouth. "That's not possible," she almost shrieked. "Check him closer", she demanded of the dark-haired Eratur who was holding a cloth to Dyrk's right temple.

"I don't see any other cuts, m'lady" the Eratur said. "This one isn't that bad either. A nasty bump on the scalp, and some swelling near his eye. I think he's all right. He's been summoned to the Lord's tent, though, so you'll have to go back to your friends."

It wasn't quite the victory scene that Dyrk had remembered from his previous years of watching the competition. Then it had always been a joyous celebration as friends and family mobbed the victor, taking his armour off playfully, and hoisting him on their shoulders. The chosen girl would be in the middle of it, sometimes carried gently by an older Eratur. Neriah had to walk back to the spectator's benches with the dark-haired Eratur, sleeves still smeared with Dyrk's blood, while he was taken off in a cloud of suspicion.

What was he suspected of? The answer was rather obvious at first. He had been entered under a false name in order to hide his attendance from his father. Of that he and Madwin were certainly guilty. But that didn't explain Cassius's reaction upon learning the name of his father.

He was seated just outside the Lord's tent with the blond-haired Eratur, which Dyrk learned was Thur Idrod. Dyrk hadn't seen Madwin go in, but he could tell from the raised voices that his headman was inside. He couldn't pick out much of what was said, but at one point he could clearly hear Madwin say, "Control your voice, Cassius! The boy is sitting right outside your tent."

Dyrk made an attempt to ask Idrod about what was going on. Idrod declined to say anything, simply saying that Madwin was the proper one to question. Shortly after that, another Eratur, broad-shouldered with greying hair, arrived and tried to gain entrance. Idrod stopped him.

"Hold there, Daynen, Cassius is in a meeting by invite only."

"Then the Lord will have to invite me immediately," Daynen said brusquely.

Idrod entered the tent, and the voices died down. Daynen scowled at Dyrk and then stood at attention in front of the flap. Then Dyrk remembered. Thur Daynen was Bayern's father. If he was here, was there some sort of plan afoot to rob Dyrk of the victory and give it to Bayern?

Idrod admitted Daynen, but it was only a few moments before the grey-haired Eratur exited the tent and took his leave with a nod to Idrod. Dyrk glowered at him as he left. It was getting dark.

"Is he sore about what I did to his son?" Dyrk blurted, unable to keep it in any longer.

Idrod simply chuckled. "Good show, that was."

It was another half-hour before Madwin finally left the tent. He looked haggard and frustrated. He nodded to Thur Idrod, then seized Dyrk none too gently by the shoulder and made him walk in front. Dyrk's nerves had not calmed down since before the competition, and they were again churning his stomach and making his heart race. His legs were like rubber as every joint shook. The adrenaline had taken its toll on his body, and he knew he couldn't walk for long.

Thankfully, it didn't take long to get to their fairground tent. The Vekh servant woman was nearby, and on hearing Madwin enter his tent, followed behind with a lamp and wordlessly stood at attention.

"He needs stiches," Madwin said, and sat quietly while the servant obeyed. Dyrk had received stitches before. It wasn't pleasant, the feeling of a needle piercing the skin right beside a wound that already smarted. Luckily this time the wound wasn't within his view, which for some reason made it easier to bear. He sat on the bench and did his best to resist flinching as the servant worked.

"We will be staying the night here," Madwin said to the woman as she applied some salve to the stitched wound to ward off infection. "Please go to the Upper City, to the Squire's Tap board-house and have our things collected." The servant nodded, hung the lamp, and left.

"Cover your left eye," Madwin immediately ordered him. Dyrk obliged. Madwin moved a finger in front of his right and watched the eyeball respond. "Thur Idrod swore that you lost your right eye in that fight," he said. "Either he was mistaken or you were very lucky. I think both."

Alone with Madwin, Dyrk erupted forth with questions. Madwin didn't seem to listen, as he sat down too with his head in his hands, and Dyrk's voice trailed off.

Madwin flattened his hands together and placed the fingertips against his lips. "Why would you ever want to become an Eratur?" he asked simply.

Madwin put so much emphasis on the question that Dyrk knew it would be improper to respond instinctively. He was supposed to carefully consider the query and give a measured response. He drew a deep breath. "Thur Madwin, I wish to serve the king in whatever capacity he should demand of me. If he calls me to the office, then I am willing to serve the people."

Madwin seemed to have changed. He always used the eloquent grammar and extensive Melandarim vocabulary in his speech, but for a moment he had lost it. He grumbled angrily, inveighing against the king with a cuss word Dyrk had never heard pass his lips. "For one second think about yourself. Forget tradition. Forget your family. Forget what the nation thinks about you, what the crowd wants to see. What do you want from life?"

Dyrk was taken aback. Madwin had always seemed to ask questions for which there was a right answer, even if that answer was obscure. This was the first time he had asked such an open-ended question. Dyrk could not formulate any response that would satisfy the criteria in his mind, an answer that was right, and true, and in accordance with what he had been taught.

"Riches, pleasure, a pretty girl," Madwin cut into the silence. "Wide open spaces, glorious death in battle, or power over men. What is it? What drives you?"

The entire day had been a whirlwind. Feelings and emotions that Dyrk had never experienced before had pumped through his being. He was left utterly exhausted by it all. Yet he had to find the reserves necessary to sort out the tightly wound mystery that lay before him. The reaction at his victory, the discussion at the Lord's tent, and now Madwin's irrational behavior, what was going on?

But for a moment, he put that aside and tried to think of an honest answer to Madwin's question.

"I'm not sure if I'm allowed to say this," Dyrk ventured, seeing Madwin squeeze his eyes shut as if in pain. "But I want to please Arren and His Servants. If I must point to something on earth that exhibits this desire, it would be the honour and praise of those who worship them."

Madwin creased his brow. "Very well," he said, not at all sounding like he meant it. "But what if those two things were in conflict? What if you could have one and not the other?"

Dyrk took a deep breath and plunged in. "Thur Madwin, forgive my saying so. Often you bait me with situations and questions that take a roundabout way to a point you want to prove. Sometimes I won't understand what you are trying to say until a good deal later. Is this one of those times?"

Madwin arched his brow and broke out into a grin. "Yes, *jadweir*, you are correct. You should know by now that I am unable to speak plainly. I will do that for you just this once.

"You are going to the College. I will tell you no more than that for today."

CHAPTER 6:
RAYVE

Rayve swung onto the first branch of the great oak tree, sitting there for a moment before standing up and reaching for the second. His favorite climbing tree had been used by other children for decades, as could be seen by the worn bark on the limbs. Most of the other trees in that city green had been vandalized by older youth, their bottom limbs chopped or snapped off. But that particular oak had branches stouter than Rayve's legs, too thick for anything but a woodsman's axe. He didn't know why he loved climbing the same tree over and over again. He knew it had something to do with the way that he felt when he was close to the top. He felt free, a boy in charge of his own destiny, who had a mind to go wherever he wished. But that illusion faded once his feet hit the ground again, the dream all but broken when he returned home. The times that Mother would try to crush his spirit, he would remember and think of that place high up in the branches, surrounded by leaves, where his eyes were unfettered and his mind released.

There he would peer across the well-kept houses in his neighbourhood to the glistening parapets of the King's keep to the north. He could just make out the guards' spears as they trundled across the battlements, or when they stood within the turrets. Every day he scanned the banners that flew from the standards. The numbers and colours were different from day to day, denoting those Eraturs who were staying as guests under the King's roof. During Grand Councils there were as many as a hundred banners flapping in the wind, resplendent in their various brilliant colours. On that day, Rayve saw a servant on the battlements, taking down banner after banner. It was the end of the Rhov-Attan, and the visitors were returning home.

But Rayve's eyes also turned to the west, to the poorest part of the great city. At times he wondered what it would be like to live there. All the adults told him that it was a terrible place. The water was said to be putrid, the food usually spoiled. Unsavory men roamed the streets, looking to enslave any children who wandered too far away from the watchful eyes of their parents. Ropers they were called, because they carry ropes tied in a noose ready to snare their prey. But he also knew that bands of children roamed free in that quarter of the city, without parents to watch over them. Groups of orphans and runaways would wander the streets, doing both honest work and stealing to make a living. It was that life he dreamed about, when alone in his room or high atop the tree as he was now. Most of his friends wanted to be a King's Eratur, or a famous judge, a ship captain, or a powerful Lord.

This time the twelve-year-old boy would not gaze at other parts of the capital city. He was more interested in the strange man that he now realized was frequenting the neighbourhood. Perhaps the man was a Roper from the slums, but he doubted it. Questionable people would always be challenged by the city's guards if they set foot into a more affluent area such as that one.

High up in the branches he was well hidden in the leaves, and by positioning himself could look through gaps in the canopy any direction he desired. Now he looked down towards the other end of the green, at the long stone bench that was beside the pool. There the man sat, always closest to where the bench met the low wall around the pool. There he was quite unobtrusive, and the less perceptive could walk through the small park and not even notice him.

Rayve had first noticed the man two weeks ago. The boy had joined with a few friends to play a game of rabbit-and-fox. He almost ran into the man as Rayve slid into a hiding place by the fountain. The man didn't even flinch as Rayve stumbled at his feet. A long brown robe covered him from head to foot, patched in one place that had become threadbare. In the shadows Rayve thought at first that the man was wearing a cowl to shade his face, but once his eyes adjusted to the light he saw that the man's head was bare, and had dark hair and a dark beard. The face was handsome, with defined cheekbones and glittering eyes. His mouth was pursed in a subtle grin that made Rayve a little uneasy. One hand was laying palm-down on his knee, the other supported his bearded chin with one curled finger.

"Ex… excuse me, honourable sir," Rayve had stammered, and then made himself scarce. As far as he knew, the man had not reacted to his intrusion in any way. He was not there the next time Rayve came to the green with his friends. But over the past two weeks, the times that Rayve came there alone, just to get away from home, he spied the man sitting in the same position, observing.

This was the fourth time Rayve encountered the man, and now wanted to get a good look at him. Why would he loiter here? What was he doing? Could he really be some kind of Roper who was simply waiting for his opportunity? The Ropers were, according to the stories, a gang of child-abductors who would sell the pilfered children to the Vekh as slaves. At first the story had really frightened him, but his classmates informed him that it was an honest lie told by parents to keep them out of trouble.

There was something eerie about the way the man sat. He remained almost completely motionless. Rayve figured that sitting on that stone bench would be quite uncomfortable, and he himself would be fidgeting in no time. The man remained still, except for an occasional movement of the right hand from his chin into his cloak and back again.

After ten minutes of studying the man sit there without moving, Rayve began to get bored and started to move to look elsewhere. But then he noticed the man reach into his cloak. Rayve watched with interest as the man pulled the hilt of a sword into view. With both hands, he tightened the coloured ribbons that were wrapped around its hilt.

Rayve was fascinated. He knew at a young age that only certain people were allowed to carry blades longer than eight inches in Karolia. He himself had seen a sword unsheathed only once, when the Headman of his ward had visited his mother's house. Thur Brullin carried a Karolian-made Andrast bastard sword, bearing the traditional double-edged straight blade. The headman had spoken with Rayve for a short time about how he was getting along at home with his father gone for so much of the year. During the conversation, which Rayve was eager to avoid, he had asked to see Thur Brullin's sword. The green and black ribbons wrapped around the hilt identified the Headman's house as House Arlavi. Other engravings and filigree on the hilt captivated the boy's attention. He wanted to stare at the weapon for hours, there was that much detail in the Headman's blade.

In the shadows, Rayve could not see what colours the ribbons were on the stranger's hilt. He could see that the handpiece was long enough to grip with a hand and a half, the pommel small and smooth so not to injure the palm of the second hand. The crosspiece was straight, but angled slightly towards the point. He so badly wanted to go and look at the stranger's sword, so amazed was he at the smithwork that went into each weapon.

But why can't I? he thought to himself. Father had said on several occasions that a man with a sword could always be trusted. If ever he thought he was in trouble, he was supposed to look for anyone bearing a sword of Karolia, and he would be safe. What made that man any different?

He wrestled with himself, worried that the man could be dangerous, but finally curiosity won him over. Swords weren't something that he could see every day, especially when his mother didn't want him to have anything to do with them. He climbed down the tree slowly and deliberately, giving his conscience time to change his mind. The man was still sitting there next to the pool.

Rayve approached cautiously, stopping ten feet in front of the man. The stranger was motionless again, having covered the sword, and now sat in the same pose he always did. The cowl was not covering his head. The boy began to feel less uneasy as he saw that the man's expression was gentle.

"I… I noticed your sword, honourable sir. I was wondering if - um - I would quite like to see it, sir," Rayve stammered.

The man's eyebrows raised a little. For an agonizing minute Rayve stood there, feeling his cheeks starting to burn. What was he doing asking a stranger to show him his sword? But in that neighbourhood, there were never any bad people. The guards always kept them away.

In a smooth motion, the man reached to his side. The ringing sound of steel sliding on steel was soft, but it still made the boy flinch. Once the blade cleared the sheath, he could see that it was about four hands long, shorter than Thur Brullin's but just as stout. The stranger laid the weapon on the ground with two hands, and Rayve bent to his hands and knees to look. The hilt had engravings like the Headman's did, but they were scored with black and silver instead of gold. Runes of an unknown language ran in two lines up the flat of the blade, on either side of the groove. The handle was thin and straight, wrapped in ribbons of red and light green, symbolic of House Melikar, Fifth of the Houses of Ruling. The gem in the pommel was the most intriguing. It was a pale yellow oblong jewel, the size of a pebble Rayve would skip into the Lower Pool in the early mornings when nobody was looking. It seemed to reflect light in a strange and ever-shifting way, as if clouds were constantly swirling within.

"These colours are those of House Melikar," he picked up the courage to speak. "That means that you and I-"

"This blade is not my own, dear Rayve," the voice was powerful yet comforting to the boy, reminding him of memories of his father. He didn't even realize that the stranger knew his name. "This sword belongs to none other than yourself."

Alarmed, Rayve sputtered, "But I - but good sir, I am not permitted to carry a sword until I am a soldier! To do so would bring judgment." His eyes never left the sword. His own! How could that be! Of course he was House Melikar, but there were many of the house that were allowed to carry swords. Maybe it was one of theirs?

"You may not carry it yet, my son. But in time, I promise you, in time you will wear it with pride."

"Where will it be until that time?" Rayve asked breathlessly, too excited to think of anything else.

The man bent down to pick up the sword. "I have cared for it since you were born, and I will continue to do so." The sword slid effortlessly into its sheath at the man's side. "You have much to learn first."

"Who - may I ask who you are, good sir?" the boy could barely remember his manners.

"You may call me Hajwan, my son. But you must be going home. You have lessons with your scribe in a short time."

Rayve picked himself up. "Yes I do," he said. He thought for a moment, and then asked, "Will you be here tomorrow, Hajwan? Could I look at my sword again then?"

The man smiled, a warm smile that banished any remaining doubt in the boy. "I will be here."

He couldn't tell his mother, he thought as he scurried home. She hated anything to do with the military that kept his father away from the home all year save a few days. She always talked about her husband becoming an officer in the City Guard, but Rayve knew his father would have none of it. He always wanted to be where the action was. She didn't want her son to ever touch a sword.

He knew he should be asking reasonable questions. How did this man know his name? How did he know that he was of House Melikar? How could he be so presumptuous to think that Rayve would become a soldier, or an Eratur, and had prepared a sword already for that event? But the young boy's mind refused to dwell on such practicalities. The rest of the day went by in a blur, and he slept fitfully, all night thinking about him striding into battle, his sword shining in his hand.

The next day he tried to sneak out of the house early, but he was caught by his mother and given a stern tongue-lashing about neglecting his chores. He cleaned the chamberpots, fetched the water, and chopped the firewood in a hurry, evoking more harsh criticism when the water sloshed onto the kitchen floor.

Finally, the time came for mother to go and spend time with the other ladies, chatting and trying on new dresses. It seemed that mother spent all her good times with her friends. She would come home to him happy and smiling, until she saw her son again. He always felt hurt that he couldn't make his mother smile like her friends did.

Rayve raced to the green as fast as his legs would take him. But to his dismay, the man was not there. Instead, there were three of his playmates sitting by the pool and playing with floating sticks. Deflated, Rayve joined his friends, and soon he was absorbed in his play. Every now and then he took a glance at the stone bench, but no Hajwan.

His friends left the green one by one, going home for the midday meal. Rayve stayed near the fountain, knowing that his mother wouldn't be home to give him lunch. He usually prepared for that by eating as much as he could for breakfast and slipping a few biscuits and dried prunes in his pocket for a snack. But still his stomach rumbled uncomfortably.

He didn't even jump when a hand was placed on his shoulder. It was almost like he was expecting it, anticipating the arrival of the man who by all rights should still be a stranger. A peculiar sensation came over him, and the smell of leather and rust-oil came to his nostrils. "Good day, Hajwan," Rayve said.

"Hello, my son," Hajwan removed his hand while Rayve turned around on his seat. His cowl was down around his shoulders, his handsome bearded face had a barely perceptible smile. The man's face did not project sternness or toughness like his father did. It was softer, almost a little sad even. Rayve felt an instant connection, like Hajwan had the parts of his father that he always wished he had.

They sat at the stone bench again. Rayve had so many questions for the man. Who was he? Where did he come from? Where did he get that sword from? He was too polite to ask any of those, and instead waited for Hajwan to speak.

But Hajwan didn't talk right away. He pulled a bundle from the small bag he carried, and unwrapped it on his lap. Inside was some fresh bread, cheese, two apples, and two strawberries. With a knife, Hajwan deftly cut some of the bread and cheese and gave them to Rayve.

"Thank you," Rayve did not forget his manners.

"You have many friends," Hajwan said, cutting some cheese for himself. "Do you see them every day?"

"Oh yes, sir. Except the days that I am at my lessons."

"What do they do for you?" The man's question was an unusual one. When Rayve hesitated to answer, the question was followed up. "What do you hope to get from them when you spend time with them?"

"I guess we just have fun," the boy responded, still a bit confused. "We just spend time together so we're not alone."

Hajwan cut another piece of bread. It was delicious, soft and moist, baked with sugar. "So otherwise you feel alone, then."

"My mother isn't home much," Rayve said, rocking back and forth comfortably as he ate. "Even when she is, she doesn't play with me and rarely talks with me. My friends are better for that."

"What things does she say to you?"

The man's tone of voice was so kind and considerate that Rayve didn't think the question was needlessly probing. "Usually she just gets mad at me for what I'm doing wrong," he replied. Was that too harsh? No, it was, actually, quite accurate.

Hajwan slowly shook his head. "One plants a beautiful sapling, full of goodness and life. Then they trample on it, and demand that it grows. 'Put forth your branches,' they say, scarring its bark. 'Delight us with your blossoms,' they mock as they strip its leaves."

The poetry fascinated Rayve. The scribes taught him much about the literature of men long dead. This was the first time he heard someone making living art, with himself as the subject.

"Your mother is not a bad person," Hajwan said. "She pursues her own ends, satisfies her own needs. Your father is the same. Is their pursuit of fulfilment and happiness an evil?"

Rayve was slightly disappointed. He would rather not talk about his parents. "No, but-"

"But why do their desires cause you to feel left out?" He voiced Rayve's unfinished question. He held up one of the strawberries. "Have you looked beneath the soil at a strawberry patch?"

Rayve shook his head.

"Their roots are interconnected, entwined, enmeshed. They don't depend solely on one or a few stalks or leaves. Each plant draws on the roots of another. Should the roots in one area fail, the nearby plants still feed it life."

"Are you a priest of Harophin?" Rayve asked. Harophin was the Servant of plants and growth, and his priests became either educators or philosophers. They often used metaphors from the natural world.

Hajwan smiled. "Yes and no," he said kindly. "I build on what he teaches." He bit into the strawberry.

"Thank you for lunch," Rayve said.

"I will see you again in a few days," Hajwan spoke, wrapping the last of the loaf of bread in the lunch-cloth.

Rayve couldn't wait. In fact, he wished that Hajwan would invite him to accompany the man. Anything was better than returning home to an absent father and self-absorbed mother.

CHAPTER 7:
HIGHER LEARNING

The bench just outside of the Rector's office was padded. Comforts like that were a rare occurrence at the College. It seemed to Dyrk that much of the furniture had been intentionally designed and built with discomfort in mind. After two years at the College, he was used to it. He laughed out loud when one of the new initiates complained of sore muscles after his first night on one of the hard cots.

He had been summoned to the Rector's office at a strange time of day. Normally the chief administrator of the College would hold personal meetings after instruction was over, in the early evening. A twinge of nervousness wouldn't leave the pit of Dyrk's stomach, but he quieted his nerves with the facts. He was doing well in most of his instruction, lagging behind in none of it. Siegecraft had been the toughest, but his friends had helped him fill the holes of the mathematics training that was lacking from his schooling in Tanvilon. He was a good singer, he excelled in horsemanship, and his combat skills were coming around. His favorite courses were those in history and legal tradition.

He recalled another time he had sat on a bench with his nerves all a-flutter. It was almost two years ago, in Madwin's tent. Things seemed to hang by a thread there. He had been declared the winner of the Contest, and by right was admitted to the College. The reason behind all the controversy still did not make sense to him. His thoughts traveled back to the morning after he had won.

He saw Neriah that morning, for the first time not wearing her dancing dress. Kureth, Vannis, and Hilla came together as a group near the stables again, to provide the necessary chaperones. Neriah was dressed in a grey cotton skirt and a white blouse under a dark outer corset; it made her look a bit older than the other two who were dressed in summer frocks. He also noticed that Neriah's hair was intricately styled, with two small braids tied together at the back, restraining the rest which was loose and flowed nearly to her waist. Two small white wildflowers were fixed just behind her left ear.

They walked and talked, spending the cooler morning in each other's company. But it finally came to saying goodbyes. Dyrk had decided to leave for Tanvilon the same day, and he would have to leave very soon if he was going to make it home by the next night.

Again, Kureth drew Hilla and Vannis a short distance away so that Dyrk could talk to Neriah one last time.

"I guess the time has come to say goodbye," he said.

Neriah nodded, her eyes again descending to the hem of her skirt.

"But I don't want this to be the last time I see you," he blurted before thinking it through. "When can I see you again?"

Her eyes widened and her lips parted a little without saying anything. Finally, she managed to venture, very quietly, "You would like that?"

"Yes."

She raised her hand to her right cheek, sliding an imaginary strand of hair behind her ear. It seemed like it took effort, but her eyes lifted to look at him and she gave a pretty smile that he would never forget. "I would like it too," she said. "When will you be back in Doleth Sarin?"

"I'd like to be back within a week," he said, making his plans on the fly. He had no reason to come back except for her. But that was enough of a reason as far as he was concerned. "I do need to see my family."

"Harwaith is right on the Great East Highway, west of Doleth Sarin. Ask for Vecton the wainwright, we are easy to find." She fidgeted with one of the ties on her dress, straightening them out between her fingers. She stole another glance at him as she chewed her lip. "Should we expect you next Taephin's Day[1]? Does that

---

[1] Friday

work?"

He was jolted back into the present. A scribe brushed past him and knocked on the door to the Rector's office. The door opened, and the man was admitted. Yes, that had been one of the best days of his life. But the next one didn't go so well.

He set out that same day on his own back to Tanvilon. Madwin had things to finish in Doleth Sarin and would be staying a few more days. The late spring rains made Dyrk's travel less than enjoyable. On the evening of the second day he rode Tanakh through the quiet streets of his hometown and up the country lane to his home. His parents were both in the sitting room of their comfortable house; it was just after dinner. A fire burned in the fireplace to ward off the chill that the rain brought. His father immediately guessed where he had been, promised some extra work as punishment, and then curtly said, "The matter is closed."

Then Dyrk told them of his victory and his admission to the College.

His father's face went ashen. His mother began sobbing uncontrollably and withdrew to the next room. Maryk turned from Dyrk, faced the fireplace, and put his bearded chin in his hands. The special shoe that he wore over his maimed foot shifted back and forth on the floor. He swore under his breath, and Dyrk could hear him say some very nasty things about Madwin.

"I don't understand why this is so difficult for everyone to accept," Dyrk said loudly, hoping his mother would hear. "I had hoped you would be proud of me but now you're ashamed. I want to serve my country just as you did, Father."

That elicited even stronger sobs from her mother in the dining hall. His father half-turned his face to him and cried, "If that's what you intend to do, then go. Get out of here."

Confused and hurt, Dyrk had packed up his things and left without spending the night. He did say goodbye to his brother Gavon and his three young sisters. But he didn't get to say goodbye to Elzabi, Nabir, or Hagris, his father's faithful bondservants who lived in other houses on the property.

He spent the night at the tavern in Tanvilon. The keeper's wife supplied him with bedding, her eyes full of unasked questions. Dyrk preferred the company of Januz, who still didn't seem sober despite being without a drop of alcohol for six months. Januz was still homeless, so he slept at the ward tavern. The man began to repeat the story of the evil beast that lived in the old mine in the hills, coming out at night to eat children.

"Oh, I killed it," Dyrk said matter-of-factly.

"Ah? You did? When was that?"

"Eight years ago. Ran it right through the midsection."

Januz stroked the stubble on his chin. "Reckon that's why I haven't seen it since then. Well good work, lad. The children are safer now. Maybe you'll make a soldier yet once you get out there and grow up."

Dyrk shifted on the padded bench. The ramblings of Januz had cheered him up that night. After the shock from his parents, he needed it. He still could not rationalize their reaction. Was it because of the injury that his father had sustained, and they were petrified that the same thing would happen to him? After two years of no responses to his letters, Dyrk was convinced that it was something more serious. But he had no way of knowing.

He didn't like to think of that day. He would rather dwell on the first days with Neriah and her family.

He returned to Doleth Sarin immediately after spending the night with Januz. The College wasn't due to start its next group of initiates until Taephin's month, which gave him about nine weeks before he had to be in Geherth Altyr. In the meantime, he had to find a way to make a living. There were no handouts in Karolia, even to the champion of the Combat of Squires.

It didn't take him long to find a job at the livery stable. His experience with horses gave him an appraising eye and before long the owner, Farnich, was counting on him for a second opinion on many transactions. Dyrk stayed in one of the poorer boarding-houses, a far cry from the quarters he had shared with Madwin at the Squire's Tap.

Dyrk struggled to think of gifts to bring with him to Neriah's house. Typically, a boy would bring flowers to the home of the girl's parents, but he couldn't possibly impress Neriah with that, given her skills with floral arrangements. He settled on something a bit more practical. On the morning of Taephin's Day, he bought a small box of citrus fruits, an expensive delicacy since they had to be imported all the way from Ancharith in snow-filled barges. That would be for the family to enjoy. For Neriah he bought a new quill and ink. He figured if things worked out, they would want to correspond while he was at the college.

He had arranged for the day off from Farnich in exchange for handling the chores on Nedrin's Day[1]. He took Tanakh and headed for Harwaith. The weather was overcast, but not raining. After an easy hour's travel, he easily found the town, just as Neriah had told him. A passerby pointed out Vecton's shop. The home was a simple lofted hovel connected to a workshop and small smithy.

Heart churning and knees knocking, he walked up to the door of the hovel and knocked. An upper window swung open almost immediately and a ten-year-old boy's head poked out. "He's here, he came!" he began shouting, and disappeared from view. A commotion was audible in the house, with many voices clamoring and the sound of furniture being moved.

The door finally opened. A woman stood blocking the doorway. Her appearance contrasted strongly with Dyrk's own mother, who was tall, delicate, and stately but rather severe. This woman was squarely built with broad shoulders and thick legs visible under her dress, the hem of which did not quite reach the floor. Her face was both hard and kind at the same time, giving Dyrk the impression of a woman who showed her love for her family by working diligently day and night. She looked to be less than fifty years old, which in Karolia meant she was still of childbearing age. Her thick, curly hair was gathered in the back but fell over her shoulders.

She had a business-like expression on her face, but it quickly turned into a mischievous smile as she looked Dyrk up and down. Her lower lip was a bit larger than her upper one, making the smile

---

[1] Nedrin's Day is Saturday, the day of the week when most businesses close.

seem clumsy, but it was joyous all the same.

"And who might you be?" she said in a teasing voice. "My daughter said there might be a young man stopping by today. Have you seen him?"

Dyrk introduced himself. The woman did not budge from the door, but she appeared to be waiting for something. Behind her, various children began to sing and poke fun at their eldest sister, who was still out of Dyrk's field of view. He presented his gift of oranges, and the woman invited him in.

The visit didn't go quite as Dyrk expected. Neriah's mother, Ryesse, peppered him with questions, about his family background, schooling, goals in life, and even religious convictions, all the while peeling potatoes and carrots. This was rather unusual to Dyrk, who expected the father to take the lead in such things. Vecton, her father, popped in from time to time but always seemed to be distracted by something. He was a thin, balding man with a hawk-like face, large mouth, and beady eyes, whose appearance changed drastically those rare times he smiled, ear to ear. Vecton didn't talk much, leaving that up to Ryesse. Neriah herself was unable to spend much time with Dyrk. She was preoccupied with her younger siblings, some of whom cried for attention while others continue to tease her about her "boy-Eratur".

As Neriah had warned, the house wasn't furnished to the same standard that Dyrk had grown up in. Indeed, there were nine people crammed into a space scarcely larger than the servant house that Nabir and his family of six lived in on Maryk's property.

After a couple hours, and some orange slices shared amongst all the children, Dyrk took his leave. Neriah came to the door with him.

"Thanks for putting up with them," she said once they were out the front door. The sky had clouded over, and a light rain was beginning to fall, but thankfully there was an awning under which they stood. Dyrk made sure that he was still within view of Vecton's shop doorway as they paused there. Tanakh gave a brief nicker as he stood in the rain.

"It was really good of you to answer all of mother's questions," she continued, sounding apologetic. She struggled to make any eye contact with him.

Dyrk assured her that it was no problem, and embellished things a bit when he said he enjoyed the visit.

"I... I keep thinking," she stammered, struggling for words. "This whole thing is like a fairy tale. This last week. I mean, you winning the competition and all, and, well, us..." she trailed off.

"What are you saying?" Dyrk tried his best to sound gentle and caring, but he could not hide the worry in his voice.

"Oh, it's just, I keep thinking that I'll wake up and find that it was all a dream," she said. "I woke up this morning thinking it was only that, and I could just get on with life. But then here you are." A tear slid down her cheek. "There's so much here that doesn't make sense."

Ryesse came out of the workshop gate with a rug that she beat against the side of the house. The rug seemed quite clean already.

"What I mean is, I've been told so many times not to get my hopes up. I went to the festival with the goal of performing in the dance. No more. I didn't expect a ribbon. I was just happy to be there. And even if by some chance I did get one, a girl shouldn't hope that it will turn into anything. I didn't expect to meet you, and..."

The tears were flowing freely now. "Valeron knows I'm making a mess of this," she said out loud to herself, extending a sleeve over her left hand to wipe her face.

"You're doing just fine," Dyrk reassured her. "But why are you crying?"

She took a deep breath. "You're from a town far away. You're from a different type of family. You're going to be doing big things. You'll be one of the leaders of the kingdom. Dyrk, there are so many things that are going to take you away from here, from me. And it's wonderful that you're doing all that. But we need to be realistic, and not start something that we have no right expecting to work."

Ryesse started shouting at one of her children from outside the workshop door, still in full view of the couple.

"I hope you're not saying what I think you're saying," was all Dyrk could put forward through the lump in his throat.

"Do you remember just before the combat? You asked me if I wanted you to quit the competition?"

Dyrk nodded.

"You're doing it again, taking my words too far." Her gaze, usually kept down, now looked straight at Dyrk. Those dark brown eyes imprisoned him all over again.

"You just need me to understand the fears that are going through your heart," he said softly.

The rain had stopped. Ryesse was now sweeping the walkway in front of Vecton's shop, despite the fact that no dust was being moved by the broom.

Neriah returned her eyes to their natural position. "Thanks for hearing me out," she said.

Dyrk reached into the saddlebag at his feet and took out the ink and quill. "Should there be distance between us," he said as he gave them to her, "let's conquer it. I am always just a few strokes of a pen away."

A week later, Dyrk made another visit. There was still a feeling of awkwardness, but he did his best to act comfortable. He played a game with Neriah and some of the older children and took a tour of their backyard garden. Again, Vecton spoke very little to him, instead he was darting in and out of the house for this or that reason. Dyrk and Neriah spent some time together under the awning while Ryesse found an excuse to do her washing within sight.

But after their goodbye, as Dyrk was getting Tanakh ready to go, Vecton strode out of his shop and purposefully approached him. They made a bit of small talk about Tanakh, but then Vecton's face lined with concern.

"Young man, you have my blessing," he said. "But it appears to me you are setting her up for some disappointment. Life doesn't go in a straight line. You've got some tough lessons to learn yet, I'm afraid, and it pains me to see my daughter have to go through more loss."

As far as Neriah's loss was concerned, Dyrk understood what he was talking about. At the age of eight years old, Neriah had lost her older sister and playmate to an illness. At fifteen, Neriah had taken ill herself several times during her schooling. In the following summer, she had gotten worse and was bedridden for weeks. Her parents had finally paid for priests of Taephin, who were the best physicians in the land, to see her, and they reported that she had kidney trouble. From then on, her diet had to be closely managed, and she had to take certain herbs. She bruised very easily, and often woke up with severe cramps in her legs. While the other girls her age were learning crafts, chasing boys, and going to school, Neriah struggled just to get through each day.

Dyrk wasn't sure what Vecton meant by the comment about tough lessons that he had still to learn. He pondered it on the way home but did not arrive at a satisfactory conclusion.

He visited Neriah at her parents' house each week on Taephin's Day before the time came to pack up and leave Doleth Sarin for the college at Geherth Altyr. Farnich, the owner of the livery stable, told him that he was welcome back anytime. Dyrk did not expect that to be necessary.

Dyrk inhaled sharply. Someone else was coming down the hallway. He looked up from where he was sitting. It was Bayern. The dark-haired squire walked past Dyrk without looking at him, and sat on the other side of the bench, as far away as possible. Dyrk's mind raced. What was Bayern doing here?

As expected, Bayern had gained admission to the Eratur's College and had started the same time. Dyrk recalled how furious Thur Daynen had been with the outcome of the Competition. As a result, Dyrk had expected Bayern to be rather hostile towards him. Now, as he thought back, he really couldn't point to anything that Bayern had done to him in their time at the College, at least not openly. Last year, they had gotten together for a rather icy conversation in which Bayern congratulated him both for his ingenuity during the fight, and the fact that he wasn't grievously wounded by the hilt-blow to the head. Of course, Bayern didn't offer any apology for the vicious act, and Dyrk didn't ask for one.

Dyrk thought back to his initial days at the college. It had been an adjustment, but a welcome one. Dyrk appreciated a regimented life, always knowing what was expected and when. He excelled at the academic demands, but struggled at times with the physical ones, especially when it came to combat prowess. Even now, he was only slowly building mass onto his lanky frame. He had to exert more effort than some of the well-built boys.

His toughest time had been on a three-day journey to Andon Ridge. They had crossed the Elgolin River and entered the hills and forests in the Korlani foothills to the west. There the instructor and his helpers found a suitable cliff. The group of twelve initiates was told that they had to treat the cliff as a fortress wall. Their assignment was to use whatever means at their disposal to scale it. The instructor and his helpers stationed themselves up top, armed with bows and cloth-tipped arrows. Anyone hit with an arrow was "dead" and removed from the exercise. Dyrk had gotten into a rather heated argument with two other boys about the plan, and when he conceded defeat, he had trouble putting his back to the task of felling the trees and building the siegeworks. He was accused of trying to sabotage the effort. Dyrk did his best to apologize and do what he could to restore trust, but things didn't get much better. Their best effort, a three-stage ramp, failed when it crumbled sideways as the first initiates charged up.

But he was having good times, too, at the college. Dyrk was a little shy about singing, but he was told he had one of the best voices in his class. In Karolia, tradition derived from Melandar's writings maintained that a woman's singing triggered sensual thoughts in a man, and therefore she could not sing within earshot of a man other than her husband and children. Hence, men were the only ones able to sing in public. Eraturs were required to be accomplished singers so that they might lead soldiers or communities in song. Dyrk was chosen several times as a baritone soloist. He was even summoned to Altyren with a small group to perform at a royal dinner. There he met Prince Amarion, who complemented him on his singing.

The door opened. Bayern was called in. Dyrk continued to sit there, stewing in silence. Did his father ever get called into these strange meetings during his days at the College? Concerning fhis father, Dyrk no longer had any desire to go home to Tanvilon. He had kept in touch with Gavon, who was completing his studies with

Arene the scribe, and was hoping to be accepted into one of the Scribe's Colleges.

No, the few times he was able to travel, he always went back to Doleth Sarin, where he took day trips to visit Neriah and her family at Harwaith. The initial fascination of "boy meets girl" had worn off, replaced by a more homely, contented feeling whenever he was with her. Other boys talked about their girls with a fervor that bordered on obsession, but that wasn't the case with Dyrk. He sometimes wondered if it meant there was something deficient in his love for her. But he could easily imagine himself, as a respected headman in Saringon, with her as his wife. The two of them even spoke tentatively about marrying last time they were together, agreeing it made most sense to wait at least until he finished his fourth year at the College, and they knew what the options for his first assignment would be.

Another difference between his relationship and those of the other boys is that Dyrk didn't worry much about Neriah being scooped up by someone else. He felt secure in Neriah's dedication to him, just as he was committed to her. Other young women he talked to were all fascinated at his love story, the fairy-tale outcome of the Competition that they all had dreamed about as adolescent girls.

But now he sat and waited for the outcome of the mysterious meeting he had been summoned for. The door opened, and Bayern walked out. The young man again didn't look Dyrk in the eye as he hurried down the hall. Dyrk took a deep breath. It will be okay, he said to himself. I've faced these things before, and I've come out on top. After all, if Bayern was called in for the same thing, it couldn't be anything bad.

He was called into the office by the Rector's assistant.

The office was opulently draped and furnished. A corner of the room was separated from the rest by long curtains that were drawn shut. The Rector sat behind a desk, and he looked visibly uncomfortable. A bad sign. The assistant shut the door behind him and then stood at attention to take notes.

"State your name for the record," the assistant prodded Dyrk as he motioned to a chair to sit down.

"Dyrk son of Maryk house Teren," Dyrk said evenly.

Dyrk was sure he noticed movement behind the curtain once he declared his name. Who might that be?

"And how are you finding college life over these past two years," the Rector smiled weakly, clearly making small talk. Dyrk gave pat answers and waited for the hammer to fall, whatever it would be.

The hammer did fall. And it crushed him completely.

"Son of Teren," the Rector said slowly and evenly. "Some matters have come to our attention that make you ineligible to continue with your instruction at the College."

It took several moments for it to sink in. But once it did, Dyrk engaged his fight reflex, rather than flight.

"Exactly which 'matters' are you referring to?" Dyrk demanded. He noticed again some movement behind the curtain, and perhaps a muffled cough.

"I am not privy to discuss those," the Rector said. Dyrk was so furious he could have run him through right then and there.

"So you're saying," he spoke through gritted teeth, "that I have been declared ineligible for reasons that I am not entitled to know, and therefore completely unable to defend myself? How in the name of Kemantar is that just?

The Rector cleared his throat. "Enrolment in the College is a privilege, not a right. That privilege can be revoked for any reason whatsoever, with no right to appeal."

Dyrk's face was growing hot. "With all due respect, sir, you are making a big mistake."

He then noticed that there were two documents on his desk. Both had official seals affixed to them.

The Rector lowered his voice. "To be honest, son of Teren, you show exemplary qualities other than the matters I cannot discuss. For that reason, I am prepared to soften the blow with an offer."

Dyrk thought about ripping the door open and running out. To commit some sort of act of violence. To shout from the rooftops that this was not fair. Why should he even dignify this unjust process with his participation?

Then he recalled a discussion with Thur Madwin years ago. "But what if those two things were in conflict?" Madwin had said, speaking in veiled riddles as always. "What if you could have one and not the other?" He wasn't sure at that time what was meant by the two things that could not be had at the same time. Now Dyrk guessed that Madwin had spoken of both honour and Eraturhood. It was paradoxical that the two were in conflict.

He sighed. Justice would not be won through violence or other rash actions. Who was he to resist the iron wheels of society, even if those wheels were crushing him? "Tell me about your offer," he said, doing his best to keep his tone civil.

"I have one order here," the Rector said, pointing to one of the documents on his desk, "that discharges you from the College in dishonour. You have failed to meet the stringent requirements and are no longer fit for the King's duty. You will also not be eligible for citizenship. But the second," he waved his left hand over the other document, "authorizes an integration into the army. You would gain credit for time spent at the College. In a little more than a year, you could be back in Doleth Sarin with your royal service completed and be eligible for citizenship."

Dyrk placed his fingertips on his temples. "So either I go quietly and maintain my rights of citizenship, or I make some noise and be branded a criminal," he interpreted.

The Rector was sweating despite the cool morning air coming through the disused fireplace chimney. "If you insist on putting it that way, yes."

Dyrk had a sudden urge to walk over to the curtain and fling it aside. Someone was ruining his life, and he was betting that the person behind the curtain was responsible. Again, he reminded himself that he stood on the edge of a knife. His entire life, at least what was left of it, could be ruined by one misstep.

"I will accept your offer on one condition," he tried to control the emotion in his voice.

"I cannot..." the Rector started but Dyrk kept talking anyway.

"I want – no, I demand – that you tell whoever is bringing these accusations against me, to be a man and accuse me to my face."

The Rector eased back into his chair, appearing relieved. "Very well," he said. "I will ensure that the person who brought these matters to my attention is notified of your challenge." The document on his left was given one last seal, rolled up, and given to Dyrk. "You will report to the military base at Trebier on Telmanitar's Day, seventh week of Harophin's Month[1]."

"That's only six days. That's not enough time to walk the Sojourn of the Ancients," Dyrk responded curtly.

"No, it isn't. Expediency demands that you forego that formality."

Dyrk set his jaw. "Every soldier in the army is given the right to walk the Sojourn of the Ancients before they report for duty in peacetime," he insisted. "You just lectured me about privileges and rights, Rector. Now you are treading on my rights."

The Rector looked as if he had just resumed his gastric difficulties. He nodded to the secretary, who unrolled the document and made some alterations. After the Rector had initialed it, Dyrk took the completed copy. He turned his back and left.

He couldn't show his face to the rest of the initiates. He was so close to tears and he couldn't let them spill out. Nothing would be more unbecoming to an Eratur than crying. Knowing his colleagues were in their classes, he went straight to the barracks and had his spartan quarters cleared out in fifteen minutes. He gave his surroundings one last glance. His heart was heavy with crushing disappointment. Down the stairs he walked, heading for the stable.

Caevin, one of the initiates, was cleaning out one of the stables as discipline for some youthful indiscretion. He came over while Dyrk was saddling Tanakh and stowing his gear.

"Going somewhere, Dyrk?" he asked, leaning on the wall and biting off the tip of a carrot.

"Please leave me alone," Dyrk responded flatly. There was no way he could talk to anyone and remain composed.

"Suit yourself," Caevin returned to sweeping out a stall. Dyrk thanked Taephin that he was granted at least a small mercy. Taking

---

[1] Thursday, May 9, 2796

the reins of his Belorin cross warhorse, Dyrk prepared to ride through the outer gates of the Eratur's College for the last time.

"Oh, by the way," Caevin spoke up as Tanakh was led out of his stall, "The Rector's assistant came down a little while ago and mentioned you had forgotten this." He held up a small pouch. "Insisted you would be coming by and asked me to give it to you."

Dyrk grunted his thanks and made a hasty exit.

On the outskirts of the city, he stopped for a bit and re-read the document. The date he was to report had been changed to add six days to his reporting schedule. Twelve days! It normally took two weeks to do the round trip. He was going to be pressed for time. He looked at the pouch that Caevin had given him. What was this? Some sort of bribe? Indeed, he opened it to find two gold half-crowns, the standard lump-sum paid to every man who completed his royal service. But Dyrk hadn't completed it yet, and he was due to receive the same amount once he was finished his military service.

Then he saw a tiny scrap of paper stuck in the pocket of the pouch. "For expenses on your journey," was all it said.

Dyrk stored the pouch in his riding coat and looked across the river towards Altyren, glistening in the distance to the south. Two hours ago, he was waking up in his cot at the college, content in the false knowledge that the day would be like so many before it – filled with learning, training, developing his skills for the service of the kingdom. Now he had been tossed aside like refuse. His skills, his aptitudes, his desires – had they not all pointed towards the very place he was now riding away from?

Instead, men like Bayern would be placed in those positions of power and influence. Or even Caevin, an immature initiate who still snuck out at night to go drinking, which was why he was shoveling horse manure instead of going to his classes. What about the young man from Ekrenned who was tone-deaf? The half-Derrekh from Resgild who still couldn't name all sixty houses of Karolia? The liberal-minded lad from Altyren who said Arren was a figment of the imagination? Surely the Servants could see this injustice.

But the Servants were silent. Kemantar was a motionless statue that was only visible to Dyrk's eyes as a faint gleam on the skyline of

Altyren. The Servant of Justice had a prominent place within the capital city. Underneath his soaring likeness sprawled the highest law courts of the nation. Dyrk had attended a few sessions during his time at the College, as part of his instruction in civil law. He had always seen things through an idealistic prism, and the courts were the pinnacle of the system of Karolian law that could solve any and every dispute in the nation fairly.

In a few short hours, that prism had shattered. If the Rector of the College could dispense with elementary principles of justice at a whim, depriving him of his entire purpose in life, was the rest of the country any different? Did all of the judges in their flowing robes have curtained offices hiding men who wielded power from the shadows? Indeed, was Eraturhood itself something achieved through privilege, connections, and pledges of personal loyalty, rather than strength, integrity, and a commitment to serve?

His mind began to turn on everyone. Madwin had probably jumped through the right hoops to get through the College. Lord Cassius had greased the right palms, his Lady Yarevis had slept with the right people. Maryk had stolen the right horse. Thur Daynen…

A possibility struck him like a hot wind to his face. Maryk had boasted about taking a Tevledain war-horse during his ride to the Battle of Rocavion. Now that Dyrk thought about it, there was no way that Maryk could have afforded one just after graduating from college. To the best of Dyrk's knowledge, his father had come from a middle-class family. Had Maryk stolen the horse? Thur Daynen only rode Tevledains in parade and in battle. Well, only in parade, Dyrk corrected himself. He had heard that Daynen had never served in the military. Perhaps Maryk had stolen the horse from Daynen? Had history repeated itself when Dyrk had stolen the Tevledain right out from under Bayern? Was Thur Daynen the one behind the curtain in the Rector's office?

Whatever the case, Maryk must have done something that was at the root of Dyrk's downfall. In his thoughts, Dyrk no longer referred to Maryk as his father. He was a relative, an acquaintance, but no longer had the right to be called father. Maryk had all but disowned his eldest son after he enrolled in the College. He had hoped Loriah his mother would have talked some sense into him over the following months, but Gavon had reported that she was even more closed off about their firstborn son than Maryk was. Both of the short letters Dyrk had sent home during his time at the college went unanswered. Dyrk guessed the messages were tossed, unread, into the fireplace at home.

Dyrk steered Tanakh towards the edge of the road. The thoroughfare between the cities of Geherth Altyr and Navren Altyr was one of the most well-traveled roads in all Karolia. The wide, paved highway was teeming with traffic: on foot, horseback, and carts. The proportion of carts were relatively low compared to the roads in Saringon, because of the ease of transport on the waterway of the Elgolin River. The sudden adjustment to matters present reset Dyrk's mood as it sank in again just how his life had fallen apart in a few short hours.

Why go on at all? He had set Tanakh on a course towards Navren Altyr only because that was the logical route towards the town of Mar Athel which marked the beginning of the Sojourn of the Ancients. But who was he fooling? Twelve days would barely permit him to get to Mar Athel and back. It was time to face the facts, report for service, and hopefully die there. The rest of his life had no meaning.

He recalled some words of Madwin. "Suffering produces one of two things," he had said. "Callousness or empathy."

Empathy? What a load of horse dung. Dyrk resolved to prove Madwin right, just not in the way the headman intended.

Thoughts of Neriah suddenly flooded his mind, which only increased his bitterness. He had failed her. Her mother had gone around Harwaith telling everyone who would listen that her eldest daughter was to be marrying into the nobility – who knows, she could even be the provincial Lady someday. Dyrk's disgrace could not be any more amplified than appearing before Neriah and her family. He would rather go home and face his own mother's sorrow and father's scorn than set foot in Harwaith.

Why wait for military service to kill me off? His mind was straying into dangerous territory and he knew it. He forced himself, as he often did, to focus on the task that lay directly in front of him. Leave the distant future to the capriciousness of the Servants.

The first thing he had to do was to get to Navren Altyr. It was the fourth-largest city in Karolia, behind Altyren, Elbing, and Halidorn. In many ways it was an extension of Altyren itself, as it lay just beyond the bridges to the islands that Altyren was built on. It sprawled amongst some of the best farmland in Karolia. It housed a lot of light industry that supported the massive population on the island. Most important was the production of paper, produced from domesticated white poplar trees that were cultivated nearby like any other crop. Karolians depended more than any other nation on the written word, for their governance, religion, and commerce.

Dyrk decided he would pursue two things in Navren Altyr. First, he should not be carrying gold on his journeys, or with him into military service. The bank in Saringon would demand that he be a registered citizen of the province, but that was not the case in Navren Altyr. They served many rich foreign merchants and so had a system for non-citizens to deposit.

Two half-crowns was a fair amount of money. It was the traditional price for a *duoma*[1] of land, though the only *duoma* you could purchase for two half-crowns today would be uncleared land far away from any population center. A serviceable riding-horse could be had for a half-crown. The joke ran that a "ten-crown horse" was one in which the owner paid far too much for a war-horse that was merely a parade animal. In reality, Maryk charged between four to seven crowns for a trained warhorse.

Crowns were not the typical unit of money in commerce. Gold was restricted in use by the king. All gold mines were property of the crown, and it was illegal for anyone within the kingdom's borders to hold gold that was not issued in coins by the Imperial Mint. The Ring, a silver coin, was used for most commercial transactions. Ten Rings made a gold half-crown. The Ring was derived from the tradition of Eldorin's time that citizens would wear a silver ring on

---

[1] A *duoma* is a parcel of land reserved for citizens of Karolia. It is typically forty acres of fertile, uncleared land.

their little finger as a badge of status. For consumer interactions, the brass coin was common. The saying went, "One brass will get you a snack, two a meal", held true through the generations of Karolian history for the most part. The brass coin traditionally represented an hour's unskilled labour, but in Dyrk's day the price of labour was easily twice that.

After the bank, he had to make up his mind. One consideration was the post office. He should at least dignify Neriah with a note to break off their betrothal so she could marry someone else. Maybe he should send a letter to Gavon. An intense pang of loneliness swept over him. His stomach turned, and he began to feel sick. Tanakh seemed to notice and pricked his ears back, slowing his gait. The nausea passed. Dyrk clicked his tongue and his mount dutifully resumed the pace.

He had responsibilities. He could not avoid the post office, despite the pain it would cause.

After that, he continued to think of things that engaged his brain instead of his heart. He counted the days it would take to travel to Mar Athel. If he pushed Tanakh, it would take at least five days, not including that day. In the early days of the kingdom, the Sojourn of the Ancients took forty days on foot, one day for each year Treon and his people endured suspended between the empires of the Derrekh Himn and Omrid Vekh. That was shortened in the years that followed to an eight-day journey on foot, to be started and ended on Nedrin's Day[1]. Today was Harophin's Day[2] and there was no possibility he could make it to Mar Athel in time to start on the coming Nedrin's Day.

While the Sojourn of the Ancients was still done by a fair number of young men who were assigned to the army, it was for the most part just an excuse to take a holiday. They rode mounts, stayed at inns, breezed past the monuments and generally had a good time. Dyrk was determined to things the "right" way. He wasn't out for a vacation. Treon and his people had suffered through many trials in

---

[1] Saturday, a weekly day of rest in Karolian custom

[2] Tuesday

their quest to establish an independent kingdom in the name of Arren. Perhaps being reminded of the struggles of his ancestors was the very thing Dyrk needed to put his current situation in perspective.

He could start the Sojourn part way through. If he could get to Anderrol, in the northern reaches of the Rodakt highlands, in four days he could probably complete the rest of the Sojourn in time.

The countryside had changed from stately manors and vineyards to the shanties of the slums of Navren Altyr. The sun had passed its apex. On his left was an escarpment upon which poor houses had been built. Those living closest to the highway had an impressive view, though they suffered from the noise of the constant traffic. On his right was a series of warehouses and docks. This was only a small port, as the river was not deep enough for merchant vessels. Most traffic to and from the Sea-lake of Cith would dock further down the river or at Altyren itself. Yet the docks before him were busy. It was far easier to transport bulk materials by shallow-draught vessel than by cart. The broad Elgolin River was its own highway between the various cities in the heartland of the kingdom.

The road became busier as Dyrk entered the city. It had no walls or gates, so there was no place for guards to enforce particular orders or collect taxes. Dyrk almost wished to be told to dismount. Technically, he was a "sword" now that he was drafted into the army.

He asked directions to the bank. He was met with a query as to which one he was looking for. After a short discussion Dyrk was directed to a bank that specialized in Dyrk's exact situation – army recruits displaced from their original provinces. He brought Tanakh to the rail and simply left the horse at the post. Tanakh would not be going anywhere.

A man with one leg was sitting on a bench near the rail, wrinkled hands on a walking stick. A horn lay at his side and a black cap was on his head. Dyrk fished for copper coins and flipped two into the leather bag at the man's feet. His job was to watch the horses and alert the guards should anyone try to walk away with one. The man's eyes widened as Dyrk walked by.

"You aren't going to tie it up?" he craned his neck in Dyrk's direction.

Dyrk shook his head. "If you want to try to tie him up, go ahead."

The man blew his breath out through his teeth. Dyrk walked inside.

After depositing the two gold coins, he withdrew some of the money out in brass and silver coins to cover expenses for the trip. Back in Tanakh's saddle, he took a deep breath and asked for directions to the post office.

His mind was preoccupied with what to write. Thinking about Neriah made him sick again, so he just considered what to write to Gavon for now. It was against his nature to describe events that he could not explain, and even stranger for him to simply write down his feeling and emotions of the day.

He found the post office. Another copper coin, another questioning look from the attendant. The building was quite large, being a hub for the Royal Postal Service. It was difficult to house tarns and horses on the island city of Altyren, which is why all eastbound and southbound mail was routed through Navren Altyr.

As a child, his parents had described tarns as great birds, but after seeing one arrive at Tanvilon he was convinced they resembled lizards more than birds. They were featherless, covered in a leathery skin like a crocodile. Their skulls had a protrusion of bone that extended back from the crown, giving them a peculiar and even comical appearance. But tarns were anything but a joke. They could bear about as much as a standard riding horse, which meant one man and equipment but no more. This made tarns ideal for communication and reconnaissance, but rarely were they ever used for combat or transport. Only the largest tarns could carry a second rider.

The animal's high-strung personality had something to do with that. Far more skittish that horses, they did not seem to operate on the same instincts as their land-locked counterpart. Their behavioral patterns resembled a dog more than a horse, and their will simply could not be broken. The men who rode tarns were often suicidal, insane, or very brave, and usually a combination of all three.

Tarns were easily distracted. They also tended to be indifferent to, or even resentful of, anyone that climbed onto their back. There was no sense of cooperation. Even the workers that fed and cared for the tarns were as likely to be injured by a random bite or beating of the wings. Blinders were widely used but did not make much difference. Unlike birds, they depended on their sense of hearing as much as their sight or smell.

The high cost of tarns in terms of money and manpower restricted their use to only the critical functions of the King's postal service. In general, the Post assigned one tarn-rider to each province, who made a circuit once a week, visiting each Headman with orders from the Crown and collecting official reports to take back. Current news was exchanged quickly by mouth as the tarn-rider took a brief rest before taking to the air again.

The rest of the mail was transported by horseback. Along major routes, there was a postal depot every league which allowed for a change of horses and efficient drop-off or pickup of local mail.

Dyrk walked into the busy office and allowed his eyes to adjust. Across from him was a row of counters with clerks efficiently serving queues of clients. To the right there were several open doorways, guarded by signs that denied entry to those not authorized. Along the wall to his left was a tall counter furnished with paper and pencils, where several people stood and composed messages.

With a lump in his throat, Dyrk walked to his left and took up a pencil and piece of paper. A postal worker watched him intently to make sure he didn't run off with the valuable paper. He wrote a quick note to Gavon, apologizing under his breath at its brevity and lack of detail.

--

T 6 Harophin 2796[1]
Gavon:

---

[1] Friday, May 9, 2796

I have left the college. I cannot say at this time the reasons why. I will be reporting for military duty at Trebier at the end of the month. I will write to you then and there.

Do not worry about me,

Dyrk.

--

The biggest lie was his concluding statement. How he dearly wanted someone to worry about him! But Gavon was not that person. He was an intellectual resource, not an emotional one. Perhaps, if Dyrk felt it necessary to take some legal action, Gavon would be of great help. But here, and now, not so much.

Dyrk used the wax available to seal the letter and got into a queue. It occurred to him that he should have probably written both letters so that he didn't have to go through the queue twice, but then assured himself he needed the time anyway to think of what he was going to say to Neriah.

"Dyrk? My royal buddy? Is that you?" A voice boomed from behind the counter. One of the clerks leaned over his shoulder to express annoyance at the loud outburst right behind his ear. A tall, lanky young man stood behind him, an Eratur's cloak flowing from his ornamental pauldrons. He had well-manicured black hair, a fine, but not quite handsome, face, and carried himself with his shoulders straight back. His stride was effortless and confident as he came out from behind the counter.

"Eveth!" Dyrk tried his best to act happy to meet someone he knew. "Haven't seen you for a year! How is the Eratur's life treating you?"

Eveth walked up to him with both his arms outstretched. "What does it look like?" he said good-naturedly. "Didn't you know we spent four years beating up our bodies to prepare us for the rigors of pushing paper around?" They slapped right hands and touched shoulders, a common greeting among young men.

But then his face fell. "Why are you here, though? What happened? Are you on official business?"

Eveth had graduated one year after Dyrk had come to the College. Four years his senior, Eveth had played a few pranks on him at first but ended up taking Dyrk in like a little brother. He referred to Dyrk as his "royal buddy" because of his lineage in House Teren. Eveth was known as "Eveth Endlessly Repeated", since his given name matched that of his house.

It took Dyrk a moment to find the words to say, but Eveth took the initiative before he could. He grabbed Dyrk's arm, a concerned look on his face, and said, "Come with me."

He led Dyrk through one of the restricted doors and into a large room where mail was being sorted. A railing separated a small walkway from the work floor itself. "Don't go past the railing," Eveth warned him. "But it should be easier to talk in here. All right, you've got to tell me what happened."

For a brief moment Dyrk prepared himself to be minimal in the amount of information he gave, but he simply couldn't hold his emotions any longer. Just the sight of someone remotely familiar that showed concern for him triggered the overpowering need that he was trying to repress. He told Eveth everything that happened in the Rector's office, and even went through some of the events at the Contest two years ago to fill in some details. Eveth listened intently, nodding at some point and asking only a few questions to clarify. The one thing Dyrk did not mention was anything about Neriah.

When he finished, Eveth put a hand on his shoulder. "First off, I have one thing I can share with you. As a graduate, I was present at your one-year review. It was very positive. Your instructors had much good and little bad to say about you."

"Nothing that could possibly lead to dismissal?"

"No, nothing. I mean, they did mention," he smiled, "that you were somewhat obstinate, hard-headed, and rigid with your colleagues. But who wouldn't want those qualities in an Eratur? But more seriously, what have you decided to do about it?"

Dyrk shrugged helplessly. "I accepted their discharge and assignment. What more can I do?"

Eveth stroked his clean-shaved chin. "Go over the head of the Rector."

"That would be Prince Amarion. Good luck getting an audience with him."

"Yes, I can't see Amarion giving you the time of day. But this isn't right. Surely there's something we can do?"

Dyrk shook his head. "What I need most is for someone to see it the same way as I do. You've just done that. Now I know I'm not crazy."

"Well, I'm not going to stop there. You said you wanted to do the Sojourn of the Ancients?"

"Yes."

"If I know you, this won't be a country ride on Nedrin's Day[1]," Eveth referred to the day of the week when businesses closed and life slowed down. "If possible, you're going to walk in every footstep that Treon left behind, aren't you?"

"I can't, even if I wanted. I have twelve days to report."

Eveth looked towards the mail being sorted. "I may be able to help with that."

"How?"

"Every courier needs an armed escort. Sometimes we hire off-duty soldiers or rent some of the Prince's men. You're a Sword now. You qualify. You're a fantastic rider with unfamiliar mounts. The postal service will get you to Elbing in two days."

"I have no armour, no weapons. How could I even pass off as a guard?"

"I can give you your pay up front. Do you have any other funds at hand?"

"Yes," Dyrk remembered the money he had just deposited.

"Remember, you need to be able to ride fast and comfortable. Nothing more than a chain hauberk and skull-cap. A good set of hard-treated leather would be even better. Find a scary-looking war-axe and a light crossbow. The job requires intimidation, not fighting, so it's more important that you look the part than that you act it."

"Well, that would certainly buy me some time…"

"You'll have a document that entitles you to use the Service's

---

[1] Saturday

horses. Anywhere in Karolia." Eveth emphasized the last statement. "You just need to report back here in eleven days. You'll need to pick up that nag you call a war-horse anyway."

It was a good feeling that at least one thing was going for him. He went with Eveth to get the paperwork sorted out. Then he picked up his saddlebag and prepared to head out.

"You had a letter to send," he held out his hand. "I'll see that it gets delivered."

Dyrk gave him the letter to Gavon.

"Did you have any others you wanted sent?"

Dyrk knew time was pressing. He had to find an outfitter before they closed. He shook his head. "No," he said. "It can wait. Thank you for everything. You are a good friend."

CHAPTER 8:
SOJOURN OF THE ANCIENTS

Just as Eveth had said, the postal service was the fastest way to travel. Dyrk left that evening, and they exchanged horses twice before they stopped. His courier was an older man named Margab. He seemed distrustful of Dyrk at first, but that could be forgiven – having some stranger with weapons riding with you might be more unnerving than riding on your own. Margab's horse was equipped with a customized kit that included about twenty round cylinders made of brass hanging off the side. They looked similar to the document jars that almost everyone carried, including the one holding Dyrk's requisition, but the ones for the mail were much larger. Documents and letters were rolled tightly into the tubes, and then sealed to guarantee that there was no tampering before their arrival.

The mail courier was not usually a target for brigands. They did not transfer wealth, only records of it. If at all, the danger would come from foreign spies who may waylay a courier to discover troop movements or sensitive political information. But even that was nearly unheard of in that day and age where conflicts between nations, while common, rarely flared into full-scale war.

Dyrk's primary purpose as a courier guard was to provide assurance to the public that the King took the security of mail seriously. His responsibilities were quite basic: never let the courier out of his sight. He was to ride with him, sleep with him, eat with him, and accompany him to the outhouse. Other than the mail, both traveled light, since everything would be provided at the depots.

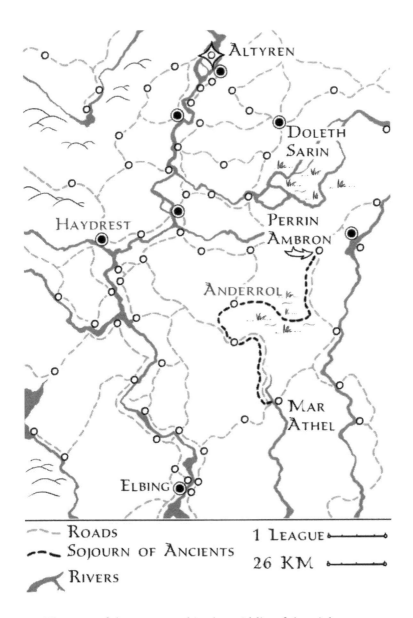

ROADS
SOJOURN OF ANCIENTS
RIVERS

1 LEAGUE

26 KM

The two of them stopped in the middle of the night at a waypost just past the border between the provinces of Halyron and Kurlen. The schedule took advantage of the slower times on the roads; they were to leave late in the morning, stop for a rest in midafternoon, and ride as far into the night as possible. The horses were able to move at a brisk canter for the entire distance between the depots, which therefore covered a league in about an hour and a half.

There were interesting privileges in riding for the mail service. Most others had to give way. They were permitted to ride hard through civilized areas when all others had to minimize the noise and dust. Patrols on the road saluted rather than scowled. Couriers going the other way were most interesting, as they had a complex code of arm signals that would warn of danger or delays ahead.

There was little chance to talk during the hectic ride. Because of that, Dyrk was lost in his own thoughts for much of the trip, and that was not a good thing. It was difficult to stay positive and dwell on the things that he had the power to accomplish, rather than what had been taken away from him. And every time he thought of Neriah, he felt a stabbing pang of guilt that he had not yet written to her to release her from their engagement.

On that decision he kept telling himself that he was certain. A tiny voice inside him said that there was still a way that the two of them could be together. But the crushing weight of the rest of his thought stifled that voice quite quickly. Neriah had been sold on a bill of goods that he was no longer able to deliver, and that was that. As her father had said, the last thing she needed was another disappointment in life.

True to what Eveth had said, they arrived in Elbing very late on Telmanitar's Day[1]. Dyrk had been sore and exhausted by the end of the first day. By that time, he was ready to fall off his horse. He bunked at the depot in Elbing. When he awoke in mid-morning, he laid in his bedroll for a few minutes, his body complaining furiously while his mind considered his next move.

He had never been to Elbing before. It vied with Halidorn as the second-most important city of the kingdom. From an economic perspective, it was quite true. Elbing was a gateway to the southern provinces of the kingdom, and to foreign realms further to the south and west. It boasted the only other bridge over the Elgolin. The city and its immediate surroundings were populated enough to be

---

[1] Thursday

considered its own province, like Altyren and Halidorn.

He was still on a tight schedule. If he was to do the Sojourn of the Ancients down to the letter, he had to leave today. It was three leagues to Mar Athel, and he wanted to avoid traveling on Nedrin's Day[1] if he could.

As he was getting up, he considered if there was anything more he could do to repay Eveth's kindness. If there was a courier headed to Mar Athel, he could even make a little more money and save the King's Post some needless hassle in finding a guard.

Dyrk got ready for the day, wrote out his morning petition to Taephin, and checked in with the clerk. No courier was headed for Mar Athel until Kemantar's Day[2]. Dyrk was disappointed to hear that mail to Mar Athel went by standard horseback, and not by relay. It would be very difficult to get there in a full day's travel.

The clerk scrutinized his letter from Eveth. "I haven't seen you before," he said, taking another glance at Dyrk's face. "How did you get this job? You're too young to be a retired soldier."

Dyrk felt there was no use making up a story. After all, nearly half of the competition winners didn't end up making it through the Eratur's College for some reason or another. "I spent two years in Geherth Altyr," he said, hoping that the clerk would pick up on what was left unsaid.

He did. His bald head nodded. "Makes sense. Margab says you're green but ride like a cavalry master. Who was your sponsor?"

"Thur Madwin son of Enoden house Ithniar. I will be reporting at Trebier by the end of the month."

The clerk sighed. "Normally I wouldn't trust this to someone I haven't met, but if Eveth speaks for you I think it will be all right. I need three spare horses taken to Mar Athel. You're going that way, correct?"

Dyrk jumped at the chance to justify his use of the Post's mounts. "Absolutely," he said. "Are all three able to be ridden?"

"They are shoeless, so you should change between them often."

---

[1] Saturday
[2] Sunday

"Very well. I'm going on my own then?"

"Yes, unless you want to wait until Kemantar's Day for the courier."

"No, I'd prefer to make it by Nedrin's Day if I can."

The clerk hastily scribbled out a note. "Then you'd better get going, it's already midday. Give this to the clerk in Mar Athel. I expect receipt of those horses by next week or I'll have you branded a horse-thief." The look on his face was half-joking, but the tone was serious.

Dyrk recalled that he would be needing equipment for the Sojourn of the Ancients. He could purchase it in Mar Athel, but knew that the prices there would be far steeper. He had seen a wilderness outfitter just down the street as he came into Elbing, so he made a quick visit. Back in Navren Altyr, he had experienced for the first time what it felt like to walk into an outfitter with a bag of silver and have them scramble to serve you. He had never spent so much money at one time. This trip wouldn't be quite as expensive, but he was in a hurry and didn't want to take the time to compare prices or haggle. He now thanked Harophin for the Rector's gift of the two gold half-crowns; his trip wouldn't have been possible without it.

Within an hour, Dyrk had purchased a one-person tent, cooking gear, a small lantern, and some tools. He sold the crossbow for half of what he paid for it. He hadn't even loaded it once. Provisions could wait until Mar Athel, and he could buy what he needed for today's trip from villages along the way.

The sun was halfway to the horizon by the time Dyrk started out. He had to double back half a league along Taneth's Highway before he took another road inland from the Elgolin River. He left behind the stone-paved highway. The road was made of dirt and gravel. Knowing the horses were not shoed, Dyrk often rode on the generous grass banks at the side to avoid gravel patches. Thankfully, it had stayed dry the past few days and traveling was easy.

He stopped for a late dinner at a village tavern as darkness fell. He asked to be served outside on the porch so he could keep an eye on the horses. When the maid cleared his dishes, Dyrk spoke to her about the road ahead.

"Don't think it's wise to attempt that at night," she said. "Especially alone. There's a lot of wilderness between here and Mar Athel, so merchants keep to the daytime."

The maid was middle-aged, but her cheeks still coloured as Dyrk politely complimented her, referring to her with an old-fashioned Melandarim term for a pretty girl. It was now a reflex for him to do so, given his rigorous etiquette training at the College.

"Are... are you an Eratur?" she asked shyly.

Dyrk shook his head. "No, but might I ask why you would think so?"

She gestured at the dishes. "There's only one man I've ever seen who stacks his dishes like this after he has eaten, and that's Thur Jenset. Most just leave them scattered about for the scullery maids to collect."

She was about to walk inside with the dishes when she leaned her head back and said, "Not to mention, you're quite able to make an old woman blush."

Dyrk's thoughts suddenly traveled leagues away to Neriah. Inwardly he beat himself up again. He still had not sent her the message. Why was he being so irresponsible about this?

I couldn't do anything about it now, one side of him argued.

At least write the letter, the other side responded. *You can send it at Mar Athel.*

He fished through his bag to pull up his verse papers. They were smaller than standard letter-paper, but they would have to do. He used his knife to whittle the pencil to a point, smoothing out a paper under the light of the lantern.

He wasn't able to decide even on the first word.

Should he start it with "beloved", which was the standard greeting to a betrothed? But could there still be love between them if he was no longer the person she thought he was? Wouldn't that sort of greeting muddy the waters? Besides, did he even love her to begin with? That last question stung him.

He had felt the stirrings in his chest and groin whenever she was close. These feelings were far stronger than with any other woman, because of the knowledge that there was a realistic chance that they could someday be husband and wife. Those reactions had faded somewhat over the past two years. His love for her was based on what he could provide for her – a good living, social status, physical security. It was also based on what she could provide for him – sexual fulfilment, children, an ordered home. Now that his side of the agreement could not be honoured, there was no reason to think that hers would be either.

He left a space for a word of address and simply wrote her name. But he could not go further. He just sat there, staring at her name. Nothing more than scratches of charcoal on some yellowed paper. Yet there *was* more. He recalled how he felt when Eveth took him aside and listened to his story a few days ago. For once, he wasn't on an island in the middle of a hostile ocean. Someone else was there. Someone else who saw him as a person, who affirmed what he felt, who genuinely sought his well-being with no expectation of reciprocation.

That, he thought, he missed about Neriah, and was keeping him from writing the last letter she would ever read from him. But if he could have his need to belong satisfied by someone like Eveth, why did he need her?

And why did she need him?

I'm overthinking this, he said to himself, and forced his pencil back to the space before her name.

A voice interrupted him. The scullery maid had poked her head out the door. "You be needin' a bed, then hon?" she said in a hospitable tone.

Dyrk folded the paper and tossed it into the brazier that was glowing at his feet, lit to warm those on the porch during the cool night. "Thank you, but I'll be heading out," he said. "I'll take my chances with the wilderness."

He regretted his decision as soon as he left the village. Tactically, he was being foolish. He was completely unfamiliar with the road and these environs. He had no idea how far it was until the next settlement. And he was in possession of three valuable horses, with only one man to guard them.

But, he told himself, the horses were just as likely to get stolen at the inn than they were out there. He pressed on. He always felt that he did his clearest thinking under the stars, anyway.

The terrain was hilly and the woods were thick. He rode for more than an hour at a time between signs of civilization. Every time a rider came the other way, which was rare, he put a hand on the haft of the war-axe he had bought in Navren Altyr. Combat training at the College included familiarity with a range of weapons, but primarily with swords and arbalests on foot, and polearms on horseback. Axes were a weapon used by trained freedman soldiers.

He used the time to reconnect with his childhood values. He had been told many times that life wouldn't be fair. This was just the first time he felt it so acutely. All the talk about working hard to overcome adversity, or fortune following the diligent, was well and good. But there was little to console him when those simple equations didn't work out. Here he was, someone who followed his religious duties to the letter, fulfilled his social responsibilities faithfully, and pursued his personal sense of integrity to the best of his abilities. And yet the Servants did not shine their faces on him. *They might abandon me, but I won't do the same to them*, he thought. *I'll show them what faithfulness looks like.*

It was nearly dawn when he arrived at Mar Athel after an uneventful journey. He woke up the night-clerk at the post office by his insistent banging on the door. Within minutes he relieved himself of the three horses. Then he found a ward tavern, paid a few copper coins to a sleepy old man, and collapsed near the cold fireplace.

He woke much too soon the next day. He was sleeping in the common room, which was shared by half a dozen other travelers. They had bedded down at a reasonable hour, and therefore they took no pains to get up quietly as the sun rose. Dyrk sat up, bleary-eyed and sore. It wouldn't be long before the innkeeper came to make sure that all the guests were out of the common room.

It was Nedrin's Day[1]. Dyrk pulled up a chair near the fireplace, which now had a small blaze, and spent some extra attention on his

---

[1] Saturday

morning petition. Nedrin was the Servant of Protection. Many misinterpreted him as a strong, warlike Seraph who defended the faithful by feats of strength. He was, in Karolian lore, the patron Seraph of all soldiers. But an honest assessment of the histories would find no instances in which Nedrin portrayed himself in that way. He protected the Twelve Fathers and Mothers at the birth of the world by being a shield against evil Seraphs. He aided the Nethariem to escape from Drukudar by clothing them in black. Nedrin prepared the faithful who followed Treon into exile for times of hardship by giving them hope and comfort. Dyrk knew there was a battle going on inside him at that moment, and he wrote out extra words of his own composition to beg Nedrin for peace in his soul. As the smoke of his verse paper went up, he felt clarity of mind, and resolved to do his best on whatever lay before him.

He ate a simple breakfast at the inn. All his gear was rechecked. He had enough food for two days which was enough for now. He was ready to begin.

Just on the outskirts of the town was a stone monument. The edifice itself wasn't particularly large or imposing, but a lot of ground around it had been cleared and planted with flowers and ornamental trees. Dirt and stone pathways wound among them towards the monument. As Dyrk arrived, equipped with nothing but his verse paper, there was a group of young men who were standing about. They were dressed similar to Dyrk, and by their speech they were likely from northern Karolia like himself. Only one carried a sword, and the colours on the hilt showed he was of House Binev. Neriah was from house Binev. He closed off his emotions at the thought.

One of the others, a tall man with youthful features and reddish hair, was reading from a small book. "It was not until the twenty-fifth year of Treon prince of Kaderish that the exiles set out from that point. With him marched over six thousand men, representing forty-three of the original houses of Tauril. Accompanying him came Alerion of Atlan's house, who had brought the Three Books of Melandar through great hardship to guide the people."

Another of the youths with short-cropped black hair and a scar near his eye gave a loud yawn and kicked a pebble at the arrangement of large stones that marked the site from which Treon's journey began. "Just another bloody war in the sad history of mankind," he said, sounding philosophical but coming off as sullen.

"It was here that Nedrin spoke with Alerion, to give words of comfort and encouragement to the-"

"Sure he did," the scarred young man chortled. The one with a sword was wandering about, studying some of the trees. The fourth was apparently victim to a late onset of acne. His face was pockmarked with red blemishes, some of which were obviously cuts from the razor which was mandatory in the military for non-professional soldiers. He wasn't paying much attention. He stood, turned away from the monument, eyes closed. It looked like he was sleeping.

The redhead paused after the interruption but then resumed. "...words of comfort and encouragement to the exiles who were about to embark upon forty years-"

"At the moment I'd like forty years in the tavern," the sword-bearer added his own comment. He was the only one wearing a hood.

Dyrk, standing close by, was sick of the interruptions and decided to finish the history by memory. "forty years of perpetual war, near-starvation, ghastly weather, and crippling sickness, all without homes or fields. They were hammered as steel is tempered, refined as silver is purified, until the promises of Telmanitar were realized and the kingdom of Karolia was born."

The acne-faced lad opened his eyes in surprise. He grinned and said to the redhead, none too softly, "Khalon, looks like we've got a zealot here."

Khalon shrugged and shut the book with a thump. "All right, looks like we're done here. When do we eat?"

Sword-boy seemed to be in charge. "Let's get a quarter-league behind us before that. The sooner we get to Talvis Ford, the better the bed we'll get, so let's hustle. The ale-maids await."

The four moved out. Thankful to have the monument all to himself, Dyrk took the time to write out the brief petition to Nedrin. A small oil lamp burned amongst the stones. After it had consumed

Dyrk's verse paper, he noticed that the ashes that collected at the bottom were the first that day.

Dyrk hoisted his heavy backpack and started out. He figured that his time at the College would have toughened him up to the point that he could keep up to the other travelers who were not as burdened. He knew he had built a lot of strength from his exercises in full plate armour. However, it wasn't long before his shoulders began to ache because of the straps. Backpacking did not use the same muscles as mounted combat. He had to admit that he wasn't an experienced traveler, either. He had relied on the outfitter in Elbing to make the best choice on his gear.

It was very warm that day. He was sweating profusely by the time he stopped; he stripped off his outer tunic before resuming. He kept up a moderate, steady pace as best he could, but there were a few times he was passed by small groups of young men who were less laden than he was. Some carried only a flask of water and a waist-pouch. Two rode horses.

Close to midday, he passed by the four men he had seen earlier. They had stopped for a rest and a bite. The acne-faced lad waved to him, "Looks like you're about to drop. Take a break."

Dyrk ignored him and kept moving. He preferred to be alone. Only when he was out of sight did he leave the road and push into the forest a hundred paces, finally stopping beside a small brook to rest. His entire body was still saddle-sore from the frantic riding of the previous days. He was feeling the effects of three consecutive nights of little sleep.

He ate a hefty meal of cheese, barley cakes, and dried fruit. He was going to save two smoked sausages for the evening, but he eventually gave in and gobbled one of them, cold. He was afraid he would fall asleep if he sat down too long, so he doused his head in the stream and went on his way.

In midafternoon he came to a marked trail that led to the right off the road. A small plaque indicated the path led to Tular's Lookout. The way was well-maintained but, judging by the tracks that continued on the muddy road, wasn't well-used. Dyrk trudged up the path for about half an hour before he came to the edge of a low bluff. There was another monument, but unlike the previous one there was no lantern.

Dyrk sat down, lit his own lantern, and wrote out another short petition. He didn't recall this one word-for-word, and silently wished he had Kahlon's book. It wasn't like that group really needed it, anyway. All of the books that Dyrk had depended on were behind him at the College.

As the smoke of the verse paper lifted into the blue sky, Dyrk looked towards the north. Treon had stood in that very place, during the third year of the exile. He had already lost his left eye during the initial battles with the Vekh of Omrid. All the territory they had won had been reversed in a series of defeats. This was the furthest back that Treon retreated, and from here began to advance northeast in the fourth year of exile.

Dyrk reflected that the ground he had covered so far was all Treon had to show for three years and many men lost. Yet he had persevered, trusting in the promises that he had been given.

Maybe those recruits were right after all, Dyrk thought. It sounded like a futile effort. He surely would have given up by now.

He put out the lamp and trudged down the path, back to the road.

Dyrk was on his last legs by the time he got to the inn at Talvis Ford. The sky was clouding over, and he was relieved to arrive before the rain started. He collapsed, exhausted, by the hitching post and rested his aching feet and chafed shoulders. There were only two horses there, but it sounded like at least a dozen men were inside. Dyrk left his equipment in a pile, stretched his complaining muscles, and tried his best to stand upright as he entered the common room.

Business was brisk; he counted sixteen, all which were young men who were, in all likelihood, doing the Sojourn as he was. The now-familiar group of four were in a corner, sipping ale and harassing the younger of the two barmaids. Dyrk limped towards the counter. Without waiting for any request, the grossly overweight innkeeper quoted him prices for a private room or space in the common room.

"I only seek permission to camp by the river," Dyrk said evenly.

The brow of the innkeeper furrowed. "Then that'll be five copper," he said, holding out his fat hand.

"Five copper? For what?"

"For staying on my land. I've got to clean up after you too."

Dyrk doubted that the man could leave his inn, much less descend the bank to the river. "The riverbank is the King's land," he retorted. "I'm only asking permission out of courtesy. It would be extortion to demand payment from those who undertake the Sojourn of Ancients…" he slightly turned his head and increased his volume so that the group in the corner could hear. "…the right and proper way."

The innkeeper did not move. In the pause that followed, Dyrk counted four chins.

"I'll pay you five copper for a loaf of bread and some firewood," Dyrk said in a lower voice, trying to find a compromise.

The innkeeper rolled his eyes. "If that gets you out of my inn, I'll come out on top."

With a loaf of bread in hand, Dyrk picked up his equipment and went down to the ford. The river there was no more than a rushing brook. It was called Talvis Ford only because there was no bridge over it. Dyrk went downstream just out of sight of the road. There he found a flat spot to pitch his tent. It was simply a sturdy length of canvas draped over a few sticks, but that made it compact and easier to carry. He returned to the inn for an armload of firewood and started to build a fire.

The rain burst forth from the evening sky to ruin his efforts. At least he was somewhat dry under the canvas. He huddled in his bedroll and ate the loaf of bread with a little cheese and his second sausage. He had wanted the full experience of the Sojourn of the Ancients, and he was getting it.

He was so tired and sore that he was already falling asleep. Before he could slip away entirely, a snap of a branch brought him back to full alertness. There was someone, or something, just outside of his shelter!

The canvas suddenly collapsed on him, and a collection of boyish guffaws erupted around him. His bedding was quickly getting soaked. He disentangled himself from his bedroll and canvas and tried to find his adversaries, but they had fled in the darkness.

Now he was truly miserable. There was no way he could get his camp back into shape in the rain. His frustration was bringing him nearly to tears again. Why would anyone pull a dirty trick like that?

Glumly, he packed up his camp as best he could and hauled his equipment back to the inn. For the time being, he stowed it in the dry woodshed, and then stomped in to find his adversaries. It wasn't difficult – the four young men were back in their corner, but the rain on their heads and mud on their boots was a dead giveaway. Dyrk strode right up to the table.

A surly demeanor came naturally to him, but he wasn't good at sounding menacing. All he could manage was, "What makes you think you can do that?"

The four looked at him, and four tankards were pushed onto the table. The one with a sword sprang to his feet and quickly got into Dyrk's personal space. He was a good three inches shorter than Dyrk, but he was compact and wiry. Dyrk knew that he wouldn't win if the conflict came to blows.

"Easy on him, Jaer", the red-headed Khalon cautioned. Jaer's chair crashed onto its back as he and Dyrk locked eyes.

The noise of the chair made the entire room sit up and notice. Dyrk especially felt the eyes of the innkeeper burning into him. "Outside," he growled at Jaer.

Both Jaer and the recruit with the pockmarked face followed him out into the rain. As Dyrk turned around Jaer poked an index finger into Dyrk's breastbone.

"Now listen here, whelp. You have done nothing but force your condescending excuse of skin into every moment of our existence since Mar Athel. We don't need a self-righteous weasel foaming at the mouth about every breach of ancient tradition he can dream up." As he spoke, flecks of spittle flew against Dyrk's jaw, likely purposeful.

"I've got three boys here who are going into their first tour of duty. Do you have any idea what they're facing? Three years of eating dust, sleeping in muck, and enduring every conceivable insult, not to mention the ever-present chance of being sent to their deaths. And you would try to make them feel bad for enjoying a few days, all for the sake of some cursed history that you sucked from the teat of a scribe?

"They are going to get a few good night's sleep, some mugs of ale and, if Taephin wills, a touch of brandy before they report. And they're going to get it without an arrogant pup schooling them."

Dyrk held his gaze for several seconds. Jaer was tense from head to toe and was coiled to strike at any moment.

"I'm sorry," Dyrk said forthrightly.

"What?"

"I realize I made your men feel bad. I'll ease up from now on."

Jaer was frozen, arrested in a combative stance. Clearly, he had not expected that. Pimple-face's eyes were wide with surprise. Jaer did his best to uncoil himself back into a relaxed pose, but he still looked a little silly doing it. "Well then," he said. "I guess we're done here. Let's go, Lohann."

Dyrk exhaled slowly. One lesson from Madwin had borne fruit, he thought. Swallow your pride and de-escalate.

The next morning, Dyrk was back on the road. The innkeeper had offered to dry his bedding and equipment by the fire, and let him sleep in the woodshed. "Might as well keep it close to the real thing," he had joked at Dyrk's expense. A few provisions later, Dyrk had what he needed and was ready for the next leg of the Sojourn of the Ancients.

While he didn't appreciate the manner in which Jaer dealt with it, Dyrk was man enough to admit that the veteran soldier was partly right. Dyrk had every right to do the Sojourn his own way, but it was wrong of him to push it on others with a superior attitude.

The next stop was the tomb of Alerion. Dyrk was still writing out a prayer when the four recruits showed up. Lohann asked Khalon for the book and read silently about Alerion's life and death. He was the religious leader behind Treon's campaign, but did not live to see any victories. He was of House Atlan, a very small clan descended from Teren's adopted older brother.

The next night was less eventful. There was another inn serving customers along the Sojourn. This innkeeper didn't object to Dyrk spending the night tenting near the local spring, and the recruits didn't bother him. Dyrk was getting tired of cold food. He made a fire and tried to make some stew for himself. He quickly figured out that, in addition to his deficient wilderness skills, his mastery of cooking was sorely lacking. By the third night, he swallowed his pride and dined on some fish stew at the tavern in the village of Anderrol. Though it needed salt and had more potatoes than anything, the stew tasted great after days of deprivation. The rain that night made things pretty miserable. He began to wonder if the various kinks and cramps in his muscles would ever work themselves out.

On the march the fourth day, he was a little surprised when Lohann, the pockmarked-face recruit, ran ahead to join him. He made small talk for a league-tenth, and they learned they were both from Saringon. Lohann was from a town in the northwest part of the province. He had participated in the Contest of the Squires last month but was quickly eliminated. He listened, fascinated, as Dyrk recounted his experience and victory from two years ago.

The Sojourn of the Ancients had left the main road first thing that morning, and now they were traveling east-by-northeast. The wide path was steadily descending. From time to time they could see that a broad valley lay ahead. Dyrk knew they were seeing the Vestelin River valley.

"Now you aren't going to go through with the whole thing, are you?" Lohann piped up at one point.

Dyrk shrugged. "I hoped to give it a try."

"I don't see what good it will do to starve yourself for a day and then drown yourself in a swamp."

Dyrk tried to be humorous. "More likely for you guys to be rid of me if I do go ahead with it. Besides, you'll make much better time if you go around the swamp."

"What exactly do you hope to gain by doing it?"

"Think for a moment what the exiles were able to do," Dyrk

answered. "The hardships they endured in many ways prepared them for that. It toughened them up."

Lohann thought about it for a bit. "Got room in that tent of yours?" he asked to Dyrk's incredulity.

"I'm sure we can make it work."

"This is more like the Slog of the Ancients," Lohann said, shaking mud off his boots as they got to higher ground. In reality, it wasn't too bad, given there was a path marked through the swamps. Both of them were insatiably hungry, having fasted since midday the previous day. The going was now a bit easier for Dyrk as Lohann carried a bit of his gear.

"Just keep thinking how good dinner will taste," Dyrk encouraged him. "As I promised, we'll go the whole hog at the inn."

"Right now, I'd be happy with some buttered bread." He slapped at an insect biting his neck.

"Okay, maybe thinking about food is a bad idea," Dyrk said. "It can't be much longer."

Indeed, the forest had begun to thicken, and the ground was getting firmer. The trip across the swamp was intended to re-enact the sheltering of Treon's people within the swamps of Garnengen, which were actually two leagues to the north but would take almost a week to cross on foot. For three winters Treon's people used the swamp as a buffer to protect them from the advances of the Vekh armies to the west. In fact, the province of Vestellia on the east side of the swamp could lay claim to be the birthplace of Karolia, as it was the first settled land never to be reconquered by the Vekh.

Daylight was fading when they finally caught sight of the town. They felt like they were in a daze by that time, weakened by hunger and the fatigue of days of travel. They stumbled into the ward tavern. They were pleasantly surprised by the proprietor, a one-legged man who claimed to have been an Eratur at some point. He told them that any who had braved the swamps and fasted were entitled to a free meal at his expense. Feeling honoured, they sat down and tucked into plates of roast beef, green beans, steamed cauliflower, and warm bread.

They were just finished their first plate and about to go for seconds when Lohann realized something. "We beat them," he said. "The other three aren't even here yet."

"Maybe they went to another tavern?" Dyrk asked.

The innkeeper shook his head. "No other place around." There were about twenty people inside, but no sign of Jaer and his companions.

Lohann stabbed another slab of roast beef with his fork. "I won't worry about them until bedtime. Speaking of which, you aren't going to make us sleep in that tent tonight, are you?"

Dyrk raised his eyebrows and shook his head. "Not in your life."

Lohann and Dyrk had eaten themselves sick by the time the other three showed up. Dyrk did his best to be congenial, but it was Lohann that poked a bit of fun. Sleep that night was long and restful, though when Dyrk stood up he was still nearly as sore as the previous morning.

"So again, tell me what we gained by all that," Lohann asked him good-naturedly as they sat down for breakfast.

"Callouses," was all Dyrk could say before stuffing his mouth.

They had one more day of travel to finish the Sojourn. They were traveling north again, and the going was tough because of some steep grades uphill. The company made the travel a bit more pleasant. They chatted about various things openly, but there were two things that Dyrk would not discuss: women, and his own family. During their traverse of the swamp, Lohann had brought up a girl he fancied back home. He had never found the courage to make his feelings known. The young man expressed his dismay that he would probably not find her still available once he was finished his military duty. Dyrk was reminded of the letter he had still not written to Neriah.

Today he realized that their steps were taking them closer and closer to Doleth Sarin. In fact, the most direct route from the end of the Sojourn back to Trebier would take him right through the city and pass through Harwaith. There was no way that he was going in that direction.

They stopped at the second-last monument. This was a crumbling tower built on the top of the ridge between the Vestelin River valley and the province of Kurlen. Below, Dyrk espied the southern reaches of the Garningen swamps.

Dyrk told Lohann the story of Treon's victories when they finally broke through the Marud Hills to the north of Garnengen and fought their way through Rianast. Four significant battles secured their gains. It was towers like that one which protected the Vestelin heartlands from counter-attacks along the Nistellion river valley to the west.

This monument also reminded the travelers of the contributions of the Warrikh people to the conquest of Treon. The Warrikh were the original indigenous people of that land. At Treon's time, they had been oppressed and nearly eradicated by the Vekh of Omrid. Those that remained rallied under Treon's banner and fought for him. Their people integrated and intermarried with the Taurilians, and ceased to be a distinct people with only a few isolated exceptions. The common language in Karolia in Dyrk's day was a dialect of the Warrikh, bastardized over the years with the influence of the Melandarim language.

Just before their final destination, the town of Perrin Ambron, was the last monument. This was the only one with a recognizable statue, a marble likeness of Treon raising his sword to the heavens. An iron rod pierced the statue's left thigh, denoting the poisoned arrow that mortally wounded him on the plains of Rianast. Dyrk looked upon the likeness of his own direct ancestor, his gaze lingering on the crown on its head. Treon had never worn a crown and refused to be considered a king. His son Tuleon continued the line of kings that was established of old by Eldorin.

Dyrk's lineage departed from the royal line after Tuleon. The elder of his two sons succeeded him as king, while Dyrk descended from the younger who died fighting the Vekh. *Ten generations later, here I am*, he thought as he took one last look at the statue. *It doesn't look like I'll amount to anything like you did.*

CHAPTER 9:
DAR-AMUND

Torrin glanced over his shoulder.

The grimacing visage visible through the horned helmet was a nightmare of pale greenish skin stretched over a skeletal face. A curved war-lance bore down on him.

Steel met steel. Torrin tried in vain to parry the attack with his own blade, but the lance hit him squarely in the back. The plate armour protecting his spine held. His mount responded to his desperate tug at the reins, driving its flank to the right into the oncoming assailant. A sickening sound erupted as horse crashed into horse, with the black mount of the Vekh getting the worst of the exchange. The war-lance spun from the Vekh's grip. A mailed hand grasped Torrin's right forearm. Torrin awkwardly flung his left arm across his body, smashing the small buckler against the helmet of the Vekh that was grappling with him. One, two, three blows and the grip released. Torrin didn't look back to see what happened to the Vekh as he spurred his horse to rejoin the others.

There were only seven of them now. What had become of the eighth?

He tried to catch his breath. He touched the spot where the lance of the Vekh had left a large gash in his white cloak. He brought his gauntleted hand back in front of his visor. No blood.

The gait of his horse slowed, but his fear did not likewise subside. He had never before been in a fight with casualties suffered. He had also never seen Pradan so concerned about their position.

The cavalry leader's sword dripped with blood. "I don't understand what they're doing," he muttered to his second-in-command, Torrin's uncle Ludonn. They watched as the group of

Vekh cavalry who had just skirmished with them melt back into the bushes. "There must be more than twenty of them, and yet they don't press the fight!"

"That can only mean that they are waiting for more to come," Ludonn spoke.

"We must try to reach the pass," Pradan ordered. "We will head into the hills."

"But sir," Ludonn's voice came from behind his full helm, "We may get boxed into one of the canyons."

"We will have to take the chance. Every time we try to approach the woods we are attacked." He turned his horse and spoke to Torrin. "You must keep pace, lad!"

"But what of Galar," said Torrin frantically, identifying the missing rider. "Shouldn't we-"

"Think no more of the dead, boy, and keep your head about the living!" Pradan sheathed his blade and glanced at the woods again. "They come! Make haste!"

Torrin froze in horror for a moment before his mount leaped off after the others. Gone! Galar had breakfasted with him that morning. He was barely five years older than himself.

Groups of black horses with lightly armoured riders were pouring out of the sparse trees to Torrin's right. Fright made him spur his horse onward into the bleak hills. Fine cloaks of white and dark blue trailed behind them as they charged into a rocky ravine. The hooves of the war horses kicked up spray from the brook. The Vekh horsemen followed, keeping up with little difficulty.

The ravine took a bend, carving deep into the hillside. The sides were now but cliffs, impossible for horses to climb. With no other choice, the horsemen continued to flee heedless down the gorge. Torrin became afraid his steed would break a leg or come up lame; the rocks underneath were a mixture of smooth river rock and slate. Out of the corner of his eye, Torrin saw a Vekh rider on top of the left embankment, riding parallel to them through the sparse trees. They were being flanked!

Around another corner, the brook ended in a steep waterfall. An alluvial ramp on the south side of the canyon was the only route of escape. Pradan led the group in that direction. Black riders appeared at the top of the embankment, sending darts towards the men with their shortbows.

Pradan quickly gave the order to about-face and fix lances. Torrin's heart sank and his knees knocked. He knw that they were engaging in a desperate, last-ditch maneuver.

The mounts jostled as they re-formed in reverse. Lances rose into the air and fell again. A cry came forth from Ludonn's helmet, shouting the first line of Nedrin's Song: *"Bae-Elohim Kel-Seth Mor-Fakhaiem.*[1]*"*

All joined with the second line: *"Nam Kel-Arkaneth Vaan-Khiem, Kham Harm Vaan-Thur.*[2]*"*

The mounts began to pick up speed in unison, but Torrin knew they wouldn't be able to gain enough momentum before the collision with the pursuing horsemen. He found himself on the flank because he had lagged in the headlong rush up the gorge.

"Vin-Ratar Pend Khaam-Zin-Kovauraeim.[3]*"*

Two rows of elongated tools of death crashed into each other. Ludonn was killed instantly, run through a chink in his armour, the next line of the Petition dying on his lips. Pradan was unhorsed. Torrin's mount reared, making a very strange sound as it began to topple sideways. He quickly realized that his mount had been speared through. His arms and legs responded to his brain and he managed to get himself clear of his fallen mount before he was pinned.

Torrin's first battle had turned into a bloodbath. One after the other, brave warriors fell from their glorious steeds, never to rise again. Sweat and tears were running down the inside of Torrin's helm as he glimpsed close friends being hewed and cut by the Vekh lances. Two seconds later, he too was fighting for his life as the riders closed in on him.

---

[1] (Melandarim) Arren Most High, look upon your enemies

[2] (Melandarim) Will you, in your power, remember your people, and thunder against them.

[3] (Melandarim) As we stand firm, we hear their cries of battle

Here I go with the rest of them, he thought. *At least I will die a soldier.*
He was not very mobile off his horse. Instinctively, he backed up
the alluvial deposit, hoping the enemy would find it difficult to
charge him on the unsure footing. The Vekh riders from above came
crashing down the slope, intent on attacking the remaining members
of Torrin's patrol from behind and finishing them off. One spied
Torrin struggling up the slope and made for him. Though Torrin
tried his best to throw himself from the path of the rider, the lance
connected with the back of his helmet. He saw stars.

Arren, he silently prayed as he struggled to his feet. *How could you
let me die like this? Is this my task? Is this all?*

An unhorsed Vekh engaged him from further down the slope,
swinging a two-handed war-axe. With the first swing, Torrin's
buckler was smashed in two. He parried the next blow, but it put
him off-balance. The axe arced towards him, its glistening edge
hungry for his life. It cleaved armour, flesh and bone. His hand fell
to the ground, still grasping his sword.

This was too much for him. This had to be a nightmare. All
sounds around him dulled. He was barely aware that his assailant
lost his footing and fell backwards down the slope. Reflexively, he
tried to swing his arm, thinking the blade was still there, but only
managed to spray blood from his useless stump.

A small bit of sanity remaining told him to make for the top of
the ridge. His feet kept going until he was behind the cover of a large
boulder. There he breathed a few deep breaths. He tried to clear the
red haze that was constantly making his head swim. It only got
worse. He took a step forward, then one step up, then another. He
stumbled on until he reached the top. By that time several Vekh had
dismounted and were halfway up the slope in pursuit.

The red haze intensified with the sudden movement, his arm
throbbing. He gripped his destroyed wrist with increasing tightness.
Stumbling on, he reached some bushes and passed through them.
He could hear the footsteps of the Vekh behind them, slowly
stalking the wounded Eratur for their amusement. Ten steps later he
collapsed. The ground under him gave way under the sudden weight,
and he began to roll over and over again down a steep decline. His

pursuers stormed after him.

At the bottom Torrin had just about lost consciousness. He had lost all strength to get back up.

He rolled onto his back and saw the Vekh closing on him warily, weapons drawn.

A flash of movement blurred across his view. The Vekh scattered in astonishment, their blades springing to life in defence. One of them fell to the ground, choking, a white-shafted arrow embedded in his neck. A dark figure passed by Torrin's vision without making a sound. If he wasn't delirious, he would have thought it looked like a shaggy grey wolf. Another form, with scales like a serpent, also came into his view, wielding a red-coloured blade in each hand. With three vicious slashes, the Vekh was impaled and lifeless.

Losing consciousness, he tried to make sense of what was happening. The last thing that he saw was the green eyes and fanged teeth of the serpent looming over him.

Pain and delirium coalesced into an endless nightmare that Torrin wished he could wake from. Awareness was crippled to a state of shock and confusion. His right arm throbbed the most, but pain emanated from other parts of his body - his head, abdomen, and left leg. Day and night held no relevant spaces of time, but it all seemed to meld into one plane of existence. His thoughts were uncontrollable, drifting from one part of his past to the next, but always returning to the horrible present, the feel of the blade slicing through flesh and bone, the sight of Pradan's head falling from his shoulders, of uncle Ludonn pierced through by a spear. Ludonn had been like a father to him for the past ten years, ever since the death of Paldonn his father.

Why am I not dead? he thought. *Why can't I join them in eternal sleep in the bosom of Arren? Why am I trapped in this nightmare?* But before he could think of answers to his own questions the whirlwind would overcome him, and begin yet again the same cycle of pain and illusion.

Days passed, though sometimes it seemed like years in his stupor. Sometimes he heard words that were not his own. They were always from the same voice, like one person talking and the response inaudible. He at times felt himself being roughly handled, accompanied by fresh spasms of pain. He just wanted to wake up in his bed in Dar-Amund, with all of this a dream, a nightmare that he could forget.

He felt warmth on his face. He managed to expend the effort to open his eyes, and an orange glow flooded into his brain. His stomach churned, and he swallowed to keep down the bile that rose in his throat. He had been laid onto his left side, facing the warming blaze. He continued to look at the fire that burned a short distance in front of him, dancing and writhing in a blur before his eyes.

"Much pain, *kyusi?*" the low, gravelly voice came from the other side of the fire. It sounded like someone with a terrible chest cold. Torrin recognized it as the voice in his dreams, who talked to the air. He couldn't see the man who spoke, blinded he was by the fire. He squinted his eyes shut as a new wave of pain shot through his right arm, reminding him of the horror of the injury he had sustained.

The voice continued, thickly accented. "It will not pass quickly. You are close to death."

Torrin kept his eyes closed tight. He swooned into unconsciousness again, and when he awoke it felt like he had only slept a few seconds. He knew time had passed, since the fire was now a small collection of glowing embers. Once his eyes got used to the light coming from the full moon, he could barely make out the form of a man sleeping on the other side of the firepit.

His arm ached. His throat ached. His leg hurt. His head hurt. His stomach was queasy. But he was still alive, he thought for the first time. *Arren has spared me for a greater purpose*, he thought, the first lucid activity his mind had accomplished in a long time. *I just hope it isn't more suffering.*

A rough blanket had been thrown over him. Somehow his armour had been removed, he didn't remember how. Under his head a bundle of cloth had been placed, but he had slipped off and a rock was grinding into his temple. That must have been causing the pain to his head, he thought as he moved it to a more comfortable position.

The blanket covered his right arm. He mustered his dwindling courage. Using his left, he slowly pulled the blanket back to get a look at it. He almost fell unconscious again at the sight, though it had been taken care of well. Burned and scarred tissue was all that was left of his hand, an ugly misshapen stump. It had been cauterized, which helped to stop the bleeding and reduce the chance of infection. A piece of cloth had been tightly tied around the arm, three inches from the severance. All the flesh below the tourniquet was either white or black, dead regardless.

He covered himself again. His fist clenched, and he closed his eyes. He had no verse paper by which he could seek the help of the Servants. His strength was so faint. His eyes teared as he pondered his helplessness, and he wiped them away. He went to fitful sleep with no comfort of mind. Yet no nightmares assailed his sleep that time.

The sound of a pile of branches hitting the ground near Torrin's head jarred him awake from his slumber. His head arose with a start. Daylight streamed through the forest canopy above, a cloud cover keeping the sun hidden. A swarthy man was crouching by the dying fire, feeding small branches into the coals. He was bare-chested and was clad only in breeches cut just above the knee. Besides his leather shoes, the only other article of clothing was a small stud through his right ear and a ring in his nose. The colour of his skin was a deep reddish-brown, like desert sand. Various markings and tattoos covered his body. A belt tied loosely around his waist had a loop for the small wood-axe that he was carrying, and a twelve-inch curved dagger was sheathed at the other hip. The man looked up as Torrin moved. Heavy brows and a scraggly goatee surrounded a scarred, squat face. The eyes had no colour, the irises just as black as the pupils were. An ugly scar pulled his upper lip into a perpetual snarl, exposing a single yellowed tooth. His black hair, while sparse at the top, fell down his back in four tight braids.

"Hungry, *kyusi*?" the man grunted, his black eyes seemed to look both at what he was doing as well as at Torrin.

The young man's stomach was queasy at the thought of food. He shook his head. "I.. I could use a drink, though," he managed, astonished at how feeble his voice sounded.

Torrin had seen but few Zindori in his life, and none that looked like this. Most that he saw were merchants or slaves, passing through Dar-Amund on the business of their masters. This man before him seemed wild, untamed, and barbaric. Under any other circumstances, he would be more than frightened to be so close to such a dangerous-looking character.

A gourd of water was thrown before him. He struggled to sit up, wincing with pain as he moved his right arm. He grabbed the gourd with his hand and fumbled with the stopper. It was wedged in too tight to pry it open with one hand. He trapped the bottle between his body and the ground and pulled with his good hand. Finally he was able to get to the life-giving water, and gulped it greedily.

"You are *zylin*, *kyusi*. Strong. Few I see can regain strength fast as you."

"Why do you call me *kyusi*?" Torrin asked.

"Zindori for young one." the man grunted, his scarred face breaking into a lopsided grin. "I know not what else to call you."

"I am Torrin son of Paldonn house Atlan," he said, and waited for the Zindori to reciprocate.

The Zindori spread the coals of the fire with a stick to allow room for him to place a small cooking pot. Torrin noticed that he used his bare hand to place the pot. Then he added a few branches to the fire and sat back.

"We are Vigheran and Erelin," he said, keeping his eyes on his cooking.

Torrin didn't know what the man meant by "we". He looked around. He could see no other. The Zindori was grinning again. Vigheran was a Roj Zindori name, but he had never heard of such a name as Erelin. It almost sounded like a Taurilian name of old. Could it be this man's family name?

He sat in silence for a time, watching the movements of the desert-dweller. The aroma of the cooking made him wonder if he could be so hungry yet sick at the same time. He wondered if the man was perhaps a Raider, one of the infamous mercenaries of the

Kuz Steppe, but he didn't see the telltale red cloak. He did see a pile of equipment at the base of a tree, but a bedroll had been draped over it, likely to keep any dew and night rain from it. The growing shadows also hid it from his eyes. At once he realized that it was not morning as he had first thought, but it was nearing dusk. How many days had he been sleeping?

After an hour of little else than occasional stirring, the man took two bowls from the ground at his side. He wrapped a cloth around his hand and picked the pot out of the fire. He poured broth into one bowl, then dumped out pieces of meat into the other. Without paying any attention to the first bowl he began to eat the meat with his hands, noisily chomping and slurping.

"I don't think I could eat," Torrin said weakly.

Vigheran paused his eating for an awkward moment, peering at Torrin in confusion. Then he looked to the other bowl and gave a short laugh. "Not for you, *kyusi*."

Torrin lay there confused for a time, watching the steam roll up from the broth, his stomach tying itself in knots from both hunger and sickness. Then who was it for?

Two soft footfalls made him turn his head towards the tree. There stood the second man, dressed in the strangest assortment of gear. Torrin could not even recognize half of it. The boots were made from a black leather, scored with designs that reminded him of Corsavan art. Greaves of strange, interlocking hexagonal plates of darkened metal made no noise as he moved. The cloak was of fur, the colour of grey wolves, and seemed to wrap itself around him of its own accord. His belt was crude: a length of rope wrapped around his waist three times and secured with a clasp of dull steel. Only a glimpse of his chain mail was visible through his shifting cloak, and that was coloured black as night, once again making no sounds with his movements. On his left shoulder perched a skin from a marmot, its head still attached. A steel pauldron, Karolian design, protected the right shoulder. It was tarnished until the shine of the metal was no more. Hard leather studded with plates protected his upper arms, typical of armour that came from the Vekh. The left gauntlet was forged of black steel, while the other was an unusual glove of hide, ending at the first knuckle to leave the remainder of the fingers exposed. Steel plates protected the wrist and back of the right hand. The hood of the cloak covered the face. The only things visible under the hood were a single, thin band of silver across the forehead and two faint pinpoints of firelight, reflections of a pair of eyes. *This must be Erelin,* Torrin thought. *What kind of nightmare have I stepped into?*

The eyes within the hood studied Torrin for a moment. The colour of the skin on the right hand, the only skin visible, was pale gray like his own. Erelin stood at a height that surpassed the tallest in Dar-Amund, a half-head taller than Torrin himself.

Erelin moved to the fire with the grace of a cat, his bizarre armour making little sound. It seemed almost that there was an invisible shroud around the man, through which sound could not escape. Even the leaves did not rustle when he folded himself to a sitting position, his back to Torrin.

Vigheran grunted a word in Zindori as he offered the bowl. Erelin took it and balanced it on his crossed legs, then removed the cowl. With the fire in his eyes and the dusk gathering, Torrin could see very little of Erelin's head, only what seemed like a hairless scalp and an unadorned circlet of tarnished silver.

Erelin stared at the broth, pausing there for a great length. Finally he tilted his head back and lifted the bowl. It seemed like forever before he put the bowl down, and impolitely wiped his face with his cloak. He passed the dish back to Vigheran, who without a word drained the last of the broth into it and gave it back.

Vigheran said something in Zindori to Erelin, his voice sounding like gravel under a boat. Erelin did not reply. His hand disengaged from the bowl and made several quick motions.

"We are safe," Vigheran said in the River-tongue, obviously intended for Torrin's ears. "We go with sunrise. He must sleep."

Erelin gave an almost imperceptible nod. He donned the cowl again. Then he turned to Torrin, who instinctively shrank back a little. The right hand, with exposed fingers, reached for his arm. Reluctantly, Torrin let him pick up his arm and look at the injury. The hooded face leaned close, sending uncontrollable chills down his spine. Erelin sniffed a few times at the stump of Torrin's wrist. Surprisingly, Torrin felt little pain as his arm was handled, but once it was left alone the throbbing started again. Erelin's fingers now reached for his head. Two firm fingertips touched his forehead, then under his nose. A strange smell filled his nostrils. Immediately he felt his eyes droop, and he fell into a deep, dreamless sleep.

The smell of smoke reached Torrin's nostrils before he saw the black billows. He had seen Erelin occasionally drop the hood of his cloak and scan the skies, a concerned expression on his face. Now he knew why. The thought of fire sent many scenarios running through his brain. They were coming close to Dar-Amund, Torrin's home, and were traveling on trails that were familiar to Torrin. He knew that the ancient fortress was just over the hill.

Dar-Amund was an isolated enclave within the kingdom of Azenvar that had survived continuously for most of recorded history. In the past, it was a valuable outpost for the extinct kingdom of Azenvar, since it guarded its eastern flank. Even when Azenvar was destroyed by the Vekh two hundred years ago, Dar-Amund remained unconquered. It regained contact with its allies when Karolia began to resettle Azenvar sixty years ago.

The people of Dar-Amund in Torrin's day, which numbered about three hundred, were without exception descended from two of the original Taurilian houses: House Atlan and House Andrem. In contrast to the Karolians, those who lived at Dar-Amund did not intermarry with the surrounding peoples. Its inhabitants could be said to be of nearly pure Taurilian blood, which gave them a long lifespan and a lifeless, grey skin tone.

Vigheran was now wearing his full armour. It was made of hardened leather, with various metal rings and studs embedded in a haphazard fashion. It reminded Torrin of the scales of a reptile. Leather protrusions protected his shoulders. His arms remained unprotected save for two metal collars on his forearms. On his head was a simple skullcap of darkened metal with leather cheek flaps. His open helmet was made to look fearsome, like a serpent, with green eyes painted into the brow.

Torrin's knees became weak when his home came into view. It was an ancient structure, built atop a steep hill. Two rows of stout stone walls protected the central courtyard at the hilltop. Most of the buildings within the structure were also made of stone, but a small village of log structures was built outside of the walls. Billowing black smoke poured from the top of the inner set of walls, adding to the plumes rising from the burning village. Parts of the outer wall had crumbled. The great gates hung open, blackened, splintered, and shattered. There was only rubble and ash left of the outbuildings: the stables, the kitchens, and dozens of homes of Torrin's friends and relatives.

The steep path leading to the gates was strewn with motionless human bodies and the carcasses of horses. Torrin saw no movement aside from the smoke and flame. He knew that they were all dead. The Vekh had been brutally efficient with Pradan and his cavalry. Torrin was sure that they would not leave a single survivor at Dar-Amund.

He sank to his knees, unable to walk. He tried to crawl for a moment, but the pain in his arm was too much. A strangled cry escaped his lips as his agony reached new depths that he had never thought possible. What more could happen to him? Why did he have to live this nightmare? Why couldn't he have died with the others?

Vigheran roughly picked him up and leaned him against a tree. "Stay here," he threatened. "You move from here, you will die!"

Torrin barely heard him. He lost himself in his pain and sorrow, unaware that Vigheran and Erelin had left him so that they could explore the carnage. His tears would not stop. A small part of him wanted to go into his home and see firsthand what had happened, but the rest of him was simply too exhausted.

Three hours he lay in torment before Vigheran roused him again. "Go, on your feet," the Zindori rasped. "No safety here."

"Is anyone alive?" Torrin pleaded, already knowing the answer. Vigheran made a guttural sound that could only be negative. "Go," he said curtly.

"I cannot go on," Torrin protested weakly. "I've lost everything. My home, my family. I have nothing left. Please, if you have any mercy, put an end to me."

Vigheran looked at Erelin for a moment. Then he bent down closer to where Torrin lay. "You have other kin, kyusi? Living close to here? An uncle, or cousin?"

"What good would it do?" Torrin replied, despairing. He stared at the sky, unfocused.

A harsh Zindori word escaped from Vigheran's clenched teeth. He grabbed a handful of Torrin's bloodstained tunic and hauled the wounded young man to his feet. With rough prodding, Torrin took a few steps and crumpled to the ground again. Grunting with effort, Vigheran hoisted the youth onto his shoulders and began to walk, seething under his breath in his own language.

Torrin sank into a trance between sleep and waking, between despair and exhaustion. He was beyond fear; Vigheran seemed capable of killing him without much provocation, but that didn't seem to register. His thoughts became less and less coherent, until finally he succumbed to numbing unconsciousness.

The fire was a modicum of comfort. Torrin stared into its mesmerizing colours, trying to collect his thoughts. The first pelting of the rain had woken him up, still slung over Vigheran's shoulders. Before long, they had stopped in a grove of trees for shelter, and Erelin built a fire within minutes. After Erelin checked his arm again, the two of them walked out into the rain, just out of earshot Torrin guessed they were having another of their one-sided conversations. Torrin was alone with his thoughts, his pain, and his confusion. For the first time since seeing the carnage at Dar-Amund, his mind felt strangely clear.

He had seen among the pair's equipment a sheaf of small papers and charcoal pencil. At first, he wondered at length why either of these would be carrying verse papers. Surely neither of them worshiped the Seven Servants and the God of Melandar. But soon his thoughts turned to the Servants themselves. Surely they had turned aside, left him at the mercy of the forces of darkness. But why had he survived? Was it for some purpose? Or did a fate await him that was worse than death, like in Tular's tale?

On impulse, he crawled over to the pile of equipment and retrieved the leather waist-sack that contained the verse papers. He carefully untied the strings with his left hand and unrolled the pouch. Once the charcoal marker dropped to his lap, he realized that he couldn't write anymore – he was right-handed.

He laughed softly to himself at the irony. The Servants let him know loud and clear that they had abandoned him. They had even taken away any means by which he could speak to them. Shaking his head, he picked up the marker in his left hand and tried to scrawl the Melandarim characters as best he could.

Bae-Nedrin Khoeth-aetar Tal-muel-goleth[1]

It took the entire page to write one line in jagged, distorted letters. Sighing, he put it aside and took up the next. Rather than writing out the entire verse, he skipped to the line in which he found the most comfort.

Auen Ratar-Aladu Kana-Esh-Baeth-e Orda[2]

"May the fallen find refuge in you," Torrin softly said in River-tongue. He folded up both papers and tossed them into the fire. "If you can smell these words, Nedrin," Torrin whispered as he stared into the twilight sky. "I could really use some refuge, too."

His two captors returned to the camp. Erelin immediately climbed one of the trees and remained out of sight until Vigheran had prepared some food. Again, Erelin only consumed broth and mash, and took an inordinate amount of time to eat. Once he was finished, he disappeared back into the branches above.

Only then did Vigheran offered Torrin a bowl, which he gratefully accepted. "You better, kyusi," he grated while noisily chewing boiled turnip. "Or you no longer zylin?"

"I'm sorry, my friend, for my weakness," Torrin said, biting his tongue as he said the word "friend". He was about to continue but Vigheran cut him off with a wave of his hand.

"You felt strongly for your family," he said, mangling the River-tongue word for "family". With another bite of turnip, he slurred,

---

[1] (Melandarim) Great Nedrin, who dwells in darkest shadows

[2] (Melandarim) May our fallen ones be remembered by you

"You must think for yourself, now, no one else." He pointed to the pouch of verse papers, which Torrin had carefully replaced in their original position. "You keep them. You speak to your gods with them, no?"

Torrin was mildly surprised. He heard that the Zindori were brazen enough to speak directly to their gods, so how did he know about the verse papers? Had they seen Torrin using them?

After they had finished eating, Vigheran wiped his face with the corner of his short cloak. He leaned closer to Torrin, absently making gestures with his knife. "Now, kyusi, you must tell us. Where you need to go? Where are your kin? We must take you to safety."

"I have a few relatives in Karolia," he said. "I think they live in Altyren."

Vigheran shook his head. "Too far," he said. "Too dangerous. We cannot travel to Karolia. Somewhere else."

"I… I have an uncle in Sorwail, I think," Torrin stammered. "or rather, I think he's a second cousin."

"His name," Vigheran demanded abruptly.

Torrin fumbled. "Raedel, I think. Uh, no, it's not Raedel, and Braedil went to, no, wait, maybe it is Braedil."

"Braedil, you sure," Vigheran sounded eager. "In Sorwail?"

"Yes, I'm quite sure. He moved around a bit, but I think the last I heard he was in Sorwail."

"Good. We leave for Sorwail at sunrise," Vigheran sounded confident.

Torrin had never been to Sorwail before. It was a port city in southern Feldar, commonly used by Karolia to resupply its merchant and military ships. "How long will it take to get there?" he asked.

Vigheran pulled his cloak around him as the rain intensified. "Two, three weeks," his voice ground like a millstone. "More if you slow us."

Torrin pondered in silence. Everything was happening to him so fast. In forty-eight hours, he had lost his right hand and all the family he ever knew. He was completely abandoned, helpless, and defenseless. Now he was heading into a strange land, accompanied by two people he had never met – two foreigners, complete strangers. By their appearance, he would expect them to harm him more than help him. The Roj Zindori had often fought with Azenvar and Karolia. They had sided with the Sej invaders during the War of Sands. Their races were uneasy neighbours at best, and bitter enemies at worse. And what was Erelin? His skin colour was similar to the pure Taurilians like Torrin himself, of which there were few left in all of Reldaan. But Erelin did not carry himself as one of Torrin's people; he was lithe, cat-like, and shifty, while the Taurilians were firm and plodding. Erelin never spoke. Maybe he wasn't able to. At any rate, it was unnerving how Vigheran would carry on his one-sided conversations, as if he seemed to hear Erelin in a language completely inaudible to others.

Both were obviously accomplished warriors. Each one carried an arsenal of odd weapons. They had easily dispatched the four Vekh that were chasing Torrin without sustaining any injury. Vigheran's blades were of Calderan craft: single-edged except for a serration on the blunt edge near the tip. He kept his long, curved knife at his side at all times, even while sleeping. There was a strange contraption strapped to the back of Vigheran's right wrist, normally kept under the sleeve but just above the gauntlet. Every morning Vigheran would carefully reassemble the device, loading a small, barbed dart. He also carried a Zindori short-bow, a small axe, and kept another curved dagger in his boot.

Erelin, meanwhile, only carried one weapon openly: a recurved composite bow made of horn, dark wood, and greenish-tinged steel. Along both arms of the bow were carved intricate runes in a language Torrin did not understand. In the few occasions that Erelin's cloak parted, Torrin could see a Taurilian short sword strapped to his left thigh. While Vigheran loaded his contraption, Erelin would lay out all his arrows on the ground, one by one, exactly the same distance apart identically oriented. Torrin guessed he was checking them for any nicks or splinters. It was a curious ritual.

Vigheran spread a bedroll beside the dying fire and made himself comfortable. Torrin did likewise as best he could with his one good hand, struggling for a time with the twine that tied it together. The mat was still stained with his own blood. They had washed off what they could to keep the smell down, but there was no removing the dark spatters completely. He pulled his cloak up to his chin. Vigheran was already snoring softly. Torrin wondered how the Zindori could sleep so easily. They were in a dangerous land, especially with the Vekh roaming the countryside. Surely one needed to be awake at any time of the night to watch for threats, but Vigheran didn't seem to concern himself with it.

Try as he might, he couldn't keep his mind from wandering to the horrible things that he had experienced over the last few days. The snarling and cursing of the Vekh began to echo through his head again. The sounds of their blades striking Torrin's armour. The scream of man and beast as they were slaughtered. The sight of Pradan's headless body gushing blood from the decapitated neck. The look on a dying Ludonn's face as he struggled in vain to complete Nedrin's song. The pitiful bluster of Torrin's own doomed horse as it collapsed. The wild eyes of the Vekh who chased him down until he could run no longer. The blades and axes that drew close to end his life, to hack him to pieces.

He awoke with a start, covered in a cold sweat. Panic gripped his heart again at the realization that reality had not changed. He gasped for breath, crumpling into a fetal position and grasping his chest with his right arm. He felt like the Vekh were coming for him, and only moments away. He pressed his head to the ground and held his breath, waiting for the footfalls of his imaginary killers. His left hand raked the damp earth. Death would be welcome, but it terrified him all the same.

He opened his eyes. There were no Vekh in sight. The fire was now only a single glowing ember. Vigheran still slept. The rain had slowed to a drizzle. High above him in the branches, two eyes stared at him unblinking, reflecting the dying light of the coals.

CHAPTER 10:
THE SCRIBE'S QUILL

--

V 1 Valeron 2796[1]

Dear Gavon:
Please understand that this is not an easy letter to write. I've been told to write to my closest relative to give my last will and testament. You see, upon arriving at Trebier, I learned that they have placed me into the tarn-riding corps. I insisted that I was cavalry, even showed them Tanakh, but they ignored me. It is abundantly obvious that the higher powers want me dead as quickly as possible.

I didn't leave the college of my own accord. I don't even know what happened, really. One moment I was in training alongside my colleagues, and the next I was on the road, with a letter of assignment. They didn't tell me the reasons for my dismissal. I concede that I'm not the easiest person to get along with. Perhaps I made some enemies there. Perhaps the enemies followed me from Doleth Sarin. At this point I don't know, and in a few days it probably won't matter. I managed to wring a concession from them that enabled me to accomplish the Sojourn of the Ancients before I reported.

The recruitment officer tells me that the survival rate of the tarn-riding training is about three in four. I am sure he's sugar-coating it. After that, many more die in the first month of active service. If you get a letter from me two months hence, I should think I'm past the

---

[1] Wednesday, May 22, 2796

worst of it, praise merciful Valeron!

Trebier is rather ugly at this time of the year. It isn't even its own island anymore, what with the river being so low. It is attached to Altyren's island by a dry slough. Though the whole island is dedicated to the Royal Army and Navy, there is still a lot of civilian traffic taking advantage of the south bridges despite the delay of the eastern drawbridge. Sorry to bore you with this, but I need to focus on other details from time to time to keep my head in order.

I know I have the option to desert, but I think it's best to die with what shame I already have, then it is to live with a double portion of it.

Gavon son of Maryk house Teren. I appoint you as the sole executor of my rights upon death. This expires upon five years survival or should I marry[1].

...neither of which is likely.

Please give my love to our sisters. They are my Lunnah, Kannah, and Rania[2], my moon, stars, and sun.

Tell Mother that I'm sorry for any disgrace I have brought upon her.

Maryk doesn't need or want anything from me.

May the blessings of the Seven be upon you, brother.

Dyrk

P.S. Don't bother writing back unless/until you hear from me again.

--

L 3 Valeron 2796[3]

Gavon:

Yes, I have survived so far, mostly unharmed. It warms my heart

---

[1] These two sentences are written in Melandarim.

[2] This is a Melandarim poetic device. Lunnah, Kannah, and Rania were the three daughters of Melandar. Their names mean moon, stars, and sun respectively. The names of Dyrk's sisters are actually Elora, Hanni, and Plessa.

[3] Thursday, June 5, 2796

to be able to write to you again.

First, about the tarns. The beasts can never be fully trained or domesticated, and their instincts are not nearly as easy to understand as horses. Breeding and raising the tarns in captivity has barely blunted the edges of their quixotic tendencies.

Tarns prefer two environs that are not amenable to us flightless humans: stagnant shallow water, and rocky crags. We riders are taught that we have the best chance to survive if we convince the beasts that we aren't really there at all, hence we spend a lot of time in both inhospitable places.

As part of our equipment, we keep an eight-inch knife in a sheath strapped to the tarn's lower neck. Its presence is a grim reminder of the constant hazard of tarn-riding. Should the tarn put itself on a course that would lead to an imminent threat to civilians, the knife represents the last resort. A soft spot just between the breastbone and the first set of scales on the neck is where the hapless rider would plunge the knife to sacrifice the beast, and himself, to prevent harm to others.

The tarns, though, are incredibly valuable to both military and governance in Karolia. They are employed to patrol our borders, deliver messages and critical mail, and provide reconnaissance to ground armies. Though we would be a fearsome advantage if used in combat, we are not to engage because we are too valuable. Better let the lads on the ground walk into a meat-grinder than lose a tarn.

Tarns are able to outlive us humans. For that reason, it isn't often that a new recruit starts with a fresh tarn. We can be thankful for that too, for the combination of a spirited beast unused to being ridden and a clueless neophyte is typically fatal. Valeron smiled upon me by giving me an old wrinkled crank.

I have named it Saen-Lairos, Swift of Wing. The creature has likely had dozens of names over its career, but it doesn't respond to names. Tarns have excellent hearing. However, they respond far more to voice tones and inflections than they do to phonetics. That is, when they respond at all. They take a certain mischievous glee in ignoring us when it best suits them. They are identified with a four-letter code branded to their flank. I pity the poor farrier that has to do the branding.

I have learned that my assignment will take me to the southern border. I will be leaving for northern Dedarrek in three day's time. I was surprised when they offered to transport Tanakh down to our garrison. It will be comforting to have him near, even if he needs to compete with an insane oversized vulture for riding time.

I hope this letter finds you well. If all has gone right, it will be forwarded to you at whatever college you are attending. Being a scribe-in-training, I expect a prompt reply.

Say hello to mother and the girls if you get a chance.

Dyrk

-

N 4 Valeron 2796[1]

Dearest Dyrk:

I cannot put to words how relieved I was to receive your letter dated L 3 Valeron 2796. Your letter finds me at the Scribe's College in Gel Sonest, Rianast. Future correspondence can be addressed here.

I was crushed by your account of your experience at the Eratur's College. I cannot imagine how alone you felt as you left that place, and your dreams, behind.

It must have been a spiritually cleansing experience to undertake the Sojourn of the Ancients. I would really like to hear a detailed account. If I know you well enough, you took it seriously and obeyed the old traditions to the last letter.

I was granted two letters of acceptance into the Scribe's Colleges. Was father ever proud! I chose Rianast, partly because I could be closer to home, and partly because I prefer the wetter, cooler summers. Halidorn is really muggy at this time of the year. Some scribes say Halidorn is preferable because the damp cold up here interferes with all the paper that we need to handle. Winter is still two months away. I guess I will find out soon enough.

---

[1] Saturday, June 14, 2796

Mother felt honoured to sew me the initiate's robe that I wore on my first day. I was unable to pass on your regards as I was in transit to Rianast when your letter dated V 1 Valeron 2796 arrived at home. It was forwarded to me here, unopened.

May I ask, if it does not pain you, what has become of you and Neriah?

I hope this letter finds you alive, well, and on the ground in Dedarrek.

Gavon House Teren

Third Canticle, Eleventh Verse, Gel Sonest College of Scribes

-

V 7 Taephin 2796[1]

Gavon:

I apologize that it has been so long, sixty days, since my last letter. Things have been very busy here. A week ago I took ill, and I am just recovering, which finally gives me the chance to spread some letter paper in front of me.

You are not well-informed about the summers in the South. Oh, how I long for a muggy day! Instead, the entire month of Valeron was nothing more than scorching winds and dry mouths.

The grasslands here are dry and brown, waiting for the winter rains to arrive from the Cith to wake them up. In my southern patrols, I go through terrain that is effectively desert. Not a thing grows there beyond the occasional tuft of kern-grass.

Saen has only tried to kill me twice. I have to be more crafty than this old vulture to keep myself aloft. I tell you, there is no experience quite like being upside down, suspended from the back of a tarn only by two leather straps, two hundred paces above the ground. The pressure on your head generates an intense display of fireworks across your vision. I check my safety straps more accurately than Tanakh's cinch and more often than I open my pants to relieve myself.

---

[1] Wednesday, October 8, 2796

I apologize for my language. I am living amongst military men. Most are cavalry. We deal with the pressures of the job, and the possibility of getting maimed and killed, in various ways. Some, like me, retreat in on ourselves. Others become more brash and loud, defying the danger. A select few maintain an air of civility, ensconced in a fortress of religious purity. Those men are blessed by the Servants, and I aspire to be like them. But they are very few. Most of us involuntarily pick up the bad habits from the loud ones whether we fight against it or not.

I'm finding that tarn-riders are a quirky bunch. We don't flock together like other disciplines. Less disappointment and loss that way. We also get transferred more often. There are fewer of us in a group, too. I am one of only four scouts for the entire South Army. I spend far more time with the cavalry boys than with my fellow tarn-riders.

Despite the fact that you need a cranial malfunction to ever put yourself on a tarn, we're pretty popular with the guys simply for what we do, day-in and day-out. We give them advance warnings, spot the caches of loot, check on the local settlers. We make their lives a whole lot easier. I admit there is also the fact that I am best placed to be scouting *them* out when they are in the field, and report anything amiss to my commander. It is the Karolian way to render respect to him who can rat you out.

The next page will go through my experience during the Sojourn of the Ancients. I hope you will find it instructive.

I would be delighted to hear of your experiences at the College. I couldn't get enough of history and law at the Eratur's College, but I'm sure you have already surpassed me in these.

Will you be taking vocal training? It is required for Eraturs, but I understand it is optional for scribes. I had always dreamed of singing the Joining of Lunnah and Tawkin with you in harmony.

It does pain me to talk of Neriah. Same as Maryk, and until I hear from mother herself, her too. I have enough here to distract me from them.

Actually, if you have access to the records, I wouldn't mind if you could look up Maryk's discharge. Something isn't sitting right with me.

Your brother,
Dyrk Son of Galion House Avderos[1]

-

K 3 Nedrin 2796[2]

Dearest brother:

I received your letter dated V 7 Taephin 2796 yesterday. That is impressive efficiency, 17 days from one end of Karolia to the other.

I apologize for bringing up matters that bring you pain. I value our correspondence and shall avoid mentioning those who evoke such hurt. But I do rebuke you as a brother in this: no one can take away your lineage as a descendant of Treon, nor are you orphaned. Hold your head proud, and do not neglect the twin red around your sword hilt, son of Teren, *almathin*[3] of Karolia.

I will share much with you about the college on a separate page. I am indeed taking vocal training. I cannot reach the deep bass notes that you can, so I think it will be you on harmony and me on melody. For once I will be leading you!

Harvest is almost complete here in Rianast. It wasn't quite as busy as it is back home, because they have many year-round crops here. But there were still many interesting events and festivals that punctuated the monotony of my courses.

---

[1] Avderos is one of the houses of Eldorin that went extinct before Treon's time. "Houseless" persons, such as the son of an outlander who meets the requirements for citizenship, are placed into one of the extinct houses. Galion is the main character of an ancient tragic myth. He was manipulated by the King of the Crills to carry the only weapon that could destroy him, the Crillslayer, to the bosom of the earth. There Galion met his death and had no heir. He was nicknamed "Galion the Unfortunate". In present-day Karolia, one would say that someone is the Son of Galion if they were a destitute orphan.

[2] Sunday, October 26, 2796

[3] "Almathin" is Melandarim for an elite armored warrior.

I will risk one thing that I hope won't upset you. I traveled to Geherth Altyr for a joint course on law with the Eratur initiates. I met a few initiates and got to know them. When they heard I was your brother, they bombarded me with questions about how you're doing, and why you had been compelled to leave. I was pliant with the former questions, but silent on the latter. They truly miss you and hold you in high regard.

Father's discharge seems to be in order. It notes that he served faithfully as a regimental leader in the Battle of Rocavion and was honourably discharged from a crippling injury suffered during that campaign. I'll hold back on any questions as to why you might doubt this.

I have also enclosed an excerpt from Professor Agrintol's dissertation on the relationship between religious and civil law, particularly when it comes to the issue of compulsory military service. I know it's something that interests you, so I copied it out.

Your brother,
Gavon House Teren

-

K 6 Kemantar 2797[1]
Gavon:

Again, I count it an immense privilege that we can continue to write. I wish you all Taephin's blessings in the new year.

Things have been difficult for me in the past two weeks. I didn't think I would struggle so much after my first one, especially with all the masculine posturing at the College about wading through the blood and guts of our enemies.

I killed a man. Just writing that makes me feel like a criminal. Instead, my boys and superiors are clapping me on the back and clinking their tankards of beer together in my honour.

The man was a Roj bandit. He was part of a group of outlaws that preyed on the ranchers in northern Dedarrek. I spied the group

---

[1] Sunday, January 26, 2797

driving off some cattle from a herd. I took my life into my hands and put Swift into a dive, pulling up low over top of their heads. But they didn't flee. One tried to shoot me with his bow, for all the good that would do. I circled around and came in for another pass, this time intending to brandish my crossbow to show them I was armed. Crossbows are impossible to load while astride a tarn, so I only had one shot. The group of them chased four animals ahead of them and made for the trees. I shot. I didn't think I hit anyone.

I sped back to the garrison and led the boys to the site astride Tanakh. Right at the edge of the trees, we found the body of the Roj, pierced with my crossbow bolt.

It's not that I feel sorry for this criminal. He made his own decisions, willingly choosing to prey on others. In that sense he got what he deserved. It bothers me, though, when I look at my hands. I now realize that they are capable of killing another human being. It was my deliberate actions. I cranked the crossbow, placed the bolt. I aimed and pulled the trigger. It was my arm strength that propelled the bolt into his liver. This rugged, savage man had fallen, curled into a ball, and knew he had a few minutes to live. What had he thought about in those minutes? Did he have loved ones? Did he weep? Did he plead to a Seraph, or directly to Arren, or gods of his own making, to save his soul?

Now his broken body lies in a shallow grave in a copse of trees in northern Dedarrek. I gave him that dignity, at least. They gave me his scimitar as a trophy to mark my first kill. I sincerely hope it is also my last.

On a different note, I have been asked if I am willing to extend my tour. If they had asked me three months ago, I would have thought that they were out of their mind. Three weeks ago, I probably would've agreed to another year. Now I'm losing the stomach for it. I will probably sign up for another two months, which will take me to the end of summer. I hope to enter the cavalry reserves after that.

Tarn-riders are paid more than any other non-officer rank. I figure it's because a good chunk of the wages flow back into the Crown treasury anyways, since upon death a single man's liquid possessions revert to the crown. It does mean that I might be able to afford a house wherever I end up.

Agrintol was right to point out that it's a stretch to claim that compulsory military service is justified by Melandar's religious requirement to honour the taxes set by lawful authorities. However, I shudder to think that this generation will use it as fodder to demand their right to refuse. There are compelling reasons to maintain the draft. Primary among these is the sense that every citizen is fully invested in his kingdom. Should citizenship simply be a matter of sliding a few silver rings across the tax man's desk every year, I think society will only continue to disintegrate. Once you invest your own blood and sweat into your country, not to mention the possibility of giving your life for it, you necessarily build an indelible sense of ownership. I may be giving you a kick in the teeth here, but I even deplore the fact that scribes and priests are exempt from compulsory service. It would toughen you up!

I long for the day when we can sit by a fire and stir up these debates. May Valeron bring it about!

Your brother and friend,

Dyrk House Teren

-

Gavon's friends were gathering in a group at the back of the lecture hall, discussing the evening's drinking plans. Gavon didn't care which tavern in Gel Sonest they were talking about. He sat apart from them, towards the front of the hall. He didn't want anything distracting him from today's guest speaker, who was from the Convent of Harophin.

There were six temples in Karolia, one for each servant except Nedrin. Among other things, they served as the primary training facility for priests of that Servant. The first Temple of Harophin was built in Tuleon's time in a small agrarian town in Saringon. Over two hundred years later, under the rule of Maneros, a new site for a temple was proposed. For political reasons, it was built in the far south of the kingdom. The crown sponsored the construction of the grand facility upon a solitary mountain well south of Elbing, in the province of Lun Avel.

Priests of Harophin were trained to be philosophers and theologians. When the leading priests gathered to plan the new temple, they argued that the new facility should advance the notion of religion past the concept of a temple. They decided to call it the Convent of Harophin, to put more of the emphasis on the pursuit of knowledge rather than reverence to the Servant.

Over the next century and a half, the Convent insisted on ideological and theological independence, while still demanding financial support from the Crown. Priests of Harophin were trained there, but so were scholars of theology, religion, history, language, and law, who went to teach at the various colleges and temples throughout the kingdom.

Early in its existence the Convent embraced an adversarial approach to theology and politics, just as it existed in the judicial system. Every religious dogma, custom, ritual, could only be valid if it was continually tested by rigorous opposition. The same applied to politics. The leading scholars at the Convent became experts in deconstructing and dismantling the settled foundations of the nation, with the stated intent of confirming them.

The Convent's oppositional approach spawned one of Karolia's national sports – the debate. It began as a gentleman's sport among intellectuals, but soon gained a following amongst other segments of society. For the most part, the debates were structured so that a member of the establishment would defend the status quo, while a member of the intelligentsia, often a student or scholar of the Convent, would challenge. Over the years, the debate gradually lost its focus on the merits of the arguments and instead tended towards crowd-pleasing theatrics. Personal affronts became a regularity.

This adversarial paradigm began to affect politics. No longer did officials strive to find consensus. Instead, they placed themselves in one camp or another, supporting a set of policies and principles while undermining others. People became champions of their own narrow interests rather than pursuing the freedom and well-being of the whole. In Gavon's time, there was constant friction among various groups: rich against the poor, men against women, native versus foreign ethnicity, citizens against freedmen against bondservants. Things became difficult for monarchs and provincial Lords. Every decision or announcement that they made would make someone upset and noisy.

From the time Gavon was born, a new strain of religious thought began to emanate from the Convent. Nicknamed the "New Theology," it rarely engaged in direct challenges against Melandar's teachings, but it began to question why the word of a single man, long dead, should be the end of every argument. The core tenet of New Theology was that the nation's system of belief should be subservient to the interests of the people, not the other way around.

The current speaker, who went by the name of Encarigon, was criticized by many in the Convent as being too moderate with the New Theology. He had been making the rounds of all the colleges, packing lecture halls with students eager to strike a balance between modernizing the philosophical basis of their kingdom and maintaining the favor of the more conservative elite.

"Friends," the speaker began his address in his usual way, using warm and personal terms rather than the more formal language typically employed by scribes. "I am not here to abolish tradition. Quite the opposite. I wish for us to save it, to salvage it from improper use."

The man was clearly of Karolian descent, but he groomed himself to look more international. He wore his hair long and gathered in the back, after the fashion of the Derrekh Himn. His beard was short and carefully trimmed, with the sides shaved, similar to the nobility of the Roj Zondori. His clothing borrowed from many races, from the Corsavan sleeved robe to the snakeskin belt worn in the style of the Vekh clerics. An unassuming adolescent boy sat off to the side of the podium, barely visible. Rumor had it that the boy was his disciple. Most of the luminaries from the Convent maintained a small gaggle of disciples, usually men about Gavon's age. This was the youngest disciple Gavon had ever seen. He was not likely to be older than fifteen.

Encarigon went on. "What is our chief purpose on earth? To

honour our Creator." Proponents of New Theology did not mention the name of Arren. They felt that the mention of a name would personify the Most High and bring Him down to a human level. He must remain beyond our comprehension, beyond our reach, beyond even our attempts at language to describe Him, they said. They used neutral pronouns to emphasize that the deity transcended the human categories of male and female. Some of the extreme ones even used a neutral conjugation in Melandarim to suggest that the deity transcended the human understanding of good and evil.

"How do we honour it? To quote Melandar himself, its crown of honour is humanity. Before you accuse me of circular reasoning, consider our forefather's statement that it pleases the Creator for its creatures to live in happiness and peace. Following this logic, the happiness and well-being of man is therefore the chief aim of religion and morality. Returning, then, to the matter of convention and tradition…"

Encarigon went on to appeal for the pursuit of new conventions, backed by law, that would alleviate poverty, redress oppression, and strengthen the voices of the marginalized. Those were the concepts that resonated most with Gavon. He felt that every philosophical and religious system should be measured on how it benefited the humans that relied on it, measured mostly by the reduction in overall misery and suffering. Karolia was, in many ways, an exemplary nation in comparison to many in Reldaan. Overall prosperity was very high. Few struggled to put food on the table. But the inequality in wealth and opportunity was still a problem. He felt that a nation as rich as Karolia should not have a single person who had to worry about a roof over their head or where their next meal would come from.

Gavon knew that King Adareoth was particularly enthused with the New Theology. The king's older brother, Taristan, was less supportive. Taristan had been king before Adareoth, but had abdicated early because he was increasingly infirm from injuries suffered as a military commander. Taristan was still held in high regard by the high-ranking officials and rich businessmen, while

Adareoth was popular with the middle-class citizenry and the poor.

All of the Colleges of Scribes, plus the Temples, came down decidedly on the side of Adareoth, while the Eratur's College was more under the sway of Taristan and his nephew Amarion, who was the son of Talisman, the eldest brother of Taristan and Adareoth. Amarion, the third Crown Prince, was positioning himself to be one of the options for the next king.

Encarigon proceeded to commend the young scribes for forming their student fraternity. He launched into one of the elaborate metaphors that often graced his speech. "Consider the strawberry plant," he said, holding up his fingers a short distance apart as if he was holding the berry. "Their roots are interconnected, entwined, enmeshed. They don't depend solely on one or a few stalks or leaves. Each plant draws on the roots of another. Should the roots in one area fail, the nearby plants still feed it life. Stick together, my friends. If your families fail you, count on your colleagues. If other institutions of the kingdom become wayward, band together to correct them. Be the conscience, the roots, of your kingdom."

Encarigon concluded his lecture with an appeal to the students to be defenders of the downtrodden, the misunderstood, and those who were victims of the rigid conventions of their kingdom.

Gavon felt invigorated by the lecture. He felt that so many went to the extremes in their ideology, which wasn't productive. Here Encarigon was giving practical advice that still pushed the envelope in moving the country out of its bonds of religious intolerance and moral rigidity. Yes, this was his new intellectual home.

CHAPTER 11:
ANOTHER PLACE TO CALL HOME

The signpost had an arrow pointing in Dyrk's direction, and another pointing the way he came. The latter was marked with "Province of Kurlen". His travel was aligned with the other, which stated, "Province of Saringon".

Though he had agreed to the additional time, he was happy to be on the ground again. Or at least astride Tanakh, leisurely making their way north along the highway.

He was not happy about the necessity that he return to Saringon. Upon conclusion of their first three-year tour of duty, recruits had three choices. They could re-enlist as a professional soldier in the king's army, committing to serve three years on, one year off, for most of their adult life. This opened the road to promotions into the junior officer's ranks, though only Eraturs were eligible for senior offices. The second option was to sign up into the reserve. Reserves were required to report annually for training. They could be drafted by local, provincial, or royal declarations at any time. They would only receive pay for service time, and they had to maintain their own equipment. But they also received full rights of citizenship while active, without the need to satisfy other requirements, such as land ownership and marriage. Many poorer recruits entered the footmen reserves, while the children of wealthier citizens often chose the cavalry reserves. This was because a reservist needed money to purchase and maintain his equipment, and a horse was very expensive to buy and maintain.

The third option was an absolute discharge. With their royal service completed, young men who were discharged could return to their homes with a bit of gold in their pockets, buy land, marry, and become citizens. Some leveraged their military experience into good jobs in local policing or merchant security. A few even give up their citizenship to become foreign mercenaries for other countries. A proverb amongst soldiers reminded them all that mercenary work provided great pay, little job security, and terrible life expectancy.

Dyrk had chosen to join the cavalry reserves. In his current life situation, he felt that he owed nothing to, and was owed nothing from, his kingdom. He was estranged from his parents, so he had no ties there. Neriah was out of the picture, given the disgrace of his ejection from the College. As far as he was concerned, his responsibilities were entirely to himself. To make as good a life as he could. To find happiness in simple pleasures. The reserves allowed him the maximum privileges of society with a minimum of responsibilities. That is, so long as peace prevailed.

Every time he thought of Neriah he felt that same stab of guilt that never went away. He had failed to send her a letter. Every time he thought about it, he had some reason to put it off. Several times he had stared at a blank paper, fighting against an unseen hand to put words on it. After he got his feet under him with tarn-riding, he began to convince himself that it was too late, that sending a letter would probably do more harm than good.

That was the main reason why returning to Doleth Sarin was difficult. As a reservist, he was required to report back to his home province. From there, he was only permitted to move to another province if he applied for a transfer. The reasons for that were obvious – the provincial governments needed to know who and where their reserves were, in order to account for them at training time and summon them for duty.

The second reason to return was the fact that most of a soldier's pay was deposited in the royal bank within the soldier's home province. Given that he was paid the premium for tarn-riders, and his parents declined their right to garnish wages, the money had accrued rapidly, and he had a tidy sum waiting for him.

The journey back from Dedarrek had taken him almost three weeks. He took his time. Tanakh seemed happy to be on the road again, instead of the days on end in a garrison stable waiting for Dyrk to return from patrols and messenger detail.

Dyrk carried with him a gilded, slightly curved scimitar in an ornamented scabbard. It was a trophy of his first kill. Dyrk was a little worried that it would be confiscated, as some of the decorative work was in gold. In Karolia, it was illegal to carry gold that was not minted in official coins. Dyrk had made no effort to hide the sword, and the authorities had ignored it.

The scimitar felt heavier than his own sword, a Karolian standard-issue steel double-edged broadsword. Two red strips of cloth were wrapped around the broadsword's hilt to signify the house of its owner. He thought back to that confrontation outside the Squire's Tap more than three years ago. *Swords-only won't stop me now*, he thought.

His feeling of unease increased as he got closer to Doleth Sarin. Would people recognize him? Would they all ask why he wasn't an Eratur? Would he bump into someone awkward, like Thur Daynen, or Thur Idrod, or even Lord Cassius? He dreaded the prospect of having to explain to anyone what had happened to him over the past year and a half. He wished he could have a new face. Walk into the city as a different man. Start over.

Whenever he began to feel depressed, he always shifted his focus to things he could control. Right now, he had to plan things. He would arrive in Doleth Sarin later today, in the early afternoon. He had to find a place to stay, and a place to keep Tanakh. Then he had to make up his mind as to whether he wanted a transfer, and where. It would be an important decision, which suggested he take his time. But he also didn't want to stay in Doleth Sarin any longer than necessary.

The first decision was easy. He would keep Tanakh at Farnich's stable. That was one person he figured he could explain his situation to. Farnich was an older man, about eighty. When Dyrk had worked for him three years ago just after his victory at Rhov-Attan, their relationship was strictly business. Farnich even asked Dyrk at one point if he had ever participated in the Competition before, to which Dyrk just smiled.

He walked on his own two feet for a spell, Tanakh following

behind without the need of a lead. With the Belorin war-horse, he typically did that a few times a day to keep the strain off the horse's legs and hooves, especially on the paved flagstones. The roads were fairly busy. Fall had definitely arrived. Leaves were turning colours and swirling across the path. The wind from the northeast had all but disappeared, and rain was uncommon. Mornings were chilly. He had not yet seen frost or frozen puddles, but he knew it was just around the corner.

But now the sun was high in the cloudless sky. He knew many looked at the sun on a bright and beautiful day like that one, and thanked Arren that they were alive. Dyrk had not done that in a long time.

Sure, he had kept the rituals that were drummed into him. Writing verses every morning felt monotonous, but he had to admit it put him in a right frame of mind. The evening verse on Harophin's Day[1], the afternoon verse on Nedrin's Day[2], the special occasions throughout the year, Dyrk diligently kept, even if it wasn't convenient. His heart was rarely in the words, especially those of Taephin, the Servant of Health, Fertility, and Love. If anything, he felt the closest kinship to Valeron the Wanderer, who roamed the skies under sun or stars, just like he did on his tarn.

"Ritual and routine are synonymous with health and well-being," he said to himself. "Neglect a responsibility, and you can't expect the Servants to shine their faces on you." That wasn't quite how his father put it, but that's how he understood things to work.

The walls of Doleth Sarin loomed into view as he crested a low hill. *Time to start my life over*, he thought *If only this city would let me.*

Farnich remembered him immediately and offered him a job on the spot. Dyrk politely declined. He left Tanakh at the stables. He stayed at the same lower-class boardinghouse that he had used three years ago, paying for only a week's lodging. The next day he visited the bank before climbing the broad steps to the provincial

---

[1] Tuesday
[2] Saturday

administrative building. He had to register his reservist status. He hoped to inquire about a transfer at the same time. He had made up his mind during the night that he would transfer to Lormost province. He had ridden through much of it briefly during his hectic ride with the post office. More recently, he had spent four days there during his return to Doleth Sarin. It was a peaceful country and reasonably civilized, but it didn't have Saringon's priority on the pursuit of material prosperity. Things were traditional, quiet, and boring, just want Dyrk wanted.

He joined a queue that was waiting for a single clerk in the administrative building. While he was waiting, two men ahead of him were noisily discussing something, making it impossible not to overhear.

"They say the whole countryside of Azenvar is overrun, from Feldar all the way to the Kullion. Keor is besieged, those poor saps who thought they could survive right under Anduk's nose."

"What are Feldar's states doing about it?"

"Same as always, wait it out. As long as the Vekh aren't hurting the bottom line, they aren't going to lift a finger."

"I suppose Atlan's boys at Dar-Amund are having themselves a parade with all the targets they can choose from."

"That's just it. One Vekh was taken captive and boasted about sacking Dar-Amund. No word has come from there for over a month, so we can't say for sure that the little green monster is lying."

"Dar-Amund sacked? Impossible!"

"That's what I thought. They're probably still holed up, unable to get any word out. Let's hope so. If Dar-Amund is taken, they've got some new weapon at their disposal."

"Or treachery."

"You would think of all places, those supremacists at Dar-Amund would also insist upon ideological purity. I doubt any would give up even a shred of information, much less the fortress, even if they were tortured."

When it came time for his turn, Dyrk gave his official assignment document that authorized his entry into the Saringon Reserves. The clerk stamped a seal on the document, then wrote out a receipt, stamped it with another seal, and handed it to him. "You are placed into the ninth regiment of the Lord's Cavalry Reserve. You are to report for training at the fairgrounds on the first day of Anakdatar's month[1]. Welcome back, soldier. Next!"

"Wait a minute," Dyrk wasn't going anywhere just yet. "I also want to request a transfer."

The clerk put his finger on a paper that was affixed to a peg on the wall beside his counter. He read from the note verbatim. "In light of the recent hostilities in the region of Azenvar, all transfer requests for reserve soldiers are suspended until further notice."

He lowered his finger, looked back at Dyrk with no expression on his face, and bellowed, "Next!"

Dyrk moved out of the way, gritting his teeth. *How could they revoke transfers just like that? The realm of Azenvar is sixty leagues away, and they figure it's a massive emergency. Unbelievable!*

He had no choice now. It was time to find a job. He started despondently trudging back to Farnich's stables.

Four and a half crowns later, Dyrk was the proud owner of a house in the Lower City. It was a three-story dwelling. On one side was a chandler's shop on the street corner, with living quarters over top. Dyrk figured a candle-maker would make a good neighbour, as there were many smellier and noisier occupations. On the other side was another house just like his, built narrow and tall to maximize the street front.

The front door opened to a stone-floored entryway with a staircase and pantry. Under the staircase was access to a small cellar. Behind the staircase was the kitchen and servant's quarters. The room had only one window which opened to the back. At the very back was the servant's privy and an outside door. The second floor had a sitting room at the back, a dining room at the front, and an alcove for a desk in the middle. A back door led both to a tiny patio and the main privy. The third floor had two bedchambers, both with steep, sloping ceilings.

---

[1] February 9

The interior of the house was dirty and needed a lot of work. Dyrk purchased the house as-is, with no furniture, no utensils, no dishes, no linens. He spent his first night on the floor of the front bedroom in his traveling bedroll.

He woke up early, which was lucky, because it took him quite a while to prepare for his first day of work. He had to figure out how and where to haul water, how and where to empty the privy bucket, where to go for some fresh bread for breakfast.

All that was quite new to him. At home, Nabir's family always took care of these things. He entertained the prospect of getting his own servant. If he had a single servant who worked part-time at the stables, he could afford the upkeep with his generous wages. However, the initial outlay would drain the rest of his reserves. He had to choose between furniture or a servant.

But that would have to wait. His first day at work took some adjustments, but he could tell right away that he would enjoy his job. Sure, it involved shoveling horse dung, fodder, and feed, but Farnich involved him in the transactions right from the start. Dyrk assisted the farrier, took inventory of the feed, and exercised some of the horses. Farnich didn't train or break horses on his own, but he bought and sold horses. The value of a given horse was partly dependent on how it was trained. Dyrk, given his father's occupation, was able to quickly assess a horse's training and temperament.

The stables were able to house as many as thirty horses. It was built on the outskirts of the city, with a large paddock adjacent for exercising and demonstrating. An adjoining field was owned by a farmer but loaned to Farnich after harvest. Farnich repaid him in horse manure. A farrier rented a corner of the stable property, running a brisk business.

At the end of the day, Dyrk was invited for dinner. He washed up at home before enjoying a nice meal with Farnich, his wife Zellna, and their servant, an older woman named Gelda who was quite the cook. Zellna heard of Dyrk's unfurnished house and insisted he take some of her spare dishes and utensils. He gratefully accepted.

The days continued with Dyrk slowly adding makeshift furniture to his house. By the end of the week, he had moved into the servant's quarters in the kitchen, where there were several beds built into the wall. There he at least had a straw-tick mattress and some threadbare linens. A wooden crate was his table, a firewood stump his chair.

It was close to the end of the workday on Taephin's Day[1]. Dyrk found Farnich talking to the farrier, intending to ask his boss if he could go a few minutes early to pick something up in town. After Farnich finished, he agreed that Dyrk could go. But then he stopped him with a hand on his arm.

"Boy, I almost forgot. I had someone come by looking for you."

Dyrk tensed. "Who? When?"

"Well, it was just at the start of the Month of Waiting[2]. At least the first one was." The Karolian calendar consisted of seven months of seven weeks. This was followed by an incomplete Month of Waiting that took until the end of the year, which began on the shortest day of the year.

"Wait. What do you mean by the first one?" Dyrk asked. Farnich at his age was a little featherbrained from time to time. "There were more?"

"Just as I said. The first one looking for you came just before the Days of Waiting last year. Asked if I had seen you. Don't know who he was. Of course, I hadn't seen you in over two years other than that one time you visited me. The second person looking for you came at this year's midsummer[3]."

"What did they look like?"

"The first was scrawny, almost bald, hooked nose. I'm pretty sure I've sold him a cart-team before but didn't catch his name."

Vecton! "Yes, I think I know who that is. And the second?"

"Well, the second I know well, and so do you." He smiled. "It was your father. I assume you've talked to him since."

Dyrk didn't know which one bothered him more. Why would

---

[1] Friday

[2] This would be around December 1, 2796.

[3] This would be early June, 2797

Vecton be seeking him out? Did he want to laugh and gloat? He remembered Vecton's warning about hard lessons to come. Was it time for some good old-fashioned I-told-you-so? His cheeks burned with humiliation. Why couldn't he simply be left alone?

And then there was his father. Dyrk had sent two letters at college and gotten no response. What right did he think he had, looking for him after three years of silence?

He was walking towards the center of the Lower City, heading to a paper supplier. Rounding a corner, he was so deep in his thoughts that he didn't see the man who sat with his back to the wall, knees huddled to his chest, begging. Dyrk's foot struck him and he nearly tripped over.

The man, face covered by an improvised cowl, gave a faint yelp of pain.

"Apologies, Dyrk said. "I didn't see you."

"Poor fortune, sir, could you spare a brass for a meal?"

Dyrk knew full well that begging was illegal anywhere in Karolia, much less in town. Yet he felt bad for the poor soul. The beggar's voice had no accent, but the facial features and pale skin identified him with the Hajrekh of Loth Tund. Dyrk fished in his pouch, and was about to take out two brass coins, when a shout came from behind him.

"Hey you! Stand up! Were you just alming?"

The man bolted. Before Dyrk could react, an armed guard pushed past him in pursuit. Dyrk followed at a distance. Before long, the guard emerged from an alleyway, dragging the Hajrekh by the arm. The beggar was whimpering miserably.

"Where are you taking him?" Dyrk demanded.

"He's an outlander, probably a runaway bondservant," the guard said. "He's going to the provincial bondservant lockup. Did he beg you for money?"

Dyrk didn't answer. The guard flipped over the Hajrekh's hand and looked at the symbol traced across the knuckles. "Time you finally earned your keep," the guard muttered menacingly. "The smithies are a little short of charcoal haulers."

Dyrk was sick to his stomach. This wouldn't have happened if he hadn't been careless rounding the corner. "Wait," he told the guard. "What would it cost to redeem him?"

The guard stopped, his neck stretched to its furthest extent as he looked back at Dyrk incredulously. "You want to *redeem* him?"

"I am a registered citizen of this province," Dyrk responded. "I have the right to redeem any bondservant from the provincial lockup, don't I?"

"I hope you're not serious. If you need a bondservant, come in tomorrow and they can talk to you about more suitable-"

"No," Dyrk said flatly. "I want this one."

His name was Khaldis, born in Karolla to bondservant parents. He had run away as a teenager. Since he had neither the wherewithal or the resources to live on his own, he had resorted to stealing. Upon capture, he had been thrown into the provincial lockup. He had managed to escape during a work detail. And now he was Dyrk's property.

More accurately, his next seven years were Dyrk's property. The system of bondservants in Karolia only extended for a lifetime by mutual agreement of master and servant. Otherwise, the status of freedman was within reach to any who faithfully served their masters for seven years and did not commit any crimes.

Khaldis was twenty-four years old, the same age as Dyrk. The difference between the two was stark. Being of different races, they had different lifespans and differing rates of maturity. In the land of his origin, Khaldis would be every inch a mature adult. Dyrk was by comparison still a baby-faced stripling. Typically, a Karolian boy would reach puberty at age sixteen or seventeen. Boys from surrounding races, like the Hajrekh, Derrekh, Zindori, and Rynekar, would reach the same stage at thirteen or fourteen. A Vekh lad often grew his first beard at ten years old but was training for war long before that.

Dyrk spent the evening talking with his new bondservant in the kitchen of his home. For now, they would eat from the same pot and sleep in the same room. Dyrk did his best to impress upon him that he had a new chance at life, an opportunity to gain his own possessions by hard work, to earn respect and good relationships with others, and in time to achieve freedom. Khaldis listened, nodded from time to time, but offered little in the way of questions or acknowledgment.

The only question he asked, "Why do you live with so little?"

Dyrk lay propped on his elbow upon his mattress. "I had a choice between furnishing this place and redeeming you. It will come in time."

The next day was Nedrin's Day[1]. Dyrk woke and spent the requisite time on his weekly petition to Nedrin. He felt a bit uncomfortable by the fact that Khaldis just stared at him throughout. He went through the morning chores, impressing upon his servant that these were his responsibility now.

There would be no business that day at the stables, but Dyrk still needed to care for the horses. He took Khaldis along to keep an eye on him. Once there, he handed the Hajrekh man a rake.

"What's this for?" he asked simply, grasping the handle.

Dyrk pointed to an empty stall. "Clean it out. There's a broom there too. I'm going for the feed."

Khaldis wrinkled his nose, took two hesitant steps into the stall, and began to feebly wipe the broom against the floor. Dyrk fed the horses and gave a brief exercise to half of them. The other half he would do tonight. In all that time, Khaldis had only cleaned two stalls, and not very well.

Just let him get his bearings, Dyrk thought. It won't do any good to be hard on him now.

Being Nedrin's Day, Dyrk did not go to the market to get food. They ate bread, cheese, and cakes he had bought the day before. Dyrk spent the day showing Khaldis different areas of the house that needed cleaning and repairs. The only room he did not show was his upstairs bedroom, in which he kept the things he did not need every day. Khaldis nodded endlessly as Dyrk listed the tasks that he wanted done.

At night, Dyrk boiled a few eggs, one of the few things he could

---

[1] Saturday, a rest day

do over a fire that produced something edible in the end.

Kemantar's Day[1] dawned cold and rainy. Dyrk prodded Khaldis to fetch the water, which he did reluctantly. They darted to the market before breakfast to pick up some fresh food. Dyrk gave his servant a few brass pieces to buy some foods that he liked. "I'm hoping you're better with a fire and pot than I am," Dyrk said. "Otherwise our stomachs may stage a rebellion."

Dyrk planned to have Khaldis work with him in the mornings, when most of the menial stablework was done. In the afternoons, he would send the servant home to start working on the house. Again, Khaldis did not take to the stablework with any degree of diligence, but he began to ask more questions about the horses. Dyrk was happy to discuss his favorite subject.

That evening, Dyrk was disappointed by the amount of work done, but that was compensated by the meal that Khaldis had prepared. It was a spicy stew of chicken, potatoes, and rice. Dyrk had never tasted anything like it; there was a tangy flavour that he could not place. He complemented the Hajrekh on the good meal, but then felt he had to address the level of work ethic.

"I am going to need you to put your shoulder to the yoke," Dyrk said, using an antiquated farming cliché. Then he resorted to one of his mother's sayings. "It will feel good to be sore and exhausted by the end of the day. It purges toxins from the system."

"You want me to work more, work faster?" Khaldis said, arms buried in the wash basin. Dyrk had sat down to write a letter.

"Yes. Compete with yourself every day to do more than the one before. Anakdatar knows that the earth will only yield to sweat and effort."

Khaldis put his head down and scrubbed the stew pot.

Dyrk received a task from Farnich on Harophin's Day[2] to pick up a horse in a town to the north. Tanakh was delighted to be out again. Dyrk told Khaldis to finish up work and go home, and not to expect him back until evening.

---

[1] Sunday
[2] Tuesday

Indeed, it was a pleasant trip, but he wasn't too happy with the horse that he picked up. It was a young, strong-willed beast, quite unsuitable for riding at its current state of training. Dyrk didn't know if it would ever be more than a farm beast. Some animals were fit for no more than that.

Upon his return, he stabled Tanakh and began to walk home. He noticed that there seemed to be a commotion in the square of the Lower City. He queried a passerby.

"It's a hanging," he said grimly. "All of the lower wards have been summoned."

Dyrk's stomach turned. He hated the thought of one man's death being put on display. There were a few worthless fools that treated a hanging as public entertainment. But most dutifully responded to the summons of their headman, attending to give public assent to the sentence, and be reminded of the deterrence for whatever crime has been committed.

Dyrk thought of getting Khaldis before heading to the town square. By the way that everyone was hurrying, he probably wouldn't have time. So he strode purposefully with the others towards the event.

By the time he arrived, the sentence was already being carried out. Dyrk became nauseous when he saw the body jerking at the end of the rope. But then his eyes widened.

The condemned man was none other than his own bondservant, Khaldis.

In another moment, he was dead.

Dyrk could not sleep that night. He lay on his mattress, eyes not moving from a gently curved scimitar sheathed in an ornate scabbard that lay on the stone floor of the kitchen. It had been in his room that morning, hidden in a pile under his trail gear. Now it lay there, unceremoniously dropped at the first opportunity. Dyrk didn't want to touch it again.

He had confronted the officials who conducted the execution, demanding to know what happened, and how they could execute the sentence so quickly and without his consent.

"There was no question of guilt," the official patiently explained. "I understand your loss, but you need to know that you will not be compensated for a bondservant who commits a crime."

The official showed him the scimitar. The gold filigree on the hilt glinted in the light of the street lantern that held off the evening darkness. "Is this yours?"

Dyrk nodded grimly.

"What design is on the blade?" the official tested him. "Just to make sure it's yours."

He was dismayed by the level of distrust. "It has an engraving near the hilt that looks like a rattlesnake's head," Dyrk responded. The official partially unsheathed the blade and confirmed.

"The criminal approached a shopkeeper and tried to sell it. He was found guilty of carrying a sword and trying to fence stolen property."

"How did you know it wasn't his?" Dyrk blurted.

"It's a blade," the official replied with a hint of annoyance.

Dyrk was laying on his mattress in late evening, not feeling well. The uneasiness in his stomach had exploded into watery bowels that kept him going to the privy every so often. He could not stop thinking about the suddenness of it all. This young man had been born to a man and woman who loved each other. He had survived a childhood that probably wasn't an easy one. He had learned lessons along the way, learned to speak, read, write, and even make a chicken stew. All the effort, sweat, tears, and love that went into one human being was destroyed forever by a single act.

A faint gleam of moonlight filtering through the clouds reflected off the silver filigree on the scabbard. This was no trophy. It was a curse.

CHAPTER 12:
BONDSERVANT

She was going to lose her mind if she had to stare at these four walls any longer.

Careesh felt her infant son relax in her arms, no longer suckling. She covered her breast and put him over her shoulder. It wasn't much better outside, given the gloomy weather, but at least the grey sky was slightly more cheery than the stone walls of their living quarters. She flung a blanket over little Mejin and headed out the iron door into the cool autumn afternoon.

Two women were at the firepit in the courtyard, chatting as one stirred a pot. There were few blades of grass in the hard-packed dirt, besides the weeds that stubbornly refused to die. On three sides were stone walls, two stories high, with iron doors spaced four paces apart at the ground level. The fourth side was a wrought iron fence, ten feet high. Through it was visible a cart-path and several sheds. She knew one kept charcoal, another firewood. Beyond that a grove of trees provided the slightest solace. A ladder was against one of the trees, and a woman was picking the last apples of the season.

Careesh bounced Mejin on her shoulder and felt the satisfying release of air from his innards. She had seen enough last night. The burns would never heal. Her husband Aijen was being worked to death in the forges.

Was there nowhere for them to go? To feel safe? To make a better life for their children?

She swept a few locks of curly black hair under her headscarf but didn't touch the tear on her cheek. Oh, for the enveloping warmth of a summer day in Ancharith. She could barely recall the taste of a fresh-squeezed lime, or the feeling of running through waist-high prairie grass, barefoot, bare-headed, without feeling the cold.

She hoped Aijen regretted coming there. He never said so, in the evenings when he sat, utterly exhausted, while she used the feeble lamplight to wash his body of charcoal dust. He endured hardship so much better than she did. Perhaps it was because he had grown up in a farming family. Careesh was the daughter of a landowner. Back when her father owned land, that is.

If only she had prevailed over her husband when they arrived at the border. By law, the Karolian border officials gave them three days at the crossing to reconsider entering the Kingdom. Careesh used those days to probe her husband, making sure he had thought everything through. He was resolute. When the official came to finalize their papers, none of the cautious warnings would be a deterrent. Just after that, another man had come and said he was a physician, would she please remove her clothes. Aijen insisted he be present, but he told her to comply.

She couldn't understand a word of River-tongue then. The physician prodded her for a few seconds, but that was enough to utterly humiliate her. Then he asked her something.

Aijen nodded in reply.

"What did he ask?" she spoke when he had gone, and she was dressing herself.

"He asked if we know that you're pregnant," he said. "They have to note that on our letter."

Careesh had asked for a southern province. Aijen refused, saying that they may have to wait for months before one of their agents came by for a parcel of outlanders. He resolved to take the first official who came. Two days later, that happened.

"So where are we going?" Careesh asked once he had spoken to the official. She needn't have bothered, she didn't understand the names of the provinces anyway.

"Saringon," he said. "It's a rich province. There will be many opportunities there. But it is in the north. They need workers for their smithies. They say I'm a good fit to fill the furnaces because I am not very tall. It will also be an easier journey. We can go most of the way by river barge."

Aijen was indeed only three inches past five feet. The two of them were indistinguishable in height. By the time they arrived at Doleth Sarin, after six more weeks of tiresome travel in which Aijen was ill and Careesh gained weight because of pregnancy, they were also the same body mass.

Careesh had given birth there, in the provincial outlander quarters. Or that was the euphemism that they employed to describe this jail. Never having set her eyes on a jail before, she couldn't imagine anything worse. Their eight-by-five pace cell housed three families and three single adults. The more aggressive residents got the spaces near the windows. Aijen was never aggressive. He was much too kind.

One man in their cell was of Bajzin descent. Careesh shuddered whenever she looked at him. The Bajzin were responsible for her exile from her homeland. Bajzin raiders had descended upon their settlement in Eastern Ancharith last winter. She and Aijen had been recently married. Aijen was working for her parents in the orchards. In one fell swoop, Bajzin raiders drove out everyone in the valley. Her parents lost their land, their servants, and their livestock when they were forced to flee. With it, she and Aijen no longer had any prospect of inheritance and became impoverished. The Karolians hadn't done a thing to stop the conflict, but gladly took in many refugees to fuel their endless need for cheap labour. For all she knew, Karolia had spurred the Bajzin on for their own gain.

Daily life there was not easy. Once a day, a guard with the face of a mole-hunting dog would bring in a crate of food, usually vegetables and day-old bread. The two other women in her cell would fight with her over the best ones. There was no sense of helping each other. Well, there was one exception. Kalmak was an old, single Vekh man in their cell who worked all day and so didn't have an opportunity to pick out any food until he got back. The first night, Aijen had seen him gnawing on rotted carrots, and had invited him to share their food. Gratefully, Kalmak joined their makeshift table every evening since.

Too kind, Careesh repeated to herself. There was barely enough to go around.

It was Kalmak who told her about a possible way out. It was an evening when Aijen was passed out early from exhaustion. For some reason, Careesh didn't feel threatened by Kalmak, she figured he was too old to have any desire for a woman.

He had told her about the guardroom. Both doors to their cell remained unlocked all day and night. One led outside to the enclosed courtyard, and the other to a passageway that connected all the rooms. Guards patrolled it from time to time, and the bondservants were not allowed to be there unless they had a good reason, such as emptying the latrine pails. A stairway went up to the guardroom, in which three guards would spend their on-duty time when they weren't making the rounds or doing chores.

"It all depends what favours you're willing to do," Kalmak was rather matter-of-fact. Careesh's cheeks reddened, both with embarrassment and rage. How could he even suggest that she was that kind of woman?

In the days that followed the conversation with Kalmak, she realized she was already a different kind of woman. The glimmer of hope that Aijen had cultivated within her was all but extinguished. This cell, this city, this country, it would kill her.

Unless she gave herself up.

She knew she was still desirable. Her hair was a mass of black curls, extending well past her shoulders. She meticulously wrapped it every night in her most precious possession – a small square of undyed silk – to keep its shape and ward off lice and insects. She had smooth, beautifully bronzed skin with a healthy reddish glow, the colour of cocoa beans. Aijen praised her endlessly. She liked that; she wanted to be beautiful for him.

She barely showed signs of past pregnancy, only a small fold of skin remained. Her body had filled out some, though. In Ancharith it made her less attractive, but apparently many Karolian men preferred generous proportions on a woman.

Karolian men! Their pasty, grey skin made her want to retch. Worse, they carried themselves with an air of superiority and aloofness, giving all the appearances of religious piety and asceticism while indulging in every kind of excess. She hated them. How could she possibly give herself to one, even if only for a moment?

But over the days her resolve had crumbled. Every time she held her son, she couldn't bear to consider either of the outcomes that were available – that the little boy would be orphaned, or that his parents would somehow continue their miserable existence. If she had the potential to put an end to it, it was her responsibility to try.

She had chosen the dog-faced one. She figured there was no chance that she could feel anything for him. She thought she could compartmentalize one moment of her life away from the rest as long as she didn't feel a thing. Lock it up and throw it away, never to be felt or seen again. If it got them out of there, she would willingly bear that scar.

She felt bile rise in her mouth when she thought of last night. She had fed Mejin, put him down to sleep, and then inched out into the corridor. Dog-face was making his rounds, carrying a pail of charcoal to fill the small stove within each cell that did little more than take the chill off. He arched his eyebrows when he saw her.

"You need something?" he asked, his politeness hitting her like acid. "I have fuel here if you're cold."

She mustered all her courage, fluttered her eyelids, and gave him a nervous smile. "I hope I could see you tomorrow night," she said, and then died inside.

His response was predictable. He leered at her, eyes traveling down from her face. "I would like that," he said. "We can have a talk. Your River-Tongue is improving. I'll see you at second watch?"

She was still thinking of what to wear that night. She had only two sets of clothes, but she thought that some combination of the two would be most suitable. If she wore the dark blouse, lighter skirt, and woolen shawl, it would be the most revealing. And the easiest to remove.

What have I come to? she agonized to herself. *How could I sink this low? No, it isn't me that has fallen*, she reminded herself with her last remaining shred of dignity. *It is this despicable world.*

Evening came quickly. Before long, Aijen was snoring. Fresh salve was on the burns on his upper arm. She put Mejin down to sleep before kissing the only two persons she held dear in her life.

"I do this for you," she whispered. Her gaze lingered on her sleeping husband. He was always asking her to be patient, to bear up under difficulties. He was so good at it. She couldn't do it any longer. She broke her gaze and silently passed through the open door.

All three guards were in the guard-room. Dog-face was sitting in a chair, feet up on a table, laughing at a joke that another soldier was telling while standing up. All three fell silent as the door swung slightly ajar and Careesh peeked in.

"Ah, the maiden from Ancharith," dog-face spoke quickly, taking his feet off the table. "I tell you, mates, she's here to practice her River-Tongue." Laughter erupted again.

Careesh didn't come through the door. She didn't want the other two to see her any more than necessary.

"We'll go make the rounds," the standing guard nodded in a silent understanding, a lecherous grin on his face. "Twenty minutes?"

Dog-face nodded.

Careesh stepped into the room and out of the way as the other two left. The last guard said over his shoulder, "I could also teach you a few new words."

She silently prayed that he would slip down the stairs and break his neck.

"Close the door and have a seat," dog-face said. A fire burned cheerily in the guardroom, making it quite warm. She closed the door and sat daintily in a chair, facing him. She willed her body to begin to relax. It was so tense and closed off. Would it hurt?

Dog-face easily picked up his chair with one hand and placed it with its back to her. He spread his legs and sat down, the chair-back between him and her. His thick arms folded over the top of the backrest. His chin rested on his arms. His ugly face was very close to hers. She felt the warm breath on her face. Besides the unusual folds of skin on his jaw, he had a wart on his neck, around which tufts of hair sprouted that could not be shaved. Seeing him so close, she realized that he wasn't very old, probably equivalent to a thirty-year-old Ancharith man.

She forced herself to stop squinting. Wide open eyes were more becoming. But she could not look at him. Her hands grasped her shawl, pulling it slightly down, putting pressure on her chest. It would be over soon, she assured herself.

"Does your husband know you're here?" he asked abruptly. His right hand was descending to her knee.

She shook her head. For some reason she thought Aijen might hear her if she said anything.

Just before he touched her, the guard picked his right hand up and began gnawing on a callous on his index finger. "Have you done anything like this before?"

She was startled at his question. Why did he care? Before she thought it through, she shook her head again.

"Are you hoping this will get you out of here sooner?"

She wanted to cry. Had she been caught? Would she be punished? She didn't answer. She didn't realize that she was trembling.

"You look very afraid," he said. "Don't be." Easy for him to say! What was he waiting for? Why was he drawing this out?

She heard the scrape of the chair against the floor. She realized her eyes were closed. Upon opening them, she was surprised to see that he had backed up a short distance.

"You are a beautiful woman," he said, straightening up. "What you are offering to me, though, is not yours to give. It belongs to your husband."

She was shocked, relieved, and disappointed all at the same time. Had she displeased him in some way?

Then his words began to sink in. Her hatred returned, whip-sawing her emotions. Who was this man to say what she could do with her own body! She could give herself to him if she wanted. And he was wrong to refuse it! The irony of her feelings escaped her at that moment.

"Here's what you're going to do," he continued. "You will stay faithful to your husband. He is a hard worker. The other guards will happily take what you are offering but it won't help you."

She wasn't even listening anymore. Had she just thrown away her only opportunity? How she wished she could have lied when he asked his questions. *Yes, I've done this before, with more men than I could count! How dare you doubt me?*

"It will not be long." He was using simpler words to make sure she fully understood. "There is a better place coming for you and your son. It will not replace what you've lost in the South. But I know you will find happiness."

All she could manage through trembling lips was, "Yes, sir. Thank you."

Careesh stood up to leave. As she opened the door, she realized how sweaty her palms were. As she walked back to her cell, she took deep breaths to calm her nerves.

She didn't think it was wise to believe him. But she had to hang onto some shred of hope to stay alive. Other than Aijen's eternal optimism, the guard's words of encouragement were all she had.

Dyrk opened the pouch and slid three gold half-crowns across the counter. As the clerk checked the coins, Dyrk took a look at the names on the paper. Aijen Ot-Mejenham, Careesh Li-Aberith, and male infant. They didn't bother recording the baby's name.

The women of Ancharith kept their clan names when marrying outside of their clan. The first boy of a marriage took on the clan name of the father, and the first girl that of the mother. Most residents of Ancharith were of Kaj Zindori descent, the westernmost of the four desert peoples. Judging by the names on the sheet, his new bondservants were of that race.

The scale balanced. The coins were verified. A seal was affixed. Dyrk sincerely hoped that this would work out better than the last.

He was surprised at how few belongings the family took with them. Aijen carried a blanket-wrapped bundle for the three of them, while Careesh carried a bundle about the same size that was the baby. Aijen was short, even for an Ancharith man. Dyrk didn't mind. Height wasn't a requirement for cleaning stables. Careesh looked healthy enough, though she kept her shawl tightly around her head. He resolved to check later if there might be a problem with head lice.

Dyrk only carried his document case with the deed to the

bondservants, in duplicate. They left the administrative building, down a wide street, and through a gate to exit the Old City. He deliberately navigated through the Lower City market on their way home. "Take a quick look, Careesh," he said. "Soon you will be coming here to get food for us every day."

Careesh seemed to feel much better as she scanned the marketplace. Food was stacked up everywhere: cabbages, squashes, broccoli, leeks, and lettuce. Eggs were sold in small baskets of seven. The smells of fresh bread wafted from a baker. A stout man, apron soiled with blood, took a break on the porch of his butcher shop, reminding passers-by that he had fresh lamb for sale at a bargain.

She whispered something in her language to Aijen. He grinned. Without prompting, he informed Dyrk in River-Tongue, "Careesh is happy to see much food here, but she is noticing that most of it is green."

Dyrk understood. In their homeland of Ancharith there were oranges, mangoes, lemons, and pomegranates in abundance. Their apples, too, were either golden or red, unlike the typical green apples of Karolia. He led them to his home. An elderly Karolian woman was already there, sweeping the stone floor of the kitchen. She introduced herself as Gelda. "I don't live here," she told the new family. "I'm just here to get you settled and get you started."

Dyrk could have kissed Gelda. In fact, he resolved to do it once she had finished what she promised to do. She was old enough that it wasn't inappropriate.

It wasn't easy, Gelda had told him, for an outlander to suddenly feel comfortable in a new environment and new expectations. She would ease the young woman into the role.

Gelda had taken with her some spare bedding and other household items. She took one look at the crate that Dyrk was using as a table and gave a disgusted cough. "This has me thinking that the master of the house is still sleeping on the floor," she said sarcastically, unaware of how close she was to the truth.

Dyrk left almost immediately for the stable with Aijen. The young man impressed him immediately with his work ethic. By midday Dyrk found that all of the available stalls had been cleaned out. He found Aijen furiously shoveling manure onto a cart when Dyrk stopped him for a break. Farnich winked at him, and Dyrk nodded his head in acknowledgment. The stable master had lent him the money to redeem two new bondservants, along with some recommendations on how to select them. Dyrk had listened to his advice to the letter.

Arriving home at the end of the day, Dyrk had never smelled such tantalizing odors in his house before. It was cleaner than it had ever been. Gelda left them just before dinner, scurrying off to cook for her own master.

The only thing lacking was conversation. Neither of them were talkative in the slightest. Aijen's River-Tongue was quite good, but Careesh's was still heavily accented and she stumbled over many words. He did notice that Aijen never spoke the Kaj language in his presence, even when Careesh used it to ask him something.

Careesh seemed delighted when he told her that the plot of weeds and grass just behind the house was hers to do with as she pleased. Some city-dwellers used their back plot as a sitting area, others for a small garden, and the rest, like Dyrk, couldn't be bothered and let it grow thistles and weeds. Though she wouldn't be able to plant anything until spring, Careesh took ownership of it immediately and had it cleared in two days. On Nedrin's Day[1], she and her husband and baby spent a good portion of their rest-day on a blanket in the back, despite the weather being chilly.

One evening after dinner, Aijen took Mejin out in back while Careesh started the dishes. All of them were still eating together in the downstairs kitchen, for lack of upstairs furniture.

"I saw you speak with the man who watched over us," she spoke in broken River-Tongue. "You say something to him, and he pointed at us. What did you say?"

Dyrk lifted his eyes from the letter to Gavon he was writing. It was the first time that Careesh had initiated any conversation with him that wasn't connected to her duties.

"The guard with the ugly face?" Dyrk asked. Careesh nodded. He

---

[1] Saturday

looked back at his letter. "I told him I wanted servants that showed honesty, integrity, and dedication." He finished writing his sentence with a flourish. "He pointed me straight towards the two of you. He said you would do anything for each other. That's a good start."

It was a cold Valeron's Day[1] when a visitor came to the stables looking for Dyrk. Or so Farnich said when he found Dyrk in the field behind the paddock, exercising two horses that got along well enough not to bite at each other.

Dyrk was immediately very nervous. "My father?"

"No. I haven't seen this man before."

"You think he's willing to come back here? I'm busy with these two." Dyrk motioned to the two horses who were enjoying their freedom in the farmer's field.

"I'll send him over."

Dyrk peeked over his shoulder now and then to get a glimpse of the stranger. Finally someone emerged from the stable. He was tall and broad, a dark blue cloak with silver edging flapping in the early winter breeze. His dark beard and hair were immaculate and had streaks of grey. A gold medallion was plainly visible on his chest.

"Madwin!" Dyrk exclaimed, both excited and apprehensive at seeing him.

"Son of Teren," Madwin said, sounding official as he strode up. "It is good to finally see you again."

"What brings you here?"

Madwin shifted his gaze in such a way that he was looking just past Dyrk. The young man knew that it usually meant that the headman was about to engage in another riddle or lesson.

"We should talk. Can I treat you to lunch?"

"Absolutely," Dyrk said. "I'll just finish up with these two and then let Farnich know."

Once Dyrk caught the two reluctant horses, he led them back to the stable with Madwin striding beside him. "Did your father ever find you?" he suddenly asked.

---

[1] Wednesday

"It's unlike you to be so direct", Dyrk teased a bit. Now that Madwin wasn't his headman, he felt a bit more at ease with his presence. Dyrk's current headman, a younger Eratur by the name of Thur Jeswold, inspired a bit more reservation. "No, I haven't seen him. But I heard he was looking for me at midsummer."

"It would be good for him if he found you," was all that Madwin said. Dyrk pondered the curious choice of words.

The two of them found a tavern with an outside patio. The day was very cool, but the sun was shining. Dyrk didn't wish to miss it. They were served hot soup and biscuits with cheese.

Madwin deserved to know his whole story. Dyrk didn't hold anything back, with the exception of anything to do with Neriah. He recounted word-for-word the conversation with the Rector of the College, which Madwin seemed especially interested in.

"And you didn't see who was behind the curtain," Madwin clarified.

Dyrk confirmed.

Madwin chewed a biscuit thoughtfully. "I imagine it has been very hard on you, having something held against you without knowing what it is. I am guessing you are holding things against yourself, your kingdom, and even me."

It was all true, but Dyrk shrugged. He could not mask his cynicism. "I'm getting used to being left out of a small group of privileged people. In this case, those privileged with knowing why everyone hates me."

Madwin visibly winced. He took a moment to gather his thoughts, smoothing his moustache.

"I want to assure you that whatever has happened to you, is not related to anything you have or haven't done," Madwin finally said. "Everyone I have talked to at the College assures me that they saw nothing but the best in you."

"Wait, you went to Geherth Altyr? You asked about me?"

"I did. I was there on unrelated business."

"Well if it isn't anything I did, then what is it?" Dyrk's countenance began to fall. "If it wasn't me, that means I must be paying for something Maryk has done! What? Or does it go further than that?"

"That's for your father to tell you. And I believe that's why he was looking for you."

"I don't believe you." Dyrk let his hand fall onto the table. "I'm sorry, Thur Madwin, I mean no disrespect, but I cannot believe that. He drove me from his presence without a word. If he's looking for anything, it's to revel in my demise."

Madwin said nothing.

"In fact, I think you know full well what's going on, and won't tell me." Dyrk began to scowl and wanted to pound his fist on the table. "If that's so, you can't blame me for being very frustrated with you when the truth of why my life has been ruined is two feet away from me, but I can't crack it open."

"What makes you think your life has been ruined?"

"Have you been listening to anything I've said?"

"Yes." Madwin sat back, not showing much reaction to Dyrk's raised voice. "I have. I've heard about Eveth, your friend at the Royal Post. I've heard about Lohann, who you befriended along the Sojourn. And Farnich, your employer who thinks highly of you. Margab the courier tolerated you. Again during the Sojourn, you made an impression on Jaer and he on you. I suspect there are many more. And I see them all as important steps on the stairway of a young man's journey to maturity."

Dyrk looked away in anger. Madwin wouldn't acknowledge the wounds he carried. All this injustice and heartache, and all the Headman did was opine about growing up.

Madwin continued. "When I found you in that cave, so long ago, I thought you were dead. Any grown man would have perished under the weight of all that rock. And yet there you were, sword at your side, barely a bruise on your head. Nedrin spared you for something, Dyrk, but the Servant won't give out the details. Some may come in time, but some will never be known."

Sword at my side? Dyrk didn't hear anything Madwin was saying after that statement. His father had never told him about finding him with a sword. They had hauled him out of that mine, unconscious. Yes, it was immensely lucky that he had woken up with barely a scratch. What sword did they find with him? And where was it now?

There was no way to ask for more details about it without making Madwin suspicious. For now, Dyrk changed the subject. "Maryk didn't fight in the Battle of Rocavion, did he?"

"What makes you suggest that?"

Curse you, Madwin. Can't you give a straight answer to anything?

"He said he fought on a Tevledain. He couldn't have owned one at the time. Even if he did, there was no way that an unmounted Tevledain could get anywhere close to Rocavion in three days from Geherth Altyr. It would collapse before it got to Resgild. Either he acquired a Tevledain closer to Rocavion, or he didn't fight there at all."

"Or perhaps a man will embellish the sole event that defines him for the rest of his life," Madwin responded. "We all, especially us men, have an innate desire to be a part of a great and glorious myth, an honest myth, that defining legend of our time. Your father is no different than you and me on that score. But before you judge him, I just want you to think back for a moment. Recall how you felt when everything was taken away from you. Remember when it hit you that you wouldn't be able to be an Eratur? You weren't the first one in your family to feel that way."

Dyrk shielded himself from that thought. He didn't want to humanize his father in any way, at least not now. He could put himself in place of the Zindori bandit he had slain, or the criminal who stole his sword. But not his father. It hit too close to the mark. "It seems like you're doing everything you can to protect him."

For the first time Madwin relaxed his face and permitted his mouth to form a casual smile. "I am Maryk's headman, after all. Not yours."

He got up and threw a few brass coins on the table. "Do I have your permission to tell your father where you are?"

"No," Dyrk said emphatically.

"I will respect that," Madwin said. "It was good to see you. I'm glad to hear that you are doing well." He emphasized the last word.

Dyrk put both hands on his temples. "Madwin," he called before the other could leave.

"Yes?"

"Just not yet."

"Very well, Dyrk."

Dyrk sat at the table alone. He realized after Madwin left that there were other questions he had wanted to ask. Who demanded that Tanakh be disqualified at the competition? Why did he leave Rothai long enough for someone, probably Bayern, to cut the cinch strap? What happened in the tent with Cassius afterwards? Why did Maryk react so strongly to Dyrk's enrolment? Did mother ever ask about him?

The barmaid came by to pick up some of the dishes and see if Dyrk wanted anything else. He took the time to admire her as she leaned over, long straight hair falling across her face and over her chest. She was at least five years his senior and clearly the mother of at least one child, but that didn't stop him from indulging.

Both sets of dishes on the table had been neatly stacked.

The military doubled down on the generally accepted religious principles of abstinence for unmarried men. Rape, no matter the victim, was always punished by execution. Assault or humiliation of any woman resulted in dishonourable expulsion from the military, as did extramarital relations. At least, that was the law in theory and on paper. Laws were only as good as the men who enforced them. Dyrk had always taken them seriously. Too seriously, his mates had joked.

The code of conduct drummed into him at the College strenuously forbade even what he was doing right now, lingering his gaze on a woman who was not his wife. Most sniggered and laughed at the prohibition. Dyrk averted his eyes.

Weak men gave into those urges. Strong men controlled their feelings. The heroes never felt them at all.

He looked past the railing of the patio. The street was very busy at that time of the day. The passersby were milling about, going this way and that way, all except for one woman who was standing stock still, like a statue. The world moved around her like it didn't acknowledge her existence. And she ignored the world in turn.

Dyrk realized that she was looking straight at him. He had no idea how long she had been standing there. She was wearing a winter shawl over her shoulders and a headscarf that partially obscured her face. Both her arms were limp in front of her, hands on the handle of a small basket from which an arrangement of white winter-blooms peeped out. Someone brushed against her. The headscarf peeled back for a second.

It was Neriah.

CHAPTER 13:
SORWAIL

The days began to blur into an amorphous stretch of time. While he had no desire for excitement, boredom was almost as bad. Torrin concentrated, minute by minute, on things he could do to relieve his pain and discomfort.

He told himself that he should be thankful to Vigheran and Erelin that he was asked to carry very little. He had been given a steel water canteen that he recognized was plundered from Dar-Amund. He carried the pouch with rune papers, flint and steel, and a few other items for personal hygiene. Other than that, a thick bear skin was his only burden.

Erelin had killed the bear with his bow. Torrin was absolutely incredulous as he figured there was no way a bow that size could pack enough power to pierce the bear's skull or do enough damage to its midsection. Once he came up to the carcass, he saw that he wasn't wrong. The arrow had pierced the bear through the roof of its mouth, driving the arrow directly into the brain. Quite a shot.

The resourcefulness of these strange men continued to amaze him. They carried only a small amount of preserved rations, which they used sparingly. They hunted and gathered as they went. Erelin often led them on small detours to hunt game.

They had stayed there a day to skin the bear, smoke some of the meat, and scrape the hide. Though it smelled terrible, Torrin welcomed the hide. Not only was winter coming, but they were going up in altitude. His thin coverings at night were insufficient. His clothing was too, being only the undergarments of his armour. Vigheran had brought back a cloak and some walking boots from a corpse at Dar-Amund. Torrin reluctantly wore the boots, but he had refused to wear the cloak as it was stained with blood. Vigheran had burned it.

Torrin did his best not to slow them down. He was able to keep up to their brisk pace for about two hours at a time, but then tired quickly. Whenever they stopped, Vigheran stayed with Torrin while Erelin went ahead to scout. Though Vigheran seemed perturbed by his delays, he didn't say anything.

The country they were going through was familiar to Torrin. He also knew how unpredictable the weather was in that region. The Sea of Winds to the east regularly sent cyclonic storms up the Istrith River valley. Thankfully, at that time of the year, the storms were not as severe and frequent. They had already endured two days of rain and wind so heavy that they had made little progress.

Torrin was still undecided as to whether the two men were his captors, or companions, or guardian Servants in disguise. He usually felt like he was a prisoner. Yet they took good care of him and checked on him regularly. They pushed him but did not force him to go beyond his limits. Vigheran rarely talked except to give orders or explain what Erelin was doing. Erelin still had not made a sound. In fact, Torrin could not even remember Erelin moving his lips to form a word. It was now plain to him that Erelin was mute. He communicated by a combination of subtle hand signals, facial gestures, and body language, but always with Vigheran.

Erelin only interacted with him to check on his health. Every night he inspected and smelled Torrin's severed arm. He felt Torrin's temples, pushed at various parts of his chest and abdomen. Once, after a particularly cold rain storm, Erelin checked his ankles and toes. It was all very strange. Almost as strange as Erelin's nightly ritual of lining up his arrows. Once, without anything else to do, Erelin had lined up a series of wood chips, left over from their gathering of firewood, identically aligned and oriented.

Torrin was able to make all these observations and evaluations only in the times that he was not deep in the throes of depression. A great many things would trigger flashbacks of that fateful day. A particular sound of rock on rock made him think of the embankment upon which he lost his hand. The metallic sound of

Vigheran's knife-scabbard hitting his canteen sparked memories of the jangling tackle on the Vekh horses as they galloped in pursuit. Even the smell of smoke from the campfire brought back images of Dar-Amund, outer walls crumbled, smoke billowing from every structure, corpses scattered all about.

Not a day went by when he attempted to do something with the hand that wasn't there. Now and then he had fallen flat on his front when he tried to grab for a handhold. The pain was there, but strangely was most intense in the part of the arm that no longer existed. In the middle of the night he often woke to a throbbing sensation shooting up his arm. He knew about infections. Vigheran and Erelin were being diligent in cleaning and checking the wound. Erelin often produced some herbs at the end of the day that he had picked up, making a salve with some boiling water and applying it to the exposed parts of the stump.

That day was the coldest he could remember. They were keeping high to the mountainsides as they traveled southeast. Though snow had not fallen upon them, they were now trudging through three inches that had fallen the day before. The air was crisp and clean. From time to time he could see through the trees, beholding a commanding view of the countryside to the east. This was the first day that he saw the ocean, gleaming far off into the distance.

At evening camp, Erelin usually darted off to do some hunting, or exploring, or both. Vigheran and Torrin had come to a silent agreement on setting up camp; Torrin would scrounge for firewood while Vigheran would do all the work that required two hands. This night, when Torrin returned with an armload of fuel, Vigheran had already started a cheery blaze. However, he had first dug a pit about twelve inches, and put rocks around it.

"You aren't smoking meat tonight, are you?" Torrin asked, recalling the interesting structure that had been set up to smoke the bear meat.

"No. Others may be close," Vigheran responded. He fed only a small bit of wood into the fire at a time, slowly building up the hot coals that would warm their dinner.

Vigheran turned his black eyes on Torrin. "You know little for one so old, *kyusi*," he said.

Torrin bristled and instinctively put on the demeanor he wore during debates at Dar-Amund. "First, I am well educated. Second, given my current situation, I don't think it's unreasonable that I have a lot of questions. Finally, I was the youngest *Almathin* in my troop." He recalled the meaning of his nickname. "Why do you always call me *kyusi* if you think I'm old?"

Vigheran flashed his teeth in the widest smile Torrin had yet seen. "It was for play. You see, you are old. But act young. Near you, I am young. But act old."

"I am forty-two. By my people, I am barely a man."

"I am three tens and nine. Not useful any longer to my people." Vigheran's smile was gone. He pointed into the darkness. "You are like the wolf. Live for ever."

Torrin figured now would be as good a time as any to try probe for more information. "Why doesn't he talk?"

Vigheran fed another branch in. Then he made a motion like he was grabbing a small object right in front of his mouth, and then throwing it away. "Gone."

"His tongue? Why?"

The coals shifted. Vigheran only shrugged.

"You mentioned your people. Who are they? The Roj?"

Vigheran didn't move, but Torrin could see him stiffen. "That people gave me birth, yes. No more. And now no more questions today, *kyusi*."

He moved the small iron pot into the coals. Torrin rejoined the silence that too often reigned.

Sorwail was built on a tall bluff that extended into the Sea of Winds. Far to the south, a chain of mountains sank into the ocean, producing a long peninsula that provided protection from the strongest winds and storms coming from the ocean. Just south of the settlement, the sea was scattered with various merchant vessels at anchor. The city, boasting over ten thousand inhabitants, was built on the bluff with a stout wall facing the land. Extending over the countryside was a semicircle of cultivated land.

This land was named Feldar, but there was no corresponding government of that name. The region had always been open for conquest and exploitation to any who would brave the weather, the bandits, the wild creatures, and the rugged terrain. Small city-states rose and fell over the years. Some allied themselves with the fading kingdom of Azenvar to the west, but most remained isolated and aloof. None survived for long, either. Sorwail was the exception.

The city was originally built almost a thousand years earlier. It was destroyed many times, but never by an invading army. Earthquakes, hurricanes, and even a tidal wave were responsible for its destruction and reconstruction. Yet it remained a vital port for any ship navigating the Sea of Winds.

Because of its independent character, the people of Sorwail were thoroughly mixed. Bay-tongue, River-tongue, Corsavan, Calderan, and all four Zindori dialects were spoken there. One could buy anything, and sell anything, without any argument from the oligarchic authorities, provided you paid the steep port taxes.

The night before, Torrin had witnessed another sight that gave him clues to the origins of his companions. In their secluded camp, in which Vigheran lit no fire, Erelin had pulled off his cowl and circlet. He ran a small razor over his head, scraping it over and over again. In the darkness Torrin could not see what he was removing. He had simply assumed that Erelin was naturally bald. The razor was also used on the eyebrows and chin.

In the meantime, Vigheran had taken great care to make several preparations of herbs and berries that he kept with him. One paste he kept until the next morning, and then with a leaf spread it over all of his exposed skin. Torrin gasped as he saw the markings on his skin disappear wherever the paste was spread.

Now the young Taurilian from Dar-Amund strode with his two strange companions along the road towards the gates. Only this time, his companions were not quite as strange. Vigheran, devoid of visible markings, still carried his weapons openly. His hair was no longer tied back in the fashion of the Roj, but flowed freely from his scalp. His earrings and nose-ring were removed, leaving imperceptible holes. Torrin still could not believe he was not yet forty; the scars and wrinkles on his face made him look like an old man.

Erelin no longer wore the circlet. His mismatched armour, and his fur cloak, had all disappeared into his belongings. Instead, he wore a dark hooded robe. Underneath was a flowing light tunic, but in its billows Torrin could see the black links of his fine chain-mail hauberk underneath. The recurved bow was unstrung and covered in a sack that made it look more like a housewife's broom than a weapon. Torrin wondered why Erelin had not offered that cloak to Torrin instead of the bear pelt.

This was the first time that Torrin saw Erelin's face uncovered in full daylight. It was unnerving. His eyes reflected light so intensely that, depending on the angle, they sometimes appeared completely white. He had no eyebrows, no facial hair. The skin was so lifelessly pale and grey that he resembled a corpse. As much as it unsettled Torrin to be around Vigheran, Erelin was downright frightening.

They mingled with the light traffic heading into the town and passed through the gates. The closer that they came to the city, the more that Erelin shrunk to the back of their trio. Torrin began to feel like an awkward mother hen, with a seven-foot-tall chick hiding under his wing. At the wide gates, Vigheran showed a stack of furs, including the bear pelt, to the customs officer. He paid a small tax to enter.

The buildings were a motley mix. Some were clearly built to withstand, hopefully, the natural disasters which plagued the city. Others did not, being built with a resignation that it would get knocked down in a few years only to be put back in place. A wood-frame building leaned against a stone one. A canvas roof was spread beside a marble dome. Expertly laid brick adjoined mud walls.

One thing was obvious with the city: sewage flowed downhill. The further they climbed, the cleaner, neater, and richer the buildings became. Torrin could see down to the water's edge on the north side, and it appeared to be a ramshackle shanty with narrow paths littered with garbage and refuse.

Vigheran led the three of them to the south side of the city. This was the commercial hub. Instead of the organized market that

Torrin had imagined, stalls were haphazardly arranged along a wide boulevard. Merchants set up right on the street, wedged themselves in nooks and crannies, or blocked doorways and alleys. Some vendors were nothing more than a young boy or girl with some trinkets, flowers, or treats. In the middle of the marketplace, a Vekh minstrel cycled through a series of instruments as he entertained the shoppers day-in and day-out, earning enough copper for a bed and a meal. Torrin had expected that Vekh music would be harsh and discordant, but upon listening to the minstrel found it to be lively, pleasing, and very skillful, if not a little haphazard.

Vigheran did all the trading. Erelin found the darkest alcove to stand in while waiting. First, the furs were sold. Vigheran came out of another shop with a light green cloak, used, but in good shape. Torrin accepted the cloak gratefully. He was surprised to hear the Roj talking in an even, almost normal voice, without the glottal vibrations, though still with the heavy Roj accent. "This place is where you find your cousin. We may be many days. But you start looking now."

Torrin looked around him in doubt. There had to be hundreds of people milling about the merchants. How would he ever find Braedil in all this? He hadn't seen his relative for twenty years. He was a strange older man, about a hundred and fifty years old by Torrin's recollection. Braedil had stopped by Dar-Amund for a week two decades ago. He got into many arguments with his relatives. After he left, Torrin had asked Ludonn about it. His uncle hadn't divulged much, simply said that Braedil had some strange ways of doing things and didn't like the idea of living in Dar-Amund.

Braedil was shorter than the average member of the House of Atlan. That made things more difficult. From Torrin's recollection, he had sported a full beard and long, unkempt hair, still black despite his age. That still wasn't much to go on. He racked his brain in an attempt to find more identifying features.

Vigheran pointed towards the north. A long building with four dormer windows facing south rose just behind the structures on the boulevard. "We will be there, kyusi. Stay and eat each night with us. If you find your cousin, go with him. Then you will not see us again."

Torrin was not only shocked by his words, but also at his own reaction to losing the only two people he had known for the past three weeks. "You would leave me just like that?"

Vigheran grunted, returning to his gravelly voice as he bent his head to Torrin. "You no longer need us, so we go."

"How would I thank you?"

Vigheran gave his wide grin, which still gave Torrin shivers. "Not needed, *kyusi*. But we see you tonight when you do not find. You ask more of your questions then."

Torrin gulped. Despite the unpredictability and fearsomeness of these two, being on his own was just as daunting. Only for the afternoon, he told himself. I can make it until then.

It was the fourth day. Torrin felt he would rather be on the road again, than strolling up and down that foreign marketplace. He was getting to know many of the vendors, as they were with him. It wasn't hard to pick out an ashen-faced one-handed man who did nothing but stroll up and down the marketplace all day. He realized now that there were two Vekh minstrels, who switched at midday. By now he had their repertoire memorized. He still enjoyed their performance nonetheless.

He had added to his circuit every day. He now strode around the docks, among some carpenter's shops, and up the hill to a beautiful fountain. But always he came back to the marketplace. If he was going to see Braedil, it was there. He wondered how long it would be before Vigheran and Erelin gave up. After all, there was no guarantee that Braedil was even living there.

One woman had caught his eye yesterday. At first he figured it was only because she was Taurilian like himself. She had kept her shawl tightly around her, and so he couldn't really see what she looked like or what else she was wearing.

However, he now realized that there were a few other Taurilian women about the marketplace, yet the one from yesterday still stuck in his head. Today he saw her again, ducking into a bakery. The shawl was a different colour, but it was still wrapped tightly around her head. He also noted how briskly she walked, as if in a hurry. She was, like most Taurilian women, quite tall, probably over six feet.

He stayed close to the bakery, waiting for her to come out. He crossed his arms and leaned against a wall. He was still wearing his thin under-armour tunic, with the green cloak over top. He folded his arms, hiding the stump of his right arm in the cloak.

The woman walked quickly out of the bakery and passed by within a few feet of him.

"Greetings, lady of Atlan," Torrin said in as even a voice as he could muster.

The woman ignored him and kept walking. But Torrin could see that her eyes had darted to him, just for a second. She wasn't old, probably twenty or thirty years older than him. Her long strides carried her quickly. There was definitely something familiar about her, but he just couldn't place it. She did not break her stride and disappeared down the street.

Torrin sighed. This was fruitless. He felt a wave of anxiety come over him again. He hated to be alone.

He decided to start walking towards the fountain again. It reminded him a little of home, but not enough to hurt. The sound of the water playing across stone never lost its positive effect on him.

The next day he walked his circuit as before. It was blustery but not raining. The sea was rough. He didn't do the usual seaside stroll for fear of getting soaked.

Vigheran was always in the inn when he got there in the evenings. The Zindori paid for his meal and allowed him to sleep on the floor in front of his rented bed. Private rooms were unheard of in most inns, being a luxury that few could afford. This inn had sleeping closets for the rich and floor space for the poor. There was just enough room on the floor of Vigheran's sleeping closet for Torrin to make himself comfortable.

Torrin had no idea what Vigheran did all day, only that they never saw each other in the market. He also didn't know where Erelin was, for the most part. Twice he showed up in the evening. He would have a brief one-sided discussion with Vigheran and leave. He did not sleep at the inn. In fact, Torrin realized that he had never seen

Erelin sleep at all.

Torrin was walking past an alleyway when he heard a sound. It reminded him of a cat hissing, but it may have come from a person. There was a child blocking the alleyway, selling dried fish.

A hand emerged from the darkness above the boy's head and beckoned to Torrin. The boy seemed oblivious, hoping that he could sell some fish to this one-handed man. "Excuse me," Torrin said as he gingerly made his way past the child into the space between the buildings.

His eyes adjusted to the poor light in the narrow alley. His heart thudded in his ears as he realized the distinct possibility that he was about to be robbed or beaten. But when he could see, he found that the only person in the alleyway was the woman that had walked by him the day before. She was wearing a dark green shawl now, different than the past two days.

Then he noticed that the woman's right hand was partially hidden in her shawl, with the base of a knife handle visible in her clenched hand. He had better be careful.

"Who are you?" the woman demanded. Torrin had not pieced together what he would say if someone asked him that. However, given that the woman was at least of the same race as himself, he figured there was less of a chance that honesty would harm him.

"I am Torrin son of Paldonn House Atlan," he said, using the Melandarim order of identification. He waited for her to reciprocate.

"What in the world are you doing here?" she hissed. "You're supposed to be in Dar-Amund. And what happened to your hand?"

"Dar-Amund was destroyed. I am the only survivor."

Her eyes widened for a moment, then suddenly narrowed.

"I don't believe you."

Unable to come up with anything else, he resorted to sarcasm. He raised his right arm. "I've been dismembered by Vekh and survived twenty leagues in the wilderness. Sure, don't believe me."

"Keep your voice down," she whispered. "Very well, what is your lineage?"

Torrin started reciting his ancestors, beginning with his father. He was two-thirds of the way to Atlan when she stopped him.

"Is there anyone else with you?"

He shook his head. "Forgive me for being intemperate," he said softly, "but I'm answering all the questions. Can you give me something about yourself?"

"No." Well, she was honest at least.

"You walk by the fountain every day," she went on. "Meet me there at the second hour of the afternoon. Alone."

He stared at her blankly. She pulled the shawl tightly around her, strode up to the low wall at the end of the alley, and hoisted herself up. She disappeared from sight. Torrin was impressed that she could do that in a dress.

He spent half an hour waiting at the fountain. He began to despair that nobody would be there. He studied every face that passed by, hoping to find one that looked like the woman he had talked to, or someone similar.

A cloaked and hooded man with a white beard was slowly going through those present near the fountain, offering blank verse papers. Most declined. When it was Torrin's turn, he replied, "I don't have any money."

"It is free of charge," the man said in an insignificant voice. "Do dignify the Servants with your petition."

Torrin took the paper with his left hand. The cloaked man went on, and shortly disappeared from view down a street. The paper felt good in his palm, a reminder of the medium by which he offered praise to the Servants.

He turned the paper over. On the back was written:

Enter the fishmonger's shop on second street. Ask to see the mackerel.

If it wasn't for the desperation of his situation, Torrin would have laughed. What sort of band of thieves was he dealing with? The mackerel? He'd been traveling with a swordfish and a shark for three weeks, what need did he have for a mackerel?

Dutifully, he followed the instructions. He may well be walking right into a trap, but it just didn't seem plausible that his enemies would set so elaborate a trap just to steal – nothing. He had no possessions worth stealing besides his clothing, which wouldn't fetch more than a few brass pieces.

And if there were men who wanted him dead for some reason, well, it probably wouldn't be much worse than staying with Erelin and Vigheran for the rest of his life.

A small Corsavan man presided over several vats of shellfish at the front of the fishmonger on second street. Torrin mustered his courage and asked, "Do you by any chance have any mackerel?"

The shopkeeper chuckled. "Word travels fast," he said in slightly accented River-Tongue. "It's in the back. Pick out what you want. Six copper each." He jerked his thumb over his shoulder.

As Torrin made his way to the back through the smelly shop, the fishmonger said over his shoulder, "I don't exchange Karolian coinage, by the way."

Not a problem, thought Torrin. He parted the curtain and entered the back. A large vat was full of fish, still in a net. Other fish were hanging, decapitated, on hooks. A pile of fish heads was on the floor. The awful smell made him queasy.

The back door opened. A man with a white beard entered and took two purposeful strides towards him. Before Torrin could react, the man had grabbed his left wrist and was, without a word, leading him out the back door.

"Wait," Torrin said, digging in his heels. "Who are you?"

The man put his finger up to his lips. Seeing his face clearly, Torrin saw the family resemblance and guessed that he might be Braedil.

"We are not safe yet. Come along and listen to everything I tell you."

Inwardly, Torrin felt that this was all ridiculous. But then it was all he could do to follow the path that the man led him down with breakneck speed. They made multiple turns through narrow alleys, darted across a main street, and vaulted a garden wall. He then put a sack over Torrin's head and spun him around a few times.

"What was that for?" Torrin asked once the spinning stopped, his head still whirling.

The man didn't answer. The vice-like grip on Torrin's wrist resumed. He had completely lost his sense of direction, which was probably the intent of the sack and the twirling. Disoriented, he had no idea where he was when he was finally pushed into a doorway. The sound of a heavy wood door closing told him that he was inside. The sack was removed. They were in an unassuming basement flat. It instantly felt homey and welcoming to Torrin.

"Kryna, I brought home the mackerel," the bearded man called.

The woman that Torrin had seen in the marketplace came into view. She no longer wore the shawl, and now he could now see that she had the red-brown hair that was all too common amongst the descendants of Atlan. He had been accurate when he called out to her in the marketplace.

Nothing made him feel more at home than the fact that she was finally smiling.

Paranoid. That was the first word that Torrin would use to describe Braedil. His niece, Kryna, was more reasonable but respected the odd precautions that Braedil demanded she take. After they had introduced themselves, they sat down to a meal and asked Torrin to tell his whole story.

He figured that any mention of Erelin and Vigheran would send Braedil into a tizzy. Yet he couldn't avoid that part of the story. There was no way that he could have made it all the way to Sorwail without help. He referred to them as "two mercenaries", which was likely accurate, but avoided any further detail. He also omitted the part about Vigheran entering Dar-Amund and coming out with plunder.

Kryna cried openly when Torrin told of the fateful fight in the gorge. Braedil, on the other hand, seemed to listen with a sort of nervous energy, shifting this way and that way in his seat. He prompted Torrin to continue every time he stopped to collect his thoughts.

"*Ropu*[1], let him take a breath," Kryna once admonished Braedil.

The two of them lived together in that basement residence. Only two small windows, both covered, offered any evidence that the

---

[1] An informal term of endearment for an older male relative, such as a grandfather or uncle

outside world existed. One corner of the main room was littered with books and papers. A small desk overflowed with them, and beside it was a low couch with a blanket crumpled up in disarray. The only enclosed space other than the privy closet was a tiny bedroom in which Kryna slept.

Braedil had never married. There was likely no woman who could promise an eternity of putting up with his idiosyncrasies. He had been living in Sorwail for twenty-five years, which is the longest he had ever spent in one place. Kryna had grown up in Altyren. She had come to live with her uncle four years ago, when her sea-faring father was lost at sea. Her mother had died when she was young, and she had no siblings.

They worked as translators, partly for the government of the city-state, and partly for a local bookseller who reproduced various works in different languages. Breadil knew four languages fluently and could read and write in five more. Kryna was his assistant and apprentice. Fortunately for Braedil and his predilections, he could do most of his work from the comfort, and squalor, of his home office.

"I don't normally take such precautions," Braedil said magnanimously as Kryna rolled her eyes. "But over the past few years I have been noticing a very disturbing pattern. The house of Atlan is being slowly, systematically, killed off. The destruction of Dar-Amund now proves it beyond the shadow of a doubt."

"He believes my father's death was part of it," Kryna said, "but there's no evidence. His ship was lost at sea and never seen again, so there's no evidence one way or another."

Torrin was dubious of Braedil's theory. "The Vekh have overrun all of the territory of Azenvar. There's no way that they were specifically targeting Dar-Amund."

Braedil put both hands on the edge of the table, arms locked. "Tell me, my boy, how long has Dar-Amund stood without falling to the enemy?"

"Over a thousand years," Torrin answered.

"And then suddenly, just like that, the Vekh are able to overcome it. One in a thousand. It's a complete coincidence that the rest of the

House is being eradicated across Reldaan at exactly the same time."

"But what threat are we?" Kryna interjected. "I mean, the threat of Dar-Amund to the Vekh of Kardumagund is obvious, but why go after the rest of the House? We are simple people, no consequence to anyone. I can't understand why someone would profit from our death."

Braedil ignored her, possibly because of the crushing weight of her logic. "Take those two mercenaries, for example. They may be part of it."

"Oh yes, *ropu*. The ones dedicated to the destruction of our house would save our cousin from the Vekh, nurse him to health after catastrophic injury, and transport him twenty leagues to safety. Yes, I can see that they are dedicated to our destruction."

"Make sure you are not seen by them again, boy," Braedil wagged his finger at Torrin.

"I do see the wisdom in staying away from them," Torrin said. "But as Kryna said, there's no way that they have been hired to kill me. They were very kind to me, in their own way."

"And do stop calling him a boy," Kryna pleaded. "He has reached manhood, fought in battles, survived so much more than he should be faced with at his age."

Braedil waved a dismissive hand towards his niece and started to clear the dishes. "We do need to start discussing what we will do with this boy, or man, or cabbage, or whatever, in the long term."

"Why can't he stay here with us?" Kryna stood up to help. "At least for some time."

"Out of the question. He will attract attention."

"So you're just going to throw him out on the street."

"Of course not. That would attract more attention."

Torrin wished he could get in a word edgewise.

"You know better than anyone that our relatives are few and far between," Kryna said, her voice becoming a little shrill. "Where do you expect him to go?"

"He could stow away on a ship to Corsava. They won't find him there."

"Are you out of your mind? Oh, why do I even ask that

question?"

"Can I speak?" Torrin finally interjected.

Braedil was already up to his elbows in dishwater. "Let the boy speak," he scolded Kryna.

"I do think a ship is a good thing. It would be the best way for me to disappear from here and not draw any attention," Torrin said. "But I don't want to go to Corsava. How often do ships go to Karolia?"

"Karolia? That's exactly where they would expect you to go," Braedil answered. "How about Verania? The coasts of Draaf are very nice in the summertime."

Kryna ignored Braedil. "In the winter and spring, ships leave for Karolia every week," she said. "The storms over the Sea of Winds and the Istrith make it difficult in the summer and fall. We're nearing the end of the storm season now, so there's bound to be a few ships waiting to sail up the Istrith."

"And sail right through the heart of a Vekh invasion? Brilliant, just brilliant," Braedil sputtered, spraying dishwater as he made sweeping hand motions.

Torrin hadn't thought of that. Braedil was correct for once. "How long would it take to get there overland?"

"Well, it would take about seven weeks…"

That would be manageable, thought Torrin.

"…to get to Dharbur. From there, if you took the pass of Takorran, which would be sheer stupidity in winter, you could be through Rynek and into Karolia in another seven weeks. If you survive. Going through the Sea of Sand would take twice as long, and you only need to get through Raider Territory. Going the north route will bring you right through the Vekh invasion."

Kryna protested. "Don't be an idiot. They haven't even crossed the Kullion River yet. They won't conquer Lyssia by that time."

Braedil waved a wooden spoon at her like a scribe about to discipline a student. "If they rolled over Dar-Amund like a tarn treads on a dandelion, Lyssia will be conquered in a week."

"All right," Torrin was fed up with arguing. "The first step is to see if any ships are planning to sail for Karolia. I'll take my chances if they feel confident that they'll make it. If not, we'll sit down and make another plan. But please, let's stop this arguing."

"Arguing?" Braedil arched his eyebrows at Kryna.

"Oh, Torrin, we do this every night," she laughed. "You'd best get used to it."

Torrin woke up feeling better than he had in at long time. He was with people he trusted, despite the fact that they were a little strange. He had a full belly, a good set of clothes, and at least a plan. Kryna had taken a look at the stump of his right arm. She had snipped off a few pieces of dead skin, put salve on to protect against infection, and bound it up.

He put his heart into his petition the next morning to Harophin. "May this peace in my heart grow like the forests," he said as the smoke of the verse paper rose.

He hoped that writing with his left hand would improve rapidly, but sadly his letters still came out like a three-year-old's. Since verse papers were small, it was difficult to write with one hand but not have the other hand to keep it in place. He found that he could use one of Braedil's books to hold the paper, with his right arm holding the book.

The interactions between Braedil and Kryna made him uncomfortable at first, but now he was starting to become endeared to them. The way that Kryna laughed at the conclusion of the debate left him with a cozy feeling that storms could always be weathered through love and loyalty.

He spent the most part of the next day inside. Braedil went out in the morning to his bookseller friend and said he'd be back by noon. Kryna darted out from time to time, always telling Torrin to stay inside until she returned. Just before lunch, Torrin asked Kryna if he could take a walk. She agreed, provided he stay in the alleys and away from busy streets. "Don't tell Braedil," she said with a wink. "At least not yet."

He hadn't gone far. It was just nice to get some fresh air. He got his bearings on some of the landmarks he recognized and determined they lived halfway up the slope on the north side of the city.

After lunch, he took another rest, and then opened up one of the books he found in Braedil's office. None of them were written in River-Tongue, but many were in Melandarim, which he knew well.

The book in his hands described the history of the realm of Belorin. The history began with Beronin, a young tribal chieftain of the southern steppes, meeting with Melphar, the son-in-law of Melandar. Beronin in time would marry Melphar's daughter Poenna. Their eldest son was named Belorin, after whom the realm and the people were named.

When Braedil came home, he noted the book Torrin was reading. "Keep it," he said. "I love seeing young men reading books in Melandarim. So few these days are taught the mother language of our culture."

Books were not inexpensive. Outside Karolia, paper and bindings were costly. More costly was the time it took a scribe to painstakingly copy every word from one book to another, sometimes translating it in the process. Torrin noted in his copy many translator's notes written in the margins. He asked Braedil about it.

"That work was originally written in Melandarim," Braedil said. "It was translated into Belorin and the original manuscript lost. This is my attempt to restore the original, but many things remain unclear. What you have there was my first draft, I wrote a more complete version later and it has been copied eighty times." He finished that statement with his chest puffed in pride.

That night, Kryna and Braedil argued about whether Torrin should get himself outfitted for the journey to Karolia. Braedil thought it too soon, too dangerous, and too presumptuous, considering they had not yet found a ship that was heading in that direction. But Kryna prevailed. Braedil counted out eight Corsavan silver pieces.

Corsavan silver was actually an alloy of silver and copper, minted in smaller sized coins than Karolian silver Rings. As a result, the exchange was usually five and a half Corsavan silvers for one Karolian silver Ring.

Torrin went out on his own that morning and purchased what he needed. He bought the needed supplies for a short walking journey. Even if he was to be on a ship, he might need to travel once at the port.

He selected a good set of traveling clothes that would do in the summer, a winter rain-cloak with sleeves, a used backpack, and a good knife. He added a compact set of eating utensils. He was getting used to doing many things with one hand, but handling money was not one of them.

He got back to the house, sorted out his new and old gear, and packed. He included the book that Braedil had given him. He had often lost it amongst Braedil's regular shifting of his notes and other books; he could now keep all his things together in one place.

Braedil approved of his readiness. "It's wise to be prepared to leave suddenly, if need be. You weren't followed, were you?"

In all honesty, Torrin hadn't checked. "No," he said.

Kryna came back in mid-morning the next day to tell Torrin that she had found a ship that was planning to brave the Istrith for Calsyx. She encouraged Torrin to go meet the captain and arrange passage.

It was another cold and blustery day, with an occasional drizzle. Apparently, that was the default weather in Sorwail in winter. The sea was whipped into whitecaps, and the distant ships bobbed up and down. Torrin followed Kryna's instructions and came to a warehouse near the docks.

The meeting with the ship's captain left him disappointed. Knowing that passage to Karolia would be in high demand given the unstable situation, the captain demanded the equivalent of eight gold crowns for a single passenger. Torrin took his leave without bothering to negotiate. There was no way he could ask Kryna and Braedil to part with a king's ransom in order to get him to Karolia. The ship was not due to leave for another week. Perhaps the captain would be more amenable closer to his departure when he had an empty ship to fill.

He made his way back to the house. Upon pushing the door open, he realized that it was not latched.

He fell to his knees.

A trail of blood was smeared across the threshold. Torrin hid his eyes with his left hand. He was not quick enough to avoid the searing of that horrific sight into his consciousness. He peeked out from behind his hand only to confirm that, yes, there were two lifeless bodies in the house.

Eyes closed, he fumbled to his left for the backpack he had stood against the wall. Then he stumbled outside, back into the grey, unforgiving weather. He was too stunned to cry.

He didn't know how long he walked. All he knew is that if he stopped, his rubbery legs would give out and he would collapse. He knew that he had to keep moving.

His only conscious thought was recalling flashes of Braedil's paranoid ramblings. *The old fool had been right, and all I did was laugh at him. And now I'm responsible for his death.*

His shins bumped into a stone ledge. He realized that he was at the fountain. His knees buckled, and he fell on his side. His eyes stayed open but the rest of him descended into nothingness, a comatose existence suspended between life and death.

The sound of the water was the only thing that reminded him he was still alive.

Someone put a hand on him. He figured it was a patrolman that would want him to move along. He didn't respond.

"Get up *kyusi*," a guttural voice pierced the veil of white noise created by the fountain. "Not safe here."

CHAPTER 14:
STARTING OVER

The basket fell to the ground. Neriah turned and hurried away through the thin traffic on the street.

Dyrk vaulted the railing on the patio and dropped onto the cobblestone. Several passersby stood back, startled at his audacious exit from the tavern. He tore off after her at a full run. The basket remained where it was on the street as he dashed past.

Neriah ducked between two buildings, her headscarf and braid flowing behind her. Dyrk followed. She didn't make it far, half-collapsing against a stucco wall, face against it, sobbing uncontrollably.

Dyrk ran towards her. Instinctively, he reached out both hands and planted them against the wall, one on either side of her. He wanted to prevent her from escaping, but it also brought the two of them closer than he had intended.

"Get away from me!" she wailed, writhing against the wall.

Neriah had not changed much. Perhaps she had put on a little weight, but Dyrk couldn't be sure. She still wore her brown hair in a thick braid. He was reminded of her full cheeks, the small nose, and those soft brown eyes that could so easily captivate him.

But now he could not help noticing much more. The pose that froze them – his arms outstretched, figuratively pinning her against the wall in the cage of his embrace – woke an intense base urge in him. He hated it, he resisted it, yet it was there and forced its way past every wall he had built. She was so vulnerable, so helpless, compared to his physical strength. The graceful curve of the skin of her neck. The unmistakable outline against her dress of forbidden fruit. The thought of how close he was to that cradle of life, that priceless treasure sealed and locked away. It threatened him like a wild animal, coming out of every pore of his being. His arms flexed as he fought. He felt like his sleeves would explode in tatters from the pressure.

But like waves of the ocean, the first swell that he detested so strongly was followed immediately by a second. She was weeping. She was helpless, distraught, pleading with him for something. He wasn't listening as to what. He was overtaken by an immense urge to protect, to gather her up, to embrace her with one arm while fighting her unseen enemies with the other. This one he welcomed, even though it was no less primal than the first. The realization had not yet dawned on him that the enemy was himself.

The third wave of emotion was weaker, but more prolonged, and ultimately forced the tears from his own eyes. He saw in that huddled, shaking, feminine body a reflection of himself. Someone torn apart by loneliness. Another person who issued a silent scream to the rest of the world: *Am I unfit to be known? Will anyone reach out to me, beyond politeness, mutual benefit, family responsibilities, or societal expectations? Reach inside to my very being and tell me that I am worthy, I am desired, all of me, without a single part left out.*

"Young maiden, do you need help?" The male voice, stern and worried, pierced the raging ocean of emotions that had forced him to arrest all physical movement, lest his body act without his permission. A guardsman stood there, two paces away, blocking the alleyway to Dyrk's right. His hand was on his sword hilt.

Dyrk suddenly realized that things did not look good for him. He had chased a woman down the street, she had pleaded with him to stay away, and now he was standing over her in a manner that could easily be interpreted as threatening. He did not know what to do. The shame began to rise in his face, intensified now that another man saw him weeping.

Neriah turned her tear-streaked face towards the guardsman. "Good soldier," she said, her jaw quivering. "This man has permission from my father. I am so sorry for alarming you. I am not in danger."

The guardsman relaxed his hand on the sword hilt. "M'lady, I will be right around the corner should you need me," he said, gingerly dropping a basket of white flowers on the ground. As he walked away, he muttered under his breath, inaudible to both Dyrk and Neriah, "She's not the one in danger, all right."

Once he was around the corner, Neriah turned to Dyrk, face twisted in rage. Her left hand clutched the loose shoulder of her blouse with which she was wiping her nose. Her right hand began to beat on his chest with a closed fist.

"You killed me! You destroyed me! How could you show your face here again?"

Dyrk almost relished the blows. Despite her apparent helplessness that triggered his deepest emotions, she had the strength of her mother and could put considerable force behind her fists. He took them as a penitent man might take lashes, knowing that with each stripe, each drop of blood, he was in some twisted way repaying his debt to society, purging the criminality from his being. If only it were that easy.

His arms were still planted against the wall. She could easily duck under them and escape, but she didn't.

"Who was she? Who took you away from me? Was she pretty? Thin and lovely? Healthy body and glowing, dark skin? Did you kiss her, bed her, wed her? Is there a trophy at home waiting for you?"

Dyrk bit his bottom lip. The feeling he had in the Rector's office, of his life turning on a single decision, came back to him with vengeance. This moment was even more important than that one.

"What's her name? Do you love her? Please, I beg you, save my soul and just say yes."

Dyrk took a deep breath. Very deep. It was long past time that he said a word. Awkward as it was, he finally forced something through his lips. It came out distorted, and he realized that his own jaw was trembling.

"I have never loved anyone else," he said. And though he meant it, he wasn't sure if he was digging his own grave.

Her eyes narrowed. Dyrk had never seen her this upset before. Nowhere close, in fact. Her anger was so acute that the rational part of him, which had retreated to a corner under assault from his emotions, raised its feeble, trembling hand, and asked him if he had cornered the wrong woman.

"You don't know the first thing about love," she cried. She thrust her right hand at him again, but this time with two fingers directly into his breastbone. "I'll tell you what love is.

"Love is a man who knows he isn't a very good craftsman, who earns nothing more than a modest living for his family, who is not held in high regard by his community, who saddles a borrowed horse and rides for days through rain and storm, looking for answers for his daughter. To Doleth Sarin, where he finds nothing. To Geherth Altyr, where he is so out of place they think he's there to steal something. Only the fact that he knows a name saves him from getting thrown in prison. He continues to Trebier, following the few clues he has. And then he trudges back home, returns the horse, and holds his daughter all evening because she feels her life is over, gone, discarded."

Dyrk could hold her gaze no longer. He raised his eyes instead of lowering them, staring at the thatch on the building they were leaning against. His arms still hadn't moved.

"I hoped you had died!" the last word came out with a viciousness that stung Dyrk. Her voice was cold and biting. "I may have been able to live through that. But not this. Not what you've done to me."

She stood up a little taller. Her words still pierced him like ice. "You have a tough relationship with your parents. I get that. Perhaps they never taught you about love. So let me give you one more lesson. Imagine a poorly educated housewife, a mother of seven, now pregnant with the eighth. She buys some letter paper. She writes some letters. She diligently follows them up with more. She finally gets a reply from a scribe in Rianast. And she hides that letter from her daughter, knowing it will destroy her. Every morning and every evening she remembers it's there, and asks herself if it's more loving to maim your daughter with the truth or keep her whole and ignorant. It took her four days," she held up four fingers. "Four days, curse you! It took her four days to give that letter to me. I forgave her for that. I can't forgive an eternity, but I can forgive four days."

Dyrk started to say something, but she put two fingers on his mouth. They were not gentle. Her nails scratched the bristly skin on his upper lip.

"So help me, I will rip your tongue out if you say a word!

"I never asked for an Eratur. I never asked for a cursed ribbon, may it burn at Morthuldan's feet. I don't care if you never get past hoeing vegetables. In fact, I would prefer that you empty latrines for a living! At least you would come back to me, smelling of the refuse of the earth, instead of treating me like it!"

She put her hands over her face again, and her shoulders shook. Dyrk didn't know if he risked serious injury by breaking the silence, so he continued the impossible task of finding the perfectly appropriate thing to say.

Her hands lowered, stretching her face and revealing her eyes together with the red flesh on the inside of the lower eyelid. Her hands parted a bit to say a few more words.

"When you left the college, I'm sure you felt terrible. I'm sure you felt disgraced. You felt like the world was against you. But you put me with the world. You put me outside of yourself. You blamed me in part for what happened to you. You proved that you are an island, an impenetrable, unassailable fortress. And there's no room in there for me."

Before Dyrk could say anything or react, she ducked under his arm and hurried away. "Don't come after me," she warned over her shoulder, and disappeared down the street.

The basket of white winter-blossoms was left there in front of Dyrk. Collecting his thoughts, he realized that he had said only one statement in that whole exchange. It was clumsy, it was a negative inference, but it was true.

His arms hurt. He removed his hands off the wall and saw that he had pressed them so hard that they were cut from the stucco.

He still had to prove that the inverse of his statement was true. To her and to himself.

The guardsman chuckled as he passed by. "Shall I call a medic?"

The furniture had come slowly. Dyrk had found a carpenter who often refurbished used furniture; he had asked to be given the opportunity to buy a few items before they were restored. The old woman who ran the candle shop next door offered a bureau of drawers with a changing table on the top. She didn't need it anymore, she had said, but a young mother could use it.

Dyrk had built a desk. Or rather, had found the lumber, the nails, and the tools for it, and Aijen had rescued him for the rest. Aijen proceeded to make a stout, rough table from which they all ate together, still in the kitchen downstairs.

Dyrk had offered to Aijen that they could take the second bedroom upstairs. Aijen had refused, and explained, "You are a young man, master. You will get married soon, have children. Then me and my family will need to come back down here. We are happy here, there is no need to get used to something else just to come back."

Indeed, the kitchen was not nearly as dreary as Dyrk had first thought when he moved in. Aijen and Careesh had cleaned the place, especially the grime on the back window that now let in the rays of the morning sun. It was winter now, but Dyrk imagined the back door could stay open during the summer, providing additional light and air.

The desk was the only reason he had to be on the middle floor. He wrote often to his brother Gavon. He sent a few letters to some of the friends he had made in his tarn-riding days. He corresponded with Eveth, the Eratur at the Royal Post who helped him get to the Sojourn of Ancients. He even responded to an inquiry from Caevin, an acquaintance at the College, as to how he had managed. A letter Dyrk sent to Trebier addressed to Lohann, his companion during the Sojourn, was never responded to.

The letter from Caevin had taken Dyrk by surprise. Caevin claimed that he had left his juvenile ways behind, and he was now in his fourth year in good standing. But it was his description of a passing encounter with the Rector that Dyrk chewed on, reading and rereading. It went as follows:

Yesterday I bumped into Rector Rogen and his scribe in the hallway outside the south armoury. He stopped me and sent the scribe ahead. He said he knew that I had been friends with you. He then asked if I knew anything about how you're doing. To be frank, Dyrk, I wasn't much of a friend to you, and I honestly know nothing of what has befallen you since. I could tell him nothing. He looked like he was about to leave, but then turned to me without that usual expression of passing a gall stone, and said, "A lot of people have been asking about him."

Dyrk's mornings had evolved into a routine. He washed, lit the lamp on his desk, and wrote his morning petition. He would then spend a short time, maybe half an hour, reading old letters or composing new ones. Careesh brought him breakfast at that time, the only meal they did not all eat together.

Careesh got up earlier than anyone else in the morning, fed Mejin, and then left the house to get the daily bread from the baker. Dyrk had never wanted anything more than warm, fresh bread with a bit of butter for breakfast.

This morning, as expected, Careesh came up the stairs with a plate of steaming fresh bread and a pat of butter just as the smoke was clearing from Dyrk's morning petition. She put the plate down. Normally she quickly disappeared down the stairs, as if she didn't belong there. But that morning she lingered. Dyrk looked up from re-reading Caevin's letter.

"There was a fire," she said. "In Doleth Ambron. Many buildings burned. The soldiers were called."

Dyrk wondered for a second about the random piece of information. Then he realized what Careesh was doing. Bondservants would typically read the morning's news on a public board in the marketplace or listen to the early-morning Crier as they did their shopping. A distinguished Karolian gentleman would start his day by receiving an oral recollection of current news from a trusted bondservant. It gave rise to the common saying, employed just before sharing some juicy gossip, "I heard this morning, straight from my bondservant…"

Nobody had told Careesh to do that. Dyrk was very surprised that she could even read River-Tongue or understand the rapid-fire delivery of the Crier. "Thank you, Careesh. I appreciate it."

She smiled and returned downstairs.

He found out later from Aijen during their workday that she was not yet able to read and write. She was, however, interacting with other bondservants who got the morning bread, and asking what she could do to better serve her master. A fellow servant had read her the notices.

That day was Taephin's Day[1]. Dyrk would only work the morning, because it was his turn to care for the horses on tomorrow's rest-day. At lunch, Dyrk told Aijen he would not be going home for the midday meal. He saddled Tanakh and rode away into the cold winter air.

He left the city, heading west. Snow was on the ground. It usually did not snow that early in the year, but when it did, it often hit hard, piling up high. The snowfall had come three days ago. It was melting quickly, receding every day.

The Great East Road was mostly clear. As Tanakh plodded westwards, Dyrk struggled within himself as to what to say. Would he even be given a chance to say anything at all?

He entered Harwaith. Dyrk would not call it a typical sleepy town. It was along the Great East Road, the main route between Altyren and the realm of Lyssia far to the east. It was a minor commercial center for the surrounding farms. This part of Saringon was some of the best year-round farmland in all Karolia, and so every available piece of land was owned and cultivated. The town itself was not large, probably twice the size of Tanvilon. The buildings were made mostly of timber frames with walls of wattle-and-daub.

He wished Tanakh could slow his gait, but he was already moving as slow as the high-strung horse was able to. Dyrk didn't tie the horse up as he got to the thatched hovel with the cartwright's shop attached. He could hear the ringing of someone beating on heated steel.

He did not knock on the door. He walked around a pile of melting snow and into the cleared open-air workshop. Vecton was at his forge, shaping a part for the axle of the wagon he was repairing. His back was to Dyrk. The hammer stopped.

---

[1] Friday

"She doesn't want visitors," was all he said, neither resuming his work nor turning around.

"I didn't come to see her," Dyrk replied. "Not yet."

Vecton put down the hammer and turned to Dyrk. With no one to work the bellows, the fire pit was beginning to cool, but Vecton made no move towards them. His scrawny arms crossed across his chest. The two tufts of hair near his ears were singed by the heat.

"I just wanted to thank you," Dyrk said, standing up straight even though inwardly he felt very small. "You looked after Neriah when I failed her. You really went quite the distance to get answers for her."

Vecton slowly nodded, his hawk-like face lined with deep concern. Then he drew a sharp breath. His beady eyes darted, and he turned to the bellows. Over the sound of air rushing into the furnace, his raised voice carried. "What makes you think I did it for her?"

Dyrk was speechless. He waited for Vecton to finish to explain what he meant. After pumping many times, the wainwright leaned his arms on the collapsed bellows. "Come to think of it, you're part right, I did do it for her, but she wasn't the only one."

"What do you mean?"

"You seem to have a real problem with accepting that someone might actually do something for *you*."

Vecton resumed pumping the bellows. A window in a dormer of the hovel opened. Neriah's voice came forth, slightly muffled. "Daddy, please tell him to go away."

Vecton stopped pumping and gestured towards the open gate of the workshop. The two men walked back to Tanakh.

"Young man," he said in a fatherly tone. "I do not withdraw my permission. You seem to be learning some of those tough lessons I talked about. But you did disappoint her, and I can't say if she will recover from it."

He gave a slight grin, which nevertheless still split his thin face in half. "You may visit *me* anytime. Though I'm not sure it's worth it to ride four hours just to spend thirty seconds with a crusty wainwright. Something tells me you will, though."

Two days later, Careesh reported the news that Saringon had called in two regiments of infantry reserves to reinforce the northern border and be mobilized to march to Lyssia if needed. Dyrk gave her instructions that he wanted to know about all of the provincial reserve callups and where they were headed.

On the following Nedrin's Day[1], Dyrk made the trek to Harwaith again. The gate to Vecton's shop was closed, being the rest-day. Ryesse met him at the door before he could knock. She was advanced in her pregnancy. She had put on a lot of weight compared to the last time Dyrk had seen her. Her face was a little swollen. She didn't appear as tough and unyielding as the first time he met her. She seemed more weary than anything.

"I need to go to the market," she said. "Walk with me?" The question sounded more like a command. Dyrk agreed.

As they walked, Ryesse first made some small-talk. Some of it was about her pregnancy, which Ryesse complained was her most difficult one yet. They chatted about the weather, about the shortage of onions that year, and about Dyrk's bondservants. He asked how the pregnancy was going, to which she responded with a series of gestures that implied prolonged sickness.

"But Dyrk, someday you'll understand what a privilege it is to carry a small person around for three-quarters of a year."

They got to the market. It was much smaller than the Lower City Market in Saringon. There was room for only four or five farmer's stalls. There was only one bakery, one butcher, and one dry goods shop. The last store advertised itself as a buttery, which sold cellar-ready foods. Everything was closed, except the ward tavern just down the street. Dyrk realized that it was Nedrin's Day.

"I didn't come to the market to buy anything," Ryesse said. She had a glum look on her face. "Someone doesn't want you anywhere close to the house. I need to sit."

They sat on a wooden bench that was normally reserved for customers who were waiting for an order from the butcher's shop.

---

[1] Saturday

Ryesse settled herself in like she was preparing to nest on an egg.

"Now. You are going to start from the day before you left the College. You are going to tell me everything." Ryesse spoke in a stern voice as if she were Dyrk's superior officer. He felt more compelled to obey her than anyone he had served under.

Ryesse listened to him with an attentiveness that Dyrk had never experienced before. His relationship with his own mother, Loriah, didn't seem unusual until he began to spend time with other families. Loriah was very tall; she always exuded a sense of elegance no matter what she was doing. Her beauty was, Dyrk now realized unflatteringly, mostly external. Despite having five children her body never seemed to change. She was strong but slim, graceful but imposing, all at once. Her hair, nearly to her waist, was a beautiful shade of amber. It had a natural wave to it, though she usually straightened it with an iron. She was, to a young Dyrk, the very image of a queen.

For the most part, Loriah was aloof and distant to everyone, including her husband. She never spoke of her feelings, her inner desires, or dreams. Though she spent considerable time on her clothing and appearance, she had no reaction to the compliments that were heaped upon her.

Dyrk recalled when his youngest sister was born. It was only a few weeks before his ordeal in the mine. Tradition dictated that, from the first signs of labour, the male members of the household would leave the house until well after the baby arrived. Several women from the community moved into the vacated space to assist with the birth.

Plessa was due to arrive in late spring. Normally Maryk would move himself and the boys into one of the vacant servant huts, but that year he decided that they would bunk down in the hay barn. It was without a doubt the best memory Dyrk had of his father.

Maryk was presented with the new baby girl on the veranda of the house. There he spent his first precious moments with his new daughter, but it wasn't Loriah who brought her out, it was the midwife. As the baby was taken back inside, Maryk hobbled back to the boys in the barn. "Mother is doing well," he assured them.

From the hayloft, Dyrk could see through the windows of the house, into the sitting room. Those days, he often saw his mother there, sitting on her own, lap empty. The baby was given to her from time to time for feeding, but then she handed the responsibility off immediately. She must be so tired, he thought then.

His mother seemed to have a double measure of detachment from her eldest son. Dyrk noticed it especially when it came time to discipline the children. She would correct Gavon forcefully, and regularly raised her voice to scold the girls, but for Dyrk she did not lift a hand. He could not remember his mother hitting him once. It was always Maryk that got the task of setting Dyrk straight, often well after the matter.

He did remember with fondness the clothes that his mother sewed. She was an accomplished seamstress, but her skills and interests lay with formal wear more than work attire. For the most part the family were clad in sturdy, well-made work clothing made by their neighbour. However, on feast days, the family was resplendent in Loriah's finest garments. They were the envy of the community when they gathered together. On that count, Dyrk did not feel left out. He still had a fine brocaded tunic she had made for him, now far too small for him, in his belongings.

Now he was sitting beside a much different woman, though of similar age. Ryesse typically chatted up a storm, and often blathered away when she should be listening. She was open and honest about herself and her feelings – too open and too honest sometimes. She was dressed in simple garments of rough cloth that wouldn't be out of place in a bondservant's clothing chest. Even before the current pregnancy, her body had some unnatural proportions, the battle scars of a victorious woman. She kept her thick, curly hair tied in the back. Dyrk would not call her pretty.

His first impression of Ryesse was quite different than how he regarded her today. At first, she came across as pushy and nosy, even a bit obnoxious. Now he realized she was simply being protective of her eldest daughter, who at that time was rather young to start a courtship. The more he got to know the woman, the more she opened up and accepted Dyrk into the family, and her heart, almost like another son.

But she was not chatting now. She was attentive to Dyrk's story and weighed every word thoughtfully. He had never experienced that level of intimate conversation with an older woman before.

"When was the first time you tried to write a letter?" she asked. He had gotten as far as starting the Sojourn of the Ancients. She didn't say to whom. They both knew who she was talking about.

"I had told myself to do it several times, but the first time I put pencil to paper was at the inn on the way to Mar Athel," Dyrk replied. Then he realized – that was four days after being expelled from the college. Neriah's words echoed in his head: "I can't forgive an eternity, but I can forgive four days."

"Do you know what stopped you?"

Dyrk nodded. "Shame."

Ryesse shifted positions with a groan. She put two hands on her distended stomach. "My husband once said that shame is very useful when you can truly identify something you've done to be ashamed of. Go on, what happened with those boys at Mar Athel?"

Dyrk continued, but as he did, he marveled inside. Here were a man and woman, neither receiving any education after their twelfth year, scratching out a basic living in one of the most prosperous places in the world. They were clumsy with the Melandarim language, knew little history, and had likely never picked up a book on philosophy. Yet they were the wisest people Dyrk had ever met.

He finished his story. Ryesse asked a few follow-up questions. Then she pulled out a folded letter that she had wedged into the sash of her dress.

"It's from early this year. You should know what he wrote about you. I'd like to know if it's accurate."

Dyrk opened the letter.

--

K 2 Anakdatar 2797[1]

---

[1] Sunday, February 16, 2797

Ryesse:

May Taephin's embrace be upon you. I hope this letter comes as you and your family enjoy good health.

I was forwarded your unaddressed inquiry dated T 1 Kemantar 2797[1] two days ago. I apologize that it took this long for it to get to me. Please understand that the College deals with numerous inquiries into all manner of things from across the kingdom. I assure you that when I saw your name, it has remained my utmost priority to respond to you as soon as possible.

I will share as much as I am able. I am aware that my brother may consider this a significant breach of trust, but answers are owed.

Vecton was correct that Dyrk was removed as an initiate from the Eratur's College last year during the month of Harophin. What he was told concerning the removal was, to my knowledge, incorrect. No reason has been divulged to any party, including the accused. The official records state nothing more than:

He has failed to meet the requirements of the college and is therefore unfit for the King's service[2].

The authorized witnesses listed are:

Rogen House Lyrus, Rector of the Eraturs's College

Amrioth House Ithniar, Scribe

Amarion House Teren, His Majesty's Commander of the Western Armies and Third Crown Prince of the Dominion of Karolia

Amarion's presence on that list was necessary because all expulsions for conduct unbecoming must be authorized by a Prince. It is likely that Prince Amarion is not even aware of this, as his office would affix his seal in his absence.

As your husband was able to discover, Dyrk was assigned to the tarn-riding corps. I can tell you that he survived his training and was garrisoned in northern Dedarrek. He wrote that he was nearly killed twice and is suffering from a prolonged illness. The last letter that I

---

[1] Friday, December 27, 2797. Since the year starts on December 22, this is at the beginning of the year 2797.

[2] This line is written in Melandarim.

have from him is dated V 7 Taephin 2796[1], which is two months ago. It is apparent to me that my brother is suffering great personal anguish. He is, to put it bluntly, not in his right mind, which is understandable given the circumstances. With myself excepted, he has cut off contact with his parents and everyone else.

I am sorry to hear that this includes your daughter.

If there is anything else I can do to help, please do not hesitate to write to me.

Gavon son of Maryk House Teren

Third Canticle, Eleventh Verse, Gel Sonest College of Scribes

--

Dyrk gave a long exhale. Reading about it brought back traumatic memories which made him weak. His hands shook as he folded the letter and gave it back to Ryesse.

"Slightly embellished, but true," Dyrk finally said. The comment about him not being in his right mind stung. Yet, if he put himself in Gavon's robes, he would have probably thought the same thing.

"Are you angry with him?" Her voice pleaded. She left unsaid, *please don't be.*

"No." Dyrk was sure of that. Gavon had done the best with what he had at the time. Dyrk's next letter had been written prior to that one. It must not have arrived yet. "I am glad that your family got some answers."

"Dyrk," Ryesse said, her voice suddenly trembling. He looked up and saw that she was crying. Her eyes studied the stonework at her feet. Dyrk for the first time saw the compelling likeness to Neriah when she did that.

"What is it?"

She fumbled with her hands, finally resting them back on her stomach. "I feel partly responsible for all this. I made a big fuss out of you being enrolled. When I got that letter, I realized that I had been foolish. I was – no, I *am* proud of you for what you've

---

[1] Wednesday, October 8, 2796

accomplished. The way you carried yourself through various tests and trials was inspiring. I don't need any stamp of approval from the College. You were already an Eratur to me, and you still are.

"Oh, how Vecton told me to stop. That silly little man, how much I love him. He's always right, you know. He can't straighten a cartwheel or add up expenses, but he is wiser than any lord."

It broke several protocols, but Dyrk no longer cared. There had been a few passersby while they were talking. Now they were alone in the town square. Dyrk put one hand on hers, still on her pregnant stomach.

"Thank you," was all he said. It was forgiveness and gratitude wrapped in a single statement. She stopped crying and squeezed his hand.

She got up and they began to walk back to the house. "Just so you know," she got practical again. "Nedrin's Day is not the best for you to stop by, at least not yet. We always have big gatherings every week. Some worship the Servants through burning verse papers and visiting temples. We focus on being together. Nothing makes me feel closer to Arren than a festival, so why not have a festival of our own every week, I always say."

Dyrk recalled that Neriah mentioned their custom. He had never visited Harwaith on Nedrin's Day before, as the College always held religious classes that day. "I'm hoping I can join you some day, it sounds wonderful," he said.

He wanted to say, *how I wish I could be a child again, and grow up in your home. I don't need a four-bedroom house with marbled floors, tall windows, and a slate roof. I want a simple home where the people who live there just can't wait to be with each other again.*

He mounted Tanakh and began the lonely trek back to Doleth Sarin.

The second, fifth, and ninth reserve cavalry regiments were summoned the following week, along with another four regiments of footmen. Dyrk was apprehensive at the news. If the reserves were being called up, he preferred to be in the first regiments heading out. Those were least likely to see battle, and the first to be rotated back home.

Pre-emptively, Dyrk had his weapons sharpened and armour refitted. It was a long wait for both as there was high demand for these services during mobilization. He went through Tanakh's tack with care, paying special attention to the cinch strap. He would need everything in good condition regardless, as he would be reporting for training in a month.

On the last workday of the month of Nedrin[1], Farnich took Dyrk aside. "I happen to have connected a buyer and supplier for a war-horse," he said. "I need to head out in a week's time to pick up the mount from the supplier. He's the best war-horse trainer in Saringon, I think you might know him. I was wondering if you'd like to go and pick it up."

Dyrk's face gave the answer. "Are you asking me or telling me?"

"I won't make you do it. I know things aren't right between you two, just thought you might like the chance."

"Thank you for understanding. But no, I prefer to stay away." That was not what Dyrk needed right now.

Careesh was ill, so Dyrk went to the Festival of the New Earth on his own. This festival marked the last calendar day of the year before the Month of Waiting. It symbolized the expectation that the Servants would one day return to the earth in power and remake it. Aijen raised an eyebrow as Dyrk prepared to leave the house at sunset, clad in only a simple tunic and a long grey hooded cloak made of rough material. Aijen had never seen Dyrk wear it before.

"You look plain for a festival," he noted.

"Next year, you'll see why, when you attend," Dyrk replied.

Festivals that were held indoors were always in the local tavern. Every ward had a tavern attached to it. Historically, the public tavern served two purposes. The first was to control the sale and consumption of alcohol. Under the laws of Treon's day, the ward's tavern was the only place in which it was legal to brew, sell, and consume it. In Dyrk's day, these restrictions on alcohol were no longer in force. The second purpose of the ward's tavern was to

---

[1] Friday, November 28, 2797

provide meals for the local poor and destitute, as well as to travelers. The practice to hold gatherings, ceremonies, and administrative meetings in the ward's tavern continued.

The Festival of the New Earth was the only festival with a dress code. No fancy clothing, no jewelry, no ornaments, no headwear. It began at sundown. Those who participated, which in these days was less than half the ward, gathered in the tavern. There mingled Lord and bondservant, young and old, men and women, Taurilian and foreigner. The uniform dress code broke down distinctions that were present every other day of the year.

A time of food and fellowship was followed by a religious service dedicated to Nedrin. Dyrk had always enjoyed that festival before, but that year his heart wasn't in it. Ever since he left the College it felt like the Servants had abandoned him.

The next day he found out that he had been called into service in the provincial cavalry.

CHAPTER 15:
PURSUIT

Erelin seemed especially agitated. At least, as agitated as an extraordinary mute mercenary could be.

As far as Torrin could tell, there were signs that there had been a falling-out between his two strange companions. Ever since they left Sorwail, they had not spoken to each other at mealtimes. The only occasions that Vigheran said anything to Erelin were in the tone of voice that a superior would use to an underling.

Likewise, Vigheran spoke far less with Torrin. He didn't tolerate questions anymore.

They had left Sorwail in haste, reaching the forest by nightfall and pushing well into the night. Torrin was completely numb to all emotions for another day after that. It was only when they stopped for the second night that he curled up in his bedroll and cried.

Four days later, they were still heading due west at an exhausting rate of travel. The terrain was difficult but Erelin always found them an efficient path that led through the maze of hills, ravines, and patches of trees. If he was ever put on a forced march, this would be it. Struggling every minute of the day to keep up gave him some measure of welcome distraction.

If there was one thing that Torrin regularly thanked Braedil for, it was the gear that his relative had paid for. Braedil's obsession with being prepared for a disaster had borne fruit. Torrin had all he needed, including verse papers and the book on Belorin history that had been gifted to him.

Torrin was ruminating over the message that he had found in his verse papers that morning. It was the first time he had opened the verse paper pouch since Sorwail. The message was written in a fine

Melandarim script, small enough that the entire message fit onto one paper. Torrin had flipped through all the other papers, front and back, which were still blank.

We are being pursued, it said. Melandarim sentence structure did not permit the longer, complex sentences that were possible in other languages. *Be alert and ready to run. Fire is your best weapon. Do not forget. Someone close to you wants to kill you. Burn this.*

He was getting jaundiced to the constant references to danger. This was, in all likelihood, a message from beyond the grave, Braedil's last paranoid rambling to him.

Oh, how he missed them! He had known them only two days, but he felt like he had lost close family. Again. He could not believe that there could be such cruelty in the world. In the rare moments that he was able to ascend beyond his miasma of despondency and trepidation, he could rationalize the destruction of Dar-Amund as an act of war by an invading army. There was no justification, none whatsoever, for the cold-blooded murder of an old man and young woman, both innocent and harmless.

He hadn't burned the message. Braedil was dead. Torrin was far from Sorwail now. This was the last thing to remember him by. He chided himself for being critical of the constant arguments between Kryna and Braedil. He would give anything to be with them right now, bickering away.

The pace had slowed today, to somewhere between full speed and frantic. Torrin was much stronger now than on his journey towards Sorwail. The days spent in town, resting at either the inn or Braedil's house, had done him a world of good. The clothes and equipment that Braedil had paid for were also proving their worth. But there was no way that even the strongest man could keep up that pace. He figured Vigheran's increased intemperance might be due to the fact that the Roj Zindori was, finally, tiring from their speed.

Erelin showed no signs of flagging. The first day out of Sorwail he had resumed his unusual gear. As before, he would often scout ahead of the other two. However, Torrin recently noticed that his silent companion was also disappearing into the wilderness along the tracks they had just made. What was he looking for?

That day much of the march was uphill in clear, cold weather. As they crested a ridge in the dying daylight, Torrin saw a commanding view of the terrain in three directions. Far to the east he saw the ocean. Thankfully a low cloud hid Sorwail from view. To the south the ridge progressed into a low line of mountains. Westwards, he saw a forested valley, with a lake edged in ice. Distant lines of smoke could be seen from several places around the lake. Further to Torrin's left, a small river snaked south.

Erelin and Vigheran stood for a time, having their longest discussion since they had left Sorwail. It seemed to Torrin that they had at least agreed on something.

They descended into a copse of spruce trees and camped earlier than they had on previous days. Being winter, the days were short. For the past three days they had roused in the dark and walked until Torrin could not see his hand in front of his face.

A small fire was quickly burning. Vigheran soon had their typical meal cooking, a spiced stew of turnips and bear meat. It was nutritious but never settled right in Torrin's stomach. He didn't dare ask the surly Zindori any questions anymore. With a bit of light left, he opened Braedil's book on Belorin history. Oh, how he wished he could still be in Sorwail, browsing the many books in Braedil's office as the old man chattered away.

The Melandarim script in the book was bold and firm. The Karolian influence was unmistakable, given the inflections on the soft consonants and the utilization of punctuation.

A chill went down his spine. He fished in his belt-pouch and opened Braedil's note. It used Taurilian inflection. No punctuation. The script was fine and curved, in contrast to the book's blocky characters.

Perhaps Braedil was able to write in both modes. Besides, who else would be able to write in Melandarim?

Erelin strode into view and sat across from the fire facing Torrin. Vigheran started to pour out the stew. The circlet gleamed as the firelight danced off of the silent one's eyes, which were looking straight at Torrin. The hood descended. Erelin picked up a bowl.

The pale grey skin on his face tightened in a menacing glare. Pale grey – the unique hue of the ancient Taurilians who fought beside Melandar and followed him into exile.

As Vigheran bent over his bowl, Erelin made a subtle gesture of his head towards the fire. Torrin folded the note and tossed it in.

The implications rushed over him like an ocean wave. He took his bowl and equipped himself with his spoon as he pondered. Erelin wanted him to know that someone was pursuing them with the intent of killing him. Vigheran did not want him to know, or, more likely, was simply indifferent to his plight. Erelin had often explored behind them, looking for the pursuers. Vigheran may be out of sorts because he was perplexed and looking over his shoulder. Some things made sense now. Questions abounded all the more.

"Fire is your best weapon," he recalled. Torrin set out his bedroll a little closer to the campfire, which by now wasn't more than glowing coals. What kind of pursuer would be more afraid of a burning branch than naked steel?

On the next part of their journey, they descended into the forested valley but steered well south of the lake and the settlement there. They crossed the swift-flowing river at some rapids. Torrin did not see another soul. In fact, there was little evidence that anyone had ever been there.

They began to climb again. The land was becoming more alpine. Snow was now six inches thick and covered the whole ground. When they stopped for lunch, Vigheran finally ventured a comment to Torrin.

"I hate cold and I hate wet. When we get to the desert I will be ahead of both of you."

Torrin already figured that they were heading for Dharbur, and Vigheran's statement all but confirmed it. Far to the west of their position was a tall mountain range, the Zelmandi Mountains. Beyond it lay the land of Belorin. That realm extended from the lush grasslands around the Kullion and Lorin rivers, all the way south to the blasted wasteland of the Sea of Sand. The land gradually changed from the former to the latter. Near the Sea of Sand was a large valley with a small inland salt sea, a veritable oasis in the midst of the unforgiving terrain. Dharbur was a city built on that oasis. It had changed hands many times throughout the history of Belorin, often reverting to an independent status that continually made and broke alliances with neighbouring realms. At the present time, it was self-governed, but on friendly terms with Belorin.

The people that lived there reflected its fractured history. The primary inhabitants were of the race of Pej Zindori, the only one of the four Desert Peoples who were nearly extinct in Torrin's day. They had been mercilessly oppressed over the centuries by the Roj Zindori. Because of that, the Pej often found more in common with the Belorin peoples than their desert brothers.

The Belorin were a people seeded by a precursor tribe of Rhomakhiem from Haned in Melandar's time. Rhomakhiem, or Unspoiled Men, refers to any peoples that were unaffected by the plague that turned the original Taurilians into Vekh. Melandar's granddaughter married one of the Rhomakhiem, and their son was named Belorin. He forged a people who would ever be astride their horses. Over the years, his descendants established a realm that spanned a vast plain between the Kullion River and the Sea of Sand.

The skies darkened that afternoon. The wind began to blow fiercely. Even in his winter gear, Torrin had trouble keeping warm. Just after the sun set, Erelin rejoined the other two and led them into a small cave at the base of a cliff. It wasn't much more than an overhang, but it got them out of the wind. He carried the carcasses of two wild pheasants.

As a storm began to rage, Erelin cut down a few saplings and propped them across the cave opening. Torrin tried to help as best he could by adding pine branches to the barrier. Vigheran just huddled in his cloak in the cave.

Torrin really started to worry when he saw Erelin make the fire. That was always Vigheran's task. Their situation became clearer when the Zindori collapsed onto his side. He was sick.

With the fire started, Erelin gave the cooking pot to Torrin and then strode outside for more firewood. Torrin filled the pot with snow and set it beside the fire to melt. He was surprised by the amount of firewood Erelin was piling up. Perhaps there was some premonition that the storm would be a long one. He glanced over at Vigheran, who was shivering uncontrollably. He heard the impact of an axe as Erelin began to fell another small tree.

Erelin dragged in a length of the tree he had just cut down. Torrin jumped past, out the opening, and into the darkness to get the branches that Erelin had just cut off.

Suddenly, Torrin's ears were assailed by the most bloodcurdling scream he had ever heard. It was not human. He jumped back, hunting knife in his left hand. His knees began to shake. The scream stopped as suddenly as it started. It had come from between himself and the camp. He was out in the open. He had to get back.

He slowly began to move to his right. Maybe if he circled, he could get around whatever made that sound. He froze. Something was moving on the snow only a few feet in front of him, but he couldn't see a thing in the darkness.

With a swiftness that defied expectations, Erelin vaulted into the night air in front of Torrin, facing away from him. Something was chasing him. A blade flashed forth in his hand, thrusting and slicing. Torrin made a break to his left, running as fast as he could towards the cave. Dashing through the opening, Torrin pressed himself against the stone wall, as far away from the opening as he could get.

Erelin loped through the opening behind him. He sheathed his sword. Then he took two steps towards the fire and sat down beside it, facing the opening. He looked alert, but not afraid. Vigheran groaned.

"What was that?" Torrin gasped.

Erelin looked in his direction, the eyes glinting opaque yellow like a cat's. Then he looked down. He was feeding more fuel into the fire, making it far larger than they normally would for cooking.

Torrin had been in the wild before. He heard the howls and cries of wolves, mountain cats, and tarns. This was nothing like that. He became aware that there were two points of light dancing, disappearing, then reappearing in the darkness outside. It resembled two stars, but as he watched, he had never seen stars glow with such a cold, blue light before.

Erelin picked up a burning brand from the fire and tossed it through the opening. There was a dash of movement, and the two stars disappeared. Torrin gasped. He caught a quick glimpse of the hindquarters of some creature. Though he did not get a good look at it, Torrin guessed that it was about the size of a large dog. A series of vicious spikes bristled on its back and down the length of a tail. The scream erupted again, now to their left.

Torrin covered his ears. He couldn't take that scream. He waited until it trailed off before he took his hands off again.

Erelin had covered Vigheran with all of their blankets, Torrin's included. The sick man was still shivering. The tall Taurilian calmly picked up one of the pheasants and began to pluck the tail feathers.

Torrin controlled his breathing until he stopped shaking. His eyes hurt from being open so wide. He blinked a few times to moisten them. Finally, his heart rate was close to normal, and his thoughts began to process what had just happened.

The floor of the cave was mostly smooth stone. The wind had pushed a clod of dirt and dust into one corner. He needed answers. With his hands, he scooped up a handful of the dust and poured it at Erelin's side. The cat eyes looked at him and narrowed. After two more handfuls, Torrin bent down and wrote the first letter of the Melandarim alphabet.

"What. Was. That?" Torrin demanded.

Erelin had already started skinning the bird. He picked up one of the tail feathers he had set aside. Using the quill end, he wrote in the dirt. He wrote five characters. Torrin had to turn his head to read it properly.

"Gryphon!" he exclaimed, and then almost laughed. "You expect me to believe that? Those things are myth!"

Erelin shrugged and resumed plucking.

"You're serious!"

Erelin gave an almost imperceptible nod. Gryphons were the name for ancient mythical demon-beasts that hunted the earliest men, soon after they came forth from the caves of the Pelgori. They supposedly had supernatural powers from the Seraphs that possessed them. Greatest of these was the demon-bear Bresjekh, who was slain in the legends upon Tawkin's heroic escape from Kardumagund.

Torrin's incredulity erupted in sarcasm. "I suppose there are dragons circling overhead and you have a flaming sword."

Erelin put the carcass of the bird, bone and all, into the pot. He started plucking the tail feathers of the second one without so much as glancing in Torrin's direction. He obviously disliked the task.

Torrin had to admit he had felt a strange foreboding feeling for some time before they stopped. Or perhaps not - maybe he was just reading into his apprehension about the coming storm. He looked at Vigheran, who had stopped shaking and was fast asleep. He knew the Zindori normally slept with one eye open. Probably an ear open, too. Right now, he was too sick to hear or see anything. This was his chance to get as much information as he could out of Erelin.

"Tell me why you're with him," he blurted. Might as well start somewhere.

Erelin spread the dirt out and wrote four characters.

"Bondservant? He's your bondservant?"

The head barely moved, left and right. (No.)

"You are *his* bondservant?" he asked in disbelief.

No reaction. This was strange. He had never heard of Zindori taking bondservants before. They took slaves, but usually imprisoned them for life. The contract between a bondservant and master, with rights and responsibilities for each, was exclusive to Melandarim societies.

Torrin pointed outside. "Is that what killed Braedil and Kryna?"

Erelin shrugged.

"How are we going to kill it?"

(No.)

"Then how are we going to get out of here?"

Erelin wrote *daylight*.

"Will it chase us?"

(Yes.)

Torrin could read nothing in that impassive face. He felt his anger rise. He could now put his finger on one reason why he felt so at home with Braedil and Kryna. They, like himself, knew fear. Theirs was not an unfeeling existence like these two monstrous men. His emotions were stirred by thinking about his dead relatives.

"Are you afraid of it?" he asked, aware that his question was a challenge. He was unprepared for the answer.

(Yes.)

"More than the Vekh?"

Could that possibly have been the slightest sign of a smirk on Erelin's face? No, Torrin had imagined it. He felt he had pushed the boundaries enough, so he changed the subject.

"Are we headed for Dharbur?"

(Yes.)

"Why?"

Erelin hesitated to answer that one. He added a few more branches to the fire. Torrin began to feel anxious. At the rate they were burning wood, the fuel they had gathered would not last through the night.

Erelin wrote *money*. It was one of the few words in Melandarim that had no good tense. Torrin was undecided as to whether the word indicated unbridled greed or the prudent acquisition of necessary resources.

"Will I die there?" There was no logical progression to the question. Upon learning from Vigheran that they were heading for Dharbur, he began to think that he was heading to his death. Something was there, waiting for him, intent on ending his existence.

Erelin wrote on the ground. It was a simple Melandarim phrase, but it was a well-known part of Nedrin's Verse. *I will protect you*, it said.

It wasn't a denial. But Torrin's loneliness eased, just a little bit. Whoever wanted to kill him, had to get through one other person first.

Erelin took Torrin's bedroll from the stack of blankets that were heaped on Vigheran and gave it to him. Torrin heard his stomach growl, but he wasn't about to protest.

"Do you need me to stand guard?" Torrin asked.

(No.)

The pheasant wouldn't be ready for some time. Maybe Erelin

would wake him up when it was time to eat. He chewed on a trail biscuit before turning in. His frazzled nerves kept him from sleeping well.

Vigheran was too weak to travel the next day. Erelin had expected it. He had allowed the pheasants to stew all night. They hadn't had a tasty meal like that since Sorwail. Torrin noticed that part of their makeshift shelter had been torn down to feed their fire during the night. The snow was heaped up, covering almost half the opening. Yet it felt warm and snug in their shelter.

Throughout the day, Vigheran recovered quickly. By midday he sat up and had some of the leftover pheasant broth. Erelin and Torrin spent the day gathering more firewood, rebuilding shelter, and melting snow to fill their canteens. Erelin left for an hour and came back with some fish for supper. That evening was uneventful. They left the cave early the next morning.

Torrin did not see or hear the Gryphon again for many days of traveling. Yet the sense of foreboding did not leave him. Erelin continued to scout in front and behind. They built defensible camps, always stockpiling plenty of firewood for the night.

Torrin counted sixteen days since Sorwail before they came to a settlement. Most of their travel was through alpine forest that rose high above the coastal rain forests below. They went through several days of temperatures just below freezing, followed by several days of rain and sleet as they descended in elevation. Thankfully, they had not encountered any truly frigid weather, which wasn't uncommon at that time of the winter. For the past week, the ocean had been on their left with mountains to the right. Torrin realized that the water was the Bay of Schiar, a deep inlet from the Sea of Winds.

The settlement was built at the furthest western extent of the inlet. Torrin could see from a distance that the buildings were of unfamiliar construction. The village was not large, possibly two or three hundred persons at most. It reminded him, as he wrinkled his nose, of a Pej Zindori village. The Pej living in Arghand and Belorin typically built their simple homes out of mud and animal dung. They did not use stone, and rarely used wood. They kept to a simple, agrarian life, having no ambitions to build large cities or civic buildings.

Vigheran had picked up his spirits over the past few days. His body markings had slowly reappeared, and now were as obvious as before he had applied the paste. Torrin thought that his two companions must have patched up their dispute from Sorwail.

"We near Vanreikh," he said. "It is Roj Zindori territory. Only fit for Roj or greedy merchants." He produced his rare toothy grin. "I am both. You are neither. I will go alone, get supplies, come back here."

He left them on a rocky hillside, upon which a few scraggly evergreen trees struggled to survive. The skies were dark, but other than some light drizzle they had not been subject to heavy rain yet today.

Torrin now questioned what he saw and heard that night in the cave. It was probably a mountain lion after all, he thought. Perhaps the moon had reflected off its eyes. Erelin was just trying to scare him with tales of a Gryphon.

While Vigheran was gone, Torrin's attempts to engage Erelin in conversation were not as successful as before. Learning nothing and getting bored, he drew his knife in his left hand and began to practice. Footwork, lunge, step back, parry, sidestep, jab. His balance was disrupted by the fact that he was using his left hand. The footwork that had been drummed into him during his training was predicated on using his right.

He had been trained mostly with spear and small shield. Those were the primary weapons on horseback. He had some experience with blades and blunt weapons, very little with knives. He was about to do another practice thrust when he noticed Erelin had approached him and was standing behind him.

A little startled, he turned around. Erelin was holding out his hand. Torrin gave him the knife, hilt first. The mute Taurilian produced his own long-knife from his boot – his left boot – and handed it to Torrin, hilt-first.

The hilt was shaped for a left hand, and the balance was different. He still felt somewhat off-balance, especially when lunging and thrusting. Erelin mimed a different thrust technique, and Torrin did his best to copy.

After his patience ran out, Torrin gave up. "Tawkin was lucky," he said, referring to the hero of old. "When they cut off his right hand, they had no idea he was left-handed. No such luck for me. I guess I won't be doing anything more than skinning a carcass."

Torrin returned to their small camp. Erelin scaled the ridge close by and stared off to the east, back the way they had come. Opening his canteen, Torrin took a long drink. He put the canteen back into the crook of his arm and fixed the stopper back in. It slipped from his arm and began to bounce down the hill.

Just what I need, Torrin thought, and sprang after it. It continued to bounce and roll down the rocky slope. Further and further he climbed down the slope, wishing it would stop. At the base of the embankment it finally wedged in between two rocks. He bent down to pick it up.

Something large hit him from behind and sent him sprawling onto the rocky ground. He hit his chin and elbow. Dazed, he reached for a handhold to hoist himself up. A heavy weight pressed on his back, and he could hear raspy breathing.

His eardrums were nearly shattered by a bloodcurdling scream originating from a few inches behind his head. All other noises stopped. The scream slowly receded as a severe ringing noise took its place.

Visions were playing about his head. He thought at first that he saw one of the cellars built into the ground just outside Dar-Amund. But then he realized it was something else, a simple home underneath prairie sod, with windows and a door opening into a ravine. The door was open. Inside was a single room, in which many people were sleeping. Only one stuck out, because of the hair.

A woman was lying on a sheepskin cot, covered by fur blankets. Her face was in view. The skin was not like his own. It was a healthy brown. Yet the woman had some Taurilian features. She was quite young, about Torrin's age. Most unusual was the hair. It was cropped short for a woman. It had no colour – it was as white as Sorwail alabaster.

As Torrin watched, a beast began to lope through the door. It resembled a canine, though thin and emaciated. Vicious spikes protruded from the back of its head and ran down the spine of its back. The creature's coat was black as charcoal. The eyes, barely visible from Torrin's perspective, shone a cold blue. It was softly making its way towards the white-haired woman. Nobody stirred.

He was jolted back to reality by the sudden shift of the weight from his back. He instinctively rolled to his right, grabbing for his sheathed knife with his good hand. Then he saw it. A large rock was between Torrin and the Gryphon, but he saw enough. It was on its back. Its eyes flared with blue intensity as its head snapped around. It was speared through its rib cage with Erelin's sword.

Torrin tried to stand up. He could hear nothing at all but the ringing in his ears. He swooned, shut his eyes, and toppled right back to his knees. A hand grabbed his coat and roughly dragged him back to his feet. The pain in his head was immense.

Finally, he could open his eyes again. He scanned around for the Gryphon but saw nothing. Erelin was picking up his sword from the place where he had seen it struggling. The ringing in his ears was slowly subsiding but still he could hear nothing else.

He tried to ask Erelin where the Gryphon had gone, but his voice made only a dull vibration. Erelin still looked at him, pointing into the trees to his right, and Torrin realized he had indeed spoken.

Erelin saw him struggling. He sheathed his sword, took Torrin by the arm, and led the way back to the camp. With relief, Torrin found that he could start to hear their footfalls over the ringing. It took over an hour of sitting by their campfire before he felt back to normal.

Erelin made him take off his coat to check him over for injuries. There were none other than several bruises from landing on the rocks. Erelin then made a gesture that he was not to leave the camp. When he returned with an armload of firewood, Torrin tried his voice again. This time, he made sounds as normal, though it hurt his ears to talk.

"Did you kill it?"

(No.)

Torrin was incredulous and crestfallen at the same time. How could it survive being run through with Erelin's sword?

"Why didn't it hurt me?"

Erelin gazed at him intently for a moment, then shrugged. He then bent down to the ground, cleared the grass off a patch of ground, and wrote three words in Melandarim in the dirt. *Talk Roj no.* He began to heat some water for their dinner.

Torrin realized that Vigheran wasn't at all aware of the first encounter with the Gryphon. He nodded but remained perplexed. "Why shouldn't Vigheran know? Shouldn't he be warned?"

No answer.

*One of these days I would like to talk to someone who is willing and able to talk back, knows River-Tongue, and isn't some sort of sadistic kille*r, Torrin thought.

The sun was beginning to set. Vigheran had not returned. The pot bubbled as Erelin fed more wood into the fire.

"I saw a strange vision while the thing was on top of me," Torrin said. Erelin raised a hairless brow but did not look in his direction. "The Gryphon was hunting something, someone. I saw a house, it may have been Zindori or Belorin, but it was definitely in a dry climate. People were sleeping inside. The Gryphon was headed for a woman."

Erelin stirred the pot. His eyes were closed.

"She had really strange hair, it was white."

The spoon clattered from Erelin's hand. Both cat-like eyes stared at him, pupils so large that the eyes themselves appeared black. Quickly he bent over the patch of soil and wrote on the ground. *Anything more?*

"No, that's all I saw. You got it off my back before I could see anything else."

Erelin stood, put both hands on his head, and turned around. His elbows were sticking out at right angles. He seemed to be in anguish. It was the strongest display of emotion Torrin had seen from him yet, even though his face was turned.

Torrin saved dinner by taking over the spoon. When he looked up, Erelin was sitting with his head in his hands. It was several minutes before he came back.

"I take it you know that woman," Torrin ventured.

(Yes.)

"Then the vision was for you? Is that why it didn't kill me?"

(Yes.)

Erelin bent down and re-wrote the words, *talk Roj no.*

CHAPTER 16:
FORMING UP

Aknock on the door just after sunrise was answered by Careesh. She came upstairs to where Dyrk was sitting at his desk, finishing breakfast.

"The man at the door, his name is Jeswold," she said. "He wants to talk to you, says it is important."

Dyrk came downstairs to find his headman, Thur Jeswold, with the ward's scribe, at the door.

"Good morning Thur Jeswold, scribe," Dyrk nodded in greeting.

"Dyrk son of Maryk house Teren," Jeswold said, for the benefit of the scribe. Jeswold was quite young for a headman. He was maybe fifteen years Dyrk's senior. Most Eraturs spend at least twenty years in the Royal Army first. Yet Jeswold's hairline was already receding, and he had never taken to the facial hair that most Eraturs grew liberally. He looked more the part of a priest than an Eratur.

"You are of the ninth regiment, Saringon cavalry reserve, correct?" the Eratur said, a friendly look on his face despite the formality of the conversation.

Dyrk nodded. So did the scribe.

"You have been transferred to the eighth. You are required to report next week Kemantar[1] for form-up."

Dyrk felt complex emotions at the sudden news. He recalled how he felt upon being expelled from the College, and subsequently assigned to the tarn-riding corps. Was this more of the same? Was someone pulling the strings to get him into the line of danger?

But then he remembered that the first reserve units called up

---

[1] Sunday

were also the first to come home. Border skirmishes often began with a lot of movement and counter-movement. Only when one belligerent pinned another down would there be a pitched battle with a lot of casualties. That was usually left up to subsequent call-ups.

But would it be just another border skirmish? From what he understood of the news, troops were being sent to Lyssia to reinforce Karolia's ally against the Vekh rampaging the now-extinct realm of Azenvar.

First called up, first to go home, he reminded himself.

"Thank you, headman. I will report as assigned."

"Are you equipped? Your mount?"

"I can assure you that I have one of the best mounts in Karolia."

Jeswold smiled. "You cavalry boys are cock-sure. We'll see how confident you are when the slings are spinning and the arrows are flying."

It wasn't a threat, it sounded more like advice. Dyrk didn't take it personally.

Jeswold continued. "I figure I may be pressed to lead one of the regiments at some point. They usually call up combat-capable Headmen during a complete mobilization. I understand they're short on junior officers. That means you'll probably get some fresh-face from the College."

Dyrk did not like the sound of that.

Close to the end of the workday, Dyrk sent Aijen home without him and saddled Tanakh. It would be a late night, but he had to go to Harwaith as soon as possible. Time would be short.

He pushed Tanakh hard on the trip. He arrived at their destination with some sweat on his mount. Instead of going to Vecton's house, he first stopped at the inn and paid the stableboy a brass to give Tanakh a rub-down and some grain.

At the door to the hovel, he sucked in a deep breath. He had dreaded to take this step, but it was time. There was not going to be any opportunity to keep fighting for her while he was out on campaign. Smells came from inside. They were probably sitting down to dinner. They were having fish stew.

He knocked. His heart raced. The door was opened. His heart leaped for an instant when he saw it was a girl, but in the next moment realized it was not Neriah. It was her sixteen-year-old sister Alnarah.

"Daddy says to wait a moment, he'll be out."

She was about to turn away, but then looked at Dyrk and said, "You know, you're really persistent. I would have taken you back by now."

Dyrk waited on the bench outside. Vecton came to him after a few minutes and sat down beside him.

"It's late," was all he said. It wasn't a reproach, merely an observation.

"I came as soon as I could," Dyrk said. "My reserve regiment has been called in. It's likely I'll be headed to Lyssia in a few weeks."

"I see."

"Vecton, I think it's best if you withdraw your permission. I don't want Neriah bound by anything while I'm gone. That's not fair to her."

Vecton gave a long sigh and sat down on the bench. He stared off into the evening sky for some time, leaving Dyrk in awkward silence.

"That's a decision I want the two of you to make together," he finally spoke.

"What do you mean?"

"I've told her that, in order for the two of you to break things off, you need to arrive at that decision together. No unilateral decisions."

"What?"

Vecton looked at Dyrk, a sadness creasing his face. "I don't want her to repeat your mistake. Whatever life brings, you need to face it head-on. Own your decisions." He looked back at the sky. "She's getting ready."

"Ready for what?"

"You'll walk with her down to the river. Talk things out. See where you stand."

"Don't one of you need to come with us?"

Vecton shrugged. "She'll be with a man as dedicated to preserving her honour as I am. If I didn't trust you with my daughter, I wouldn't be sending her with you."

Dyrk's mind raced. What would he say to a woman compelled to be with him? He hadn't expected that. Could Vecton find a crueler way to break things off between them?

The door opened a crack. Neriah poked her head out, covered in a headscarf. "Daddy?"

"Yes, dear."

"Is he here?"

"Yes."

"All right. I'm ready, Dyrk. Let's go."

Dyrk read absolutely nothing in her tone of voice. It was flat, emotionless. He felt he could not get enough air, and yet was self-conscious about making too much noise breathing.

The two of them began to walk towards the river.

"Where's your horse?" she asked.

Small talk, Dyrk thought. *Better than nothing.* "I left him at the inn for grooming," he replied. "He was pretty tired. I pushed him hard to get here by dark."

His heart fluttered at being so close to her. He had to stop it. This wasn't right. This couldn't go on. This was torture. It had to end as soon as possible.

"Daddy said we need to come to an understanding," she ventured. He could hear her voice trembling. Their feet crunched in the well-trodden snow at the riverbank. The moon was out, which was their only light. It was at half wane.

"How are we going to do that?" Dyrk put his thoughts to words.

"Why don't we go one at a time and tell each other how we feel right now?"

That seemed good to Dyrk. "All right. Who is first?"

"You. You're supposed to be the leader."

He hated hearing that. He was thrown out, banished from any place of leadership. He was not qualified to be the head of anything.

He drew a deep breath and tried to sort out his thoughts. He wished they could sit down, look in her face. But Vecton was cunning. He wanted the two of them to speak to their own feelings independent of each other, not the ones they felt only when staring into each other's eyes.

"Very well. But we will do it one at a time, taking turns. I will tell you one thing I'm feeling, and then you will." Dyrk felt like a child playing a game.

"Agreed," she said, sounding mechanical.

"I feel like I've failed you. First in not living up to the promise of my potential achievements, something I now know was misplaced. But after, I let fear rule me. I failed you by shutting you out."

She let that digest. Then she spoke. "I feel like my heart is shattered into a thousand pieces. The man who said he loved me abandoned me when he needed me most. He only wants me in his life when times are good."

The moon illumined her face as they walked, but she did not turn her head to him. "What would happen at the time I needed you the most? Would you abandon me then?"

Dyrk was about to answer when she stopped him. "I'm sorry," she said. "We're supposed to be telling each other how we feel, not asking questions. I broke the rules."

It felt so good to him to be with her, interacting like that, even if she wasn't being warm. But wasn't this just prolonging the agony? He took his time, choosing his words carefully. The safest path was something in between; something that would protect himself from the inevitable crushing disappointment, but still leave the door a crack, just a sliver, open. That left a chance, however slim, that she would burst it open. Wasn't it right to leave the choice up to her?

"I feel-" he said, thinking again of the Rector's words when he was tossed out of the college. He stumbled over his words. "You deserve-"

He squeezed his eyes shut. He was an Eratur running away from a battle, casting his weapons aside as he threw off his armour and begged his enemies for mercy. And he hated himself for it.

Or maybe, just maybe, he could stand in front of the door and try his best to kick it down. He would be unprotected. He might get cut down. But no warrior worth his salt entered battle without understanding the potential consequences and facing them with courage.

He noticed that he had stopped walking. Neriah looked at him, that forbidden glance that they were supposed to try to avoid. Her nose was wrinkled, her eyes bore great sadness. Her mouth was downturned in an expression that combined a wince with a frown.

"Kemantar knows I'm not telling the truth," Dyrk said. "Let me try again." They began to walk again, eyes forward.

"Your father is right. I have never understood that someone would do something for me. Either it had to be because I could do something in return, or it was some act of charity. When I was released from the college, I met a former fellow student who helped me. He didn't do it for something in return. He also didn't do it for charity. I realize that now.

"When I saw you in Doleth Sarin a few weeks ago, the walls around me finally crumbled. I could see for myself what injuries those walls caused to the ones I love. I- I feel so many things for you, Neriah. Now I can't bear to let you go."

When he finished, Neriah stopped walking. Dyrk followed suit. She pulled the end of her braid in front of her and untied the ribbon that held it together. She took several steps down the bank to the riverside. There was a small lip of ice and snow at the edges, but otherwise the frigid water was flowing freely. Dyrk took a step to follow her, but she put up her hand to stop him.

She held the ribbon between her two hands. Dyrk saw it was dyed red. The ribbon from the Contest. She crumpled it up and tossed it into the river. It was quickly lost from sight in the black waters.

Without turning, she spoke in a clear voice above the sounds of water flowing. "So ends a bond founded on expectations and undeserved favor, brought to its end by self-pity."

She turned back to Dyrk. One tear-streaked face beheld the other. "Can we build a new one, in which we pledge to commit our whole, imperfect selves to the other, come what may?"

Dyrk's heart had just fallen to his knees and then risen to the stars all in one moment. He reached out his hand, and she put her own in his so he could help her up. He didn't let go of her hand.

"Absolutely," was the only word that he could manage.

Neriah returned to her customary reserved stance, lowering her eyes and lifting her other hand to smooth the hair at her ear. Her other hand stayed within Dyrk's. She was standing very close to him, but to one side. "I hate to say it, but those weren't my words. They were my father's. I couldn't come up with anything so profound."

"Doesn't mean that they didn't come from your heart," Dyrk assured her. He closed the last distance between them, putting one hand on her shoulder. It felt so good just to touch her again.

She nodded. "He said them to me as a question. I said them as..." her voice trailed off.

"A declaration," he finished.

As they came back to the hovel, no longer touching, they saw that Vecton was still sitting on the bench under the awning. Ryesse had joined him. As the young couple approached, Vecton got to his feet. Neriah slid onto the bench beside her mother, into a close embrace.

"What is your decision?" Vecton asked, looking at Dyrk. The attention of the women was on him too. He had never seen the older couple so anxious.

"I-, I mean we, do not wish for you to withdraw your permission," Dyrk announced, and then couldn't stop a witless smile from blossoming on his face.

Vecton returned his smile with a grin of his own. "I figured the ladies would need a cry regardless of the decision," he said. "Let's find some spiced sausage and cheese."

The ground outside the training yard was churned up by countless footsteps and hoofprints. Dyrk joined with a throng of nervous-looking young men as they assembled outside the gates. They were open only a crack. A young Eratur was calling down a list of names, and those called stepped forward and through the gate, leaving the others behind to mill about.

This was the form-up. There would be no training or riding today. It would simply be a meeting of the regiment and the assignment of tasks. Full training would be in a week.

Foot regiments were in groups of sixty. The typical heavy foot soldiers worked in teams of three within their phalanx. They were equipped with convex pavises, pikes, heavy arbalests, and stabbing shortswords for close combat, though not every soldier carried every item. Seeing a heavy phalanx in action was an amazing sight – pavises shielding the unit in front and above, pikes defensively fixed, crossbows being loaded and fired in sequence between gaps in the shields.

Light swordsmen were also in groups of sixty per regiment. Their formations were more spaced out, since they needed more room to swing their weapons and move on the battlefield. The spaces also provided room for the front-line men could retreat behind the second they when exhausted or wounded. Like the heavy infantry, they were arranged in fighting teams of three.

Cavalry were organized in regiments of twenty-four. The parades were deceiving: gargantuan parade horses bearing men ensconced in thick plates of armour so stifling that they could barely move. With the exception of a single unit of heavy cavalry that had poor range and therefore were rarely brought into battle, Karolian cavalry were quite different on the battlefield. Light cavalry were equipped with bows and light spears, tasked with harassing the enemy. Medium cavalry were better armed and armoured, but still prized movement and range over weight and protection.

Dyrk had been equipped as medium cavalry. Tanakh was, in comparison to many war-mounts, tireless and agile, but his build did not allow him to reach the pursuit speeds of the light cavalry. Dyrk was also a poor archer, especially from horseback.

Dyrk found out quickly that regiments were being re-formed from professional soldiers, reserve soldiers, and service soldiers. Service soldiers, often called recruits, were those who were fulfilling the three years of King's service in order to get their citizenship. They were young, green, and inexperienced. Professional soldiers agreed to stay in the army after their service. Reserves, like Dyrk, had completed their service in the army and enlisted to be called up by province or kingdom to respond to local emergencies or hostilities with foreign powers.

The professional soldiers and service soldiers were already in the training yard. Reserves were being called to fill out each regiment.

The gate opened a crack, and another Eratur emerged with a list. He read off nine names. Dyrk was not called. Nine reservists accompanied the Eratur through the door while the rest waited apprehensively. Dyrk struck up a conversation with one of the other reservists, finding he was from the "upper province" near Tanvilon, Dyrk's hometown.

All eyes went to the gate as the next Eratur stepped through. Dyrk drew a sharp intake of breath. It was Bayern. The dark-haired son of Thur Daynen wore the pauldrons and cloak of a full Eratur. This was impossible! Bayern hadn't completed four years at the college yet!

"Dyrk son of Maryk House Teren," was the first name that Bayern called. He held his hand up to shade his eyes from the winter sun, thick arms bulging in muscle beneath his short-sleeved tunic and blue-and-silver cloak.

Dyrk felt like he had just been trampled by a horse. Did the Servants have any mercy? He had made new beginnings. He was starting to take control of his own life, his own destiny, slowly healing from the wounds of the past. Now here was a transparent reminder, a bright flare of the bonfire of shame he was trying mightily to extinguish. Why Bayern? Anyone but him!

Dutifully, Dyrk stepped forward and answered the summons. Bayern tipped his head and opened the gate to admit him. More names were being called, but Dyrk didn't hear them. A small group of reservists gathered around him. He was too lost in his own thoughts that he didn't hear at first that the others were talking about him, hands covering their mouths.

"Unfit? Really?"

"Yes. Shown the door with assignment papers in hand."

Dyrk turned his head. The two reservists dropped their hands, shut their mouths, and glared back at him. One was older, about forty, a dirty-blond shock of hair atop his ruddy face. A lump on the bridge of his nose showed that he was no stranger to injury. The other was a spring chicken like Dyrk. He had a cold look to his blue eyes.

Once the group numbered ten reservists, Bayern escorted the group to a corner of the training yard. Archery targets were hung there, unused. A group of men were already standing, congregating in two knots, one older and one younger.

Dyrk recognized a face in the younger group. "Lohann!" he shouted, rushing forward. The lad had grown a beard to hide the mottled skin on his chin, against regulations. Bayern would no doubt require him to shave it off. Lohann smiled when he saw his acquaintance. The two struck hands and touched shoulders.

"Dyrk, where have you been? I asked about you once I got to Trebier, but nobody could tell me where you had gone."

"Tarn-riding," Dyrk said with a grimace. "I survived, though, and now I'm back here. Did you get my letters?"

Lohann sighed. "I had a cushy posting in a fortress in Loth Bevren. Mounted patrols. We were out of the way, so mail didn't always get through. Nothing happening in the outlands there, so I just sat tight, trained, and bided my time. Then *this* had to happen," he waved his arm around the training yard. "Cursed Vekh couldn't stay in Anduk, had to ruin my service with a call-up."

"Hey, you know this guy?" The older reservist with a bump on his nose cut in, not being friendly. He spoke to Lohann. "You flunked out of the College too, then?"

Lohann's eyes narrowed. "No, I'm in service. I haven't flunked out of anything." Dyrk noticed that Lohann took a small, barely noticeable, step back from him.

"Not wise to hang out with the unfit," the reservist scorned, mangling the Melandarim word that was on Dyrk's discharge record. "Might rub off on you."

"What is your problem?" Dyrk challenged. "You barely know a thing about me!"

The man gave a low, unfriendly grunt. "We're going into battle, young scruff. We need to know if our fellow soldiers have our backs, or if they'll turn tail and bail out on their comrades."

Aggression dictated that Dyrk settle the matter with fists. But not in the training yard. That would get both of them labeled dishonourable. "I don't need a slip of paper to prove my worth," he said defiantly. "I survived ten months on a tarn. I think I'm above accusations of cowardice."

Broken-nose turned to another soldier, a professional one. "What do you think, Deman? He says thin air is a cure for craven spirits!" Laughter.

"Attention!" Bayern bellowed. The men fell into two lines in random order. Lohann did not make any effort to get beside Dyrk.

Bayern strode in front of them, the picture of a veteran Eratur despite his young age. His thick arms were behind his back, pinning his cloak to reveal his fine tunic the colour of chain-mail. His pauldrons made his shoulders look even larger than they already were. A thick belt secured by a silver clasp surrounded his generous waist. He wore an armoured waist-piece with plate greaves. He looked like a heavy cavalryman taking a break, except his armour was brightly burnished and didn't have a scratch on it.

"Men, we are now the thirty-ninth cavalry regiment of the Karolian East Army," his voice carried. "Look around. You are going to be with these men for the next three-and-a-half months."

Dyrk glanced to his left. Broken-nose glared back at him menacingly.

"Training starts on Taephin's Day this week. This morning is equipment inspection. I and my regiment master will inspect your mounts this afternoon. This gives you enough time to put down your hay-burner and get a real horse." A few chuckles came from the men standing at attention.

"Our posting remains secret," he continued, sounding very important. "All I can say is that we will need to cover a great distance on horseback. No parade-horses and no sprinters. No portage." That meant that they would not be transported by ship, at least. Dyrk had worried about how Tanakh would fare on a boat.

"As with any regiment, we will have travel duties and responsibilities." He raised a list. "I have reviewed your records and made the appropriate assignments. For Regiment Master, Dyrk House Teren. For Quartermaster, Ambold House En-Reglan."

There was a twitter amongst the men. Dyrk was taken aback by his assignment. Regiment Master? That meant he was Bayern's right-hand man, responsible for discipline within the ranks.

"Thur Bayern," one soldier interrupted. "With permission to speak…"

Bayern looked up from his list and glared at the man. "Granted, Kethrol" he said reluctantly.

"Shouldn't Regiment Master go to an eligible soldier, not someone who…" he didn't get to finish his sentence.

"Regiment Master is not an officer. It could go to my scullery maid." Bayern took two steps towards the soldier who protested. "I'll have you know that your Regiment Master is the best horseman I have ever laid eyes on," he shouted, faces separated by three inches. "You would do well to learn from him, Kethrol House En-Kulvor."

Dyrk was taken aback by the unexpected aid. Where did that come from? Bayern continued down the list, assigning a responsibility to each man. Duties for overseeing cooking, stores, caring for the mounts, maps, weapons, each were assigned to one soldier after another.

Bayern moved into equipment inspection. The man with the broken nose, who Dyrk now knew was Naethin House Kromar, was assigned to armour-master. Since he was responsible for equipment, he assisted Bayern in assessing the gear of each soldier. Some were sent to the training yard's smithy to wait in line for a sharpening, or a small modification. The only weapon the cavalry recruits were not carrying with them was their mounted spear. It was impractical to store them in each reservist's home, and so the spears were kept and maintained at the training yard.

Recruits displayed their weapons, suited up in their armour, and paraded before the inspectors. When it was Dyrk's turn, he could not resist a jab at Naethin. "Glad to meet someone from the Houses of Planting," he said softly, referring to the group of houses that included House Kromar. "Can you tell apart a pike from a hoe?"

Naethin bent down to check Dyrk's hauberk but then suddenly came up, fist swinging. Dyrk half-expected it and managed to dodge. Other soldiers jumped in immediately, separating the two.

Bayern turned from what he was doing. "What is going on here?"

he demanded.

Dyrk extracted himself from the arms grasping him. "Nothing, Thur Bayern. I stumbled while putting on my armour."

He hated using the name and the title in the same sentence. As everyone returned to their work, he kept his distance from Naethin and tried to engage in talk about the equipment. That insult was foolish of him, he thought. "I deserved a knock on the nose for that," he offered.

Naethin did not answer. He continued through Dyrk's equipment like nothing had happened. "All good," he finally said. "Your eating kit is cracked. You may want to fetch a new set." He moved on to the next recruit.

Bayern finished his extensive discussion with Ambold about the quartermaster's duties before coming to Dyrk. He motioned for the two of them to step away from the group.

"Glad to see you are doing well," Bayern said without much gladness.

"Congratulations on early graduation, Bayern," Dyrk politely offered. "But I'm honestly a bit surprised you wanted me in your regiment at all."

Bayern seemed irked by Dyrk's assertion. "If you're referring to my humiliation at your hands during the Contest, I'm disappointed that you don't think I'm man enough to get past that," he said sternly. "I understand we weren't best of friends at the College, but I'm not looking for friends. I need good soldiers, which is why I requested your transfer from the ninth reserve."

"*You* requested my transfer?" Dyrk arched his eyebrows. That feeling like he was being set up for danger came to the fore again.

"Yes I did. With your upbringing on a horse farm, and your experience at the College, you are more fit than the rest of these." Dyrk was taken aback by the compliment. There were some professional soldiers there who had many years of cavalry experience.

"I have one thing I wanted to clear up, though," Bayern continued.

I have many things I want to clear up, Dyrk thought.

"At college, just before jousting practice, you told me that I had better check my cinch strap twice. Was that in reference to your, um, accident during the combat at the Contest?"

"Would you know anything about that?"

"Yes I would," Bayern responded. "My only fault is that I didn't warn you. The only one that touched your horse while you were with those girls was Thur Madwin. And he spent a lot of time checking your cinch."

I don't believe you, Dyrk thought, but nodded anyway. He settled on the one thing that he wanted to know. "Can I ask you what you were doing in the Rector's office just before I was expelled?"

"Ah, that," Bayern's face fell. "A dark day. It seems they were looking for any excuse to get rid of you, Dyrk. I couldn't understand why. They called me in because they figured we were from the same province so we must know each other well.

"They grilled me for half an hour, trying to find something to pin on you. I didn't give them anything. 'How was his singing,' they asked. 'Fine', I said. 'Did he ever call into question your honour,' they said. 'No,' I said, and on and on. After some time, the Rector appeared to think I was in league with you and so they dismissed me."

Dyrk didn't say anything, but he must have looked unconvinced.

Bayern fixed his cloak. "I'd love to keep chatting about the old days, but we have work to do. I'm going to assume that you need no pointers on how to do your job given your leadership training at the College."

"I have to confess that I'll be a bit rusty. Leadership wasn't required for expendable tarn-riders."

"I'm sure it will come back quickly." Bayern turned and strode towards his next quarry.

Bayern could very well be lying through his teeth, Dyrk thought. There was nothing to prove his story either way. But if he wasn't lying, Dyrk would be unjust to hold these things against his commanding officer.

But maybe there was a way to confirm at least one of Bayern's statements.

After equipment check, the recruits scattered for a midday meal and to fetch their mounts. Dyrk hurried towards Farnich's. No doubt a few of the others were keeping their mounts there too, but he didn't try to walk with anyone.

Upon finding the old stable-owner, he asked, "Is it still possible for me to take on that trip to Tanvilon?"

Farnich smiled. "Of course," he said. "See me on Harophin's morning[1] and I'll give you the payment. The man charges a high price for a warhorse, be sure to tell him it's not right to profiteer in wartime, will you?"

The distance to Tanvilon was a little more than a league. He had reasons besides talking with Madwin and picking up the war-horse. Farnich had urged him to give Maryk another chance. Madwin had pretty much said the same. Both Vecton and Ryesse had also at several points mourned the fact that Dyrk was estranged from his parents. So, he would try, one last time, to restore something between them. After all, if Maryk had looked for him once, he could at least return the favour.

He had not been home for three and a half years. He slept in the ward tavern in Rocavion, about a half-league from Tanvilon, and continued the next morning. The lands became more and more familiar as he turned off the highway and made his way into the hills to the north. He passed Wolben's house and thought he could see in the distance his childhood friend Breven handling some milk cows. Dyrk did not stop.

Being winter, he had on a full coat with a hood. He drew the hood about him. He didn't want to be recognized in his hometown. It was difficult enough just to go home.

He passed through the village and took the path going east. Over a hill and a creek, the estate of his youth opened up before him. There was the house, a beautiful stone two-story dwelling, which was a bit out of place in Tanvilon. The paddocks for training, the hay fields over the hilltop, the gardens, the servants' huts, the barns,

---

[1] Tuesday morning

the stables, all was pretty much as he had remembered it. A soft layer of snow covered everything.

He entered the stable and availed himself of an empty stall to take care of Tanakh. Just as he was finishing, Hagris, the young Derrekh bondservant, limped his way in. His job was to keep the stables clean, so it was not unusual to see him there.

"Dyrk!" he said, rather surprised to see him. "It has been a long time. Does the master expect you?"

"Sort of," Dyrk said. "I'm here to pick up the warhorse for Farnich. Do you know where he is?"

"He is off riding," Hagris replied. "I had no idea you were working for Farnich. In fact, I haven't heard bip about you for years."

"I've been well," Dyrk lied. "I'm not sure that father wants to see me, but we should do business. Could you fetch him?"

"Sure," Hagris agreed. "I have a pony saddled just outside. I'll ride and find him. You can wait on the patio of the house, if you like. I'll meet you there."

Dyrk made his way to the house. There was a covered veranda on the south side, facing the hay barn. It had a plank floor, two rocking chairs, several other seats, and an end table. As he paced there for a minute, he remembered how his mother would often sit out in the morning sun, rocking with a blanket over her knees, doing needlework or some other fine craft. She loved the early sun, especially when there was no wind to dry and chap her skin.

He felt an intense longing for his mother. Might she be home? He opened the side door and called inside.

Nothing.

He peered into the sitting room. He saw plush chairs, bookshelves full of books. There was the fireplace where Maryk had sat the last time they spoke. There were only dying embers in the ash.

He took off his boots and entered. He called once more, but no answer came. Was nobody home? Where was mother? Where were his sisters?

A sudden memory jolted his thoughts. Whenever Dyrk and

Gavon found themselves alone at home, they would sneak up into the attic and find some old artifact to play with. Up there was a chest, and in that chest was, supposedly, Maryk's armour and weapons from his few days as an Eratur. If, as Madwin had said, Dyrk had been found in the mine with a sword, wouldn't Maryk store it somewhere up there?

He hurriedly took off his boots and walked up the stairs. He called out again, just in case someone was in the bedrooms. There was no answer. He opened the trap door into the attic and climbed inside. The attic was rather cluttered with various dusty items, but nothing resembled a sword. He recalled that he had been up there several times after the incident in the mine, and he had never found a sword.

Maybe Maryk had put it in his armour chest?

He listened carefully a moment to determine if anyone had come into the house since he had come up there. He heard nothing. Carefully he tried to lift the lid of the trunk, but it was latched. A small lever was beside the latch with a keyhole. He kept it locked, of course. Absently, he flicked the lever. The latch clicked open. He lifted the lid of the chest.

There was no armour inside. No cloak. No pauldrons that denoted his status. All there was inside that chest was a single, solitary sword, sheathed. Dyrk gasped. It was the sword in his dream.

It was a simple blade, a double-edged broadsword that was of compact dimensions compared to some carried today. It was unadorned by any precious metal or jewels. What made Dyrk recognize it was the design of the hilt. Most modern Karolian blades featured a two-pronged hilt that curved slightly towards the point; the one before him had straight prongs, at a slight angle that had a small notch in each side for catching an enemy blade. This was more like the historical Taurilian swords of old, he thought.

The handle was wrapped in double-red. If Maryk didn't have armour, a cloak, or his pauldrons, that must mean one of two things, he thought. Either he was never an Eratur, or he was discharged dishonourably. Either way, he wouldn't be eligible to carry a sword.

So, that blade was Dyrk's. From the caves. He reached towards the sword slowly. Would it erupt in flames? Would that strange glowing man appear? Would he see some sort of vision?

Nothing happened when he touched the blade, or when he drew it. The naked steel appeared ordinary. All he heard was his own heartbeat, elevated. He re-sheathed the sword and took it with him, silently closing the chest and re-latching it. He stole downstairs. Nobody was there. He got all the way back to the stables without seeing a soul. He hid the sword under Tanakh's saddlebags and returned to the patio.

He had not been there long when he heard voices. The sound of the chattering and arguing of his sisters was unmistakable. Elora, Hanni, and Plessa came into view. They were coming from the kitchens, carrying some pastry that had just been baked. While Hagris's mother Karam did most of the cooking for the household, Loriah would often spend time there making some delicious dessert or snack. Dyrk could smell cinnamon.

Plessa, the youngest, noticed Dyrk on the veranda. She shouted his name and ran to him. She put the cinnamon swirls aside and threw her arms around him. Elora and Hanni followed, in one sweeping embrace of sisters.

"Girls!" A harsh call made them stiffen. Loriah stood there, near the front door. Her long hair had been straightened today, then bound up along a circular wire frame around her head. She often did that on days she wanted to do baking, to keep it out of the way. A stern look was on her face. "Come along," she snapped. "He's here for your father, and no one else."

The girls retrieved their snacks and followed their mother through the front door. His mother hadn't even looked at him, or spoken his name. He suddenly felt very cold.

Hagris, Maryk, and an unsaddled horse had arrived at the stables. The unsaddled horse looked much like Tanakh. Maryk was riding a white sire that was of the Akhiros breed. The Akhiros were hill-horses from southern Dedarrek, famed for their footing and hardiness as they survived wild in the southern foothills infested by wolves. Tanakh had been sired by an Akhiros.

For two lame men, they were adept riders, at least for short distances. Dyrk wondered how Maryk had been able to travel all the way to Tanvilon at midsummer. Hagris dismounted first, then helped Maryk climb down.

Dyrk took out the bag of gold he had kept close. Thirteen half-crowns. Someone in Doleth Sarin was desperate to get their hands on a Belorin cross war-horse. He re-counted them and stacked them on the end table.

Maryk hobbled up to the veranda and limped up the stairs, one at a time. Dyrk moved forward to help, but the older man waved him off. Maryk sported a neatly trimmed goatee, the same colour as his brown hair that had not yet thinned. His face was set with the same determined jaw as Dyrk's. He was of similar age as Madwin, but his hair had not started to grey. Dyrk had to admit that, would it not be for the injured foot, his father would easily look the part of an Eratur in the King's service.

"You've come for the horse," he said icily.

"Yes," Dyrk responded. Then he ventured, "It has been some time." He didn't know if he could say *father*, which would hurt himself, or *Maryk*, which may hurt the other.

Maryk took a furtive glance to the door. "The last letter agreed on six and a half crowns," he said in a businesslike tone. He didn't even look at the gold.

"It is there," Dyrk said. I've never been known for tact, he thought, so why bother? "You came at midsummer," he said.

Maryk looked like he had just been shot with an arrow. With wide eyes and a look of pain, he took another glance at the door. He took a half-step towards Dyrk and said firmly, but in a low voice, "I did no such thing, you hear me? You must have been mistaken. I'm not even able to make it past Rovenhall." That was the village in which Dyrk had stayed the night.

Dyrk felt abandoned. His sisters had given him an instant of joy, but everything else was turning into a disaster. He did notice one thing, though. Maryk was, at least, looking at him. Just that eye contact, the slightest acknowledgment, meant a lot.

"You may inspect the horse," Maryk waved towards the stable. "The usual terms apply, voided by involving it in any competitions or military action." The eyes seemed to be pleading with Dyrk, *not now*.

Dyrk settled himself with a deep breath and descended the short stairs towards the stable. It took him two hours to fully inspect the stallion. After a visual check, he took it into the paddock and led it through some maneuvers. Next, Hagris helped him fully dress the horse, and Dyrk rode it through some additional exercises. It controlled well without reins, handled the extra weight of the armour, and was agile enough for Dyrk's liking. It wasn't startled by loud sounds or nearby impacts.

Maryk had stayed on the veranda. He was watching the inspection intently with his elbows resting on the railing. Dyrk let Hagris undress the stallion and came to say goodbye.

"You do good work for Farnich," Maryk said softly when he was near. "I'm sure he's happy to have you." It was the closest that Maryk got to saying anything positive.

Dyrk swallowed. "I wanted you to know that I've been called up. Medium cavalry. I leave for the East in three weeks."

Maryk visibly choked up. "Serve your kingdom well," he finally managed. He turned his back and sat down on one of the chairs.

After Tanakh was quickly saddled, Dyrk headed for town. He had gotten nothing out of Maryk. Hopefully Madwin would be more forthcoming.

"Yes, I cut your cinch strap."

Madwin and Dyrk were sitting in Tanvilon's ward tavern. It had taken a little time to track down the headman, but the king's official had made himself available for fifteen minutes. Dyrk didn't waste any time, and Madwin did not hold back at answering his first question.

"Why would you do that?"

Madwin twirled his cup. Both were drinking spiced cider, for it was only mid-afternoon. "Maryk didn't give you any answers?"

"He didn't say a word to me." It wasn't entirely accurate, but in the context, it made the point.

"Then I suppose he is derelict in his duty."

"What is that supposed to mean?"

"It means I can go against his wishes." Madwin took a deep breath. "He wanted to be the one to tell you, but I am guessing that the circumstances weren't right."

Dyrk waited, pensively tapping his fingers on the table.

"Your suspicions were correct. Your father didn't fight in the Battle of Rocavion. He spent the battle in prison."

Dyrk's fingers stopped.

"He was dishonourably discharged from the King's service after that."

"That's not what the official record states. What did he do?" Dyrk cut in.

Madwin acted as if he didn't hear. "His injury was sustained during his arrest."

"What crime did he commit, Madwin?"

"Do you want me to stop?"

"You aren't going to tell me, are you?"

"I am already going against his wishes, Dyrk." Madwin leaned both elbows on the table. He had never looked so threatening. "Do not push things."

Dyrk wanted to respond in kind. *This is my life that has been ruined,* he thought. *I deserve to know the whole truth.* But he restrained himself. He was finally getting somewhere. He could push later. "Go on," he said.

"The official record was altered to show that he had been honourably discharged after suffering an injury in the Battle of Rocavion."

Dyrk wanted to ask, *Who did that? Why?*

"Maryk was permitted to retire to a distant countryside, to live out his days in peace."

"And then his son shows up and reminds everyone of what he did," Dyrk ventured. "Only I'm not included in the impenetrable ring of confidence on what actually happened."

Madwin put his fingertips together and leaned his chin against them. "That circle of confidence is very small."

"Who?"

"Maryk, myself, Cassius, and a few others."

"What does Cassius have to do with this?"

Madwin closed his eyes. Dyrk guessed that he was deciding on which lines to cross.

"Cassius was the military judge in Maryk's case."

Things were beginning to fall into place. Not everything, but at least in part.

"So my father didn't want me to go to the Rhov-Attan because Cassius might see me."

Madwin nodded.

"And you made me use a fake name, and tried to sabotage my victory, because you didn't want Cassius to know that I was there."

Madwin nodded again, even less enthusiastically than last time.

"Did that include you fabricating a story about Tanakh being declared inadmissible, to reduce my chances?"

"Yes."

"How did the Rector find out?"

Madwin sat back. "I don't know," he finally said. "Someone in the know must have seen you at some point."

"Who? Who else is in the know?" Dyrk pleaded. He thought about the man behind the curtain.

Madwin did not answer.

"Thur Daynen?"

Madwin shook his head.

"What part did you play in all this? How did you come to be in confidence?"

"I defended your father. I was his classmate in the College."

"Let me guess. That's why a well-spoken, highly effective headman is stuck in a backwater like Tanvilon."

This statement clearly caused pain. Madwin looked towards the door. "I wouldn't quite put it that way," he finally said, "but I think our time is up."

Dyrk was torn. On the one hand Madwin had finally confided some very important information. But there was still much that he was holding back. The headman had always relished his riddling, leaving his charges to sink or swim with minimal information and find things out for themselves. Dyrk was both angry and thankful at the same time.

"You're a fox, Madwin," he said with a frown. It was intended as both a complement and a pejorative.

The headman wryly smiled as he got up. "As you guessed, being forthright landed me here, Dyrk. You aren't the only one whose life was affected by all this."

"I ride for the east with my regiment in the new year," Dyrk informed him.

"I wish you Nedrin's protection. May Valeron speed you on your journeys," Madwin said politely.

CHAPTER 17:
REGIMENT

Setting up camp was now routine. The regiment operated like a well-oiled watermill, setting up the picket lines, the rows of tents, the cookfire. Wood was being cut and collected. Lines of sight were being determined for guard positions. Sharpened stakes were set where possible to discourage enemy mounted troops. Bayern's tent was always the first up, and Dyrk had the duty of ensuring that was done along with Broedac, the map-keeper.

The tasks were automatic: shovel snow, unfold the tent, drive in pegs, fit in supports, and raise it up. Since the snow there was quite deep, they piled it against the tent both to insulate it and to reduce the chance that wind would carry it aloft.

With the tent up, Broedac assembled a small table in the center and got to work on plotting their current position. Dyrk crossed the width of the camp to help Gadril with their two-person tent. Dyrk and Bayern had agreed that the two of them should sleep on either end of the camp, to keep an eye and an ear out for misbehavior.

Indeed, their regiment was already down to twenty-three. Dyrk was primarily responsible for that, or so the regiment thought. There had been a showdown of authority a few nights ago, after which Tajan, a reservist, was sent home alone.

Dyrk had no regrets. Bayern was sore at the loss of a valuable soldier, but he had yielded to Dyrk's judgment. It involved the daughter of the Lyssian woman who had billeted them four nights ago.

The girl was thirteen. Tajan was making lewd gestures and remarks at her. Dyrk had taken him outside.

"You are going to treat every person in that household like it's your own mother, sister, and brother," Dyrk had demanded, getting up close and personal. "This woman has taken us in. Everything you do in there reflects on the entire regiment and, ultimately, on the Crown."

Tajan had sneered in his face. "What are you going to do? Dishonourable discharge? I bet you're just itching to dish out what you took at the College."

"You lay one finger on her and I'll show you what I'm capable of," Dyrk had warned. Tajan had shrugged.

A half hour later, as the girl walked by, Tajan had caught Dyrk's attention before slapping her bottom.

Tajan was headed home first thing the following morning. Bayern signed the log that authorized the dishonourable discharge.

As Regiment Master, Dyrk was responsible for the regimental log. He would use the table in Bayern's tent after Broedac was finished. He would note the coordinates that the map-keeper had determined and recount the events of the day. Today would be a short entry. They had covered almost two leagues, which was excellent progress given their additional activities.

Most of the army was being transported to the Eastern Front by sea, docking at a temporary harbor at the mouth of the Kullion River. Many regiments of cavalry, however, were given the double task of making a sweep of the wilderness of Narval on their way to the Kullion. They had been spaced out in half-league increments, sweeping across Narval and Lyssia like a dragnet. Their quarry was a scattering of small Vekh raiding parties that had been loosed behind the main battle lines. These raiders were, for the most part, pre-emptive sabotage missions: Vekh commandos who were trying to burn caches, disrupt communications and supply lines, and divert the attention of the main armies by general raiding and looting.

Due to the vast expanse of the area, it was difficult to hunt them down and eliminate them. The regiments were given instructions to camp at their target latitude on the Paellion River in Lyssia until a specified day, and all advance at the same time. The Paellion was a navigable river that flows from the Hyrnistia Mountains, through the small nation of Lyssia, and north to the Sea-lake of Cith. It had few crossings. Bayern's regiment, the thirty-ninth, was lucky in that their assigned latitude was close to a Lyssian ferry. They were holed up at their billet on the east side of the river for three days, waiting for the assigned day to advance.

Since they started out from the Paellion, the regiment was now spending extra time to explore areas in which Vekh raiders might be holed up. It might be a copse of trees or a narrow gully. All had to be checked for any recent signs of the enemy. They did not have any experienced trackers with them, but the regiment would nevertheless be able to pick up obvious signs of camping or passage.

So far, they had not noticed anything untoward for three days. They were deep into the hilly region known as Narval, a depopulated area of scrub forest, moors, and marshes. After two more days of travel, they would have to veer their course slightly south to meet up with the Eastern Army.

They had now encamped with Mount Soareg on their northern flank. The foothills of that mountain had caused some deviations to their course, so it was important to get the right latitude in order to correct the regiment's course on the morrow.

Dyrk wrote out the log, leaving a gap to fill in their exact position. The stars were not yet bright enough for Broedac to accurately determine their latitude. Dyrk's fingers were cold. He blew on them from time to time, happy that it was a short entry. Once finished, he left the log on the small table and strode out to inspect the camp.

"I need two patrols, Dyrk" Bayern said as he passed him by. "I'm nervous about our position."

"I'll have them report to your tent," Dyrk replied.

After sundown, Bayern sometimes sent out a night patrol. Typically they did little more than find a good vantage point and scan the surrounding countryside for cookfires. Their enemy was no doubt invested in staying hidden, so there was little chance of finding them. Still, there was always the possibility that someone was careless.

"Naethin and Tenrik, Kethrol and Deriav, you are on patrol duty, report to the officer's tent," Dyrk barked above the din of the camp noise. Deriav and Tenrik were, like Lohann, still doing their King's

Service. Dyrk liked to pair up the green soldiers with the professionals wherever possible.

Naethin and Dyrk had come to some sort of grudging respect for one another after their initial skirmish in the training yard. Dyrk appreciated Naethin's can-do attitude and work ethic. Naethin recognized that Dyrk was, despite his young age, a capable leader. Naethin had remarked to him after the incident with Tajan, "While I would have handled that a bit differently, I've got to say that you showed the boys that you don't bluff."

Dyrk was a little stung by the distance between himself and Lohann. The young recruit had stepped back from him as soon as the veteran soldiers began to make hay about Dyrk's expulsion from the College. It wasn't news to Lohann, but he clearly wanted to fit in with his mates.

Sharing a tent required two men that got along. Dyrk was thankful for Gadril, an old, experienced soldier who didn't talk much. Gadril had the job of inspecting weapons and sharpening them if need be. Gadril was half-Derrekh, born outside of the kingdom to parents who later became bondservants in Karolia. As a result, Gadril had to complete seven years of bondservitude when he came of age. Ineligible for citizenship, he joined the army upon gaining his freedom and never looked back. Unmarried and unattached, he was dedicated to his craft. Dyrk wanted none other by his side in a fight.

"Pegs are loose, and pile a bit more snow," Ambold demanded as he made the rounds, inspecting the tents. The fire in the middle of the two rows of tents was already burning brightly. Lohann, the regiment cook, was hauling water from a nearby stream to fill the cook pot. There was no compelling reason at present to attempt to conceal the regiment's position.

They would keep a light guard of two men at a time. The raiding parties, if they were close by, would not be assaulting a full cavalry regiment. Dyrk looked at the sky. The clouds in the west were gradually receding. It would be a bright night.

He blew on his hands again and went to Bayern's tent to finish the log. Bayern had just completed giving instructions to the four scouts. "Who's on first watch?" Bayern asked.

"Gelchan and myself," Dyrk answered. "Is two enough?"

"Yes, but I want the fire out once the food is up."

Dyrk rubbed his hands. "It will be a cold night. The sentries could really use the fire."

"No fire," Bayern repeated firmly. "Our position isn't the strongest, and we can be seen for miles by anyone to the south."

"As you wish."

Bayern had kept things professional between the two of them, just like in their college days. Dyrk was very glad he had received confirmation from Madwin that Bayern was being truthful at least about the Contest. Without it, Dyrk's mistrust would have resulted in constant friction in their working relationship.

He walked by Lohann and asked him to keep the fire as low as possible. Then he went to check on Tanakh. The horses had been picketed for the evening out in the open where they could forage some long grass that stuck up through the snow. They would also be getting some grain once they were picketed for the night. Tanakh was being nipped by another horse, of similar build and colouring; Dyrk's mount was ignoring the annoyance.

Bayern was riding a Belorin cross just like himself. "You didn't think I'd ride a parade horse twenty leagues from Karolia, did you?" Bayern had laughed when he showed off the healthy beast. It had been his father's. "Thur Daynen just bought himself a new one," Bayern had said. Dyrk wondered if it was the one that he had brought from his father.

Supper was a stew of peas, salted ham, pearled barley, and potatoes. They still had plenty of hard bread, but that was saved for midday meals or other times that they might not want to start a fire. The scouts returned for their grub before the fire was put out. They reported a single open campfire, well to the south, that was probably one of their own regiments. Bayern's regiment had veered some distance south from their line due to the foothills of Mount Soareg on their northern flank.

Some men retired early. A few others sat around the dying coals of the fire. Tomrigal left to re-picket the horses. Dyrk started his rounds, tracing a circular sentry path a good distance from the camp. Sentry was dreary work, but at least it was his turn for the first watch. He hated waking up in the middle of the night.

It was cold. He spelled off with Gelchan, one of them making the rounds while the other sat beside the warm ashes of the fire, wishing that it was still burning. When Dyrk took his turn in the camp, he couldn't sit down very long. He had to get up to stamp his feet and get the feeling back into his hands. He would be glad to start warming up his fur bedroll.

The soldier's cloak around him was a quality piece of clothing, but it was more suited for cool, rainy weather than it was for cold, dry weather. It could be worn inside or out. The inside was lined with natural cloth, a light brown that would blend into many terrains. The outside was made of a dark blue dyed cloth, the telltale colour of the Karolian military. Dyrk, like all the others, was wearing his inside-out so as not to be conspicuous.

Gelchan came back to the center of the camp, a bit early than expected. "Dyrk," he whispered nervously. "It could be animals, but I'm hearing some sounds coming from the escarpment to the northeast."

"Wake Lohann, I'll get Gadril," Dyrk ordered. They were next on guard.

With the two soldiers up and about, Dyrk told them, "Gelchan was hearing sounds northeast, we're going to take a look. Standard signals."

On foot, Dyrk and Gelchan crept their way east along the ridge. Every crunch of snow under their feet made him wince. A small knot of fear twisted in his stomach. Dyrk had to admit he had never really been in mortal hand-to-hand combat yet. Neither had he seen an enemy Vekh. Would this be the first for both?

Coming close to the lip of a small cliff, Dyrk lay onto the cold snow and crawled his way to the edge. Once there, he and Gelchan lay completely still, listening. The snow was melting at his chest and hips, soaking into his clothes. Was this for nothing?

Down below was a wide moor that stretched into the distance from the cliff they were on. A low gully ran east-to-west. It twisted and turned, no doubt governed by a small seasonal brook that ran along the bottom. Dyrk saw a flash of movement in the gully, and the unmistakable sound of boots on gravel. He scanned the gully intently, trying to get a visual. He could not confirm who was down there.

Dyrk weighed the tactics. It was Bayern's call, of course. But it would be a poor decision to head down there in the dead of night. Whoever it was, they were moving away from the regiment's camp, to the east.

He dragged himself back from the lip of the cliff. Whispering with hands cupped, he told Gelchan to sentry himself there and signal if anything approached. He headed back to camp, woke Bayern, and reported.

After some discussion, the two agreed that it wouldn't make sense to pursue them until morning, provided they were not attacking the regiment's position. Dyrk sent another soldier to relieve Gelchan, then finally got some sleep himself. He would need the rest if there was hard riding tomorrow.

Bayern gave instructions to rouse in the dark. The camp was full of nervous energy as it was hurriedly packed. It could be their first sight of the enemy, the first taste of combat. Some of the recruits chatted excitedly. Dyrk himself had an uneasy feeling in his stomach, recalling the time he found the body of the Roj raider, curled up in his last throes of death. Lethal force if necessary but not necessarily lethal force, he told himself.

As the horses were being prepared, Bayern held council with Dyrk, Gadril, and Ambold, who were the section leaders. "May I remind you we have no visual confirmation yet," Bayern was saying. "Signs point to this being a Vekh raiding group, on foot, who were day-camping just beneath our position. They were probably trying to sneak out during the night. We'll go down there, find tracks, and follow wherever they lead, even out of our line. If we find signs of greater numbers then our own, we will break off. Gadril will lead the tracking party. I will be on the left, Dyrk on the right, Ambold behind with supplies. Ambold, leave three with the baggage if we engage. Loose formation, standard signals. I want to emphasize, men, we do not have confirmation. It could be local settlers, it could be our own men, it could even be nothing at all. Do not engage unless you confirm they're armed and hostile. Surrender is cause for quarter, but if it's the Vekh, we will not demand it."

Dyrk understood the rules of engagement. Prisoners wouldn't be ideal for their current mission, but the Code of Korhal must be respected.

They mounted up. Their train of pack animals had no hope of keeping up with a full advance, so it was essential to leave some soldiers to bring them up in that event. Tack was checked, weapons readied, tension mounted. Their lances were short, the type that could be kept on a pack animal to free up the hands of the riders for long journeys. But now each soldier kept his spear in hand, their primary weapon against any enemy, mounted or not. The men wore open helmets. They could fix visors on them if combat was imminent, but they were uncomfortable as they restricted breathing and vision.

Bayern gave the command to move out. The four groups began their descent. Bayern's took the lead. Down the wooded embankment they came, out onto the moor. Their leader crossed over the gully at a full gallop to the north, not taking the time to look for tracks or the enemy. Dyrk led his group down the embankment and took up a slower speed on the south side, eyes scanning for hostiles. Gadril descended into the gully where two of his riders dismounted. Ambold and two other riders peeled off from the baggage train and scoured the base of the cliffs, looking for the enemy camp.

Three loud knocks were audible, coming from the gully where Gadril was dismounted. The signal for enemy sighted. They must have found evidence of Vekh. Gadril's group remounted and began to move at a fast pace down the ravine to the east. Dyrk set the pace for his group and followed the same trajectory across the flat moor on the south side of the ravine. Bayern shadowed them on the north.

The nervous pursuit went on for one hour, then two. Gadril did not lose his tracks, though they left the ravine and started across open terrain in a straight line, bearing east-northeast. Dyrk could see some forested slopes in that direction, which would give the enemy cover if they reached them. They had many hours head-start, but they were on foot and would now be tired. The chase was on.

Dyrk kept to a pace that would not unduly tire the horses. They slowed to a walk whenever Gadril stopped to check tracks. After some time, another soldier spelled off Gadril and kept up the trail. Dyrk checked over his shoulder. The pack animals were far behind.

On any other day, this would be exhilarating: cantering across wide-open moors on a horse that doubled as your best friend. Dyrk was in good health, well-equipped, well-fed. *I wouldn't mind being a bit warmer,* Dyrk thought with a wry smile. But today, knowing that they were likely heading towards violence, it left him uneasy. He tried to put himself in that bravado-saturated headspace that was whipped up whenever the young Eratur-apprentices would set their minds to something.

Dyrk recalled the sashes that his fellow soldiers in Dedarrek proudly displayed, marks or symbols sewn for every kill they claimed. It was difficult, if not impossible, to believe the aggregate numbers of enemies dispatched. The Raiders must have sprouted from the ground like dandelions for that to be true, he thought.

As they slowed for another brief walk, Dyrk turned to the reservist who rode at his side. "You ever kill a man, Emgaer?"

He shook his head. "I was in two skirmishes, but never saw the enemy. Took a dart to the chest, though." Emgaer was a reservist like himself, though five years older, and had been stationed within the cavalry at a different garrison in southern Dedarrek. "What about you?"

"One raider in Dedarrek," Dyrk replied. "Didn't know I had shot him until they found the body."

He had written six letters to Neriah already. He had promised himself to write at least once a week, but the travel so far had been easy enough for him to write a little every night. One letter ended up as a combination of his thoughts from a few days. Given that his task was the regiment log, it was convenient to take out a creased letter paper and write a few lines to his beloved each time. Never again would he leave her without his utmost effort to be connected with her.

It would be nearly impossible for her to send letters his way. There would be a post depot at the Eastern Front, but unless Dyrk was stationed there for some time, there wouldn't be a way for Neriah to know to address him there. Being cavalry, they were always on the move, and it would be foolish to announce any planned movements to a sweetheart back at home.

The last time they had spent together before his departure had been precious to him. The weather had been unnaturally cold at home. The presence of all her siblings made it impossible to get any quiet time inside the house, so they had sat on the bench just outside the door. The stars appeared one by one in the sky as the sun set, spurring their conversation on. She huddled close to him for warmth. When they stood up to finally say goodbye, she extended on her tiptoes to give him a kiss. It was simple, unpretentious, with little passion, but immensely meaningful to them both. One more glance into each other's eyes and Dyrk had left.

Dyrk had sent his previous letters while they were billeted on the Paellion. Now she would have to wait until he arrived at the Eastern front. Assuming he would get there alive, he reminded himself. This wasn't training anymore.

Some abnormal, motionless shapes to his right kept Dyrk's attention for some time. Finally, he could make out a stone foundation. Probably the old ruins of some farm or house. He sent two riders to pass through it. They reported nothing more than the remains of a campsite, nearly obscured by fresh snow. It was at least a week old.

By now the sun was high in the sky. On the next pause, Dyrk saw that Bayern's group had stopped. He told his men to dismount and eat something. It was not noon, but a quick stretch was in everyone's best interests. After a very brief refresher, they were off again.

Dyrk began to despair that they would reach the hills before their quarry. Searching through trees and rocks on horseback was not easy work, and they were prone to be ambushed.

Gadril's group came to a sudden halt. Dyrk reined in his troops. Bayern began to circle around ahead of Gadril's path. What had he found? "Load up," Dyrk ordered. At a stop, it wasn't difficult for those with light crossbows to load their weapons. They used a long, steel lever to pull the bows back. This was nearly impossible while moving, and the bows shouldn't be left loaded all day. Dyrk didn't use a crossbow. It was generally looked down upon at the Eratur's College as a necessary but ungentlemanly weapon.

Once they were loaded, Dyrk nudged his group into a canter, circling around Gadril's group in the same manner that Bayern was doing. They were in snow-covered high grass. If the enemy was nearby, they could be hiding anywhere.

The sound of a horse's squeal snapped Dyrk's head sideways. Bayern's group had engaged with something. Dyrk saw dark shapes on the white snow among the horses. One of Bayern's men tumbled off his horse to the ground. Dyrk spurred Tanakh to come to their aid, raising his arm in signal to widen their formation.

By the time his group arrived, some of the shapes had begun to flee. The Vekh were slightly smaller than Karolians, wearing blackened leather armour. Their cloaks, which appeared to be bleached cloth, blended well into the snow-covered surroundings until they moved. Bayern hacked downwards with his sword. When the Eratur looked up and saw Dyrk's group fast approaching, he pointed with his sword after the routing enemy. Dyrk adjusted his course.

He was in the lead. His heart pumped as hard as Tanakh's hooves. He could hear the thunderous sound of the others right behind him. Forty paces, then thirty, to the dark shapes that were running across the snow. He leveled his lance. He didn't even realize that he was yelling, an indistinguishable shout that stimulated all his faculties. Twenty. His quarry darted sideways at the last moment, away from Dyrk's path, but he had anticipated it. Tanakh shifted their direction slightly. Dyrk's lance cleaved clothing, armour, and flesh before striking bone with a sickening impact. Tanakh responded to his spurs and knees by carrying on through the enemy. He had let go of the lance. Behind him, Dyrk heard cries and snarls as his fellow cavalry also hit home.

It was all over in a few seconds.

Emgaer let out a whoop. Dyrk turned his group around and directed them to search carefully for survivors. "We can't have any jumping out of the snow and putting one in our backs," he shouted. Riders began to crisscross left and right. Emgaer prodded one of the dead with his lance.

Bayern hailed him. Dyrk rode over. He saw that Deriav was the one who was unhorsed. He was on his feet, breathing heavy, hand on the saddle of his mount. Dyrk's stomach turned when he saw the remains of two Vekh on the snow, dismembered by the swords of Bayern and his men.

"Report!" Bayern shouted at him, his broadsword, still in his hand, stained with blood.

"Five more dead," Dyrk responded. "We're searching for stragglers. No casualties."

Tenrik, the regiment's medic, had ridden up from Gadril's group, dismounting to help Deriav.

"Assuming Deriav is all right, we have no casualties," Bayern announced. "But I still want this whole area searched. Keep an eye out for tracks."

Dyrk's hands were shaking. He gave orders to the other soldiers, then returned to pick up his lance. It was lying on the snow, but still stuck in the Vekh he had killed. He had to dismount to pick it up. With two hands, he jarred it loose from the corpse. Blood stained the snow and the leaf-shaped blade on the end of the lance. Only moments before, this carcass had been a living, breathing human being. Dyrk had ended that in an instant.

This was war. These Vekh had no doubt been sent to kill, murder, and maim any that they could get their hands on. By the actions of their regiment, they had saved the lives of others. Dyrk tried to keep things in that perspective.

He didn't collect any trophies for his second kill.

The mood that night was festive. They were camped in the ruin that Dyrk had briefly searched only a short distance before the battle. Since they had veered north in their pursuit, the regiment patrolling just north of them had seen them and camped with them. It was good to have the additional men there, to swap stories, share information, and help with the camp work.

A shallow mass grave was hacked through the frozen soil for the seven Vekh that had been killed. Deriav had some bruises from being pulled off his horse. Kethrol showed off a puncture in his chain armour, on his right side just above the belt, which was caused by an arrow narrowly missing his torso. Emgaer told and re-told his skewering of a fleeing enemy. Bayern was congratulatory to his men but otherwise remained aloof.

Dyrk stayed lost in his thoughts. He lingered over the regimental log, recording in detail the events of the day. He felt little emotion, positive or negative, when he wrote, in the list of outcomes of the battle, *Dyrk House Teren slew one Vekh irregular.*

He left the log on the table for Bayern to review and sign. Without leaving the tent, he pulled out his current letter to Neriah and began to write.

"To your parents?" Bayern's voice came over his shoulder. The Eratur ducked into the tent, cloak wrapped around him for warmth. He sat on the floor-cloth across the low table from Dyrk.

"No. To a girl."

"Ah yes, to the flowers of our nation," Bayern said light-heartedly. "We dangle a ribbon and expect them to be ours forever. They take much more grooming and attention than a parade horse, or so I'm told."

Dyrk couldn't figure out if Bayern was being poetic or trying to make a joke.

Bayern removed his gauntlets and rubbed his cold hands. "Whatever happened to that girl you favored at the Contest, anyway?"

Dyrk lifted the letter and put it down without a word.

"Well, isn't that a fairy tale," Bayern chuckled, not with Dyrk but at him. "I didn't take that little game seriously in the slightest."

"Most of the girls didn't either," Dyrk returned. "Especially not the one wearing yours."

Bayern sucked in air as if he'd just been punched. "Ah, my friend, you aren't kind enough. She was pretty for a day. The radiance of her face was due in part to my grant. And my boyish courage was due in part to her eyes upon me. That's how it works. But we enjoy the moment and move on."

Dyrk recalled the image engraved in his memory of the ribbon disappearing in the icy swirls of the river. "That may be the case for most. But relationships start with a chance meeting, whether it be here or there. It's just up to us to make them into something more."

"Well said. Is the log complete?" It was back to business for Bayern.

The booming voice continued over the lectern. "Compassion is well and good," Encarigon continued, the Disciples of Taephin hanging onto his every word. "Yet what good is compassion if both the giver and receiver starve? I've seen one peasant help another, until neither had enough food to live on. When the winter-fever came, both lost one of their malnourished children. Meanwhile, the wine-merchant next door dines on the flesh of animals. Misplaced, short-sighted compassion only enables these tragedies. Real compassion would demand change."

Rayve had to admit that Encarigon's voice was animating. He had heard a few lectures before by other lecturers, and he had looked for the easiest way to excuse himself. Encarigon could hold an entire crowd of twenty-somethings, and a sixteen-year-old boy to boot, by his grand inflections, sweeping statements, vivid metaphors, and inventive vocabulary.

"I call it a crime!" Encarigon thundered, walking up the aisle of the lecture hall, something that was not common for lecturers to do. "It's a crime when a poor woman perishes in the compassionate arms of another while a priest of Taephin sips wine at the Headman's house, discussing ways to prevent skin rashes!"

Priests of Taephin were trained as physicians. In past centuries, the people were generally cared for by country midwives and unlicensed doctors, only calling on a Priest of Taephin for difficult cases. Over the past century, the crown had, at the urging of the Temple of Taephin, cracked down on unlicensed physicians, requiring them to go through schooling in order to practice.

Midwives, too, were no longer permitted to operate unless they were under the indirect supervision of a Priest of Taephin.

"Is the profession to blame? Let me ask you this, dear acolytes. Is it right to take our best and brightest, and throw them in the same mire of poverty?" Encarigon lowered his voice and became personal, another rarity amongst lecturers. "I don't know about you, but I work to eat."

Rayve tried his best to follow his master's train of thought. He could usually make it part-way through a lecture before he lost sight of what Encarigon was driving at. The professor rarely drove his points home with practical advice. If Rayve had to find fault with anything, it was that.

But it was not a disciple's place to find fault with his master. Perhaps it was Encarigon's intent to let his hearers come up with solutions on their own.

Rayve was wearing the robes of an Acolyte of Harophin. He was supposed to dress like that whenever Hajwan took on the identity of Encarigon. Rayve accepted Hajwan's second identity with ease, given his childhood experiences with his own father. The few times his father was at home, he was just that – his father. He argued incessantly with his wife, spent a lot of time in bed, and rarely acknowledged Rayve. He had a name, his personal one. But when the man put on his sword and military cloak, he became a different person. His name became Comentus, a high-ranking title in the army. His appearance and demeanor changed – he shaved the growth on his face, stood up straight, and talked far less but with more effect.

But neither of his father's personalities paid much attention to Rayve.

Hajwan was different. In the modest home shared by the two of them in an unassuming neighbourhood of the capital city, the man lavished attention on the boy, speaking words of encouragement and advice softly and often. Encarigon also paid him attention outside the lecture halls, though it was more of a detached discussion between master and disciple.

The transition between Hajwan and Encarigon was much more

peculiar than his father equipping his military gear. Rayve would be with Hajwan one moment, then look away, and Encarigon was there the next, ready to take him on another visit to this college or that temple. In the evening, Rayve sometimes went to sleep in his bed while with Encarigon reading a book, but when he awoke, Hajwan was there reading the same book.

The two identities did not have identical facial features. Hajwan had a full beard that softened the man's countenance. Encarigon had a thin, pointed goatee that made him look professional. Hajwan's hair was full and brown. Encarigon had a high forehead and his hair colour was black. Hajwan's eyes were large, bright, and kind. Encarigon had dark eyes, the type that could bore a hole through a misbehaving acolyte. Hajwan wore unassuming clothes which were even a little threadbare in places. Encarigon was magnificent in his international ensemble. Rayve could tell that Encarigon was several inches taller than Hajwan.

The lecture wrapped up. Most of the students filed out, but a gaggle collected around Encarigon to ask him follow-up questions. One came up to Rayve and told him how lucky he was to have been chosen as Encarigon's disciple at such a young age.

Rayve was sometimes baffled by Hajwan's favour on him. It wasn't as if Rayve was particularly intelligent – his scribe had made sure he knew that. If he had some sort of redeeming quality, like strength or bravery, Rayve figured his father would have taken more of a notice of him. No, Hajwan's interest in him seemed to be unconditional, or perhaps the man saw something in him that no one else did. The boy wasn't about to complain. He was happier than he had ever been.

CHAPTER 18:
URGENCY

Vigheran had been right. As the climate became drier, his stamina increased. Torrin began to lag under the furious pace that Erelin set. He knew the two of them were arguing again, and during the seven days since Vanreikh, it did not appear that they had settled it.

Vigheran had lost the first argument. There was no road in that region, but there was a trail marked out along the Mubrich river as it flowed from the west. It wasn't suitable for cart traffic as it was normally traversed by camel. It led through a pass in the mountains to a wasteland known as the Bleak Valley. It was the most direct way to Dharbur. Vigheran wished to stay off of any marked path, but Erelin knew that going cross-country would slow them down.

It wasn't easy to deduce their conversation, but Torrin was beginning to pick up on Erelin's combination of sign language, body language, and head gestures. It was certainly easier to interpret than Vigheran's rough Zindori tongue.

Passing by the Zindori merchants on the trail was a nervous business. Each caravan had several guards, all armed to the teeth. If any of them were unscrupulous enough to waylay a few isolated travelers, Torrin did not think that their little group would stand much of a chance. Perhaps it was their kinship with Vigheran, perhaps it was Erelin's intimidation factor, but most likely their safety to date was because they didn't openly carry anything that was valuable.

They had left the snow behind on the northern mountains. Their last rain was a day after they left Vanreikh. The terrain was getting drier, dustier, and bleaker.

The next argument was being had over whether they would head north or south once they reached the mountains. Torrin himself had no idea why they would want to go through the Zelmandi region to the north. True, the Bleak Valley was inhospitable and difficult to cross. It was, however, the most direct route to Dharbur. The Zelmandi region had water, but it was well known since antiquity to be the haven for bandits and outlaws. His history book even stated that Belorin himself was killed by Zelmandi rebels over two thousand years ago.

Better to carry water and risk dying of thirst than to traipse through a hive of bandits, Torrin figured. But what did he know? He was just a maimed Azenvarim completely out of his league, in a territory that he only knew about from books.

His knees and thighs continued to flare up in pain. Oh, would he give his left hand for a good horse? Nearly so. They were constantly going uphill as they approached the mountains. When would this endless walking stop?

Torrin did not think about what would happen once he got to Dharbur. It was a foreign town to him, and he didn't believe he could have any relatives there. The only consolation is that it was closer to Karolia than Sorwail was. At least he was headed in the right direction, even if that direction required him to cross a continent for any possibility of refuge.

He thought over and over again about Erelin's reaction to his vision. He guessed that the present urgency was in some way related. Was the white-haired woman Erelin's relative, or possibly his wife? If the Gryphon was threatening to go after someone Erelin cared about, wouldn't he be walking straight into the trap if he rushed back to try to save her? What did the Gryphon really want, anyway?

In the legends of old, the demon-beasts were described as indiscriminate killers. Only a few, such as Bresjekh the bear, Dwarth the wolf, and the King of the Crills himself, were said to be intelligent and cunning. Of course, then there were the tales of men who gave themselves up to evil Seraphs: Vaezur, Kharon, and Drumeth were the three most prominent.

Vaezur had orchestrated the downfall and destruction of Tauril, and pursued Eldorin, who was leading an exodus of survivors. Once Eldorin established his kingdom in exile, Karolia, Vaezur set out to destroy Eldorin's family and finally met his end at the hand of Eldorin's son Esdarion. Kharon, Vaezur's chief lieutenant, continued the pursuit of the House of Teren, slaying them all to a single man during the ages to follow. Drumeth lived many centuries within his fortress of Delvaeth, harassing the kingdom of Azenvar throughout its existence. Even now, rumor had it that Drumeth still lurked within his fortress of Delvaeth, the power of the Seraph preventing his natural death.

All three were recruited of old. They worshipped the Darkness and gave themselves up to it. It was said that they even allowed their tongues to be torn out in order to prove that their words were of Seraphic origin.

The connection hit Torrin for a brief moment. Erelin was missing his tongue. No, it couldn't be. It would be ridiculous in the extreme to go through such great extent to re-enact an event that was, at best, historical legend.

He realized that Erelin and Vigheran had gotten some distance ahead of him again. This time, he didn't want to catch up. No, there must be plausible explanations. Didn't the Sej Zindori tear out the tongues of prisoners of war, or of slaves who insulted their masters?

Torrin stopped for just a moment, resting his hand on a rock as he caught his breath. Catch a hold of yourself, he thought. Let's just deal with one thing at a time.

When he started moving again, he saw an interesting sight ahead. A small party of men without camels had stopped to speak with Vigheran. Erelin was standing off to the side, looking uncomfortable.

The men were Zindori and wore long red cloaks with gold embroidery. Gold earrings were in their ears. Their beards were thin and pointed, their heads covered in light-coloured scarves to keep the sun off their heads. They wore wicked-looking scimitars of various curvature on their belts. Raiders! The Roj of the Kuz Steppes were part of the Wakin clan. After the Raider Wars between Karolia and the Wakin Roj, their red-cloaked fighters became known simply as Raiders. An uneasy ceasefire existed between the two nations, but the Raiders continued to harass and raid allies, including Ancharith, Rhonaur, and southern Belorin. Raiders also functioned as mercenaries to profit from internecine conflicts in faraway lands, or even for private persons as bounty hunters.

Torrin had thought Vigheran was a Raider when they first met, but now he quickly realized his error. Even other Roj Zindori had little love for their close cousins because of their brutality and ruthlessness. Torrin caught up and stood closer to Erelin. He did not like the way that the Raiders looked at him. He liked it even less that the discussion with Vigheran seemed to be getting a little heated. He did not want a fight with these mercenaries, even with Erelin and Vigheran on his side.

Finally, to Torrin's relief, Vigheran disengaged from the Raiders and both parties continued on their way. Another argument started between Torrin's two companions. Oh, if only he could understand the language. For all he knew they were discussing how best to sell him. Or eat him. He continued to look over his shoulder until the Raiders were out of sight.

Their travel that day was uneventful. If the circumstances had been different, the terrain would be fascinating to Torrin. They were traveling within broad canyons that wound through a high plateau. Jagged outcroppings of bare rock reached for the sky. Acacia and juniper were plentiful, but there was no sign of the hidden water sources that kept these plants alive. As night was approaching, they could see ahead a small but beautiful waterfall cascading down the side of the canyon and disappearing into the rock below. Erelin led them on a path that wound up the side of the canyon. They camped near the stream that fed the waterfall. Torrin guessed that this might be their last chance for reliable water for some time.

That night was brutally cold. Torrin lay shivering all night within his bedroll, even after he piled up his cloak and all his spare clothing on top of himself. At one point, in the middle of the night, he awoke to find Erelin crouched near him. He was slipping something into Torrin's pouch of verse papers. Torrin must be sure to read it in the morning.

Vigheran roused before the sun was up to start a fire. He knocked the ice out of the cooking pot and filled it with water from the stream. Wisely, their canteens had all been dumped the night before to prevent them from freezing up and splitting. Torrin continued to snooze as he smelled the unappetizing morning porridge cooking. He was not enamored with their travel diet. It was far heavier on meat and fat than he was used to, with very little in the way of fruits and fresh vegetables. But it seemed to keep them all going, albeit with a little indigestion.

Erelin strode into the camp. He laid three strange-looking fruit, each about the size of a small apple, at Vigheran's side. The Roj had obviously seen these before, he set right to peeling them with his knife. Once peeled, he sliced them into the pot and smacked his lips.

The sun was now peeking through a pass in the eastern mountains. Torrin got up, stretched, and refreshed himself in the stream. It was bitterly cold. The stream was rushing gaily, its flow larger than its stream-bed. The overflow must be due to the time of the year, he thought.

Torrin sat down and took out his verse papers. He easily found Erelin's note, written again in Melandarim. It said:

You must say – you have relatives in Ancharith.
They are rich.
The Roj will be well paid.
If not, trouble.

The knot of anxiety in Torrin's heart intensified. "Roj" was written in singular, it must refer to Vigheran. Torrin noticed something else, though. In Melandarim, verbs were conjugated based on whether the action, or the subject noun, is thought of as good or evil. The verb in the third line, "will be well paid", was conjugated in the evil tense.

He recalled Erelin's plea that Torrin not talk to Vigheran about the Gryphon. What was going on here? Was Erelin conspiring against his master in an attempt to gain his freedom? Or was he truly looking out for Torrin's well-being and warning him of Vigheran's intentions? Torrin understood the rest of the note. He was being asked to participate in a ruse that he had rich relatives in Ancharith that would compensate Vigheran well.

He tossed the note into the fire. It smoldered and smoked.

"Do you know yet where we are headed after Dharbur?" Torrin asked Vigheran as the porridge bubbled. It actually smelled appetizing that morning.

Vigheran grunted. "Not known yet," he said.

"If you are headed further west, I would very much like to continue on with you," Torrin ventured, trying to sound convincing. "I have family in both Altyren and Ancharith. Both own land, and I'm sure they would compensate you well for bringing me there safely."

Vigheran's eyes shifted. He tapped the spoon and laid out the bowls. "We shall see," he muttered. "Long distance to both."

Torrin figured it was safe to mention Altyren. There was no way that Vigheran would think about heading into the heart of Karolia. Being honest with himself, he really didn't know where his Karolian relatives lived. There was an estate reserved for the House of Atlan at Altyren, but he didn't know who lived there.

He remembered the family tree that Braedil had put together to prove his theory that the House of Atlan was being exterminated. There were many names on there, seventy or eighty. Most lived, or had lived, in Dar-Amund. At least five of them were noted to reside in Karolia, but Torrin recalled that three of them had been crossed off. He couldn't find himself on the list, presumably because he was still a child the last time Braedil had visited Dar-Amund.

As Vigheran and Torrin began to eat the sweetened porridge, Erelin walked over to the cliffside and scanned the path that they had taken yesterday. As he sat down near the fire, he made a signal to Vigheran that made him put the bowl down with a vexed look on his face. Then they finished their breakfast in haste and silence.

Vigheran got quickly to his feet. "Wash the pot, *kyusi*. We are hunted."

Dutifully, Torrin took the pot to the stream. His anxiety continued to tighten. On his way back, he half-whispered, "Who's hunting us?"

"We go north," Vigheran said, ignoring his question. North

meant the dangerous Zelmandi region. Erelin was re-stringing his bow. Torrin filled the canteens. Vigheran kicked dirt over the fire. There was no way that they could hide their campsite in time.

"Now listen, kyusi. You need to be good at hiding. Not being seen. Not being heard. If we run, you run. If we stop, you stop."

As they hoisted their packs and made final adjustments, Vigheran had one more piece of advice.

"We will have enemies ahead and behind. We hope they fight each other." Erelin was already nearly out of sight, scouting their path to the north.

The Zelmandi region would be a barren, rocky wasteland if it were not for numerous streams that cascaded from the mountains to the east that bore the same name. Wherever water flowed, life flourished. In the long spaces between, it was as bleak as Torrin had ever seen. The landscape was crisscrossed with several intersecting chains of hills, some running southwest-to-northeast and others running perpendicular. This resulted in a lot of boxed canyons. Within the first morning, Torrin counted eight caves in the rock faces that they passed.

After the first hour, they slowed their pace to a more sustainable rate. Vigheran had Torrin march just ahead. The Roj would stop now and then to listen for signs of pursuit. Torrin would mimic as he was ordered. Erelin mostly scouted ahead. Twice the tall Taurilian came back to them and diverted them to another route.

It was nearly midday when Vigheran, during one of the spells in which he was listening for sounds behind, motioned for Torrin to start climbing an embankment to their right. A small cleft in the rock wall was inhabited by bushes and few scraggly trees, evidence that a rivulet occasionally flowed there. Torrin began to climb up. He didn't see Erelin anywhere.

The two of them got into the bushes within the cleft. Vigheran motioned for him to lie down. The Roj crouched behind a bush, equipping his shortbow and nocking an arrow.

Torrin waited breathlessly. He began to panic as he thought about their tracks. They were not making any effort to hide signs of their passage. Yet perhaps, if their pursuers were not expert trackers, they might go unnoticed in the rock and gravel through which they traveled.

Four men came into view, traveling in two pairs. They no longer wore the red cloaks, but Torrin recognized them as the Raider mercenaries that they had met earlier on the road. They moved quickly, warily, weapons drawn, though not in a stance that suggested they expected imminent combat. One kept on the edge of the cliffs away from Torrin's location, while the other was headed right for their hiding spot.

The two closest to him suddenly ducked for cover. A moment later, an arrow clicked off the stones near where they had stood. Torrin held his breath. He had no idea where the arrow came from. A hoarse shout from one of the Raiders below alerted the other two. Then Torrin spied a lone figure on the eastern side of the gorge, further along the path that he would have been taking. It was Erelin. He had nocked another arrow in his bow. The arrow was loosed, deflecting harmlessly off some stone near where the mercenaries had taken cover. Erelin turned and disappeared from view.

He was surprised that Erelin had been standing in the open. He surely had the ability to stay hidden. But as the Raiders began to move from cover to cover to pursue their quarry, Torrin understood. Erelin was drawing the enemy away.

It did not take long for the Raiders to move out of sight up the canyon. Vigheran kept Torrin still for several more agonizing minutes. Finally, they left their hiding place. The Roj picked up both arrows as they made their way across the rocks.

They crossed the canyon and cautiously headed north, Vigheran alertly searching both ahead of them and at the western rock wall. Torrin guessed he was looking for a way up. Before long, they found a fissure from which a rivulet poured into the canyon. Torrin was thankful that the climb was not too arduous; two hands were much more useful than one to clamber up a rock face. Some of the rocks were slippery, and there were a few hair-raising moments in which his feet slipped out from under him and he slid back towards the canyon from which they came. Without a word, Vigheran gave help only when it was most needed.

Once they were at the top, Torrin could see why they had preferred to travel at the bottom of the canyon. Their path traversed very little level ground. Rocky hills, cliffs, and outcroppings dominated the landscape and made progress slow. Sometimes their only path was to go up or down rockslides. This not only presented difficulties in footing, but also made a lot of noise as the rocks clattered down the hillside. They were gradually heading west, but the going was difficult. They took a rest in a narrow valley, beside a spring of water that fed a small grove of low trees.

As they rested, Vigheran kept looking at the ridges around them, and cocking his ear to listen. He seemed tired and more surly than usual. Torrin was more interested in the small area they had stumbled into. Almost immediately he noticed that some of the trees had been cut down and branches snapped off. He looked on the ground for tracks, but his untrained eye could not pick anything out. He began to scan the nearby rocks. Was someone watching them?

Vigheran bent down to fill up his canteen at the spring. A brief movement caught Torrin's eye. Instinctively, he put both hands onto Vigheran's back, grasping the scabbard of one of his swords, and pulled the man down. An arrow came out of nowhere, grazing Vigheran's side. Bits of leather flew into the air. Torrin was knocked aside as Vigheran lunged for some cover. Torrin went in an opposite direction. It occurred to him that Vigheran might not know where the arrow came from, so he shouted and pointed.

Adrenaline kept Torrin thinking clearly. Only one shot had come. It did not originate from high above them, but it came from a jumble of rocks a short distance up the valley they were in. The distance was only about thirty paces. *What can I do? I can't fight, I can't shoot a bow. About the only thing I could do is hold a shield, and I don't even have that.*

That gave him an idea. He picked up some rocks and began to hurl them, left-handed, towards the place that their assailant was taking cover. It took a few attempts, but he was getting closer. He planned a route and took a deep breath. If he couldn't fight, he could at least distract their enemy. He bolted for the next rock. He didn't see it, but he heard the sharp sound of a shaft spinning through the air. He clambered to his knees behind the rock. It must have missed.

He peered over the rock just in time to see Vigheran leap over the barrier behind which their enemy was shooting from. His dull red Calderan blades swung in succession, one downwards, and the other crosswise. It was over in an instant.

The two of them scoured the rocks for other enemies. Finding none, Torrin took one glance towards their defeated assailant. He was not dressed well, a combination of rags and furs kept in place by several ropes around his body. What wasn't covered in blood was filthy. Torrin wasn't a stranger to blood and death, but it was always in the context of war. This man tried to harm them unprovoked, and so met his end. He would have done the same to them given the chance.

A bandit camp was behind the rocks. Torrin counted seven bedrolls. That underlined their urgency to get moving again. Vigheran threw a hide-covered shield in his direction. This might come in handy, Torrin thought, though for the moment he had no ability to tie the straps onto his left arm. He secured the straps onto a loop on his backpack. The Zindori pocketed a few odds and ends as he rifled through some bundles.

"We move, *kyusi*, but no tracks." He pointed back the way they had come.

"I'll follow you," Torrin said. *A little gratitude might be in order*, he thought.

They moved down the rocky stream bed that was formed by the spring, heading almost south. After a hundred paces or so, Vigheran climbed out of the ravine to the west with Torrin right behind him. Only once they were out of sight of the valley did they stop again for a moment and catch their breath.

Vigheran unslung his canteen. He held up the leather strap, which was almost torn through. Torrin realized that the first arrow had sliced through the strap, narrowly missing Vigheran's flesh.

"You impressed me, *kyusi*." The Zindori's still appeared ill-tempered, despite the rare compliment.

That's probably all the thanks I'll get, Torrin thought. "Where is Erelin? How will we find him again?"

"We meet him ahead. No fear of that."

"Will he kill those raiders?"

Vigheran cut the strap just above the tear and threaded the new end through the buckle on the canteen. "No. They are not bandits. Good fighters. We must go."

They made camp for the night at the base of a tall spire of rock. While their camp was hidden, the spire was visible for many miles around. Torrin guessed that the landmark was previously agreed between Vigheran and Erelin as a rendezvous.

They had not acquired any game that day. Vigheran did not light a fire. Supper was a loaf of hard bread and one strip of smoked venison between the two of them. Venison was tough and tasteless, but it made the old bread a little easier to swallow. Despite the heat of the day, Torrin missed the hot meal that they usually enjoyed after nightfall. Even just a cup of hot water would make him feel better.

They were camped under an overhang. It was not quite a cave, but it was sheltered in case it rained. Torrin spread out his bag to sleep. Vigheran remained sitting cross-legged. He was perched on a low rock with a good vantage point, staring east into the fading night.

Torrin was very tired. It felt like he was being woken as soon as he put his head down.

"Get up, *kyusi*, we are in danger." Vigheran's voice was a hoarse whisper.

He opened his eyes but saw nothing. It was nearly pitch-black. He willed himself to spring into action. "Do we pack up?" he whispered.

"No time." Torrin felt his right arm being pulled at the elbow. Two straps were tightened over his forearm. To his relief, he could tell by the sound of the breathing that it was Erelin strapping the small bandit shield to his arm.

But the shield was strapped on his right arm! He was trained to use it on his left!

A warm leather object was pressed into his left hand. Erelin's boot-knife, with its reverse grip. He knew he would be useless in a fight like that. Why was he being armed?

"Come," Vigheran hissed.

Torrin felt lucky that he had fallen asleep in his full traveling clothes. He had no armour like his companions, but at least he wasn't half-naked. He followed the sounds of Vigheran. He had to reverse the knife in his hand in order to use his fingers to feel along the rocks in the darkness.

They were moving up to high ground. They scaled a rockslide and hoisted themselves onto a ledge along the pinnacle of rock. Torrin's eyes were now adjusting to the darkness. The night had clouded over, and only a thin sliver of the moon gave feeble light from the western horizon.

Torrin heard a sound below him of a string slapping against wood. Tense as he was, his reaction was immediate. He threw himself to the floor of the ledge they were on. An arrow struck the rock wall above where they had been standing. The Raider mercenaries must have found them!

They had a little cover in that place. There was one easy route of access along a ridge that ran to the northwest. If they tried to escape that way, they would be exposed for quite some distance. Otherwise, the only access to their position was up or down the rock-slide.

Vigheran roughly grabbed him by the back of the collar and wrenched him into a sitting position. Feeling exposed, Torrin lifted his shield. He was nudged closer and closer to the edge. Then he heard the sound of wood stretching and bending, right beside his ear.

Then he understood. Vigheran was using him and his shield for cover. He lifted the buckler a little more, to give the maximum protection.

Both his companions loosed arrows in quick succession. Vigheran's gave the sharp sound of wood flexing as it fired, but Erelin's bow was almost silent. Torrin could barely hear what sounded like a hollow horn of bone being knocked. Both reloaded, both flexed their bows, and waited. Torrin sweated. Minutes passed by.

The impact of an arrow felt similar to someone kicking his shield. Torrin fell backwards. Both bows fired again. A raging stream of Zindori curses erupted from below. He ran his left hand, still holding the knife, along the outside of the shield as he lay. An arrow was lodged into the upper right.

"Up!" Vigheran hissed. He resumed his position. "Watch." The Zindori's monosyllabic orders gave Torrin little in the way of details.

Torrin adjusted his position somewhat and gave Vigheran another angle to fire from. His heart beat rapidly. Were they in trouble? If this was the group of Raiders that had been following them, there would be four enemies. Even counting Torrin, that meant they were outnumbered. More seconds passed by. Torrin could almost feel the tension in Vigheran's bow, inches away from his right ear. The shouting below had not stopped. Rocks were hitting rocks. They were coming up! Why didn't Vigheran have a bead on them?

I may be maimed but I'm not useless, he kept telling himself. *I've been in combat before. I've trained my senses and reflexes. How can I help my allies?*

Two more arrows hit nearby, one striking rock and the other deflecting off the top of Torrin's shield, narrowly missing his head and sending splinters into his face. Vigheran fired. Erelin did not. Torrin's breath came in ragged spurts. More noise from below. He could not see anything down there. He glanced along the ridge, then did a double-take. He had time to shout a warning to his companions as two figures sprang out from behind a rock. The enemies covered the remaining distance in two strides, leaping the last interval with blades flashing.

Torrin met one with his shield, matching the movements of the blade with his right arm. A blow hit his buckler, driving him off his feet onto his back. He swung his knife in a futile gesture as he fell. It sliced through air.

Erelin's bow sounded, its hollow-horn tone registering distinctly in Torrin's ears. Steel clashed. Vigheran shouted. A boot planted near Torrin's hip. He wrapped his good arm around the leg, trying to do anything, anything at all, to help his companions. Vigheran snarled in pain. Sounds of something ripping came from above

Torrin, and the foot was wrenched from his grasp. The noise of rocks clattering and falling reached his ears. He struggled to get up.

He was on his hands and knees. He could now see Vigheran lean over the edge, fist clenched, no weapon in his hand. A loud click came from his arm, followed by the sound of a dart ripping through the air. Another cry of pain came from below. Vigheran recoiled as a scimitar just missed him, striking the rocks beside him. The blade raked across the front of his body as the Zindori flung himself backwards.

Torrin spied the shape of the Raider attacking from just below the ledge. He lunged with his feet and stabbed with his left hand. His feet gave way under him as he stepped on loose rocks. The knife in his hand was nearly wrenched from his grasp. His adversary lost his balance and toppled backwards down the rockslide. If it wasn't for Erelin's hand grasping his tunic, Torrin would have followed to the bottom.

Erelin pointed him along the ridge from where the first Raiders had attacked. Vigheran was already limping his way across, hunched over. Erelin brought up the rear. His bow was still flexed, and he scanned the rocks below. After eighty agonizing paces in the open, they were finally able to climb over some broken rocks. Another rockslide opened up before them, but this was going in the other direction. Gratefully, Torrin slid down it quickly. Anything to put distance between himself and their murderous pursuers.

At the bottom, Erelin suddenly left them and disappeared in the darkness. "We wait," Vigheran said softly.

Torrin could barely see a thing. He could hear Vigheran's rasping breathing beside him. His first thought was to check himself for injuries. Everything had happened so quickly, it was possible that he could be bleeding and hadn't felt it yet.

He undid the straps of the shield. Part of it was dangling already, a chunk torn off by the scimitar blow he had blocked. He tossed it aside. He felt his head, his right arm, his torso, his legs. All seemed in order. He had bruises on his right arm and a stubbed toe, that was all.

"Vigheran, are you hurt?" he asked. He received only a grunt in response. That did not sound promising.

It did not take long for Erelin to return. He had a satchel and canteen that Vigheran had left behind, and Torrin's bedroll. Erelin handed the canteen to Torrin, then took a brief pause beside Vigheran; Torrin guessed he was checking for injuries. Vigheran gave a few words in Zindori and then cursed in pain. Erelin began to hand more equipment over, including one of Vigheran's swords. Erelin's boot-knife was taken back.

"Distance," was the only word the Zindori uttered in River-Tongue.

They began to move again, Erelin in the lead. Torrin was carrying all of his equipment again, plus the extras that had been handed to him. He hoped they didn't have to travel far. In the dark night with little illumination, it was difficult going. He skinned his shins as he stumbled.

After two hours of tough going, Vigheran told Torrin to wait again. Erelin scouted forwards and then came back. He led the three through a grove of scrub trees, and to a rock overhang on the other side. Torrin could hear water trickling, but he didn't see any flow. In less than a minute, Erelin had a tiny blaze going and was building it into a fire.

Torrin noticed that someone had camped there before. Erelin had lit the fire in an existing firepit that had ashes in it. A small pile of branches was nearby for firewood. It was not ideal to camp in a place in which the previous inhabitants may return, but at least the firelight would not easily be seen.

Vigheran was unstrapping his armour. He had splashes of blood all over himself, but it was most obvious in the dripping coming from his left arm. Erelin, too, was stained in several places but it was hard to tell what was a wound, and what was the blood of their enemies. Gingerly, Vigheran rolled up his sleeve to reveal a nasty gash just above the elbow. Erelin set to work on it immediately.

Torrin expected Vigheran to be upset over their narrow scrape and his injury. Instead, he seemed almost exhilarated. He said some words to Erelin as the wound was being tended, and then turned his head to Torrin.

"You hit one, *kyusi?*" Torrin wasn't sure if it was a question or statement.

"I'm not sure," Torrin answered. "I think I knocked him down, that's all."

"Two are badly hurt. Maybe dead. They will not pursue."

Torrin was relieved. "You are *zylun*, Vigheran," he remembered the Zindori word for strong.

Vigheran flashed his teeth.

They didn't stay there long. The sky cleared and the sliver of moon rose into the south sky. It was bright enough to move on. It wouldn't be long until morning anyway.

Vigheran had suffered some damage to his equipment during the fight. His leather chest armour had a cut across the front. Some straps and belts had been severed. One of the pieces that protected his shoulder was bent at an angle; with a few deft movements Erelin wrenched it off and stored it for later repair.

Erelin, for the most part, seemed unhurt. Torrin suspected that there might be an injury to his right arm, as he favored it and kept it bent beneath his cloak as he walked. There was a long tear in his wolf-skin cloak.

As the sun came up, they stopped for a little more food without a fire. Torrin didn't like to stop while it was still so cold out. He shivered uncontrollably as he sat.

"Not traveling all day," Vigheran assured him. "We will be safe tonight." The sound of a safe night's sleep was music to Torrin's ears. It had been twenty-six days since the last time he had slept soundly in Braedil's house. The memory again brought the sorrow of his loss to the forefront.

The landscape had begun to change again. The rocky crags and cliffs gave way to rolling hills and grasslands. This allowed them to make very good time. A low series of hills on their left, to the southwest, caught Torrin's attention because it had horizontal black streaks across the rock formations. He was also beginning to connect the landscape with the vision that the Gryphon had given him. He resolved to ask Erelin about it later.

Coming over a hill, Torrin was surprised to find several cows grazing in a green patch near an isolated wetland. He wondered for a moment if these cows had escaped, but then recalled that the Belorin of that area kept wide, unfenced ranches and let their cattle roam free. His stomach rumbled. If Vigheran had turned aside and slaughtered one of the cows for their meal, he would not have complained.

But they went on. Erelin checked the sky often, which was clear in all areas except for an ominous thundercloud to the north. As the day went on, the sun became uncomfortably hot. Both Vigheran and Torrin shed most of their clothing, but Erelin continued as he was. Vigheran tied a cloth to his head. Torrin wondered if that would be a good idea; his fur cap would be too warm but it also wasn't healthy to have the sun beating on his head. Just to think, that very morning he had been struggling to keep warm.

They stopped often for rests. Torrin's stubbed toe throbbed, but otherwise he was comfortable with the pace they were setting. He guessed Vigheran was weakened from blood loss.

It was mid-afternoon when they came to a small settlement. The black-striped hills were now to the southeast. The settlement was made entirely of mud huts. Torrin saw a well in the middle. There was no inn in sight.

As they entered, Torrin was surprised to see that there were very few Belorin there. Most were of the Zindori race. Yet they were quite different from the Roj, in that they were short and squat. He recognized them as the Pej Zindori. They had not been blessed with the physique of powerful warriors, but they were some of the hardiest pioneers and farmers of the ancient world. They were oppressed and relocated by many peoples, especially the Roj Zindori. Some lived as far north as Arghand and Lyssia, but the only region in which they were a majority was the southernmost steppes of Belorin.

Vigheran walked through the village and stopped at a house at the edge of the settlement. Instead of knocking, he shouted a two-syllable word in Zindori. A deadbolt was drawn back, and the door was opened. The weathered face of an old Pej woman peered out.

After a short conversation with Vigheran, which included a question directed at Torrin, she held out her hand. Vigheran placed two Corsavan silver pieces in it. She drew back the door and let them in.

It was a modest dwelling, but after being on the road for almost four weeks it was as good as a comfortable inn to Torrin. The hut was one room. Two beds in the back were nothing more than raised dirt platforms with boards on top. A charcoal fire was smouldering despite the heat. Torrin ignored the flies as he breathed in an aroma that he had not smelled before.

The woman's son also lived there; both his legs were missing from the knee down. He looked at the stump of Torrin's right forearm and gave a nod of understanding. He was sitting in front of a contraption that Torrin recognized as a crude loom. He was weaving a horse blanket from black and brown yarns.

Without asking for permission, Torrin deposited his gear on the floor and sat down on a chair that was beside a low table. A chair! To sit on an object made for a human! He told himself that he would never take for granted the simple pleasures of life.

They had little to do for the rest of the afternoon and evening, but that was all right with Torrin. He was happy to be off his feet. He wrote a long-overdue petition and threw it into the cooking fire when the woman wasn't looking. Vigheran had sat down with a bucket of water near the doorway and washed the blood and grime from his body. Torrin reminded himself that he should do that tonight. Erelin had left the house for some errand.

Two hours after they had arrived, they sat down to some lentil stew and fresh black bread. Torrin had never eaten so much in his life. It had been three days since hot foot had filled his belly, and almost a month since he ate bread that wasn't the dry, hard-crusted trail variety. The woman offered him a cup of warm milk which he accepted gratefully. He didn't care what animal it came from.

After dinner, the woman cleared the clay dishes from the table. Vigheran took his leave to do some errands. Erelin was about to get up from his stool when Torrin put a hand on his arm. He took out his verse papers and pencil. Erelin sat back down.

Torrin was confident that the woman couldn't understand

Melandarim, so he spoke in that language.

"We are at some distance from the woman in my dream," he said. It wasn't possible to ask direct questions in Melandarim, only to present incomplete phrases.

Very close, Erelin wrote. *In two nights I will go. I will be back by morning.* Torrin guessed that Erelin was planning to go check on the woman. He felt relieved. He had never met the woman but felt a certain degree of responsibility to keep her from harm. He changed the subject. "The four Roj were after something," he said, referring to the Raiders.

Erelin took the pencil and wrote. *Mercenaries. Money.*

"We don't have money. Vigheran spoke with them earlier as friends."

Not friends. Erelin tapped the pencil on the table for a bit as if considering what to write.

The Roj must not hear. Torrin nodded. His blood ran cold when he saw what Erelin wrote next. *Money for your head.*

His thoughts returned to Braedil and his wild theory that the House of Atlan was being exterminated. That did not make sense. Who would profit from the removal of one of the ancient houses when Karolia had many stronger houses that were more of a threat? He finally said in a weak voice, "No-one would pay money for me."

Erelin underlined his last statement as if to emphasize it. Torrin's mind raced. So those Raiders were after him all along! He had recalled them looking at him intently as they finished their initial exchange with Vigheran. They were identifying him!

Another past event fell into place for Torrin. Erelin had asked him to tell Vigheran about rich relatives in Ancharith shortly after the encounter with the Raiders. Was that to convince him that it was more valuable to keep Torrin alive than to turn him over to the Raiders?

"Nothing will prevent Vigheran from turning me over at Dharbur for money," he said.

Erelin wrote, *I will protect you.*

"I don't understand why you do that."

He was mystified when Erelin tapped the verse papers with the pencil, then wrote, *Because you protect me.*

Erelin got up and threw the two verse papers they had used into the cooking fire.

CHAPTER 19:
THE BATTLE ON THE CLIFFS

The Thunya was a canyon through which the Kullion River flowed on its way to the Sea-Lake of Cith. It was uncrossable all the way from the Arghand Marshes to the river mouth, save the bridge at Keor. This ancient structure, made of huge slabs of stone, was still standing after millenia of commerce and conflict.

The Vekh of Anduk, after ravaging the land of Azenvar last summer, had pushed across the bridge and into sparsely populated Narval. The Karolian Eastern Army, allied with the Lyssian Militia and a small number of Belorin mercenaries, were pushing them back. There was no saving Azenvar. That ancient realm was done for good.

It was during the reign of Talidon, about seventy years ago, that Karolia had sponsored an attempt to revive the kingdom of Azenvar. The ruins of Keor were colonized, in addition to fortified towns in the Irbon Valley and in Haned. Karolia was overjoyed at the news that Dar-Amund remained unconquered and would continue to guard the eastern flank.

But the dark fortress of Delvaeth still brooded on a spur of rock overshadowing the Istrith River. In years gone by, Delvaeth had been put to siege many times, but had never been entered by any man who lived to tell of it. Delvaeth and Dar-Amund had continued on as the two polarized beacons of good and evil in the land.

With the rise to power of Anduk, and the alliance of both Vekh nations of Kardumagund and Omrid under its Emperor Zered, the Vekh overran Azenvar over the past two years. Rumors persisted that even Dar-Amund had fallen, which many saw as an ill omen.

Dyrk understood that the overall objective of the war was to contain the Vekh within Azenvar. Karolian naval superiority would take care of the rest, asphyxiating the movement of supplies and troops over the Sea-Lake of Cith and the Istrith River.

The thirty-ninth cavalry regiment had arrived on Anakdatar, fifth week of Kemantar's month[1]. They camped with two other Karolian cavalry regiments that had already completed their sweep to the south of the line Dyrk's regiment had taken. Dyrk stayed with the men to set up camp while Bayern went to find their divisional command tent to secure a standard. The division was led by an Eratur with the rank of Comentus, or Captain. Bayern had the rank of Prium, which translates to First Officer or Lieutenant. That meant he would not normally be in charge of anything more than a regiment. It was the minimum rank for any Eratur that was joined to the army. Professional soldiers who were eligible citizens could also ascend to the rank of Prium through reliable service and exceptional leadership.

In Bayern's tent the next morning, they discussed the situation. They had been joined to the Sixth Division of the East Army, part of Battle Group Rudin, which was the north front. The Battle Group now had two full brigades of medium cavalry, each with four regiments, or ninety-six men.

The Vekh armies were hemmed into a semi-circle, about a half-league in diameter, around the bridge. They were retreating forces over it, day and night. Bayern suspected that tomorrow there would be a push to encircle as much of the remaining Vekh army as possible, and to eventually destroy or capture the forces caught within.

"I hate to get ahead of myself, but this has the makings of a glorious victory, son of Teren," Bayern said as they reviewed their tactics. They knew their standard formations well, but there was now the added complication of fighting alongside footmen and other cavalry. This presented a far narrower corridor for escape and necessitated tighter formations. "We'll need to practice these formations this afternoon," Dyrk said. "We haven't tried them since

---

[1] January 20, 2798

training – the boys may be a bit off."

"We won't be put into a frontal assault against entrenched positions," Bayern said as he turned the map towards the sunlight coming through the flap of the tent. The map was a hasty hand-copied facsimile that Bayern brought with him from the commanding officer's tent. "If all goes well, we won't see anything but the backs of the enemy."

"They must have set up some positions," Dyrk pointed out. "The East Army would have overrun them immediately if they hadn't."

Bayern pointed to some marks on the map. "They have the high ground here, here, and here. Yes, they have set up trenches and stakes. They have light archers, few heavy crossbows. Some halberdiers and light cavalry have been seen. It looks like they were prepared for Lyssian militiamen, and then the big boys showed up."

Dyrk was uneasy. It was never wise to underestimate an enemy. "Their horsemen would be the first to cross over if they were abandoning their positions. I'm worried that they are better prepared for us than we think."

"That may be," Bayern didn't sound convinced. "Our Army Group is, as we speak, penetrating along the cliffs towards the bridge. We will get up at third watch, proceed along today's path, and once we are at the front, continue the advance right at daybreak."

"What's our support?"

Bayern looked smug. "We have four brigades of heavy infantry, another of light. The heavies will alternate providing fire support and advancing. We will also have eyes in the sky."

"What will be protecting our flank?"

Bayern blew air through his teeth. "That's the tough part. We'll be strung out a great distance and open to a flank attack. I'm sure they will leave a heavy on a ridge at some point that should give us some protection. However, let's remember that we want them to attack us. They'll need to pull back units from their entrenched positions which is our primary objective."

"So we're bait."

"Yes. We are. Another glorious day in the Karolian army. Now, keep in mind that we won't have our exact orders until we are ready to ride tomorrow."

"How are they not expecting us?"

Bayern rolled up the map. "They are. They just can't do much to stop us. Have you ever seen a full brigade of cavalry in action, Dyrk?"

"Not beyond a parade ground, and I bet you haven't either."

"It's a fearsome thing," Bayern was used to ignoring Dyrk's barbs. "Ninety-six *almathin*, in multiple spearhead formations. A sea of lances and a wall of impenetrable steel. Unstoppable. The army group has already advanced two league-tenths[1] and they've barely suffered a scratch."

"But now they know we're coming."

Bayern slapped his shoulder. "You have got to be the most dour and pessimistic regiment master I've ever had."

"Thank you. Pessimism keeps men alive, or so I've been told," Dyrk allowed himself a smile. "We're leaving the baggage behind?"

"Yes, they will be absorbed into the Sixth Division's baggage. Tell the men to store all personal items in Gimmil's bags. That's the black mule, right?"

"Yes it is."

"Then let's get an early sleep. We're up in the middle of the night."

Marching while it was still dark was unnerving. Add to that the fact that they were advancing through hostile and unknown territory, and it was terrifying to soldiers who were not battle-hardened. *If I'm feeling this tense,* he thought, *what might the service recruits be feeling?*

The regiment had gotten up at the start of the third watch, six hours before daybreak. Preparation was laborious, considering they had to equip the full armour kit on their horses. Visors were fixed. New shields had been acquired, kite-shaped, to replace their small round bucklers.

The orders came in. Their regiment would be joined with another

---

[1] Two league-tenths is about 5 kilometers or 3.5 miles

new regiment, and two existing professional regiments, to form the brigade. Dyrk was glad for that. The professionals would make their job much easier. Just do what they do.

Theirs would be the first brigade to sortie at daybreak. Dyrk did not like the sound of that – defenders would have guessed the path that they would be taking the next day and would have something nasty prepared. The one advantage on his side was the eye in the sky.

Reconnaissance tarn-riders were immensely valuable but not particularly reliable. The tarns did not like to circle endlessly over a small area and would take off from time to time. They also couldn't stay aloft for more than a few hours. Despite the unreliability, their aerial scouts provided a significant advantage as they could discover Vekh hidden in the path of an advance, or enemy units moving up for a flank attack. That could save many lives.

The breath of the horses created dense clouds as they formed up in the cool night air. Once their groups formed up, they dismounted to wait for the call to move out. Their boots sank into an inch of mud. There was no snow on the ground, but some had drifted up against rocks and hillocks. The melt created a mire wherever there was soft ground.

Dyrk checked his equipment. He was using the sword he had taken from his parent's house. It was nearly the same dimensions as the regulation blade. He had used it through the training, and it seemed to balance very well. Better, in fact, than his own sword. All it needed was a little sharpening. The telltale crosspiece identified it as his sword moreso than the twin red strips around the hilt.

The soldiers milled about, giving some last-bit grooming to their horses and final encouragement to their mates. Tension was thick in the air. They had all written their letters last night in case of casualties. Now was the infernal wait for the order to move out.

This is not where I want to be, Dyrk thought. It's contrary to every survival instinct to put one's self into danger. But this needed to be done. They had prepared for this for all their lives. They were getting impatient to get this over with. All this standing around was the toughest part.

Finally, mercifully, the order came. Dyrk repeated the order, and the regiment mounted. There was little moonlight as the sky was overcast. It would not be a good idea to light torches to lead the way, so every rider followed the rump of the horse ahead, all moving in a twin line after Bayern and Deman, his standard-bearer.

They moved at a slow walk. Some light infantry were ahead of them, and ranks of heavy infantry were behind. The "heavies" were well-armoured, with plate breastpieces, full-length chain hauberks, and scaled greaves. The front two rows carried their pikes on their shoulders and their shields at their sides. The back row lugged the heavy arbalests.

Dyrk felt bad for the light infantry. They were swordsmen and mace-men, all of whom wore less armour than the heavies. They were the ones out in front, in loose formation, blazing the trail for the advance. The ground they were covering had been won yesterday in a coordinated assault. The soldiers who made the assault had already been replaced by the night-watch troops. Dyrk's battlegroup was headed to relieve the night-watch and continue the advance. Fresh troops were deadly troops. Tired troops were dead.

They passed through some rough terrain. They were keeping close to the edge of the cliffs on their left. Those cliffs plummeted over a hundred paces down to the Kullion River below. Over each ridge, Dyrk awaited the sound of the light infantry engaging an unseen enemy. Nothing came. A heap of rock loomed on his right. Only when he was right next to it did he hear the buzzing of flies and realized that it was a pile of Vekh bodies and equipment, awaiting burial or the torch. His breakfast wasn't sitting well.

Shapes moved on a hillside to his right. The cliffs were on his left, so he figured that any attack would come from the right. He nervously gripped his spear, held in the upright position as the cavalry slowly marched on. What was out there? He dutifully followed Bayern's lead which did not break formation. A few soldiers started to whisper uneasily to each other. They had seen it too.

Dyrk whispered an order of silence. The chatter stopped. As they got closer, a salute came from a few of the shapes. It was their own men, a regiment of heavy infantry night-guarding on the hill. For the first time, Dyrk realized how easy it was for jumpy soldiers to mistake their own men for the enemy.

War-horses were trained to be as quiet as possible when not in danger. It was eerie to be part of a group of a hundred well-armoured mounted warriors, and the only sounds were a faint jingle of equipment and the continuous footfalls of hundreds of hooves on rock and earth. The heavies behind them made just as much noise with their clattering pikes and clanking armour.

The skies were beginning to brighten in the east. Still no engagement. Dyrk was breathing a sigh of relief. It would not be good for a green regiment to have its first taste of pitched battle in the dark.

A shout came from ahead. Sounds of steel on steel. Every rider tensed. Bayern held up the sign to hold. Dyrk repeated the sign, and so did Gadril and Ambold, the squadron leaders. They waited. The mounted regiment to their left, led by the division commander, moved forward cautiously. The division commander held the rank of Comentus; he was in charge of the advance. They stood on the next ridge but did not engage. The sounds stopped. The Comentus's messenger rode back and relayed a message to each regiment leader. Dyrk's regiment was ordered to hold. The heavy infantry right behind them began to move up the ridge to their right.

Dyrk understood the situation. They were likely being hit by skirmishers, lightly armoured Vekh who would fling spears, shoot arrows, sling stones, and disappear into the darkness. It would be unwise to pursue them with mounted troops in the dark. It was also important to keep their force concealed as best as possible. The light troops would have to take care of things on their own.

Finally, the order was given to move out again. Horses stamped, equipment clinked, and the column was set in motion. As they came over the ridge, Dyrk's line passed right by two Karolian swordsmen. The first was on the ground, motionless, unsheathed blade lying to one side. His shield had been placed under his head. The second, who couldn't have been much older than twenty, was hunched over him, calling his name over and over with no answer. The column marched on, and the darkness swallowed up the tragic scene.

The sun was now peeking over the horizon. Dyrk scanned the skies, searching for the help that was promised. Nothing beyond flocks of ravens looking for a meal. He hadn't put his visor down yet. No sense suffocating and blinding himself until the arrows started to fly.

He was surprised to look to his left and see, past other cavalry, rows of helmets, pikes, and smiling faces. They were passing another regiment of night-guard. Their task was done; within a few hours they would be getting some much-needed shut-eye. Heard above the din of horses plodding: "Push 'em into the river, boys."

Dyrk had not expected such an important battle to involve so much tense waiting, so much nervous watching, and so little fighting.

Dyrk had gone over the strategy with Gadril, who had been part of a similar formation before. The cavalry would race in front for about fifteen hundred paces, pierce through any entrenched units, and clear out any skirmishers. They would then be followed up by the heavy infantry. Flank attacks would be dealt with by supporting cavalry, who would then take the next sprint while the first regiments rested and guarded the flank. It was dangerous work for the lead cavalry, but it ensured a rapid advance of the troops and prevented any attempts by the retreating enemy to dig into new positions or solidify into formations.

Dyrk reflexively reset his grip on his lance, yet again. The final row of the night-watch came into view. About a hundred paces away, a small hillock ran across their view, with several thickets and bushes across it. A screech was heard overhead. Their long-awaited tarn swooped into view. Something was dropped, fluttering to the ground in a display of bright colour. On cue, the sound of the release of thirty heavy crossbows echoed from behind. Dyrk heard the whizzing of the quarrels flying a short distance above his head. Uncomfortably close. The bushes rippled and tore. Dyrk knew what it meant – enemies were sighted just over the next rise.

Bayern signaled a line formation. Visors were dropped. The regiments on either side were quickly moving up into their lines. Dyrk spurred Tanakh forward and fell in off Bayern's right. Gadril went left. They formed a row, sixteen across, and broke into a canter.

The remainder followed behind with Ambold. Another volley of quarrels whizzed by. As much as Dyrk was gritting his teeth, bracing for danger, he was happier to be on a horse and part of the charge, rather than facing it.

Fifty paces before the hillock Dyrk began to hear the impacts of small objects on armour. One rider cried out in pain. Dyrk didn't see it, but he knew that they were being shot at. Nobody within his field of vision fell out of line. The pace of the horses quickened.

Up the hillock Tanakh went, hooves churning, muscles flexing in the effort to ascend quickly. Several spears were raised from the bushes, a ragged and futile effort to stop the cavalry charge. Many of the enemy were already fleeing. A spear was hoisted up just on Dyrk's right. Emgaer, directly on Dyrk's right flank, fell out of line to avoid it. Dyrk stiffened his hips in the saddle, communicating to Tanakh to hold up. The mount tossed his head as Dyrk shifted his grip on his spear to an overhand hold. All he saw through the holes in his visor was a brief movement within a knee-high trench that had been cut into the backside of the hillock. He thrust downwards with his lance. Once, twice. Both times he hit gravelly soil. Tanakh shifted sideways. More movement. Thrust again, and again. The urgency increased - the enemy's spear could not be brought around on himself or his mount. Most of the rest of the line moved past. He was dimly aware that Emgaer was on the other side of the hole in which Dyrk was hewing with his lance, aiming a light crossbow across his body. The crossbow fired.

Keeping his wits about him, he knew he had to form up. The footmen were close behind, shouting as they ran. They would mop up. Dyrk spurred Tanakh with his feet into a dead run. Emgaer followed suit.

The gap in the lines had been filled by Ambold's trailing horsemen. Dyrk caught up and fell in where the trailing group would have been. Emgaer joined him, breathless. He wasn't giving victory shouts anymore. Saliva dripped from the mouth of his horse. Dyrk gave himself a chance to fill his lungs with oxygen. He shifted his grip on his lance back to the forward position. He could see that about a third of the eight-inch iron blade was broken off. Blood dripped from the jagged end.

The line continued on at a measured pace. Dyrk scanned the bushes and ridges carefully, as best he could through the holes in his visor. His shield he kept in front of him. The plates on Tanakh's head bobbed up and down. A cry came from his right, together with several sounds, like pebbles striking steel. "Arrows!" someone shouted. Dyrk raised the shield, across his body as far as it could go. How he wished he was left-handed! A rider fell out of formation just ahead of him, the mount reacting in pain. *Maintain the line*, the concept was being repeated over and over in his head. He spurred Tanakh ahead to fill the gap.

Whoever was shooting, they were not his target. Thankfully, the missiles had stopped coming.

It seemed they were headed for a gully of crumbled rock, what was likely a dry stream bed that spilled into the river far below. That gully could be hiding a hundred pikemen, Dyrk thought to himself. That was his responsibility, not the skirmishers to his right. The line moved on.

The gully was empty. Bayern held up his sword, reversed formation, and the regiment began to head back at a slower pace. Standing stock-still in the open was a good way to lose a cavalry regiment. Bayern never used a lance. His arms had to be free to give signals and orders.

"Ambold, see if they need aid," Bayern pointed his sword to his left, up the escarpment from which the arrows had come. An entire regiment had gone after them. Ambold and five others were only halfway up when the other regiment appeared over the rise. They had broken off pursuit.

Dyrk hurriedly checked through his five men. Emgaer was winded but all right. An arrow had deflected off the nose-armour of Rethen's horse, startling it. The mount was wide-eyed and stressed. The other three had kept the line and were in good shape.

Those enemy skirmishers could return at any moment. Everyone nervously scanned the ridge just to their left. A few reloaded crossbows with levers.

The heavy footmen were now visible. The other cavalry brigade was making their way along the top of the embankment to Dyrk's left. It would be their turn next to lead the advance. Now would be an opportunity to give the horses a breather, though most were barely winded. Dyrk looked overhead. No sight of the tarn.

Dyrk's regiment gathered at the foot of the embankment. The footmen marched by. Many of the horsemen dismounted for a quick breather. The remainder nervously fingered their weapons. The tarn had still not returned.

Naethin showed off the arrow that was embedded in his shield. Another reservist had been hit in the helm by a thrown weapon; he was not injured but the impact had stunned him and caused him to fall out of line. So far, no serious problems, Dyrk thought. Time to mount up. Those skirmishers were out there somewhere, and now it was their turn to screen the footmen.

Bayern led the way up the embankment. It was not a high ridge, and they did not have a great view from it. Higher hills raised in the near distance, blocking their terrain behind from their view. Dyrk despaired when he saw how many hiding places there were.

Over the next thousand paces, they were assailed twice by arrows and rocks. Some riders exchanged fire with their crossbows. No one was hit on either side, and the cavalry restrained itself from chasing after them. All the while, the comforting sound of the footmen marching nearby assured them that they were making progress and achieving their goal.

They switched again with the other brigade, charging out in front. This time was far less eventful than the first. They saw or heard nothing ahead of them, but the flanking cavalry continued to be harassed. They would have one more turn as the flankers before they would be done for the day, Dyrk figured. Man and beast were tired, both by the marching and by the tension.

They formed up on the flank once again. The sun was past mid-morning, as far as Dyrk could determine in the cloudy sky. He opened his visor for a bit of fresh air.

The tarn swooped low overhead. Another marker fell, now only a hundred paces to their right. The skirmishers have been spotted. This was their chance! Bayern motioned with his sword to spread their formation, and the regiment broke off the flank and headed into the heath. Dyrk could already see figures running away. They had the enemy on the run! He remembered his visor and clamped it shut.

It was not easy to proceed over the broken ground, rocky gullies, and hilltops. Over every rise, Dyrk gripped his shield and braced for impact. Cries of pain came from his right. All he could think of was to eliminate these harassers who had caused them so much grief for the past few hours. Each rider was spurred on by his fellow soldier to continue the chase.

Dyrk rode over a rise and saw at the top of the next embankment a lone Vekh, his sling swinging in circles above his head. The skirmisher launched the missile and turned to flee. Dyrk tried to climb the embankment after him but Tanakh stumbled. Another rider rode across the top from his left and disappeared from view. As Dyrk slowly navigated Tanakh up the embankment, he heard a cry of pain that was suddenly cut short.

"A little more, Tanakh, we're nearly done," Dyrk encouraged, seeing that the horse was labouring as they climbed the rise. More hooves thundered by. There was no formation anymore, just a haphazard melee as the cavalry chased down the skirmishers.

Once he was at the top of the embankment, Dyrk looked around and spotted Bayern with many others disappear down a deep gully. They were getting dangerously far from the footmen. Dyrk spurred Tanakh after them. Many more followed on either side and behind.

He came into the gully to see Bayern and four others at a stop, fighting furiously with several Vekh that they had pinned against a rock wall. Before Dyrk could help it was over. Bayern stabbed his sword down into a twitching Vekh body for good measure. Dyrk stopped near the entrance to the gully and lifted his visor.

This was the first time he got a good look at the skirmishers. The dead Vekh were lightly armed with bows and slings. They wore light armour made of leather with steel rings embedded. Their entire outfit was all in a dun colour, which blended well with the surrounding terrain. The cavalry had been assailed by throwing spears as well, but Dyrk did not see any there.

Bayern was steering his horse further into the gully, searching among the broken rocks for more enemies that may have hidden. Most of the regiment had followed. Dyrk had stayed at the entrance of the ravine "It isn't safe here!" Dyrk shouted.

The tarn screeched above them. All looked up. Another marker was loosed. Dyrk had only a moment to realize – the marker was headed straight for them!

He pulled up his broken lance and dug his spurs into Tanakh to get his mount moving. He looked ahead and was frozen for a split second as he beheld the sickening sight of Bayern's lifeless, headless body falling listlessly in the saddle, blood pouring over the war-horse's flank. Men carrying poleaxes and halberds surged across the ground around Bayern's horse. Others sprang from the lip of the gully on top of Dyrk. Horses screamed, men cried out. Dyrk was caught between joining his mates in the gully and fleeing for his life. He was surrounded on both sides before he could react. A poleaxe swung into his view from his left. The shield was torn from his hands, and it felt like his left arm had been crushed. Tanakh pitched upwards and then to the left. Dyrk lost his grip on the lance. His visor clamped down of its own accord, from the sudden movement. He reached across his body for his sword, but Tanakh pitched again, this time to the right. Dyrk was dimly aware of a footman to his right that was thrown off-balance by Tanakh's movement. Something hit him in the lower back. Whatever it was, it was lodged into his armour and was yanking him to the right.

Dyrk's sword was finally unsheathed with a ring. *Ride, Tanakh! Get going or we're dead!* He ducked low over the saddle as another halberd slashed dangerously near. He swung blindly with his sword. It connected with metal. Tanakh reared again, shifting to the right. Shouts and snarls of Vekh came from either side. Dyrk saw a flash of steel to his left. He stabbed with the sword in that direction, cutting through air.

Tanakh took two, long loping strides forward, away from his immediate assailants. But something was very wrong. Dyrk gripped his sword as the horse began to collapse. One more wild swing to his right bit through a wooden haft and connected with something solid. He spared only a thought for Nedrin that the Servant might save him in his last moment. Tanakh tumbled onto his left side. The rocky ground rushed up to Dyrk, and the impact of it on his helmet knocked him senseless.

Ears ringing, he picked up his head. He seemed to be in a different world, one in which everything was moving slowly and deliberately, where the sounds around him were dulled by an intense thundering in his ears. He was dimly aware that he was unable to get up, his left leg pinned under something immovable. He could see figures moving around through the haze. They were on foot, wielding long, wicked-looking pikes with a steel bill on the backside, with which to unhorse cavalry. One was standing above Lohann. The young man had lost his helm and was covered in blood, lying beside his dying horse. He held up his hands in a futile attempt to stop the cruel point of the halberd that sped towards his chest and ended his life.

Dyrk closed his eyes and retreated into merciful blackness. He could feel very little of his own body. He did not try to get up. *Taephin, care for Neriah*, he prayed. *Console her in her grief.*

Footsteps thudded close to him. He squeezed his eyes. It barely registered on him that the footfalls were made by hooves, not feet. More shouting. Dyrk did not want to open his eyes and witness more death, more killing. Even with his eyes shut, the vision of Lohann, helplessly holding up his bloodied hands, replayed over and over.

Something tapped the armour on his back. Clear as day, cutting through his consciousness, he heard the voice of Naethin in a strangled cry. "No. Looks like those bastards got them all."

Dyrk's eyes snapped open and he gasped a ragged breath. His lungs filled with air. Pain shot first up his torso, then he could feel the fire coursing down both his leg and his left arm.

"Wait! Live one here!"

Dyrk watched, helpless, as two of his comrades got on foot and put their shoulders to the motionless bulk of Tanakh. He felt blood rushing into tingling flesh as his left leg was freed. He began to cough, uncontrollably. An acrid taste was in his mouth.

The two men helping him were arguing. Dyrk could tell urgency in their voices. "I can ride," he tried to assure them numbly.

"By Nedrin, we've got to get out of here, Naethin!" Deriav's panicked voice came from near Dyrk's ear.

Dyrk tried to stand. His legs were like rubber. His left leg refused to respond. He fell over.

Another voice, distant, hollered something undecipherable.

"One, two, three, hoist!" Naethin shouted. Dyrk was being carried through the air, and then unceremoniously dumped on his stomach across a horse which sidestepped in dismay at the burden.

"Go! Go!"

The bumps from the movement of the horse began to jolt him, sending shooting pain up his limbs again. His head was hurting from the blood rushing to it. He began to think, for a second, that he was at the fairgrounds in Doleth Sarin, struggling upon the back of a gargantuan Tevledain warhorse, trying to get into the saddle. One leg over, grab the saddlehorn, other leg in the stirrup – where was the other leg? Brace hands against the withers, sit up.

The breeze on his face felt good. His body naturally timed itself to the rhythm of the walking horse. Feet in the stirrups. Right foot, good. Left foot. Where was his left foot? He could see his foot, but he couldn't move it.

"You are one gutsy steer," he heard a gruff voice below him and to his right. He looked down. Naethin was on foot, leading the horse upon which he was now riding. His comrade was breathing hard, marching as fast as he could in full gear.

"Almost there," Naethin assured. Other mounts were on Dyrk's right and left, but he didn't see who they were.

"Bayern," Dyrk moaned.

"Gone," Naethin grunted between heavy breaths. "I'm in command now."

Dyrk had enough presence of mind to go through the regimental command structure. Naethin in command? What about Ambold? Kethrol? Gadril? Himself? What had happened?

"How many left?" He managed to ask.

"Five. And I'm going to collapse if you don't shut up."

They were now passing through other men. He saw well-armoured foot soldiers, shielded by pavises, heavy crossbows at the ready. They were safe. As safe as they could be well behind enemy lines, that is.

Naethin finally got him off the horse by a low scraggly tree. Dyrk was laid against a shield that was propped up by a rock. He felt parts of his armour being removed. "Quite a hole in your back, but no blood," an unfamiliar voice commented.

"Where's Tenrik?" Dyrk asked for his regiment's medic.

"Dead, I'm guessing. I'm from the twelfth regiment," came the reply. Dyrk looked at the face of a strange man. "Can you feel your legs?"

Dyrk finally took the time to have a good look at his own body. He went over each limb with the man who was helping him. His right arm was fine. His left arm hurt terribly, but he was able to move it. He couldn't grasp anything with his left hand. The left leg was numb. When the medic began to probe at it, he asked, "You got this pinned under your mount?"

"Yes."

He withdrew his hands. "I'm impressed. I can't find anything broken. You're swelling up something awful around your left knee, though. Torn ligaments. Looks like your armour took a blow in the back but it missed you."

Dyrk looked around. Deriav was sitting nearby, helmetless, his head in his hands, making some awful sobbing sounds. Naethin was checking equipment on his horse. Someone else was lying on his back not too far away. The medic that had been helping Dyrk was now splinting that man's leg. Then it began to sink in. His regiment had been decimated. Eighteen men that he had breakfasted with that very morning were now corpses. His horse, who had been his constant friend for five years, was gone. He had a serious knee injury. He wanted to cry like Deriav.

Naethin crouched next to him. "Well, boss," he said. "I may be in charge, but I could use some help. What are we supposed to do now?"

Dyrk tried to refocus his thoughts. He had to concentrate on the here and now, he told himself. "Review with me who we have left."

"Myself, Deriav, and Broedac are still standing, though Deriav is a mess. Broedac lost his mount but took Ambold's. Rethen got thrown by his horse. He has a broken leg and may have broken his back as well, we'll see. We left the bodies out there," he motioned weakly to the west. "They were hacked up pretty bad." He nearly choked up.

Dyrk saw his sword leaning against a rock, in its sheath. He was surprised it had made it back. He remembered unsheathing it and figured he had lost it. "Are you sure the rest are dead?"

Naethin cursed, not at Dyrk, but at their situation. "Yes, I'm sure."

"We can't risk any men to go back for the bodies. We'll make our way back with the troops when they're relieved," he said. "We'll have to report to the Comentus that we lost our Prium, our regiment leader. We'll probably be decommissioned and assigned to new regiments."

Then he noticed blood around Naethin's eye, coming from a small cut just beside the bump on his nose. A bandage was around his leg. "What happened to you?"

"I'll manage."

Dyrk realized that Naethin had put in blood and sweat to get him out of harm's way. "Thanks for getting me out of there."

"Don't thank me yet. We're not out of this."

Dyrk sat in Bayern's tent, making the last entry in the regiment log. His left leg was stretched in front of him, wrapped tight. A cloth bag filled with snow was on his knee to keep the swelling down.

He wrote another line: *Kethrol, son of Jareos, House En-Kulvor, killed in action.* It was emotionally draining, but it had to be done. *Emgaer, son of Emathor, House Tomas, killed in action.* Another mother in grief, a father bereft of the child of his youth. The last one took the most effort. *Lohann, son of Eldann, House Vaneth, killed in action. May Telmanitar bear their souls to heaven.*

His cheeks were wet. It didn't count as crying if he kept doing things while the tears flowed, he figured. He was about to close the book. It seemed so incomplete. Less than a quarter of the pages were filled. He dipped the pen in ink and wrote one more line.

The heroism of Naethin son of Daeron house Kromar should be noted. He saved lives in selfless devotion to his brothers.

He felt like he had not slept during the night. His memories played over and over in his head, not only of the violence, but also of the times he had shared with these men. He wouldn't admit it, but it wasn't the first time he had wept. First thing in the morning, he had written and posted a letter to Neriah. That allowed him to collect his thoughts and gain the courage to write the log.

He pulled himself to a standing position and picked up his crutch. He looked out at the camp. Labourers were taking down many of the tents, salvaging equipment to be used for other soldiers. Bayern's tent would be next. Dyrk was awaiting his next assignment, though he was unsure if they could use him given his injury. A warrior-scribe was striding towards him.

"Dyrk House Teren?" The scribe asked, reading off a slip of paper.

"That's me."

"You are wanted in the Comentus's tent."

"I'll go with you."

Dyrk didn't feel completely immobile. He could put weight on his leg. He figured he could ride, though uncomfortably. But in his current state, he could not fight. He wondered what was in store for him. It was unusual to be summoned to the Comentus's tent just to be reassigned or declared wounded.

Upon arrival, he was told to wait just outside. After an Eratur strode out of the tent, Dyrk was shown in. The tent was, like most Karolian officer's tents, rather bare. It was tall enough for a half-dozen men to stand erect. A table stood in the center on which to spread maps or write notes. A cot and foldable chair were along the back. No commander worth his salt wanted to give the impression that he was living in luxury while his troops slept in mud.

There was only one man in the tent, who was standing at the table. Several lists were spread out in front of him. A map had been turned over so that Dyrk couldn't see it. The scribe had said the officer's rank was a Comentus, or captain, who usually commanded a full division of five hundred soldiers. A Comentus was one rank below an Almentus, who was equivalent to a provincial lord. This man must report directly to Lord Rudin, the Almentus of the northern battle group.

"This is Dyrk, house Teren, the tarn-rider," the scribe said. The way he was introduced gave Dyrk a pretty good indication of what the meeting was about.

"You've had experience riding tarns," the captain said, He had a silver medallion around his neck, his badge of office. Otherwise, he was equipped quite plainly, wearing the cloth under-armour hauberk of a heavy foot soldier. A dark blue cloak with silver trim was around his shoulders.

"That's right, I was a reconnaissance flyer in Dedarrek for ten months."

"I understand you aren't fit for combat duty."

"That's a fair statement, sir."

"Do you think you're fit to ride messenger duty?"

Dyrk thought about it. Being up in the air for hours at a time, without any way to move his leg. It would be painful.

"Glad to hear it, soldier," the Comentus went on without receiving an answer. "The southern messenger has taken ill, and we're quite desperate." Dyrk saw the scribe wince at that remark. Warrior-scribes were not only the recorders of information, they were also the gatekeepers, and they were always cautious to give out any more information than absolutely needed, especially in a war-time situation.

"I'm not confident on my range, sir, but I think I am able to do a short-term flight."

"You'll be doing the southern route," the captain said, expecting Dyrk to know what that meant. Seeing Dyrk's blank look, he added, in a low voice, "Here to Mount Arrasheth, to Holbern, to Ben-Panith, to Dharbur."

Dyrk didn't know some of those names, but he recognized Dharbur. That was almost fifty leagues[1] from there. "Sir, I don't

---

[1] Fifty leagues is about 1300 kilometers or 800 miles

know if…"

"You can navigate by sun and stars?" It was a half-question, half-expectation.

"Of course."

"At Dharbur, you are expected to make your way back to Navren Altyr by whichever route you see best."

His heart leaped. "You mean going home?"

"Yes. You will be decommissioned upon reporting at the Royal Post at Navren Altyr. You will report to Thur Eveth for decommissioning."

The scribe was writing furiously.

"Any questions, son of Teren?"

Dyrk tried to remember all the elements of the comprehensive orders he received when delivering messages in Dedarrek. "Disposition of cargo upon grounding or threat of capture?" he asked.

"Destroyed immediately upon any credible threat."

"Am I to forward messages upon request from the forward destinations?"

"If it does not compromise your primary mission, yes."

Dyrk's head swam. He had a million questions, but he couldn't articulate any of them. "That is all, Comentus."

"Very well. I will leave the two of you to review the route." The Comentus strode out.

Dyrk exhaled deeply. He was back in the saddle. But he was also going home.

CHAPTER 20:
BELORIN

I t was a clear night. Apparently, most nights were clear in this part of Belorin, Dyrk thought. He could get used to the weather, at least in the winter.

He was well-rested. He had arrived in Ben-Panith in the evening two days ago. He spent a full day resting up for the final leg of his journey. It would be the longest, so he was leaving well before sunup. He thought back to the start of his trip, four days ago.

The first part of the journey had been harrowing. Getting on a new tarn is always a life-threatening exercise. This mount was bigger than Saen-Lairos, the tarn he had ridden in Dedarrek. It was stronger and had better endurance, that was obvious. But it also had a predilection for diving and landing wherever it pleased. The two of them spent an hour in the frigid marshes of Arghand, Dyrk unable to dismount because of the waist-deep ice-cold water and thick mud. To make matters worse, the marshes were thick with Vekh armies marching southwest to prepare for a summer campaign against Belorin. Dyrk felt it was only by sheer luck that they were not discovered and ambushed.

He arrived at Mount Arrasheth to find it nearly besieged. It was an old stone fortress that was lately maintained and garrisoned by the Karolian Military. It was used as an eastern foreign outpost, as it was well outside their borders. It lay in the middle of the land of Arghand, a sparsely populated area that was between Belorin and Lyssa but claimed by neither. The military garrison there was well-supplied, well-equipped and entrenched in excellent positions. It was, however, surrounded on three sides by Vekh armies. It appeared that the Emperor of Anduk was content to bypass the fortress on the way to attack Belorin.

Dyrk's leg was bothering him less than he expected when in the saddle. Once he landed, he found that the knee swelled up to the point that he couldn't straighten the leg anymore. It was all he could do to hobble around. He received an ice treatment and some herbs during his overnight stay at Mount Arrasheth.

He was not privy to the information that he was carrying, but he got the impression that he was bearing good news. The fight at Keor must be going well, despite Dyrk's personal defeat there. Judging by what he saw in Arghand, Karolia would need victory in the north if it was to help its allies in the south. Since no land-based messengers were able to get out of the fortress, Dyrk was laden with all the correspondence he could carry for the trip to Holbern.

He had never seen the capital of Belorin before. He was less than impressed. There were no stately buildings, no manicured boulevards, and no formidable fortifications at Holbern. In size it did not even rival Doleth Sarin. But despite their lack of architectural achievement, Dyrk took an instant liking to the Belorin people he met there. They were hardy, no-nonsense folk who loved the wide expanse of their homeland. While they did not place the same value on education and social structure, they eschewed the material comforts that the Karolians were becoming accustomed to. They rarely built expansive homes because they were often on the move. The prosperity of a Belorin citizen was measured by the number and quality of his horses and cattle, not his dwelling-place.

Dyrk's third stop was Ben-Panith, the southernmost permanent Belorin settlement. Many Belorin lived well south of it, especially on the Eber Plateau, but they were isolated and semi-nomadic, rarely forming settlements. Navigating to Ben-Panith was very difficult. There were few, if any, landmarks on the open plains. Dyrk had other struggles on this leg of the journey, too. His mount decided to descend again, but this time swooped down towards a startled steer. Try as it might, the unfortunate bull could not get away from the airborne predator, and Dyrk could do nothing to turn his mount's attention away. A sickening crunch, one last bawl, and the steer was lifeless in the talons of the tarn. Dyrk gulped. If the tarn decided to do that to a human being, well, that's what the suicide knife was there for.

He rested beside the dead bull for a spell. Perhaps the owner was nearby, and he could at least apologize and offset the cost with the meager amount of money he was carrying. But nobody came. There was a possibility that they were afraid of a six-hundred-pound flying predator which had just proven its ability to maim and kill.

Thankfully, the sky was clear, and he could steer well by the sun. Despite its random descents, the tarn was responsive to making small adjustments to its course on the request of the rider. He was still off by a half-league. If it were not for the northern spur of the Zelmandi mountains that came into view, he may have missed the town entirely. He arrived tired, sunburned, and windburned.

The extra day layover in Ben-Panith did him wonders. He had no messages to deliver there, other than a small favour for a Belorin lord in Holbern. The town was a hub for military and civilian traffic for the entire southern steppes. Its garrison was well-equipped to resupply any military excursion, including tarn-riders. This was the last place before Dharbur, fifteen leagues[1] to the south, where there was a dependable year-round water supply.

The starry skies greeted him as he ascended from Ben-Panith in the early morning. He hoped he would get away with only two rest-breaks for the tarn, but he had to remember that he wasn't in control of those anyway. He steered by a few compass-segments off Valeron's Star, going as close to due south as possible. He rose in altitude until he got a tail-wind. This allowed him to make good time until sunup.

At daybreak the tarn spotted a small wetland, and they descended for a rest break. Dyrk had been told not to expect any potable water, so he had with him an extra canteen. Indeed, the small amount of water in this isolated wetland was still and stagnant. Not worth drinking for humans, but the tarn enjoyed it immensely.

Before the sun was up, it was below freezing. He was tightly bundled up, including his face. At his first stop, he shed most of the

---

[1] Fifteen leagues is about 400 kilometers or 240 miles

clothing but kept the face-scarf. He had been warned of the winds carrying stinging sand, even at higher altitudes, which could blind the unprepared aerial traveler.

On he traveled. The terrain became more and more bleak as he progressed. Thick rolling grasslands with frequent copses of brush gradually gave way to wastelands of rock and sand with a few tufts of tall grass. At this time of the year, there were green patches here and there where water from the infrequent rains had collected. Wildflowers occasionally produced smaller patches of colour. He spotted more wetlands randomly dotting the landscape. He figured that these would be completely gone by summertime.

Steering south by the sun was a little more difficult than by stars. Thankfully, there would be some landmarks near Dharbur by which he could correct his course, provided he arrived while it was still daylight. Dyrk could not find a tail-wind anymore. Cross-winds made his exact position even more uncertain. A second rest break during the heat of the day took advantage of one of the last wetlands that they would see, and Dyrk took the time to refresh himself on the landmarks on the map. So far, he had been fairly successful with navigating to places he had never visited before simply by maps, instructions, and the clues the Servants had left in the skies. He assured himself that he would be hard-pressed to miss the salt sea that lay south of Dharbur.

But a smooth trip was not in the Servants' plans. Several dots appeared below as he flew, another dispersed herd of cattle owned by local ranchers. The tarn spied movement below and began to dive. Dyrk's heart lurched into his throat as he plummeted hundreds of paces in a few seconds. The tarn pulled up to glide at high speed, only fifty paces above the desert floor. They passed by a few bawling, startled cattle, then Dyrk saw what the tarn was headed for. A horse was running along the path of the tarn, and they were closing quickly. In horror, Dyrk realized that there was a rider on the horse.

He frantically sawed at the reins. No reaction from the tarn. He took the knife out of its sheath on the neck and beat the handle against the back of the tarn's skull. It shrieked, pulled up slightly, but then it beat its powerful wings and sped on. In one more desperate attempt, Dyrk lashed the reins over the tarn's eyes. The rider dodged to the right. Dyrk's head and shoulder were smashed against the tarn's neck as the beast spread its wings in a banked turn. It was changing course to pursue.

Dyrk didn't have time to think. He had already exhausted all of the options that he had been taught to regain control of an unresponsive tarn. He frantically sliced through the straps on his knees, freeing his legs to give him the leverage he needed. He circled his left arm around the heaving neck, plunging the point of the knife into the soft spot at the base of the neck. The tarn stiffened and drew back violently. The wings began to beat irregularly, and the two of them began to whirl in the air, losing what little altitude they had. Dyrk clung with all his might to the tarn's neck and stabbed again, dark blood gushing onto his hands. The ground rushed towards him.

For a second, he dangled within a realm of suspended animation. His thoughts were clear while the world around him slowed to almost nothing. He had experienced this before, a long time ago, in the mine as a child. He thought to himself, is this a dream again? If not, how can the Servants explain this sudden run of terrible fortune? Here he had escaped certain death at the hands of the Vekh, only to die there in the Belorin steppe at the whim of a half-crazy bird of prey. The Servants sure did have a morbid sense of humour.

He was crushed into the leathery body of the tarn. The force made him feel like he was being squeezed like a ripe orange. The knife flew out of his hand. The leathery skin scraped against his own. His shoulder was the first to hit the ground. The back of his head was next. His ears heard nothing but ringing after that. His chest continued to heave erratically, giving him the only assurance that he was still alive.

He felt something cool on his face. He opened his eyes and gasped for breath. The bright sun seared his eyes when he tried to open them. He sucked a little water into his lungs, which caused him to choke. He turned on his side, coughing and sputtering. His hands were caked in blood and dirt. His knee hurt. There was a sharp pain in his abdomen. His shoulder ached. But otherwise he was alive.

A hand was on his stomach as he lay on his side. His ears heard a voice, a woman's, speaking words he did not understand. He wiped his hand on his legs and then tried to get the sand off his face, but only made things worse.

"A Karolian! You crazy idiot! What possessed you to do that?" the shrill voice suddenly shifted to fluent, but accented, River-Tongue.

He tried to slow his breathing enough to say a few words. Finally, he managed, "not your enemy."

"That will take some convincing," the voice said.

Dyrk raised his head, but sand was in his eyes, stinging them whenever he tried to open them. "I can't see," he complained.

More water hit his face. He held out his hands, and he got enough water to clean them off. He wiped the grit out of his eyes. Finally, he could open them.

She was a middle-aged woman, old enough to be his mother. She was thin and fit, not very tall. Her hair was either very short, or it was put away underneath the leather cap she was wearing. Her skin was a healthy brown like the Derrekh, but not so dark as a Zindori. Her thin, bony face held a look of concern mixed with anger. Other than the crow's feet around her grey eyes, the wrinkles on her face were more likely from weathering than age.

Her clothing was made almost entirely of well-crafted leather. Only the shirt was made from cloth. She was not wearing a dress, but to Dyrk's surprise she wore leather leggings like a man, with a loose protective leather covering on the outsides of the legs. She had a large wooden canteen in one hand.

Her River-Tongue had an accent that Dyrk had heard before. A few Belorin traders plied the great roads in Karolia, and the ladies especially gave positive complements about the charming twist that they put on their language. Karolians were particular about phonetic accuracy, but the Belorin were less concerned with separating consonants and enunciating compound vowels.

Dyrk sat up. The pain in his abdomen intensified. He noticed now that he was bleeding. He lifted his shirt. A long gash in his skin was thankfully not very deep. He guessed that on impact the hilt of the dagger had dug into him.

"Can I get-" he was about to ask, but she pressed some cloth against the gash.

"While we're waiting for my spooked horse to calm down and come back to us, why don't you tell me what in Kemantar's name you were doing?"

"I'm a soldier in the Karolian army. I was on a mission to Dharbur," Dyrk explained, leaving out the purpose of his mission. Messengers should always be coy about what they were doing.

"Yes, you were. Not anymore," she said with a little levity. "That tarn's not going anywhere but up in smoke, now."

"I'm sorry I frightened you."

"How did that thing die? Did you get hit by something in the air?"

"I killed it. To stop it from hurting you." Dyrk winced. Everything around him was moving as if he was still in the air. His stomach began to turn from motion sickness.

"What?" The woman didn't seem to comprehend.

"Tarns aren't easy to control. They sometimes do their own thing regardless of the rider's commands. Sometimes that means they attack animals, or even people. I killed it when I saw it was about to hurt you."

The woman's eyes went wide. "Well, you are about the bravest buck I've ever met. I've never heard of a horseman taking out his own panicking mount from under him, much less an airborne one."

"Horses don't have three-inch talons and a beak that can dismember a human being," Dyrk responded wryly.

"If it be true that you are a Karolian soldier, then you are welcome in my house," she said, but her eyes held a warning. "If that be true. Out here there isn't any law. We deal with thieves and bandits internally, as they say."

Dyrk tried to get up. "I am so surprised that you are even breathing, much less getting on your feet," she marveled. "You took a tumble that would split most skulls."

"I'm getting used to near-death experiences," Dyrk said. "Can I use a bit more of your water?"

She gave him the canteen. His mouth was so dry. He took a long drink before using another sprinkle to wash his hands and face again. He noticed that blood was seeping through his tunic. She helped him bind his face-scarf tightly around his abdomen to stop the bleeding.

"It'll need stitches," she said. "Give me your sword and any other weapons you have on you."

Dyrk wasn't sure he heard right. "Pardon me?"

"Your weapons. I'm taking you prisoner until I can check your story. We may be trusting folk but we're also cautious."

Dyrk didn't know whether to laugh at this woman. Here she was, probably half his body weight, unauthorized by his nation's rules to carry a sword, and she figured she can put him under arrest? His face began to colour in humiliation as he complied. He loosened his belt and threaded off the scabbard, handing it to her.

"My knife is still on the tarn," he said. "There's also a light crossbow."

She took his sword. With several fingers to her teeth, she blew a shrill whistle. "Why don't you go over the carcass, then, and give me anything meant for killing." She freed a loop of leather at her waist that was holding a small axe in place and used it to secure the sword. The axe she slid into a loop on the other side. Dyrk almost laughed at the sight of a wispy woman wearing a broadsword.

He limped his way gingerly over to the body of the tarn. Some parts of it were still twitching. He unsecured the first of the two cargo bags and dragged it a short distance away. It held the message canisters. She could have his weapons, but she wasn't going to touch the messages, he thought. He tried to get the other cargo net, but it was pinned under an outstretched wing of the tarn. He reached in under the wing, the smell of blood and tarn sweat thick in his nostrils. He was able to find the clasp and unhook it. He pulled with all his might, weakened as he was from the fall. It sprang free, and he fell back.

The crossbow was broken. He tossed it aside. There was no need for the quarrels, either. Some spare fodder for the tarn was useless. He sat on the dirt, sun beating down, as he sorted through the rest of the gear. He put aside his knife for his captor and retied the bundle.

The horse had returned. The woman had a hold of the bridle but was waiting for him to come back. She was standing upwind of the carcass. Dyrk figured the horse would probably be spooked again if it caught smell of the tarn. He hobbled his way back, dragging the two bundles on the ground.

"Aren't you a pitiful sight," she said with more mirth than consolation in her voice. "Why don't you get in the saddle and I'll start leading the way home. You have ridden a horse before, right?"

Dyrk could not smile at the irony. He tried to assure himself that the situation demanded it, but it felt shameful all the same for a soldier of Karolia to give up his weapons to a woman and have her lead him on a horse. *Nobody can see me now*, he thought, *and nobody is writing a book about this.*

They headed southwest. The woman continued to chatter on and off. She mentioned of the need to come back and burn the corpse of the tarn; couldn't risk disease spreading to the cattle. She had seen a tarn once before, a Belorin messenger who landed at the farm for some water. It had spooked all the horses and cattle something awful.

They had gone a fair distance when she stopped talking and slapped her head as if punishing herself. "Here I've fixed you up, taken you prisoner, brought you halfway home, and we haven't even made introductions. My manners are slipping." She stopped walking and gently patted her horse's head. "I'm Rothell clan Enoath. What might I call you?"

"Dyrk," he said, trying to decide if his patronymic or house name would be less awkward. "House Teren."

"It is good to ride with you, Dyrk," Rothell spoke a common Belorin greeting, despite the fact that he was riding while she was walking. They started off again. After a dozen footfalls, she spoke loudly over her shoulder. "House Teren? Isn't that your king's house?"

"Very distant relation," Dyrk said.

Rothell launched into all the family relations that were living with her. It sounded like a substantial number. Belorin households did not take bondservants like Karolians did, but extended families often stayed together and took care of their own elderly and infirm.

"Most of my little ones are grown up now," she said. "I have one left who could still be called a child. Do you have any children?"

"No," said Dyrk. "I just barely finished my royal service."

She waved her hand disdainfully. "You kingdom types take forever to settle down, with your military service and this and that. Us, we had better be nursing young ones before we're two decades old."

Dyrk felt his colour rise again. Despite the air being cool, the sun's rays were very strong, and he was becoming uncomfortably warm. A breeze brought some relief now and then. Rothell took off her cap and shook out a mess of short-cropped chestnut hair. It didn't touch her shoulders. Dyrk also noticed that she no longer handled the bridle when leading the horse, it obediently followed her.

"Almost there," she said. "You probably didn't see our place from above because most of it is under the sod."

Ahead, a wrinkle in the plateau signaled a stream bed. As they came closer, a narrow cut through the flat ground opened up before him. On the far side of the depression Dyrk could see doors and windows sunk into the earth. Some had timber awnings over the doors. Judging by the three horses seeking shade under one awning with a wide door, it was a stable. As the creek bed came into view, it was bubbling brightly with a brisk flow of silty water.

"This creek dries up in spring," Rothell swept her hand over the ravine. "This here is our winter grounds. Very good grazing nearby. We avoid the mud and winter pox in the north. You Karolians probably live above-ground in stone houses, am I right?"

"Most houses are made from wood," Dyrk corrected her. "But yes, I haven't seen many living underground where I come from."

"It's not so bad," she said. "Stays cool in hot weather."

Dyrk saw other people moving around. He began to feel self-conscious again. "Can I walk?" he asked.

"Can you? You didn't look like you were doing much of it back there."

"I should stretch out my leg."

She stopped the horse and reached up to help Dyrk dismount, further embarrassing him. He made sure to carry his messenger bag. Those documents could not leave his sight. He had thought to himself while riding if his current circumstances would qualify as "grounding or threat of capture." Dyrk felt he was in no danger. The Belorin were close allies with Karolia. He determined it was premature to start destroying the valuable documents. He was not far from Dharbur and could still reasonably reach it within a few days.

A young girl came skipping towards them from one of the sod huts. She was wearing a cotton frock with a leather bodice. Dyrk was relieved to find that some of the females there don't dress like men. The girl shouted a greeting to Rothell in Belorin, followed by a query while pointing at Dyrk. He could understand a little conversational Belorin, and from the words he determined that the girl referred to Rothell as her aunt.

"He doesn't understand prairie-speech, child, so why don't we practice our River-Tongue?" Rothell responded.

The girl's face glowed as she spoke directly to Dyrk. "I can speak your words well," she said, slightly halting and heavily accented. "Welcome to our home."

"Well, he's not welcome yet," Rothell said with a satisfied delight. "He's our prisoner for now."

She didn't look concerned in the slightest. Rather, the expression on her face revealed that she considered it more of a game. "Why, what did he do, Auntie?"

"Fell out of the sky. Fetch your father."

The girl's expression became confused, but she obeyed and ran off.

Dyrk scanned the homestead. A small garden was planted near the spring, not producing much more than beans and greens. A large corral was fenced in against the west-facing slope. There was at least a half-dozen doorways beneath the sod of the east-facing slope. Some were double-wide and tall, such as the stable. Others were low and narrow, and he doubted if he could walk in without ducking his head. Most had wooden awnings built in front of the doorways. He could see several people in the shade under the awnings. An old man rocked in a chair with his whittling on his lap, staring at the newcomer. A teenage boy looked up from scraping a cowhide stretched on a rack. A toddler was oblivious to everything else as he chased a chicken around.

The young girl ran into the stable, and before long reappeared with a tall, thin man. His clothing wasn't much different from Rothell's. He wore his beard thick and untrimmed, though he wasn't past the prime of his life. The hair on his head was a sun-bleached blonde, his beard was darker. He walked towards Dyrk with a smile on his face and extended a hand. Not sure what to do with it, Dyrk grasped it and found his arm being pumped up and down.

"Good to meet you, stranger," the man said in accented River-Tongue. "You can call me Orben, clan Enoath. Lieutenant of the Belorin Home Guard, Southern division, second company."

Dyrk responded in a Belorin greeting that he knew. Seeing Rothell's surprised expression, he added in his own language, "that's about the extent of my knowledge of Belorin. My name is Dyrk of House Teren." He figured he should reciprocate with his rank and military designation as Orben had done. "Eighth regiment, Saringon cavalry reserve."

"My daughter says you fell out of the sky. What, may I ask, is going on?"

Dyrk explained to him his situation with as much detail as he used with Rothell.

"Well, that's easy enough to verify," the man said. He had pulled out a leather object from his pocket. He slapped the cap onto his head to ward off the sun. "If you're a Karolian messenger, you kingdom types always carry a letter of appointment."

"That's why I needed you," Rothell stated matter-of-fact. "You're the only one that can read their script."

Dyrk sorted through the saddlebag that kept the messenger equipment. There were several large brass canisters, linked by a metal chain. The only free canister was his own personal document case. He pulled it out and unscrewed the cap. He flipped through several documents and gave one to Orben.

The Belorin turned away from the sun and narrowed his eyes as he read. "Looks in order," he finally said. "Give him back his weapons, Rothell. Let's not unnecessarily harass an allied soldier."

Orben rounded up another man and the teenage boy to go deal with the carcass of the tarn. Dyrk was finally eased into a rocking chair just across from the old man who was whittling. Rothell fetched an older woman who went over Dyrk's injuries. She brought Dyrk in through a low door. Inside were a series of bunk beds built into the wall, a curtain providing the only modicum of privacy. Dyrk was laid in a lower bunk to get stitched up.

He was offered a shot of liquor before the stitching. Dyrk was used to drinking beer, but the distilled grain spirit made him cough and splutter. The woman chuckled at his expense and poured a little of the spirit on his cut, making him yelp in pain. He gritted his teeth as the needle pierced his skin six times. Finally the wound was closed and wrapped with some new cloth.

Dyrk thanked her and returned to the rocking chair. The man had resumed whittling like his afternoon was no different than the previous one. A fire pit was smoking out in the sun, and he noticed a younger woman attending to it from time to time. She was wearing leggings similar to Rothell's but her leather top was sleeveless and form-fitting. *Does anyone dress decently here?* he thought. The toddler trailed behind her, calling her mama in the universal language of infants.

The shadows from the awnings, facing east, were getting longer. Two riders appeared on the south horizon. One was a middle-aged man, husky and weathered. His curly red-brown beard was full and untrimmed like Orben's. The other was a woman, wearing clothing much like Rothell. Because of the distance, and the cap that she wore, Dyrk couldn't really tell her age. Rothell spoke with them for a bit, before they took their horses to the stable and had them quartered. A half hour later, the two of them exited the stables and approached Dyrk. He felt like he was an exotic animal being gawked at by passers-by.

The man introduced himself as Koeric, Rothell's husband. The woman's name was Saris. He could now see that she was quite young, and he couldn't help but notice her attractiveness. She had large, green eyes that brimmed with laughter and a pretty mouth that was slightly curled on one side, making her default expression one of condescension. At first he thought that she had no eyebrows at all, but as she got close he could see that they were so lightly coloured that they were nearly invisible. She had removed her riding jacket and wore only a thin-strapped bodice with laces keeping it together along the front. Bare flesh was visible beneath the laces. Dyrk stared at the ground in embarrassment. He had seen more of this woman in a few seconds than he had seen of Neriah in four years.

"And this is your daughter?" Dyrk asked innocently, motioning towards Saris but trying not to look at her.

She giggled, and said, "You go ahead and think that."

"I would imagine you would eventually like to make your way to Dharbur, soldier," Koeric said.

Dyrk nodded. "Do you go there often?"

"Every few weeks. It's the closest market for cattle and horses. I might be able to organize a trip there in a week or so."

"I really appreciate all your help," Dyrk said politely. "Once I'm on my feet, I promise you I'll earn my keep."

As they walked away, Saris removed her cap and shook out her hair. It was cropped shoulder-length like the other women, but Dyrk was very surprised to see that it was a brilliant silvery white. He had never seen hair that colour on a young woman before.

That evening was an experience for Dyrk. Once the sun dipped low over the horizon, the extended family came together around the cooking pit, where a side of beef had been slow-roasting all day. They ate together under the darkening sky, laughing loudly, and observing few manners. Afterwards they began to tell stories or sing songs. Most were in Belorin, but they came up with a few in River-Tongue for Dyrk's sake. Dyrk was embarrassed again as the women joined in the songs. It was counter to tradition in Karolia for a woman to sing around a man that wasn't her husband.

As the night wore on, the Belorin began to retire to their beds.

Dyrk turned in early as well. They offered him a spare bed in the sleeping-shelter. He had trouble sleeping. Though he was used to sleeping in a camp with dozens of men, sleeping in the same room as a woman made him very uncomfortable. After two hours of sleeplessness, things got worse. Saris entered the bunk next to his and began to hum softly to herself. He could hear the slide of leather on skin as she disrobed. All this, coupled with the unfamiliar musty smells of cow-hide and muskrat fur, kept him wide awake long after the others were softly snoring.

He recalled the tale of Ter-Athel and his Eleven Companions. Blessed and guided by the Servant Anakdatar, they saved Tauril in the days after Tawkin had restored the kingdom. Afterwards, Ter-Athel and his descendants supposedly lived in the deepest forests of Feldar. The mark that Anakdatar gave them was that their hair would never bear colour. That people were named the Alwemkind. In subsequent centuries, they came once to the aid of the kings of Azenvar, but they were otherwise never seen again.

However, he thought, the Alwem would be pure-blooded Taurilians and would therefore have grey skin. Saris's coloration was not dissimilar from the other Belorin. It was probably just some sort of hereditary quirk. He had seen in his day some of the Derrekh bondservants have a streak of white amongst their usually dark locks. Women with that morph were considered especially attractive in that culture. But he had never seen an entire head of white hair in a young woman.

When Dyrk finally did get to sleep, he had terrible dreams all night. Over and over again, the scene played in his mind, of Lohann, helpless and bloodied, holding up his hands in a futile defence as the Vekh plunged the point of the poleaxe into his chest.

The next day, Dyrk did his best to pitch in. His injuries prevented him from joining the men and women who rode out to watch and herd the cattle. Instead, he stayed on the homestead and helped in the stable, which he had cleaned out in no time. He surprised many of the Belorin with his knowledge and aptitude with horses.

The young mother dug out the firepit and started another slow roast, this time of a whole wild pig. Dyrk thought that last night was a special occasion, a feast. But now it looked like the Belorin did this every night.

Close to the end of the day, Dyrk sat down on the rocking chair across from the old man. He took out his equipment and did his best to clean it. As he rubbed a cloth over his scabbard, the adolescent boy came forward with wide eyes. His name was Toic.

"You have a sword," he said simply.

"You haven't seen one before?" Dyrk asked, a little surprised.

Toic shook his head. "I can use a bow, throw an axe, and fight with a spear," the boy said proudly. "But I've never held a sword."

Though it was against his nature, Dyrk reminded himself that he was in another country, with another set of customs. He extended the sheathed blade, hilt first. The boy drew the weapon, mouth agape in wonder.

The old man muttered something in Belorin. Dyrk wasn't sure, but it sounded like he was saying something about lopping one's own arm off.

The boy took a few practice swings. Dyrk winced as he could tell the boy was wielding it like an axe. To humour him, he gave a few pointers and instructed him on the thrust. Then he took the weapon back. He began to clean the rest of his gear. He polished the metal splints on his military boots. The boy didn't go anywhere, but he sat on the floor and watched in wonder as Dyrk went through each part of his armour.

Toic ran his hand along the chain mail hauberk after it had been cleaned. "Metal skin," he said softly in Belorin. He turned it over and exclaimed in surprise, "It's broken!"

Dyrk recalled the blow he had taken in the back during the ambush in which Bayern was killed. He figured that the billhook of a poleaxe had grazed him and caught his armour but not his flesh. A jagged hole was left in the back of his hauberk. Some of the adjoining links were beginning to unravel. He should get that fixed before the entire hauberk comes apart, he thought.

Dyrk finished with his open-faced helmet. Toic tried it on, and it slipped over the young man's eyes, to the laughter of them both.

Supper was just beginning. Dyrk joined in for another night of feasting and merry-making. He realized that he had not written a petition since the morning in Ben-Panith, so he wrote one out before eating that night. It was Anakdatar's Day[1], so he thanked the Servant that Holds Up the World for his tireless vigil against the depths of the earth: the violent oceans of the deep and the destructive magma of the underworld. He threw the petition into the fire.

Rothell noticed him doing that. "You Karolians burn a lot of paper talking to the Servants," she mentioned. "You might not know it, but many of our songs are doing the same thing. You write to Arren, we sing to Him."

Dyrk was again uncomfortable with the notion that one could sing directly to a Servant, much less to Arren Himself. He pondered as they began to sing together. Some swayed, lifted their hands, or even danced as they sang. How could they be so bold?

"How about a story and song from Karolia?" Toic piped up at one point.

"Well, that's a great idea," Rothell laughed. "We took him prisoner, why don't we get some use out of him?" Others chimed in their encouragement. Dyrk took a deep breath. He racked his brain. He had better stay away from any of the tales about Belorin; he was surely to make a fool of himself if he did so. He also thought better of telling the tale of Ter-Athel and his white-haired companions.

Dyrk settled on a safe tale that he knew well – the War of Kalthund. He began by describing the frigid land of Kalthund and the brave and hardy men that lived there. Tuin's son Drukudar was on the throne in Tauril after murdering his father. Drukudar was deceived by his own son Drukhor to conquer Kalthund. Melandar, Drukudar's brother, sent his two sons-in-law, Julin and Ruthlin, to help in the invasion. There the two were captured by a young Kalthunite chieftain named Tawkin. In captivity, Julin and Ruthlin became friends with Tawkin. When Drukhor had Tawkin captured, Julin and Ruthlin led a daring raid into Drukhor's stronghold in Kardumagund to rescue him. There Julin was mortally wounded. Before he died, Julin asked Tawkin to take his place and care for his

---

[1] Monday

childless wife, Lunnah.

Dyrk then began, in his deep baritone, Tawkin's song of mourning for Julin. Singing was a key part of an Eratur's training, and Dyrk had been praised for his vocal talents before his dismissal. He could feel two dozen eyes upon him as he sang. Singing on his own for an audience made him nervous, but it was preferable to singing with women. As it was, he finished the dirge without anyone else making a peep. Several of the younger children were weeping quietly. Rothell brushed a tear aside.

"I'm sorry, I didn't mean to dampen the mood," Dyrk apologized.

"That was amazing," Koeric said.

"I've heard stories of the Order of Eraturs in Karolia," Orben stated, his face glowing in the firelight. "They not only fight, but they sing, they lead, and they defend their nation's virtue."

Dyrk was sheepish. "I am no Eratur."

Toic gushed, "You seem like one to me."

"Hush, Toic, don't embarrass him," Rothell scolded her son. She turned to Dyrk. "Well, whatever they call you, it's plain to me that you're all that."

Saris clapped her hands. "Let's liven things up," she enthused and jumped to her feet. "How about some dancing?"

Here was yet another moral dilemma for Dyrk. At least he had an excuse. He pointed to his knee, wrapped in cloth, and begged to be relieved of the activity. The old man produced an instrument that resembled a series of pipes and picked up a lively tune. Away they danced, switching partners and twirling around each other in the twilight. Dyrk was especially glad to be exempt when he saw how near Saris got to Toic when the unfortunate boy was passed off to her. Neriah would rightfully slap him if he ever drew that close to her.

That night, Dyrk mercifully fell asleep immediately, tired as he was.

He awoke with a start. Peeking through the curtain, he could see through the window that it was still dark. Nobody else was stirring. *In fact*, he thought to himself, *I can't hear anyone else at all.* He reasoned that since he was awake, he might as well relieve himself. He slipped on his trousers and tunic before pushing the curtain aside.

The door was open. Dyrk's heart leaped into his throat.

A blue glow surrounded a creature that slowly stepped through the doorway. It had the appearance of a large, thin dog, its coat as dark as blackest night. Spikes rose from its spine and two vicious horns crowned its skull. Most frightening were the eyes, that burned a cold, piercing blue. The maw was agape without a tongue.

Dyrk reached to the wall beside his bunk. His hand gripped his sword. *What is this unearthly thing?* his thoughts raced. *Am I dreaming?*

He rose slowly, unsheathing his sword as he did so. The beast looked in his direction. A bright red light lit the room. It took Dyrk a few seconds to realize that the light was coming from his sword.

A voice came from the beast, reminding him of the troll that had spoken to him so many years before. "You! What are you doing here?" the voice demanded. The dog's mouth had not moved.

Dyrk thought of several possible responses and counter-questions, but a voice came from him, seemingly of its own accord. "Thalnuris. This family is under my protection. Begone."

He lifted the sword higher to underscore his command.

The beast coiled to pounce. "You would deny me my prize?"

"At this time, yes." Dyrk wished he could have said something more definitive.

The beast gave a piercing scream that normally would have deafened Dyrk. He lifted the sword and advanced. In a flaming arc, the blade swung towards the creature, which sprang directly out the door and was gone. Dyrk chased it outside, but in the starlit night he could not see his quarry anywhere.

The sword dimmed, and eventually faded completely. He stood outside in the darkened homestead. What was that thing? And what was going on with his sword? Was his mind re-enacting the dream from so many years ago?

As he turned around, he also asked himself, why didn't anyone wake up? The Belorin seemed to be a people who were always alert. That scream would have woken up an entire city. He re-entered the sleeping quarters and listened quietly. His heart eased as he heard the easy breathing of two dozen sleepers.

He grabbed his cloak and returned outside, shutting the door quietly behind him. There was no way he could go back to sleep. He had to protect this family from that – that thing, whatever it was. He sat down in one of the rocking chairs. He was soon lost in thought. What was the prize the beast was talking about?

"I didn't know Karolians sleep better in chairs," Saris's voice jolted him awake. It was morning already. He had fallen fast asleep under his cloak in the chair, the sword sheathed across his knees. He rubbed the sleep out of his eyes. He tried to mumble something about fresh air.

"Well, you sure gave me a fright," she said. "You were able to get out the door without waking me up. That takes real skill. I always sleep with an eye open."

He smiled weakly. "I try to be quiet." He tried to look past her. The simmering attractiveness of the young woman already made things difficult for him. It was made all the more trying by her choice of clothing. At least it wasn't as bad as the first night, Dyrk thought. She was now dressed in supple leather trousers of dark colour, fitting close at her thighs. Her top was a light cotton short-sleeve blouse with the neck left untied, revealing the cleft between her breasts. She had a leather riding jacket in one hand and some protective leather garment for her legs in the other.

"I take it you're riding after the cattle again today," Dyrk attempted small talk, wishing she would leave.

"Yes, I'm going with Koeric to look for some steers to take with us to Dharbur."

Dyrk didn't like how she used the word "us" when talking about the journey to Dharbur. "You don't refer to Koeric as your father?"

"I was an orphan," she said simply. Her mouth was turned down. She began to put on the jacket.

Dyrk tried to apologize. "I'm sorry, I did know."

She picked up the chaps and began to walk towards the stable. "I guess you didn't need to know," she muttered as she walked.

On the one hand, Dyrk felt bad that he had said something to offend her. On the other, maybe she would leave him alone and stop flaunting herself around him. He didn't like the way it made him feel.

He got up out of the rocking chair. Time to wash up and start another day, he thought. Hopefully it wouldn't be long until he was in Dharbur. He didn't know at this point how he was going to get back to Karolia, fifty leagues[1] away, but he resolved to take on the challenges one at a time.

Three days later they were ready for the trip to Dharbur. They were taking only a few head of cattle to exchange for needed supplies. Koeric, Saris, and Dyrk would be riding with them, plus a pack horse.

Dyrk figured he could have found his way on his own if he needed to. The stream that flowed through the homestead was running from west to east, and more than likely would end up in the salt sea south of Dharbur if he followed it. But there was no sense in taking chances. The five days that he had spent with Rothell's family allowed him to recover from his injuries sustained upon the tarn's demise. His knee was still not well, but his limp was not as pronounced.

He had done a lot of thinking about the encounter with the Gryphon. He knew the old stories well. The similarities to the demon-possessed creatures that threatened the early Taurilians were unmistakable. He figured that his dream was a result of the images he had conjured up in his imagination when he heard the stories. He was unnerved at the thought that he had sleepwalked. That could get him in big trouble at some point, he thought.

An alternate theory was forming in his head. He recalled his two recent near-death experiences, and noted he had the sword with him both times. Madwin had been surprised that he survived the cave-in within the mine as a child. Was the sword protecting him in some way? Was there some sort of connection between the misshapen ogre in his childhood dream, and the Gryphon in his most recent one? In both situations the sword immolated, and his enemy became powerless to stop it.

---

[1] 800 miles

The overnight trip was relatively uneventful. They slept under the stars. The morning found them drenched with dew as the temperature had dropped precipitously over the night.

As they started riding, Saris took the lead while Dyrk and Koeric took up the rear. Dyrk took advantage of the situation to ask Koeric a few questions about her. Specifically, whether Koeric knew her parents.

"No, I never met her parents," he answered.

"How did she come to you then?"

He gave a short laugh. "You probably won't believe it if I told you."

"Try me."

"Well, she didn't come to me. She was adopted by my father. I was six years old when she arrived. She grew up as my sister."

Koeric already had several grandchildren. "That would make her well over forty years old then," Dyrk said.

"Yes. She grew up very slowly compared to the rest of us. The man that dropped her off, denied that he was the father. Was really desperate that someone look after the infant, though."

"What did he look like?"

"He was Taurilian, like you, just with less colour in his skin. Very tall. Bald. Seemed young at the time, I figured he was a teenager. He came by a few times in the first few years to check on her. Haven't seen him in, oh, twenty years or so. I figured he got into mercenary work and probably got himself killed."

Dyrk's curiosity was piqued. "What makes you think he was in the mercenary business?"

"Well, the last time I saw him, he was carrying some professional-looking weapons. Nothing like the Belorin or Karolian military would carry. And he tried to give us some money."

"Tried?"

Koeric tipped his cap. "My father didn't ask for payment, didn't want it. Saris has pulled her weight like any full-blooded Belorin woman. We're family."

CHAPTER 21:
DHARBUR

Torrin peeked out of his bedroll into the cool desert air. Yes, the sky was brightening in the east. Morning was near.

Torrin had slept uneasily during the night, knowing that Erelin was not watching them as he usually did. They were camped beside a small wetland. The water in the pond was not good enough to drink, but a small trickle coming from the rocks to the north allowed them to fill their canteens. The wetland had supplied them with their dinner, two waterfowl that graced their stew pot and produced a wonderful aroma.

Erelin had told Torrin that he would not be watching them that night. Torrin knew that this meant Erelin was checking on the white-haired woman in his dream. Over the past two days, the mute Taurilian had led them into the plains of Belorin, supposedly to get well away from bandit territory. Today they would turn south to head for Dharbur. They would, if all went well, reach it in two days.

To Torrin's relief, Erelin strode into his view as he got dressed. Torrin could not read any expression on the other's face, covered as it was by a cowl. But the fact that he was there made Torrin think that the worst had not happened.

As Vigheran went to refill their canteen, Torrin came alongside Erelin who had just finished re-packing. He was laying out his arrows in his curious manner, side by side, perfectly spaced. Without prompting, Erelin wrote on the ground.

She was not there.

Torrin was disappointed. Erelin had come so far to see to her safety, and now she wasn't even there. Erelin continued to write.

She is safe. Traveling to Dharbur.

Torrin breathed a sigh of relief. Whatever business Vigheran had to do in Dharbur, at least Erelin could see to this woman's safety at the same time. He ventured a personal question.

"Is she your daughter?"

(No.)

"Wife?"

(No.)

"You know I'm going to keep asking until you tell me why she's so important to you."

He wrote on the ground, *safer for you*. Then he kicked dirt over the characters as Vigheran approached.

Torrin had seen many parts of Belorin before. However, he had never gone so far south as Dharbur. His first surprise was the spectacular formations of stone that came into view on their left. They were streaked with repeating layers of red, white, and grey. The brilliant colour of the formations during sunset gave the valley its name, the Red Valley. These he studied in wonder as they prepared for their last camp, they hoped, before Dharbur.

The next day dawned clear and bright. It was still cold at night, but not as bone-chilling as it had been in Zelmandi. As they walked, the landscape changed with each rise that they topped. Torrin was unprepared for how lush and green the valley was. They had walked through many leagues of rocky desert, seeing little more than scraggly trees, hardy bushes, and patches of brown grass. Now an expanse of green grass spread before him, with exotic trees growing close to the waterways that cut through the upper valley. Irrigation ditches crisscrossed the land on either side of the larger streams.

Farms were built near the waterways, while the green hillsides were dotted with grazing animals. As they walked down the road that wound through the farms, he could see that their growing season was reversed. Crops were now actively growing in the wettest time of the year. They would be ready for harvest in the drier spring months. He wondered how the landscape before him might change during the dry, hot, summer months.

Erelin and Vigheran had changed into their city gear again.

Vigheran's body markings, however, were not covered. Torrin guessed that he wouldn't stand out quite so much in a place like Dharbur, which had a substantial population of Roj Zindori.

Vigheran had already told Torrin that morning that he was not to head into the city itself. They planned to stay at an inn just north of the city. Torrin would stay there while the other two would venture out to conduct their business. Torrin had mixed feelings about this. He wanted to satisfy his own curiosity about the city, and he also wanted to be with Erelin when they found the white-haired woman. However, staying in an inn sounded like an inviting prospect after their extended time on the road. It might also keep him out of danger. Finally, he was wary of Vigheran's intentions at Dharbur, and this at least confirmed that the mercenary wasn't planning on selling him into slavery, or something even worse. At least not right away.

The smells of the strange vegetation captivated Torrin. He passed groves of trees bearing fruit that he had never eaten before. The farm animals were familiar, except the cows were of a smaller variety with taller horns than he was used to. There were many more sheep than other types of animals.

An impressive structure was built into the east side of the valley. It was a long chute, supported off the ground by columns at regular intervals. Sometimes it was anchored to the cliff wall. Torrin realized that it carried water for the city, which was built on a hill beside the river ahead.

From this distance, the city did not look impressive. Most of it was composed of low buildings of mud and brick. Its defences were limited to some low brick walls, criss-crossing the city in a haphazard fashion. The aqueduct was the most impressive feature. It entered the heart of the city and emptied into a large pool. From there, several small canals carried water through the city and eventually exited on the south and west side.

The three of them stopped in the late afternoon in a collection of huts and businesses that catered to the livestock trading industry. There was no point driving the animals into the city unless it was necessary. They secured a rare private room at an inn there. It was costly, but Vigheran seemed to think it was necessary. After a hot meal, Erelin and Vigheran briefly discussed something.

"*Kyusi*, it would be good for me to rest," Vigheran said, using his normal-sounding voice that seemed to take effort. "Erelin wishes to look at the animals. You may rest with me or go with him."

Torrin was happy to go. He had a good idea of what Erelin was really looking for.

They exited the inn, stepping into the warm air of the desert evening. The sound of many cattle lowing, sheep bleating, and horses whinnying coalesced into a constant din. Business appeared to be wrapping up for the day. Erelin selected for himself a good vantage point on a corral fence. Torrin sat on the same fence, on a lower rung. He knew that he wouldn't be of much help finding their quarry as Erelin was taller and had the better eyes.

"Do you think she'll be here?" Torrin asked.

Erelin shrugged. The expression on his cowled face was difficult to read, but Torrin was beginning to see subtle differences that proved the tall Taurilian had emotions after all. He looked worried.

Torrin began to feel some affinity to this man. For the first few weeks after they met, Erelin came across as an unfeeling, detached killer motived solely by money. But subsequent events showed Torrin that he was indeed human. He especially remembered the outpouring of emotion when he described the vision of the Gryphon hunting the white-haired woman. Clearly, he cared for someone, and by all indications it was a connection that went beyond any material or sexual value that she might mean to him.

Torrin asked himself several times why he wanted to find the white-haired woman so bad. His best guess is that he was being driven by empathy. He longed so much to mean something to someone. He had attached so quickly to Braedil and Kryna, two people that spoke his language, shared his history, and were committed to his well-being. Erelin had a connection with this woman that was very important to him. From Torrin's perspective, it was the only relationship that Erelin had. If Torrin felt such a drive and desire for that sort of connection, so must Erelin.

But perhaps there was something more selfish lurking under the surface. What was it about this white-haired woman that made Erelin so concerned for her safety and well-being? If Erelin was telling the truth, and his dedication wasn't for any conjugal reason, then Torrin wanted the same thing. He wanted to *be* the white-haired woman to Erelin.

"Someday, it would be really nice to actually have a conversation with you," Torrin said, slightly surprised that he was putting his thoughts in words. "I've been with you for more than a month, and I've come to trust you. You know a lot about me, my fears and aspirations. But I don't know much about you."

Torrin searched Erelin's unmoving face. The frown curled a little lower, and the brow raised slightly. Torrin took this as a sign of thoughtfulness.

"About the only thing I know about you is that you care for this woman. You seem to care for me too, but as you said a few nights ago, you do that for your own protection. I don't really know what you mean by that, but you see in me a fair exchange. Somehow. Am I right?"

Erelin absently peeled off some bark from the fencepost he was braced against. He gave a faint nod.

"But this woman, you want to protect her. I don't see anything she has to offer you. Maybe I just haven't seen it yet. But it strikes me that you love her."

Erelin visibly flinched. He broke his gaze on the crowd, shook his head, and then turned away. Torrin figured he had gone too far. Even though it was negative emotion, it felt good that he could at least elicit something, the satisfying feeling of squeezing blood from a stone. He shouldn't push things.

Erelin was looking at the thinning crowd again. He took the cowl down from his head. Torrin tried for one last connection.

"You are a good man, Erelin. I don't know what's in your past. I don't imagine it's pretty. But I do see beauty in you. I do see Arren's blessing upon you."

Erelin quickly got down from the fence. He grabbed Torrin's arm, spun him away, and pointed over his shoulder to the wall of a nearby shed. Torrin complied and walked towards the shed, fearful that he had angered Erelin. Once he got within the shade of the low building, he turned around. Erelin was still standing, hands by his side, by the fence.

Someone approached Erelin. Torrin could see it was a young woman, but her hair was gathered beneath a cap. She passed off as a Belorin given her snugly fitting leather clothing and dark skin. But as she approached, he could tell by her facial features that she was, indeed, the white-haired woman. She was striding quickly towards Erelin as if she recognized him. Her demeanor was not friendly. Erelin had drawn up his cowl again.

When she came close enough, she thrust both hands straight at Erelin's chest as if to knock him over. She had to reach above her head to do so. He took a small step back to keep his balance. "You again," she snarled in Belorin. "I didn't think you'd chase me all the way here. Can I ever get away from you?"

It wasn't the meeting that Torrin had expected. He could understand Belorin well enough. Dar-Amund had been dependent on trade with the Belorin to keep itself supplied.

She put one hand on her hip and the other pointed at his face with a menacing gesture. "I told you last time. I don't want to see you again. Especially here, where people can see us."

Erelin made a complex gesture with the fingers of his right hand, then extended his left with a folded verse paper grasped between two fingers. When she saw it, she knocked it out of his grasp. It fell into the dirt at their feet.

"I don't need you," she enunciated each word for effect. "I can look after myself. The last thing I want is for you to be telling me what to do. I won't say it again. Leave me alone."

She stormed off. Erelin bent down and picked up the folded paper. He didn't stand up but stayed in a crouch. Torrin didn't know what to say. He knew he should be afraid. This man was a trained killer, and who knows what he might do when his emotions were raw. But all that Torrin had suffered to date was making him understand the suffering of others. His own longing to belong, to have family, was reflected in the man that stood before him. For the first time, he also identified his own disability, his missing hand, with that of Erelin's, his inability to speak.

"That didn't go well," he said in River-Tongue. He hoped his tone conveyed his empathy. "Something tells me that you aren't going to give up, though."

Erelin straightened up and took a deep breath. He motioned for Torrin to follow. He looked like he was on a mission. They began to move through the thin crowd that remained around the corrals and outdoor booths in which business was done. Erelin kept hunched over for the most part so that he did not stick out in the crowd. Torrin realized that they were following the woman at a distance.

It wasn't long before they came to a tavern. A large patio was built in front, with several tables. The sound of music and dancing came from inside. The woman sat down at a table with two men. The first was a grizzled old Belorin range-rider. The second caught Torrin's eye. His skin stood out from the others, being lighter and with less colour. He was dressed as a Karolian soldier, the dark-blue of his tattered military cloak turned outwards. He was not wearing armour, but had a Taurilian sword strapped to his side, the hilt wrapped in double-red. He was young, possibly even younger than Torrin. He had a distinctive set to his jaw that made him look a little surly.

Torrin noticed that Erelin was writing. He was leaning against the wall of a feed shed, which blocked the last rays of the setting sun. Torrin joined him in the shadow. Finally, Erelin passed him the paper.

I want you to meet that Karolian.
Find out his name and anything else you can.
Tell him you want to travel to Karolia.
Be honest about your situation.
Do not tell him where you are staying.
Do not talk about Er-Elin or Vigheran.

It was the first time he had seen the spelling of the names of his two companions. Erelin was spelled Er-Elin, the ancient Taurilian method of distinguishing between two men with the same name before there were House names. Vigheran's name was clearly a transliteration of a Zindori name into Melandarim.

He took a deep breath. He was hesitant to make acquaintances with anyone. They always wound up dead, he thought. But the blue cloak called out to him like a beacon. His best chance at safety lay in the realm of Karolia, and there before him was a representative of that kingdom.

He approached the table. The woman had just stood up, tugging on the older man's arm, asking him to dance. He at first resisted her urgings. Torrin paused as the woman finally got her way, and the two of them disappeared into the raucous mirth inside.

"Good evening," Torrin said in River-Tongue as he approached the table. "May I sit?"

"Of course," the Karolian politely said, raising an eyebrow with curiosity. "Welcome, stranger. I don't see many other Karolians here, I'm pleased to make your acquaintance." He did not give his name immediately.

"Thank you. I'm not from Karolia but I'm pleased to meet a fellow *almathin*[1]." It was exhilarating to Torrin to finally use Melandarim phrases again in casual conversations. "My name is Torrin, son of Paldonn, house Atlan."

The soldier reciprocated. "I am Dyrk, son of Maryk, house Teren. And I have to say that this is the first time in my memory to have met someone from House Atlan." He gave a brief knowing smile. "It's like we are long-lost adoptive brothers."

Dyrk called to the Zindori barmaid who had just whisked by to get Torrin a tankard of ale. He did not refuse.

"I sense you have quite a story," Dyrk said. "A Taurilian not from Karolia, carrying some significant injuries. You have certainly piqued my interest."

"I am from Dar-Amund," Torrin said. As he expected, the expression on Dyrk's face widened with surprise.

"What can you tell me about Dar-Amund?" Dyrk questioned earnestly. "I have heard many stories, none of them encouraging."

"It is as bad as you have heard, and worse, I am afraid," Torrin

---

[1] An *almathin* is Melandarim for a mounted warrior, and a polite term to use amongst men who can speak the language.

said. He drew breath sharply to steel his emotions. "The Vekh have completely destroyed it. I believe I am the only survivor."

Dyrk motioned his head to Torrin's right arm with an unasked question.

"I was thrown from my horse during the fight and suffered injury," he sadly reported, keeping the details as sparse as he could for his own benefit. His ale arrived, and he used his left hand to take a long draught. It was swill compared to the spiced ale he enjoyed back at home, but he enjoyed it all the same.

"You are an eye-witness?" Dyrk questioned.

Torrin confirmed. "I saw the place burned to the ground, and the-" he choked and gripped his tankard tightly. "I saw the bodies of the slain."

"I'm sorry." Dyrk's words of support were not altogether convincing. "But if you are an eye-witness, this needs to be reported to Karolia immediately. Could you write me-" he stopped himself. He glanced at the stump of his visitor's right arm and showed some remorse. "I'm sorry, just getting carried away. Tell me more, if you can."

"I managed to escape the battle, and was helped by some, er, Feldarian villagers. They brought me to Sorwail, but I couldn't stay there. I bought land passage to Dharbur, and now I'm hoping to find my way somehow to Karolia."

"Which is why you approached me."

"Yes."

"Would you have any money for expenses?"

Torrin didn't think it was wise to tell strangers that he had a lot of money, whether it was a lie or not. "What kind of expenses would you need paid?"

"If there was some way I could bring you to Karolia, I would hope you could supply a horse and your own travel gear. I am not with my regiment. I am on my own."

"I could see about that," Torrin replied noncommittally. "I have no idea what a horse would cost here, though."

Dharbur, like the rest of Belorin, had stopped minting its own coins centuries ago. They used Karolian coinage, with the exception of the gold coins, of which it was not legal to take them across the border. For large transactions, Belorin used a Calderan gold coin, which was worth only a little less than the Karolian half-crown.

"Eight silver rings," Dyrk responded. Horses were inexpensive there, and he could probably find a good one for less than that, but he wanted to be on the safe side. "Do you know horses?"

Torrin recalled his war-horse, killed in the same encounter in which he lost his hand. "Yes, but not the local breeds. I was trained on an Eastern war-horse."

Dyrk's eyes narrowed. "What breed, exactly, did you have?"

"A pure-bred Veranian mare," Torrin said wistfully. "She was cut out from under me by the Vekh."

"Coloration? Height?"

Torrin wondered why the Karolian was asking him these details about his horse. Maybe he was suspicious, and was checking Torrin's story. "She was grey with some white dappling. Eighteen hands."

Dyrk asked a few more specific questions about Torrin's mount before he was satisfied. "Can you recall the date on which Dar-Amund was destroyed?"

"Taephin, first week of the Month of Waiting[1]. What is today's date, by the way? I've been on the road a long time and lost track of the calendar."

"It is Telmanitar, seventh week of Kemantar's month[2]. Though I have to say it doesn't look like it around here."

Torrin agreed that it looked nothing like Kemantar's month, the depth of winter. The snow would be heavy on the slopes of the Warder Mountains right now, but there in Dharbur it felt like summer-time during the day.

"You said you are alone, but there are two others at this table before I got here," Torrin said, fishing for some information about the white-haired woman.

"Those are some Belorin friends of mine. I won't be traveling with them."

---

[1] December 5, 2797
[2] February 6, 2798

"That woman. She looked familiar," Torrin lied.

"Saris? I doubt it. She does tend to meet a lot of men but if you just got to Dharbur, I don't think she's had the chance."

At least he now had her name.

"Now if you're serious about heading to Karolia, meet me here tomorrow at the third hour with the money for a horse."

"Very well," Torrin answered. He finished his ale and got up. "It was a pleasure meeting you, *almathin* of Karolia. A pleasure I have not had in a long time," he said, heart-felt. Despite the obvious signs of suspicion, Torrin was encouraged by the meeting. Perhaps there were some parts of the world that were not completely hostile to him.

Erelin stripped off most of his gear. It was important to travel light tonight. He had already strung the bow. The weapon straps were checked. He was missing his left boot-dagger, but it was better for Torrin to have it.

Vigheran carefully reloaded the contraption on his arm. When they traveled, he kept the two Calderan blades strapped parallel, vertically on his back. When he expected combat, as he did tonight, they were arranged almost perpendicular to one another, diagonal, so he could reach over each shoulder and draw them both at the same time.

Torrin had instructions to spend the night in their room and not open the door for anyone. The two mercenaries exited the inn and began walking along the darkened road into the city.

Lighting was poor. The sky was clear, but the moon was just a sliver. Most of the light came from the stars. Erelin's attentive eyes continually scanned the horizon, the path ahead, the path behind.

Their first destination was the docks. Fishing in the salt sea to the south was a viable industry, and a small set of docks to the west of the city served the small scows that went to and fro. Much fishing was done at night, so there were few boats moored when they arrived.

Vigheran arranged the terms with one of the Roj fishermen there and paid him.

They entered the city through a gap in the wall. There was very little to tell the buildings apart. All were made of the same sun-baked mud bricks. Few other pedestrians were about at this time of the night. Those that were in the streets traveled in groups. There was no sign of any watchmen.

They came to a leatherworking workshop. Vigheran knocked on the wood-plank back door that led to the residence in the back. A narrow slot opened. Vigheran had a brief conversation with the person inside. They were told to wait in the street. The door opened, then closed, and an older Roj man made his way down the street and was lost from view.

Vigheran fidgeted. Erelin stood stock-still. They waited for three-quarters of an hour. The man came back, now holding a lantern, and beckoned for them to follow. The moon, by now, was below the horizon.

They made their way to the south side of the city, where there were few houses. Warehouses dominated the south wall. Now there was nobody on the streets besides the three of them. The man led them into one of the warehouses. The floor was made of hard-packed mud. Less than half of the building was full of wares, which were mostly bundles of woolen fleeces. Close to the back, the floor changed to wooden beams. A trap-door could easily be seen in the floor. The man opened the door and directed them to descend. He stayed by the door.

Vigheran went first, Erelin second. They were in a dank cellar with a high ceiling. Bales of raw wool were stacked on one side. The musty smell of sheep tallow permeated the place. Two torches flamed and smoked on two pillars close to the center of the room. A lantern sat on a stool. One man stood behind it, cloaked and hooded. Erelin had no doubt that more lurked in the shadows.

There were no introductions. They all knew why they were there. Erelin kept back as far as he could without being suspicious, positioning his head so that the corner of the cowl blocked the light of the torch from his eyes. He picked out one, now two, figures in the shadows. He began to figure out lines of fire, angles of cover, and how they could possibly get up the ladder alive.

"You took your time," the robed man spoke in Roj. "You wouldn't be back if you didn't have good news for us."

Without a word, Vigheran reached into his belt satchel and retrieved a small object wrapped in cloths. He placed it on the stool beside the lantern. The hooded man unwrapped it. A pungent odor of acrid preservative assailed their nostrils. It was a severed human index finger.

"You are looking for more," Vigheran stated. "We can find the rest. But first you must pay twice for this one. Braedil was not easy to find."

"You think highly of yourselves. I can assure you, we will find the last one that remains."

Vigheran was tense, ready to spring at the slightest sound or movement that came from the darkness. Erelin backed up an inch further into the darkness.

"We already have him," Vigheran said. "The four you sent after him are dead. And if we don't walk out of here, you will never find him, I assure you."

A silent standoff ensued. Vigheran grew more confident as it became apparent the cloaked figure across from him did not expect this turn of events.

"How can you prove this?" the question finally came.

"We will meet you tomorrow evening. Same time. On the southernmost quay. You will come alone. Doing business is difficult with six crossbows pointed at my head from the darkness. We will bring proof of his death. Now, I want payment for Braedil. Double. And double again tomorrow night."

The man moved his arm. A bag fell to the ground with a clink. He then fumbled with another bag and counted more coins. He wrapped up the second amount and threw it beside the first.

Vigheran did not bend down to fetch the bags. He nudged them with his foot back towards Erelin, without taking his eyes off the cloaked man.

Now they had to get up the ladder. Vigheran climbed first while Erelin stood watching the rest. Then, without turning his back, he leapt, once onto a middle rung of the ladder, then again to clear the ten-foot height. Within a second, he was beside the startled old man who was holding the trap door open.

They left the warehouse, walking quickly. Back to the docks they went. They entered the fishing scow that was just ready to cast off. They joined the mass of boats on the salt sea that was just completing their night of fishing and about to come in. The scow was lost with the others. Nobody would be able to tell it apart in that jumble of boats. An hour later, as the fishing vessels came in to dock, several of them continued up the river to other docks. One punted near to the west side of the river, and two men jumped overboard into the shallows. They made their way north. Nobody followed them.

Torrin fingered the gold coin in his pocket. He had never held a gold coin before.

When he woke up this morning, Vigheran was sleeping soundly but Erelin wasn't there. He had dressed and headed down to the common room. Erelin had been waiting for him. When they sat together, Erelin had passed him the coin, motioning for him to keep it in his pocket. Torrin had recognized the imprint on it as an authentic Calderan gold coin. He wished he could hold it up to the light, just to confirm that it was real. As if he knew how to tell apart real and fake gold, he reminded himself.

"This should be plenty," he said to Erelin. "I don't know how to thank you."

They were sitting at a small table in the eating-hall. Breakfast was being served. Torrin had eaten so much the previous night that he didn't much feel like eating now. Erelin was writing on a verse paper. The maid came by with a bowl of runny oatmeal, the way Erelin liked it.

Erelin handed the paper over to Torrin, and then put his finger on his lips. Torrin read the words and his eyes opened wide.

"But- but this is false, right? I'm just saying this so he'll take me with him?"

Erelin slowly shook his head. His expression clearly conveyed sadness.

Torrin let his hand fall to the table in shock. "No. It can't be. There must be someone. Somewhere."

Erelin repeated the motion with his finger on his lips. (Quiet.) With a trembling hand, Torrin opened up the message again.

You are the last surviving male of the House of Atlan.

Tell this to the Karolian.

You must leave with him tonight after Er-elin and Vigheran have left

Do not obey Vigheran's instructions.

Burn this.

Farewell.

Many more questions threatened to spill out. Would he see Erelin again? What was going on between Erelin and Vigheran, that they were not on the same page? Who was exterminating his family? Would they come after him even if he made it to Karolia? Who should they look out for along their journey? What if Dyrk refused to take him?

Erelin got up to leave. Torrin curled his right arm on the table and buried his head in it. It was all too much for him. There had to be, somewhere, sometime, a place that he could feel safe, where he belonged. The only person to which he had any semblance of a connection had just said farewell. He was with strangers yet again, assuming those strangers would even take him.

Who could he depend on? The words that Erelin had written weeks ago echoed in his consciousness. *I will protect you.* The phrase was out of Nedrin's verse. Yet the Servants seemed distant. His inability to write was a big part of that. Oh, for the amazing gift of speaking directly to one's God. Not solely through the written word. Not through the intermediaries.

He steeled himself. If Arren wouldn't allow it, then He may as well strike him dead for trying. He would be dead either way.

He spoke in his mind, tentatively at first, but then the emotions came rushing out. Anger, hurt, frustration, and above all, the loneliness and feeling of abandonment. But then he gave up. He couldn't go on. Just like the very real circumstances of his life, his spiritual circumstances seemed utterly hopeless as well.

A woman's voice began singing softly from the table beside him in the Belorin language. Unlike the Karolians, Torrin had no issue with women singing. At first it barely registered on his tortured soul. But then he began to listen carefully to the words.

When the grasslands have no end.
My only friends are the lonely hills.
Even the distant mountains offer no help
But you will remember me.

Was this the way that Arren stopped someone from coming to him directly? He might as well send someone to interrupt me, he figured. The woman, her back to him, sang the next verse. He strained to hear the words.

The sun may beat on my brow
The darkness of night hides my paths.
Snakes and scorpions might I tread
But you will remember me.

Was this some sort of a love song? A lonely herdsman pining for his beloved? People are fickle. There's no sense hoping that they will stay with you, or even remember you.

My closest friend may turn aside
The son of my youth may curse his birth
The fellow soldier may fall away
But you will remember-

"Hey!" A Pej Zindori barmaid scolded in the woman's direction. "Singing is for evening times. Don't bother the other customers."

Torrin wiped his misty eyes and stood up. It was time he got to his feet. He had things to do.

Dyrk lingered over the letter, going over the three pages to make sure he hadn't left anything out. This was his third letter to Neriah since leaving Karolia. If all went well, he should be home by the time this letter reached her, but that's what he had thought about the last letter he had sent from the battlefront at Narval.

Saris took a chair next to him. Even though it was mid-morning, she had just gotten up. She was moaning that her head hurt, and her mouth was so dry, and she was still tired. Dyrk ignored her. She was wearing her light cotton blouse, but it had slipped off one shoulder, leaving it bare.

"What are you writing?" Saris asked, trying to get his attention.

"A letter," he responded without looking up. A self-respecting Karolian woman would never be seen dressed like that in her own house, much less a public tavern.

She persisted. "Who's it to?"

Dyrk was pleased that she asked the question. It gave him an opportunity to insert more distance. "My betrothed back in Karolia."

She stared at him for a few seconds with bleary eyes. "Huh," she finally said. "Is she pretty?"

"What do you care?"

"You're right, I don't. I need a drink." She got up and staggered away.

Dyrk wasn't sure if she was talking about water or more alcohol, but it didn't really matter to him. Saris had danced late into the night, and then had left the inn, quite drunk, in the company of a strange young Belorin man. She had returned just before sunrise. Dyrk wanted nothing to do with a woman who demonstrated such disgraceful behavior.

Dyrk had considered Torrin's offer carefully last night. He had thought about skipping the meeting with Torrin that morning. Having that man with him might slow him down. Yes, his story checked out, but there was something going on that Torrin wasn't telling him. Dyrk had learned from his father that it was best to keep away from anyone that appeared to be in some sort of trouble, because all too often they had brought it upon themselves and would subsequently bring it on you. Madwin's take had been a little different. Render help when it is needed, distance when it was warranted, and enough attention and scrutiny to know the difference. Easier said than done.

He had hoped to scrape enough money together to buy a cheap horse and ride for Karolia. He was won over by the prospect of having the funds to buy a better horse and equipment, both for himself and Torrin. So he had decided to keep their meeting that morning.

The story Torrin gave at their meeting wasn't convincing, and only worried him more. The last of Atlan's house? Surely there were a few dozen left in Karolia. After all, an estate was reserved for each of the Sixty Houses of Karolia. How did he know that he was the last? But the money Torrin supplied overcame Dyrk's reservations. Pooling their resources, they would be able to purchase two quality mounts, which would go a long way to make their journey easier. He had agreed.

Yes, Torrin would be a liability with only one hand. However, traveling on one's own was dangerous for many reasons. He kept listing the advantages and disadvantages to himself as he folded and addressed Neriah's letter. It would cost a hefty amount to get a letter from there to Karolia, but it was worth it. He was never going to abandon her again. He put the letter in his satchel and walked out the front door of the inn. After delivering the letter, he planned to head to the corrals to find horses for their journey.

Now what if Torrin was telling the truth about Atlan's house? It was Dyrk's duty to the Kingdom to preserve one of the Houses of Karolia. Especially a prominent one like Atlan. But Torrin's final request still mystified him. Why leave at night? He seemed to be in some sort of trouble, like someone was hunting him. Was Dyrk getting himself into a complicated situation that was none of his business? But again, just as he would protect any woman in trouble, shouldn't that also extend to a crippled man?

Koeric had left for home first thing this morning. Without cattle to drive, he could make it home in a day. Saris wanted to stay behind, probably to party. Dyrk slept in the open room of their inn, making sure to keep his bedroll as far from Saris as possible. He had refused Torrin's request to leave during the night. Instead, he invited the man to stay the night at their inn and they would make a start before first light. Saris had said she was thinking about accompanying them as far as her homestead, or possibly staying in Dharbur a little longer and making her way home alone. Dyrk would rather she chose the latter.

He spoke with the merchant and began to browse through the available horses. His father would have a field day there, he thought.

Many good studs for breeding with the Akhiros mare. Maybe he should bring one home for him?

What was he thinking? His father hated him. Better to bring a horse for Farnich to spite his father. Yes, that would be a better decision.

Dyrk took his time. He had all afternoon, so there was no sense rushing into a decision. He narrowed down his choice down to four mounts. Despite the complaining of the trader, he left a deposit and took each for a ride up a nearby hill. His final choice was a young, spirited stallion for himself, and an older gelding for Torrin. He did not want to take a mare with the stallion for obvious reasons.

He had instructed Torrin to purchase riding boots and some leather protective leggings. Dyrk planned to take the route through Lyssia. There was no knowing how far the Vekh had penetrated, but a winter journey through the Pass of Takorran wasn't wise. Their route would take them over the Ebur Plateau. There would be no roads but more than their fair share of cacti and thorn forests.

After their evening meal, Torrin and Dyrk packed their saddlebags with the necessary provisions and equipment. Torrin said he would return to his own inn first before coming back to bed down.

Dyrk sat down to while away the evening hours until the common room would be available for sleeping. He set up a chair, as far away from the revelry as possible. He put his visored cap over his face and tried to snooze.

"Why don't you like dancing?" The voice was Saris's. He pulled up his cap. She was leaning against the wall. Her eyes were sparkling, white hair tossed back in an unkempt tangle. A bit of sweat glistened at the base of her neck.

"You haven't met many Karolians before, have you?" Dyrk said cynically.

"No." She appeared oblivious of his intent and repeated her original question. "So why don't you dance?"

Dyrk figured that he should, at the very least, avoid the harshest response that he felt like giving. "We hold to traditions that exclude dancing together," he said, hoping that his words were kind enough.

"Well you're missing out. Come on, I'll show you." She held out her hand.

He had a brief flashback of Saris dancing with Toic back at the homestead. A rush of hormones pumped through his body, making him feel nervous. A part of him desperately wanted to indulge. The rest of him screamed for him to get away. "Thanks for the offer, but I'm not interested."

She cocked her hips slightly to the left and her head slightly to the right, in a pose that displayed curiosity. "Do your traditions exclude everything that's fun?"

"Not at all." Defending his heritage animated Dyrk like nothing else. "We play sports, enjoy a good story telling, and drink beer. In moderation."

She gave a mischievous smile. "Moderation? I haven't seen you drink more than a tankard at a time. That's not enough to wash down lunch!" She pursed her lips and half-closed her eyes. "That girl of yours back home. How do you give her a good time?"

Dyrk hesitated to answer that. He and Neriah never really set out to have a good time. They just enjoyed being together, and the company of her family. Why did everything need to be a thrill? But he felt the need to at least rebut her assertion. "We take walks, tell jokes, play games, spend time with her parents and siblings. That's good enough for us."

She wrinkled her nose as if someone had introduced a bad odor. "Something tells me she's not waiting in eager anticipation for your return."

Dyrk leaned back as if to resume his snooze.

She wouldn't take the hint. "I mean, have you ever *asked* her if she likes to dance?"

"For your information, she is a fantastic dancer," Dyrk replied, a touch of anger in his voice. "But for us, girls dance. Men sing. Never shall the twain be confused. It works great for us. I'm glad you are able to enjoy yourself, but it just isn't my thing. Now if you'll excuse me, I'd like to get some rest before I leave tomorrow."

She gave a little laugh and tousled her hair, leaning both shoulders against the wall. "You're so soft. I'm going with you tomorrow, and

I won't go to bed for at least a couple hours."

"You can't find your way back on your own?"

"I figure you might want a few pointers on how to travel across Belorin. We might as well discuss it on the trail."

She had him there. If he was honest with himself, he would really value her wisdom. If she was nearly as old as Koeric, she must have a lot of experience in the wild. He grudgingly re-oriented himself to be a little less hostile.

"We leave two hours before sunset," he said. "You'll need to pack."

"I'll take care of it later." She wiggled four fingers in his direction as she walked away. "First I need to enjoy myself." She turned and headed for the music.

She is a disaster waiting to happen, he told himself. He buried the twinge of excitement that he would still get one more day with a woman as attractive as this one.

CHAPTER 22:
THE SERAPH

"We are close to leaving for Ancharith," Vigheran's gravelly voice assured Torrin. "For tonight, you will not leave this room again. Do not open the door for anyone but us."

Torrin nodded his acknowledgment. Vigheran had taken most of his equipment this time, and so had Erelin. Just as they were heading out the door, Vigheran turned to him.

"*Kyusi*, you are a *tinvak*. A warrior." He said it with more emotion than he had displayed to the one-handed traveling partner to date. "We will be back before sunrise."

Erelin and Vigheran first went to the stables and retrieved two horses. Leading them, they took the road down to the docks again under the late evening sky. Before they got there, they turned aside to an orchard. They counted off an agreed number of rows and trunks, then enlarged a hole beneath the roots of a large pomegranate shrub. They deposited a significant amount of gear there. Erelin removed most of his armour, his cloak, and his sword. He placed a leather bag with his extra bowstrings and the sling he needed to restring his bow. Vigheran kept his leather chest armour and bracers, but deposited his leg armour and helmet. One of the Corsavan swords was left behind in its sheath. They tied the horses two trees over, still saddled and ready to go.

Again, they found several fishermen at the docks. The negotiations took longer this time, and the money that changed hands was greater. But money will often get men to do things that they wouldn't otherwise consider.

The fisherman accompanied the two mercenaries onto the boat.

It was put it into the water. Normally, the fisherman was unable to fish without a larger crew with him. But he would be making much more money tonight than an entire boat full of fish. He could buy a whole new boat, possibly even two.

The boat was punted down the river to the southernmost quay of the city. There was only one cloaked man standing there, motionless. As the boat eased up to the dock, he climbed aboard without a word. They began to move out into the salt sea.

Of the several boats that were within view upon the water, one began to shadow their movements. Neither Vigheran nor Erelin noticed it. Their attention was solely upon their passenger.

Vigheran stood with the visitor near the single mast that held only a furled sail. He took out a small object, bundled in cloths. The cloaked man took it and unwrapped it. It was another severed index finger. He examined the gruesome token. He even leaned close and appeared to smell it. Then he straightened up.

"Well?" Vigheran grated. "Is it his?"

"It is," the reply came. The voice was not like the one from the night before. It was low, powerful, and unearthly. It didn't even sound like it came from the hood of the cloak.

"Where is the payment?"

The man moved his hand forward. A small bag fell onto the deck with a satisfied clink. The fisherman's eyes were fixed on the transaction, as were Erelin's.

Vigheran bent down to pick up the bag. In a flash, he was suspended a foot above the ground, a hand tightened around his neck. Erelin didn't even have time to nock an arrow, but he did so now in a fluid motion. The recurved bow tightened with deadly force.

"Do not play games with me," the eerie voice intoned angrily. "I do not need the discarded appendages of the living. Where is he?"

Another boat was now very close, moving quietly under the power of four oars. Erelin, so intent on the two that stood before him, did not realize it until the first feet thundered onto the deck. Five men boarded, equipped with loaded crossbows. Bright red cloaks flowed from their shoulders.

A small splash came from the stern of the boat, ignored by everyone else. The fisherman had gotten away with his life and his payment.

Vigheran squirmed just to draw breath. Finally, he managed, "Will tell you." He was dropped to the ground, clutching his throat. He tried to sputter something about bringing proof before the transaction was completed.

"First-" he started to say.

"You are in no position to negotiate," the voice boomed. "Your life for the location of the boy."

Vigheran gave the name of the inn and the room that he and Erelin were staying in.

The cloaked man entered the other boat with long strides. The Raiders with crossbows remained. "I will return," the voice stated as the boat began to separate and pick up speed. It was headed for land. There was nothing visible propelling it.

"If it is as you say, you will have your payment and your life."

There was no need to mention what would happen otherwise. In fact, given the amount of money involved, everyone on the boat had a good idea of the only logical conclusion to the encounter.

The Raiders kept Vigheran lying on the deck, two crossbows pointed at his prone body. The other three nervously fingered their triggers as they surveyed the tall Taurilian, bow tightly drawn. They wordlessly urged their partners to volunteer for the task of disarming him.

Erelin slowly raised the bow. The Raiders were relieved that it was no longer pointed at their chests. The echo of air moving through the horns was the only sound that came as the arrow was released. Erelin dodged to the side as two crossbows fired their bolts harmlessly into the bow of the ship where he had been.

The boat's sail came crashing down on the two holding Vigheran. Erelin's companion got to his hands and knees, raised an arm, and with a distinctive snapping sound, a small projectile lodged itself into the face of one of the Raiders who had just fired. The red-cloaked mercenary screamed and dropped his crossbow.

Within three seconds, Erelin had loaded and fired twice. The first narrowly missed a diving Raider, but the second hit home on one extracting himself from the sail. He was aware that one crossbow had not yet fired, so he kept moving as he loaded a third time. The loud crack from the impact of metal on wood made him flinch, but no quarrel was hurled his way.

Vigheran clutched at the missile embedded into his chest. His right arm held one of his Calderan blades, but his left was now reflexively gripping the bolt as he fell to the deck. As two men closed on him, scimitars sweeping, he raised his weapon in a feeble attempt to parry. The first glanced off his sword, his arm bracer, and finally into the nearby wooden railing. The second descended on his left shoulder, slicing through armour, flesh, and bone.

With one last desperate lunge, one of his assailants was impaled on his sword. A guttural cry escaped his lips. A downward blow to the back of Vigheran's head ended him.

Erelin's third arrow missed, but it deterred another Raider from closing in on him long enough to make his escape. He threw himself into the water. The Raider ran to the railing, fumbling to reload a crossbow. The quarrels spilled out of his trembling hand. Finally, he had it cocked, a quarrel in place. He scanned the dark waters for his quarry. Nothing.

Dyrk awoke with a start. He looked around the common room of the inn. Nobody else stirred. It was difficult to tell the time, but by the fact that there were no sounds at all in the kitchen adjacent, he did not believe it was close to morning.

Something wasn't quite right. Things around him appeared slightly blurred. His hearing was dulled. Was this another dream? He sat quietly, trying to pick up the breathing of the others sleeping on the floor.

Then he noticed Torrin, a few feet away, propped up on an elbow on his bedroll. "Is it time?" he asked in a whisper. "I haven't been able to sleep at all."

Dyrk rubbed his eyes. He figured they could leave, provided Saris could wake up. That wasn't a given. Still, he couldn't shake that feeling of foreboding that hovered close by. He had felt that during the dream in which the Gryphon entered the homestead.

There was no way he could get back to sleep now. Maybe, if he had a rocking chair, he joked to himself.

He got dressed, making as little noise as possible in consideration for the others still sleeping. He told Torrin to get Saris up. He rolled up his bedroll and cinched it tight. He always kept his sword underneath a lip of the bedroll. He picked it up to strap it on his side. Was it unnaturally warm? No, he must be imagining it. He picked up his bedroll and saddlebag. Time to get the horses prepared for their journey.

He entered the stables. He caught movement out of the corner of his eye. It seemed to him that someone had just left the stables quickly. Was it the stable-hand? No, the watchman was slumbering peacefully on a pile of hay near the entrance.

It was against tradition to name a horse after one's distinguished ancestors. But there was a more recent practice of naming a mount after a historical enemy, both to besmirch the name of the enemy and to make one's horse sound frightening. Dyrk had named his horse Drudor, the eldest son of Drukudar, the first king of the Vekh. Torrin had named his gelding Valdor, which was Melandarim for "survival".

Dyrk led Drudor out from his stall and saddled him. Torrin arrived just as he was laying the blanket on Valdor. Dyrk figured he should not touch Saris's horse; she was rather particular about it.

It took them nearly an hour to get away. Saris took her time getting up, packing her things, and saddling her horse. She complained the entire time about the unearthly hour that they were leaving. Dyrk offered many times to leave her behind but she insisted on going with them.

Finally, the three were mounted. They rode north along the road through the riverside groves. A strong, dry wind was blowing from the east, making the trees wave their branches. All three of them kept their cloaks tightly around them to ward off the chill.

They had left the cattle yards well behind. The sweet smells of ripening fruit graced the air as they passed through hedged orchards. The wind had blown some sparse clouds over the eastern sky, but otherwise the stars shone brightly, and the sliver of moon gave them enough light to proceed along the road.

Dyrk had no doubts about Saris's horsemanship. So far, he had been pleasantly surprised with Torrin's knowledge of the riding equipment and how to handle his mount. Perhaps he was being truthful about his training as a mounted warrior. Dyrk's one-handed traveling mate possessed a degree of compassion and gentleness that Dyrk didn't have the patience for. This boded well for the attachment between horse and rider, but Dyrk wondered if that gentleness might be a hindrance once it became necessary to push the horse beyond its comfort zone. Dyrk observed Torrin posting naturally as they moved out in a trot.

Dyrk's crossbow had been broken when the tarn crashed to earth. He didn't want to carry a spear, either, for a long journey that could take weeks. He had bought a slim shortbow and small quiver with six arrows. The bow was tied, unstrung, beneath his saddlebags. Otherwise, his only weapon was the sword from back home.

The road took them between two rows of hedges. Dyrk's nerves tightened when he saw three figures on foot on the road at the far end of the hedges. One carried a lantern. As he came closer, two of them seemed to be night-guards. The third was cloaked but his hood was down. Dyrk noticed his horse was showing signs of fright.

A distinct voice penetrated Dyrk's consciousness. For a moment he thought it was coming from his horse.

[You must have courage]

The voice echoed in his head. He couldn't even tell what language it was speaking, but he could certainly understand it. He had been feeling uneasy ever since he woke up, but now he knew he was cracking. His horse? Talking?

"Hold there," one of the night-guards called in Belorin. "Dismount, if you will."

Despite the greeting in the Belorin language, Dyrk could tell that both of them were Zindori, either Roj or Pej. The third man in a cloak had a broad face with a thin beard. He appeared to be either of Ancharith or Rhonauri descent. None of the three seemed in any way threatening. Dyrk obeyed.

"Sorry to bother you, good travelers," the guard went on in Belorin. Dyrk tried his best to follow along. "We are looking for some escaped slaves. All we ask is that you show us your right hand and you may proceed."

Dyrk raised his eyebrow at Saris who interpreted for him. Something was not sitting well with him. He couldn't put his finger on it, but the man in the cloak, who was smiling broadly, made him feel very uneasy inside.

Dyrk showed his right hand, palm down. Saris did likewise, though the men didn't even look at hers. Then all three of the men suddenly became alert.

"Where is your friend?" one of the guards barked the question at the two of them.

Dyrk spun around. Torrin was gone. One of the guards pointed to the hedge closer to the river. He shouted something in the Roj language before crashing through the hedge. The other two followed.

Saris had her hand over her mouth. "What do we do?" she asked, breathless. "He's in trouble!"

Dyrk's mind worked quickly. He decided that he was suspicious enough of these men that he didn't want them to find Torrin without witnesses being present, at the very least. He wasn't sure why Torrin had run, but all the talk about him being the last of the House of Atlan made him understandably paranoid.

"I'll follow. Stay here with the horses," he said.

He ducked through the ragged hole that had been made in the hedge by those who had gone through previously. Branches scratched his face and tugged at his clothing. On the other side was peach orchard. The leafy cover blocked out nearly all the moonlight. While Dyrk could barely see his hand in front of his face, the lantern light bobbing through the tree trunks gave him a clue as to the direction he should head.

Something was very odd about the behavior of these guards, he just realized. If they were indeed looking for escaped slaves, wouldn't they have placed him and Saris under arrest once the third member of their party bolted? These men were especially eager to get to Torrin first and foremost.

And they had asked to see their right hands. That was the easiest way to find a one-handed man.

Dyrk thought about drawing his sword, but in the inky blackness it would be reckless. The sound of movement made him turn his head to the left. Someone was quickly making their way through the trees, back the way they had come.

Through a gap in the trees, a sliver of moonlight illuminated the man. It was Torrin! Now Dyrk could hear more footsteps, moving much faster. Dyrk headed at an angle to Torrin's path, hoping to meet up with him.

He now caught a glimpse of the cloaked man through the same sliver of light. He was rushing straight at Torrin! Dyrk broke into a run himself, holding one hand in front of him. His hand brushed a tree trunk. He adjusted his course based on the hurried footfalls. Like a charging horse, he lowered his right shoulder and collided with the man, throwing him off his feet. The sound of the hedge branches scraping against clothing confirmed that Torrin had escaped.

"Obragdon!" a surprised and enraged voice came from Dyrk's feet. "What are you doing here?"

Dyrk had no idea who the man was speaking to. He tore off in the direction that Torrin had escaped. As he forced his way through the hedge, he could hear footfalls behind him, and Saris's strained voice ahead. She was telling someone to leave her alone.

Dyrk tripped over a root and fell onto his face on the road. He spun around and crawled backwards, fumbling for his sword. The man's head and upper torso came into view. His face was contorted in rage. In one hand he carried a wicked-looking knife, curved forward and then back in on itself. The weapon glowed a faint blue, trailing a mist behind it as the man moved. Even his eyes lit up in a piercing glow.

"You would deny me my victory!" the voice thundered in an otherworldly tone and volume. The man's mouth had not moved.

Dyrk backed up as best he could in his position. The man lunged. A hollow sound accompanied the whizzing of an arrow. The man fell sideways and hit the ground only a foot from Dyrk, the shaft of an arrow protruding from his chest.

Dyrk scrambled to his feet and ran for his horse. He was dimly aware that there were three others already mounted. Three! The third held a strange bow and fired again. Dyrk didn't even have a foot in the stirrup when Saris spurred her mount to the north up the road. Drudor didn't need any encouragement. Dyrk kept his hands on the saddlehorn, hopping with his free leg to keep up as his horse began to move. Drudor was thrown off-stride as Dyrk threw his leg over the saddle.

That wasn't just any man. The wind whipping through his hair reminded him that these events were quite real. His mind was screaming at the rest of his body to be more fearful. Yet he was operating mechanically, leaning over Drudor's neck, urging the horse to a steady run without frightening it. How was he able to keep going without descending into a terrified stupor? Was he this battle-hardened already?

Gradually, Dyrk moved to the front of the group. His horse being a natural leader, the other three fell in close behind. The new person with a bow had saved him. That was enough of an introduction for Dyrk to know that this man, at least, wasn't trying to kill him. But he needed to know more, much more, before he could have any trust. After more than ten minutes, Dyrk finally reined his horse to a stop. All four mounts collected, snorting and curling their upper lips in fear.

"What in the name of Nedrin was that?" Saris gasped.

"I don't know," Dyrk responded, trying to calm his trembling hands. Torrin was also shivering uncontrollably on his mount.

The fourth man was completely foreign to him, a mix-match of many odd accouterments. Dyrk couldn't tell a nationality by any part of his gear. His head was cowled, and only the glint of a silvery circlet was visible in the moonlight. The unusual composite bow of horn, wood, and green-tinged steel was still in his hand. The horse he was riding was a Belorin mare, but he rode it stiffly as if riding did not come naturally to him. He was tall and imposing, even on a horse. "Who in Morthuldan's realm is this?" Dyrk demanded.

"This is Erelin," Torrin blurted. "He's a friend."

Saris turned towards Torrin, her face showing intense fury. "You *know* him?" she shrieked.

"Y-yes," he stammered. "He has been helping me."

"Where are you from, stranger?" Dyrk asked of the newcomer. No answer came.

"He's mute," Torrin declared.

"Thank Kemantar for that," Saris muttered.

The fact that Saris knew this man jogged Dyrk's memory. He recalled Koeric's story about the Taurilian man who brought Saris as an infant. *He was carrying some professional-looking weapons. Nothing like the Belorin or Karolian military would carry.* At the time, he hadn't believed Koeric. A Taurilian mercenary? There were very few full-blooded Taurilians left in Reldaan, only in isolated pockets where they had little chance to interbreed with the surrounding peoples. Torrin was the first that he had ever met. Those that did exist were ensconced in closed communities and wouldn't engage in activities like mercenary work. His suspicions aside, Dyrk had enough information to confirm that this man was more of an ally than a threat at this time.

"Can anyone tell me what happened back there?" Dyrk shifted his questioning.

Torrin felt his glare. "I don't know!" he cried in fright. "All I know is that we're in danger!"

"We aren't going anywhere until you tell me what's going on!" Dyrk seethed. Someone must know more than they were letting on.

Saris cut in with a panicked cry. "Someone's coming! On horseback, behind us!"

Before waiting for the others, she kicked her mount into motion. Dyrk didn't need to tell Drudor to do the same. Torrin's mount followed behind. Questions would have to wait.

Saris stayed in the lead, guiding the group over a bridge to the west side of the valley. The western slopes were more gradual than the red rock-walls of the east. Dyrk hoped it wouldn't be difficult to find a way out of the valley from there. If they were being pursued, perhaps their enemy expected them to stay on the main road.

Ten minutes later, they were well away from the river. The landscape had changed from the lush vegetation of the riverside to an expanse of dry grasses, growing tall in tufts. Bare rock protruded from the hillsides here and there. They skirted a few small bluffs before finding a path up to higher elevation. After a laborious ascent, Dyrk noticed that all four horses were dripping foam from their mouths. He called for a rest. The eastern sky was beginning to brighten.

Despite all the strange and violent events, he felt exhilarated to be back on a sturdy, fast horse. It was like his body was back in its element. He got off his mount. He soothed the beast with words of encouragement. As he did that, his mind was doing the reverse. They had just survived a narrow escape, and a woman had been put in danger. Someone was withholding information. Someone in his party might even be responsible for it. Keeping the reins in one hand, he moved over to Torrin and grabbed a knot of clothing in his fist.

"Now you are going to tell me exactly what sort of danger you have put us all in."

Torrin was in a cold sweat. He took several gulps of air. Dyrk allowed him time to calm down, realizing it was no good to pressure a man seized with fear and panic.

"He's a spy, planted by this stalker to keep an eye on me!" Saris shouted through ragged breaths. "I'd like to kill you *both*!"

"I told you, I am the last of the house of Atlan," Torrin finally managed to stutter to Dyrk. "I don't know why, but I think someone is trying to extinguish the House. If I'm the last one, it's quite possible that they're coming for me."

Dyrk let a little of his anger abate. Torrin had indeed told him about being the last of his House, and Dyrk hadn't believed it. But nobody said anything about being chased by a supernatural assassin. Everyone seemed as surprised and shocked by the sound and appearance of that man as he did – everyone who could talk, that is.

Erelin had steered his horse to a better vantage point. He began to make arm motions, indicating that something was below. Warily, Dyrk nudged his horse to come alongside. Not far away, he saw three riders appear from behind a rock. They were moving quickly. Two of them had red cloaks billowing behind them. The third was dressed only in a dark cloak. The beating of their hooves was now audible to Dyrk.

Three of them. Four of us. "Do you think we could fight them?" he asked to himself, out loud.

Erelin vigorously shook his head. He then pointed to the northwest. Dyrk knew in an instant that he was right. He himself was not wearing armour. His bow was unstrung and so only had his sword. Torrin wouldn't be of much use in a fight. And Saris, well, that remained to be seen, but he didn't expect much of a woman. He recognized the red cloaks as experienced Roj mercenaries. They were outmatched.

"Off we go," Dyrk commanded. He spurred Drudor ahead of the other three and set the pace. He knew Belorin horses well enough to know a speed that they could maintain for a long distance. The only thing he was worried about was where to find water.

"Veer to the right," Saris shouted at him from a trail position. "You'll get us into bad terrain."

Dyrk adjusted his course, a bit shame-faced. She knows this area far better than me, he told himself. They were passing through steep rolling hills, gradually increasing in elevation. Ahead, some of the foothills were pockmarked with stands of evergreen trees. Away to his right, the ground evened out and became plains. There were some faraway dots of cattle grazing. Mountains equal water, he said to himself. But it also equals rough terrain, and they could get trapped.

It was a reflexive activity of his, to count hoofbeats during a mounted run. It helped him to keep time and measure distance. They had covered two league-tenths[1] when he looked over his shoulder. Their pursuers were, if anything, gaining. They were riding their mounts hard. He had hoped to stop at some point and give their heavily-laden horses a breather, but this was now impossible. They

---

[1] Two league-tenths is a distance of about 5 kilometers or 3.5 miles.

were running out of options.

He dropped back until he was riding even with Saris. "Take the lead," he shouted. "We need to enter the hills and find a way to lose them. We can't pull away from them on open ground."

Saris veered left, to the west. Within a few minutes they entered a narrow gap between two hills. The terrain quickly changed from dusty grasslands to a rocky ravine. Dyrk's heart leapt when their ravine emptied into a broader cut that had a small brook running down the base. Water!

Though they had not made enough turns to lose their pursuers, Dyrk knew that their horses would not make it if they did not have a rest and a drink. They had to chance it. Dyrk dismounted close to the brook and directed the others to do likewise. The horses stood for a minute, steaming in the cool morning air, before putting their heads down to drink. Other than fatigue, the animals were holding up pretty well. Dyrk had always known that Belorin horses were accustomed to situations that would cause anxiety in most other breeds, but this was the first time he was witnessing it in person.

Dyrk retrieved his chain hauberk from his saddlebag and lifted it over his head. The weight was comforting, but he knew it would also make him slower on foot. He bent down for a drink of his own. Then he checked over the rest of the party.

He was surprised to find Torrin doing better. The young Azenvarim had gotten over his fright. He was praising his horse once it lifted its head from the water. Saris seemed slightly rattled, but Dyrk saw in relief that she was stringing a short composite bow. Erelin's horse was still drinking, but Dyrk could not see where Erelin was. He walked to the other side of Erelin's horse and still didn't find him.

Glancing around his immediate surroundings, Dyrk was puzzled when he saw that Erelin had scaled on foot the gradual part of the cliff on the side of the ravine, which was a pile of rocks and gravel that had broken free from the rock wall. Dyrk was about to shout at him when he heard, over the sound of his own horse drinking, hoofbeats approaching.

Saris had noted Erelin's departure as well. "Time we left him behind," she said, mounting her horse with the bow in her hand, a flat quiver now slung across her back.

Dyrk longed for some regimental discipline. Everyone was working against each other. Nobody was in charge. Hastily, he assessed the situation and determined that Erelin was right. Their enemy was just around the corner. They would barely get into the saddle before they were overtaken. He might have just enough time to string his own bow. With one tug, he retrieved the twig and fished in a side pocket for a string. "Torrin, take the horses a little upstream," he ordered. "Not out of sight."

He looped the string on one end, put his weight on the bow to bend it, and slipped the loop on the other end. Shortbows were made to be loaded and fired quickly. They were small enough to be fired from horseback. However, they lacked the punch and range of larger bows. Against armoured foes, they were little more than a nuisance. Dyrk had trained very little with the weapon, just enough to remind him that he was not a very good archer.

The enemy riders came into view down the ravine, at about three hundred paces. Dyrk was only halfway up the pile of rocks. The enemy paused, looking both ways. Dyrk figured he had an effective range of less than fifty paces. He would only get one shot off.

The three riders began to approach. At two hundred paces, Erelin shot. The bow made little sound and the enemy was caught unprepared. A horse stumbled and pitched to the ground. Its rider, the dark-cloaked man, was thrown. Erelin was shooting for the horses! He was amazed at how the Taurilian could get off a shot that felled a horse from this range.

The other two riders took evasive maneuvers. One approached alongside the right-hand ravine wall on the same side as Erelin and Dyrk, where some rocks cut off their line of fire. The other rode around to their left, flanking them. Dyrk saw the flash of steel and heard the report of a crossbow. He ducked. The bolt smashed into the rock face only a foot away from a crouching Erelin.

The recurve bow sounded again. The arrow narrowly missed the flanking Raider, who was riding for the cover of another ravine. Dyrk kept his eye on the one creeping up on them. He had an arrow nocked. He was waiting for any sign of movement. Once he saw the side of a horse and an elbow protruding from the rock face, he fired. He was not well trained with a bow and had not taken the time to calibrate this one to his liking. His aim was considerably off. Knowing he was the first target to be seen, he threw himself off the rocks. A crossbow bolt whizzed over his head.

Erelin fired again. Dyrk did not see what he was shooting at. A horse thundered by from the other direction. Surprised, he saw Saris turn her horse without a hand on her rains, shoot her bow, and then spur her horse back down the ravine towards Torrin. Dyrk began to fall back. Erelin took one more shot and then ran after them.

Torrin had stopped about two hundred paces down the ravine. Dyrk ran the distance. He took one look behind his shoulder and could not see any pursuers. Torrin was already mounted. Saris was a hundred paces ahead. Erelin and Dyrk swung into their saddles and headed after her.

She led them through several turns, generally heading north. They scaled a gentle slope and found themselves on the rolling plains again. After the climb, they took a brief rest for the horses. Dyrk listened as best he could. He couldn't hear any sounds of pursuit.

"I didn't see how they fared," Dyrk found the breath to say.

Saris turned. "Two of their horses are down. I put my arrow off the shoulder blade of the third. I don't think any of the men were hit, but I didn't see the first one."

"The one in the lead was thrown," Dyrk confirmed. "I don't think he is going anywhere."

Erelin shook his head.

Dyrk didn't know whether than meant he disagreed or confirmed his statement. "At any rate, their mounts are in bad condition. Let's hope they give up the chase."

He turned to Erelin, who again gave a shake of his head. "Nice shooting, uh-"

"Erelin", Torrin reminded him. "Good work all of you."

"Let's get some more distance," Dyrk suggested. He didn't feel like he had done much at all. Distracted them, perhaps.

He allowed Saris to lead again. They set a more measured pace.

Dyrk took the rear and checked often for pursuit. He saw none. Again, he was instinctively counting hoofbeats and came up with about six league-tenths by the time they slowed to a walk to give the horses another rest.

Dyrk walked his horse alongside Saris's. "You've been of considerable aid to us," he said. "But I do regret that you got caught up in all this. Torrin's a stranger to you. You don't need to be putting your own skin on the line for him."

Saris shrugged.

He continued. "If you head for home now, I would think that our pursuers would follow the three of us and leave you alone. You should get home tonight if you push it."

A condescending laugh escaped her lips. "Let's face it, hotshot," she said while removing her cap. "You boys are rather lost without me. None of you have traveled this territory before." She shook out her silvery hair and wiped her brow. "Though I'd love to be rid of *him*."

Dyrk couldn't contain his curiosity. "Is he somehow related to you?"

Saris gave that same cold look as when Dyrk had asked about her parents back at the homestead. "Ask him," she stared ahead of her. "He won't say anything to me." Dyrk caught both sarcasm and hurt in her voice. He wanted to also ask why she hated him so much, but now he figured he had at least part of the answer.

It struck him for a second that the two of them shared a similar burden. Both of them had significant parts of their past shrouded in mystery. Both know that people close to them have the answers but are unwilling to be forthcoming. Then he corrected himself. *Mine is nothing like hers*, he thought. *I know my parents, I know my race, my heritage, my shared history.* To have those taken away from him as well? That was a burden he could not comprehend.

Torrin, meanwhile, was feeling much better than a few hours ago. The incident in the orchard was the most frightening event in his life, and that was saying something. The Vekh in Azenvar, they were enemy warriors, bent on conquest and looting. He could understand their motivations, twisted and evil as they were. But his current adversary, the cloaked man who had chased him in the orchard, induced a different level of fear. Torrin felt like the man was dedicated to his destruction. His adversary's voice had an otherworldly tone to it. Torrin had seen the weapon that he carried, the curved dagger that shone with a blue mist. That was not just any man. Torrin was not running from mere flesh and steel. Despite what Erelin had done to him, Torrin had a sinking feeling that they had not seen the last of him.

What calmed him down were his companions. As suspicious as Dyrk was, he presented a militaristic sort of decisiveness and courage that made Torrin feel more at ease. Saris had her own contributions, being an excellent rider and familiar with the terrain. He was still with Erelin, who was a powerful mercenary, supposedly pledged to protect him. Then he remembered about Vigheran. Where was he?

As the horses slowed to a walk, and Dyrk engaged Saris in conversation, Torrin took the opportunity to ask Erelin a few things. Knowing that he was limited to binary queries, he asked simply, "Are you still with Vigheran?"

(No.)

"Did he release you?"

(No.)

"Did you escape?"

(No.)

Torrin could only think of one other possibility, and he didn't want to voice it at first. "Is he dead?"

(Yes.)

"Did you kill him?"

He had asked before he carefully thought it through. The cowl turned his way. The face was expressionless, and the opaque white eyes burned into his. Torrin shivered under the glare. He figured he had crossed a line.

"Those people chasing us. Did they kill him?"

(Yes.)

Torrin felt a mixture of relief and sadness. Vigheran had not been kind to him. Yet the rough Zindori had seen to his survival for many weeks. Torrin had even saved his life once. Erelin did not seem to fully trust him, but Torrin had not witnessed anything that would generate mistrust.

"Those people chasing us. Did they kill Braedil and Kryna?"

Erelin hesitated for a second. (Yes.)

"Do they have anything to do with the Gryphon?"

(No.)

This produced too many intersecting lines for Torrin. Things would have been much easier if he could put all his enemies on one side and his friends on another. Had Vigheran been his enemy or friend? He might never know. Was Erelin his enemy or friend? He was inclined to think the latter, but suspicions still remained. Dyrk seemed naïve enough to be exactly who he said he was. Saris, well, she appeared to be an immature but capable woman who was more concerned with Erelin's presence than their pursuers.

Torrin had been pursued for weeks. His encounters with the Gryphon had already primed him to accept that something supernatural was going on there. The sight of the man coming through the hedge was certainly disturbing, but Torrin had recovered from his fright much faster than Dyrk. It certainly helped that Erelin seemed to be in the know about the identity of their pursuers and what to do about them. He would simply need to place his immediate trust in his mute protector.

He knew that Dyrk would question him again once given the chance. How much should he tell the Karolian? Again, perhaps the best strategy was to let Erelin take the lead on how much to reveal about the Gryphon, even about Vigheran. Erelin had told him to convince Dyrk about him being the last of Atlan's House, so he would be open about that. As much as it wounded his conscience to keep information from his allies, it would needlessly worry them if he said too much too soon.

He had one more question for Erelin. He expected to be disappointed by the answer. "Those people chasing us, do you think they may have given up?"

(No.)

They made their night camp in a stand of trees along a rushing stream. The water was very cold, indicating it was a glacier flow. They discussed whether to start a fire or not. To their surprise, Erelin nodded his agreement to a fire.

They had two tents between the four of them. Dyrk decided not to set his up, given that the weather was almost assured to remain dry overnight. Saris said she would start the fire. Erelin had left.

"Where is he off to?" Dyrk asked Torrin.

"He often hunts when we make camp," Torrin guessed. "I'll take care of his horse."

"We'll do it together. At the same time, you can tell me a thing or two about your uncommunicative friend."

As they worked on their horses, Torrin started from Dar-Amund and told of what he knew about Erelin through their journey to Sorwail and to Dharbur, but omitted everything about Vigheran and the Gryphon.

"So he reads and writes in Melandarim," Dyrk confirmed.

Torrin nodded.

"I am having trouble figuring out why some stranger would go through all that trouble to save your hide," Dyrk pressed. "What's in it for him?"

Torrin for the first time became defiant. "Brave *almathin* of Karolia," he began politely. "I want you to understand that I have lost my family, lost my home, and lost my right hand. That is a lot to process. I have also been on the road in strange lands for eight weeks, afraid for my life every minute of every day. Forgive me if I haven't had the time or energy to question the motives of the one person who is responsible for my survival."

Dyrk felt convicted. How he had longed for someone to help him survive when he had lost so much. How he valued were those few people who got him through those difficult days. He softened his tone. "I'm sorry I'm coming across as demanding, but I have one more question. Why didn't you mention him when you first spoke with me?"

"He asked me not to. If you recall the visceral reaction of the young woman who was with you, I now understand why."

Dyrk sighed. "Do you know anything about his relationship to Saris?"

"Very little. All I know is that he cares about her safety a great deal."

"Is that why he's with us?"

"I expect that is at least part of the reason." He finished brushing Valdor and turned to Erelin's horse. "To be honest, I don't know much about you. Shouldn't I be afforded the same allowance for suspicion?"

Dyrk raised his eyebrows. "There's not much to tell. I'm a reservist cavalry in the Karolian army who was pressed into tarn-riding duty after my regiment was disbanded. I had to scuttle my tarn on the way to Dharbur and I ended up near the homestead of Saris's family. They took me in. I'm trying to make my way back home."

"So you barely know her?"

"Yes. You could say I'm traveling with three people who, as of two weeks ago, I had never met."

"And you've never seen or heard anything like what happened in the orchard?"

Dyrk thought about his own dreams of flaming swords and demonic beings. Best not to needlessly alarm anyone. "No, I haven't."

They returned to the fire. Just as Torrin had said, Erelin was there with a grouse for the cooking pot. After plucking a few of the tail feathers for some use of his own, he deposited the carcass near the fire.

Saris grumbled something about not being a chambermaid and began to repair a harness strap. Erelin turned his attention to his own equipment. Torrin took out some verse papers. Dyrk sighed, drew his hunting knife, and took the grouse to the stream to clean it.

Erelin was laying out all the arrows in his second quiver to dry, near but not too near to the fire. There were five of them. There was only a single arrow remaining in the quiver on his back. After that, he sat down with a small wad of wax and worked on his bowstring.

Dyrk came back with the meat and added it to the cooking pan with the vegetables. He noticed that Torrin took a long time with his verse papers. The young man was getting better at writing with his left hand, though it was still a slow, laborious process that took several sheets. Once the papers were burning, Torrin closed his eyes for some time, his face turned up to the heavens.

"What are you doing?" Dyrk asked once the other had opened his eyes.

"I cannot write the entire verse yet. My arm gets sore. I sing the rest in my mind."

Dyrk wanted to scoff but he tried to stay respectful. "The Servants don't hear what's on our minds," he said. "I also highly doubt they appreciate singing. That's supposed to be for our benefit, not theirs."

"Whether or not the Servants hear, we do know that the Most High is able to probe the thoughts and hearts of man," Torrin responded, quoting from Melandar.

"Perhaps," Dyrk said. "But it remains to be seen if he actually does it. It seems to me like he just leaves us to our own devices."

"Yet you still write your verses."

"A man might assist a maiden because she is becoming, she is kind and thankful, or is an excellent cook," Dyrk opined. "But a good man will assist a maiden for none of those reasons. He doesn't expect anything in return. He does it because that's his responsibility."

"That may be," Torrin said. "But consider for a moment that you may have things backwards. We are the maidens and the Servants the agents of our good. I am grateful for their aid."

How can you be grateful for their aid? Dyrk thought. *After all you've lost, you should be bitter and resentful.*

Dyrk continued to stir their supper while reflecting on their more immediate concerns. He was getting frustrated. He had questioned Torrin as far as he dared. Saris was useless. He suspected that Erelin knew the most, but he had to admit that he was afraid to approach the mute Taurilian. There were too many incidents to ignore. The encounter in the orchard could not be dismissed as a dream. He had collided with a real, physical person who had exhibited some startling superhuman traits. Even if he had imagined the surreal phenomenon, the fact remained that their makeshift party was being pursued by an unknown but dangerous enemy, willing to use lethal force against Torrin and anyone with him.

As they sat and ate, Dyrk again queried Saris as to her intentions. She said that she had traveled as far as the Pass of Takorran before, and she would be willing to guide them that far.

"Though it depends," she hesitated, "as to what he does." She motioned to Erelin, who had drained most of the broth from the stew into his bowl and taken it some distance away. "If he stays with you, I may take my leave much sooner."

"I hope to talk with him tomorrow morning," Dyrk said, procrastinating. "I'll let you know." Sleep on it, he told himself.

Dyrk woke up with a start. The fire was almost out. The sky was still dark. A shadow in the trees above confirmed that Erelin was still on watch.

[Come, let's talk.]

The words echoed through his head. It was an unfamiliar voice to him, making him feel guarded, but not afraid. He got himself out of his bedroll and put on his boots. He put on his cloak to ward off the chill. His sword came with him too. Then he walked out of the camp. There was a large rock outcropping about two hundred paces from the camp. Dyrk circled around it.

His actions were automatic. He did not will any of them. For this reason, he knew he was dreaming again.

On the other side of the oucropping, a man sat on a log. Dyrk immediately recognized him as the cloaked man who had chased Torrin in the grove. Dyrk sat on a rock opposite him calmly, almost as if they were enjoying a warm mug of ale on a patio. His placed his sheathed sword across his knees. The hilt was uncomfortably warm. He could even feel heat coming through the scabbard. He still didn't have control over his body; it felt like he was simply being a silent bystander.

"Obragdon," the man said, repeating the name Dyrk had heard him speak in the grove. "You are becoming quite a nuisance.

Thalnuris is also here and he longs for his prize."

A voice rumbled in return, coming from near Dyrk but not from his lips. "Urdipanior, you have overextended yourself. Turn back or be destroyed."

Urdipanior slowly shook his head. "I am too deep. I am too close. Can you not see it?"

"You have been granted leave for some victories that you seek," Obragdon replied. "But not this one. What has been decreed shall not be stopped by the hand of man or Seraph."

The eyes of Urdipanior lost their focus, staring off into the distance. "Mortal man struggles all their lives in a valiant contest against death. But death comes to them all," he said. "So I will struggle with all my power against a decree that I know cannot be broken."

"May he rebuke you," Obragdon stated.

The discussion was over. Dyrk picked up the sword and headed back to the camp. He laid down as if to sleep, cloak on, sheathed sword in his right hand.

[You must have courage.]

The words pierced his sleep so sharply that he had no choice but to wake. They were the same words, spoken by the same voice, as near the orchard just before they were ambushed.

It was the dead of night. Dyrk scrambled out of his bedroll. For some reason, his right hand gripped his sheathed sword, and his cloak was already clasped around his shoulders. He heard two loud footfalls a short distance to his left. He quickly raised himself into a crouching position. He glanced in that direction. Erelin had leapt from the tree, his bow cast aside, and had drawn his sword. He began to advance into the darkness. Saris and Torrin were stirring too.

Dyrk's instincts were to stand shoulder-to-shoulder with a fellow soldier. He drew his sword and moved quickly to catch up with Erelin. Before he could reach him, the sound of a great wind filled his ears. He was propelled back and stumbled to his knees. Through the corner of his eye, he saw Erelin thrown into the air, back towards the camp.

What was happening?! His mind was still groggy with sleep. He didn't even see their assailant. But one thing burned through his consciousness. He had to protect Torrin!

He got to his feet and took three great strides to his right, towards where he remembered Torrin had bedded down. Torrin was half out of his bedroll. A dark shape was hurtling towards him. Dyrk swung his blade with all his might.

There was the sound of a thunderclap. Dyrk was thrown onto his back. An angry red light streamed from his right side. As he got up, he heard the stretching sound of Saris's bow, followed by a loud sound of cracking wood and a curse from her lips.

Twenty paces away, he saw a cloaked figure come to a standing position at the same time. It was the same man as he had seen in the orchard! But that wasn't possible; Erelin had shot him! A long knife was in each of his hands, wickedly curved and trailing blue mist. Dyrk lifted his blazing sword and closed the distance.

His training kicked in. Strike from the right, parry downwards, upward backhand stroke. Each time his sword was met with one or both of the knives. Brilliant flashes lighted the forest. Sparks of blue and red showered over both of them. Dyrk felt an instant chilling of his right arm with each strike, numbing his fingers. But he noticed his enemy grimace in pain as the flames burned his arms and sides.

Dyrk cocked for a thrust, forgetting he had no shield. One knife turned his sword aside, the other sliced into his upper thigh. He cried in pain. Backing up, he warded his enemy off with several wide sweeps. The man's cloak was burning, but he seemed oblivious to it.

A throwing axe flew from Dyrk's left and embedded itself into the man's chest, throwing him off his feet. Dyrk immediately seized the opportunity and closed with an overhead thrust at his recumbent opponent. But the knives flashed into view, knocking his sword off its path. The momentum carried Dyrk over his target. Some unseen force propelled him further into some brush.

"You are the property of another," the man growled, rising to his feet. The axe fell from him. As Dyrk extracted himself, he saw Saris flung into the air, spinning round and round. Another movement made him look towards the fire. Erelin was back on his feet, bow in hand, making a break for the arrows he had set out to dry. He too was sent into the air, out of the circle of the firelight. Torrin was nowhere to be seen.

Dyrk was on his feet now and rushed again, this time less recklessly. The man turned to engage just as Dyrk made his thrust. His blade cut through the cloak near the right shoulder. One knife swung around and sliced into Dyrk's arm.

Dyrk's entire arm was now completely numb. His fingers could no longer hold the sword. His adversary clutched his shoulder, then suddenly drew back as if something had struck him from behind. Grasping the hilt with his left hand, Dyrk ran him through the abdomen. Fear and anger drove him on. He planted his foot on the man's chest, pushing him over as he withdrew the sword. Another thrust, then another. He had to make sure this abomination was dead, was gone!

"Dyrk, Dyrk, enough!" Torrin's voice cut through the fog. "He's dead!"

CHAPTER 23:
THE PLATEAU

Dyrk felt the tension drain slowly from his limbs. Pain began to throb in his right arm and left leg. He began to feel sick. Yet he could not take his eyes off the dead man's face. He might still be alive. He might return. It did not register that his sword had gone dark.

Then he remembered the others. "Where is Saris? Erelin?" Dyrk could still not break his gaze. "Go find them. I must guard him!"

"I'm here," Saris's strained voice came from his left. He managed to pull his eyes away just long enough to assess her situation. She was standing, holding one arm to her stomach. Her nose was bleeding slightly from one side. Her face had lost a lot of colour. But otherwise she seemed to be intact. Another shape moved in the woods. Erelin limped into view, holding his bow.

The four scanned each other's gaze one by one. It was Saris who put words to what they were all thinking.

"What just happened?"

Dyrk struggled to put words to his thoughts. "I killed him," was all he could say.

Erelin had retrieved one of his arrows that were now scattered beside the fire. With his bow pulled back, he cautiously approached the body of the man.

"He's dead, Erelin! You're putting all of us on edge here!" Torrin cried. He reached his left hand to the dead man's neck. Dyrk cleaned his sword on the grass. Erelin stood stock-still, nocked arrow pointed at the adversary.

"No pulse," Torrin said, lifting his hand and trying to shake off the blood. Only then did Erelin release the draw on his bow. Torrin bent down again, lifted the man's shoulder, and retrieved the left-handed dagger that was embedded in his back.

"Your sword," Saris gasped. "How did you do that?"

"I wish I knew," Dyrk mumbled. "What should we do with him?"

Erelin took his arrow and made a stabbing motion towards the ground.

"Bury him? Why not just throw him off a cliff?" Dyrk asked, surprised. "We don't even have any shovels."

Erelin repeated the motion.

"There's a cleft just over there," Torrin said. "We can move dirt and stones over him."

Erelin and Dyrk set to the grim task of moving the body to the crevasse that Torrin had pointed out. The three of them began to move dirt with their hands and feet.

"Dyrk, you're bleeding," Torrin said. "You should attend to that."

Dyrk's arm was dripping blood. A stain was growing on his left leg. He disengaged from working and headed back towards the fire.

"I can help," Saris said. She had already gotten the fire going again.

"What about your arm?"

"I think it's just a sprain." She extended it, wincing in pain. "I can move it. It just hurts."

Dyrk put pressure with his left hand on the cut on his hip. Saris pulled back his sleeve. "How are you not howling in pain?"

He grimaced. It did hurt. The numbness was wearing off, and with it the pain was growing. She left him for a second to fetch some water. When she came back, Erelin had also come to help. Though she showed discomfort at his presence, she bent down at his side.

Erelin made a motion as if to close the wound. Saris did so. He took some water in the palm of his hand and crushed a berry from his shoulder pouch into it. He rubbed the paste against the wound, causing grunts of pain from the patient. Then he took a brown leaf, soaked it in water, and used his knife to cut it into tiny strips. He laid the strips crosswise over the wound. After blowing a few breaths on it, he motioned for Saris to take her hand away. The wound held closed.

They turned Dyrk onto his side and removed his trousers. They repeated the process with the slash on his leg. This one didn't bleed as much, but it was a longer cut. Erelin then left Saris to finish up the bandaging. The arm was easy, but the injury to his side required Saris to wrap a strip of cloth around his upper leg.

"I'll finish that off," he offered.

"Don't be such a baby," she scoffed. "Trust me, I've gotten much closer to a man. You're nothing special." That made him even more uncomfortable.

Torrin had checked on the horses, which were frightened but thankfully still tethered. They all finished up their tasks, then sat near the fire in a group in stunned silence. Only Erelin got up from time to time, walking around the perimeter of their camp. None of them felt like sleeping. The fire burned brightly.

Erelin had just gotten up for a second circuit around the camp when Saris broke the silence. "Do either of you know what just happened?"

Both shook their heads.

She pointed at Dyrk from across the fire, tightening her other arm around her legs. "You had better know! You're one of them!"

"What do you mean?" Dyrk said defensively. He had just saved these people and gotten injured in the process. Now he was being accused?

"We all saw those flames! You're some kind of sorcerer!"

Dyrk put both hands up. "I'm just as surprised as the rest of you, believe me!"

"There's no such thing as sorcerers," Torrin cut in.

"There's also no such thing as flaming swords and getting flung into the air," Saris countered. Both her hands were on her face now. "Either I've had too much to drink, or not enough."

"That sort of power can only come from a Seraph," Torrin told them.

Saris blew out air between her fingers. "So sorcerers don't exist, but Seraphs do. Whatever."

"That fire from that blade, it was like when Esdarion slew Vynek," Torrin continued. He was referring to a legend in which Karolia's king challenged a Vekh warlord, who was said to be possessed by an evil Seraph, to battle before the gates of Aztoroth's capital Keor. None had been able to slay Vynek by physical means until that fight. Esdarion bore the Crillslayer, a legendary blade of old, which flamed during the combat.

"Yes, where did you get that sword from, Dyrk?" she opened her eyes wide.

Dyrk withdrew the sword from its scabbard just enough to see the base of the blade. It was unremarkable, the same simple Taurilian sword that he had taken from his father's armour chest. "I found it in a mine near my house when I was a child," he said. "At least they found it near me when they rescued me from a cave-in. I don't remember much."

"Fine. You picked up a flaming sword in a cave in Karolia. But what about him?" She flung her arm towards the makeshift grave. Her voice became shrill and distraught. "That was more than just an enchanted blade. He was throwing us around like we were rag dolls! I embedded my axe in him and he shrugged it off! Who was he?" Her voice trailed off as Erelin came back to the fire and sat cross-legged near it.

Dyrk chafed. Saris refused to talk with Erelin around. Torrin likewise would not question their mute companion. But Erelin had shown that he knew more about their pursuer than anyone else. He had been conscious of their enemy's power and persistence. Dyrk had been reluctant to press Erelin on anything yet. The man was a head taller than himself. He was equipped with deadly weapons and clearly knew how to use them. Dyrk reminded himself that others were in trouble. It was his responsibility to be brave.

"You know more about this than you're letting on," Dyrk said to Erelin, doing his best to not sound too accusing. "Is there any way you can tell us about what is going on here?"

Erelin's eyes fixed on him. The firelight reflected off them, causing the orbs to flash with red. Dyrk wanted to wither under the glare but he did his best to meet it with an unmoving one of his own.

Erelin lowered his head and cleared a patch of dirt in front of his crossed knees. He wrote a long name in Melandarim script. Torrin and Dyrk craned their necks.

"*Urdipanior.* Never heard of it," Torrin said.

It seemed familiar to Dyrk. It was a name, but he couldn't place where he had heard it from. He felt a sense of dread. Erelin erased the name and wrote a word. *Seraph.*

"You see?" Torrin sounded like he was vindicated. "He was a Seraph, just like Vaezur, Kharon, Vynek, and Drumeth, the demon-captains of Kardumagund!" The names he mentioned were the captains of the Vekh armies who destroyed Tauril in the time of Eldorin. Two of them pursued Eldorin to his exile in Karolia.

Erelin nodded.

"Seraphs follow two paths, destruction or deliverance, depending on whether they have rebelled from Arren," Torrin continued. "Whoever he was, I'm thinking he was responsible for exterminating the rest of my family and my house. He was devoted to destruction. I thank you for putting an end to him."

Saris interjected. "So when you shot him, back in Dharbur, he didn't die because he was a Seraph? What rot!"

Erelin twisted his head to one side as if that wasn't quite correct, but then nodded anyway.

Dyrk added, "I believe he was the first rider that attacked us later, the one whose horse you shot out from under him. I didn't think it would be possible to get up from that fall. But I guess he isn't subject to physical harm."

Erelin nodded. Saris continued to scoff.

"Then how did we kill him?" Dyrk wondered.

Erelin pointed to Dyrk's sword.

Dyrk drew a deep breath. There was a reason that Erelin knew the Seraph's name. There was some sort of connection. He summoned his courage. He was about to demand an explanation when Saris spoke first.

"Seraph or no Seraph, he's dead," She pronounced. "And we're safe."

Erelin slowly shook his head.

"But we're not," Torrin could not hold it in any longer. He sounded like he was verging on panic again. "There's another one out there. And it's coming after you, Saris."

Erelin nodded. He held out his hand in the same gesture in which he had offered the folded paper to Saris in Dharbur.

Saris was shocked at first. Her gaze flicked from Torrin to Erelin. Then her expression slowly changed to one of disbelief. "He put you up to this, didn't he?" she looked at Torrin while making a hand motion at Erelin. "This is another of his attempts to lock me up again." Her tone changed to one of mocking sarcasm. "Oh, Saris can't take care of herself, she needs some big, strong boys looking after her to keep her from getting in trouble."

"This one is in the form of a Gryphon," Torrin said. "I know it's hunting you."

She rolled her eyes. "I'm surprised it wasn't a fire-breathing marmot".

"They're right, Saris," Dyrk said. Saris's mouth froze in the middle of another remark. Now she could not ignore them. Torrin looked at Dyrk, surprised. Erelin's half-closed his eyes and gently nodded in an expression of confirmation. Dyrk continued. "Remember that night I was sleeping in the chair? When you woke me up in the morning? It came for you that night. I chased it away."

She brushed her hands over her face, distraught. "So let me get this straight. Have all three of you teamed up to scare me out of my wits? Why in the world would a Seraph be hunting me? I thought they only went after powerful leaders of men."

Erelin looked down and erased the word. Torrin relished the inadvertent compliment.

"All I can say is what I saw," Torrin said. "The Gryphon gave me a vision that it was hunting you. I am quite relieved that Dyrk found you before it did."

Dyrk stood up and gingerly walked over to where they had buried Urdipanior. He just couldn't get over his unease and wanted to make sure that their adversary was still in the ground. The cairn had not been disturbed. The pain of his injuries was only getting worse. He could really use a good rest.

He limped back to the camp. "It's starting to get light," he said. "We should probably get going." He didn't mention breakfast. None of them felt hungry. He had forgotten his resolve to get more information out of Erelin.

"Right," Saris said, happy to be moving on to a different subject. "I know of another homestead, friends of my family. I think they're about a day's ride northwest. It would be good to stop there for the night."

They got up to prepare for the day's ride. Nobody had seen the name that Erelin had written in the patch of dirt.

Thalnuris

It was late afternoon when they encountered a tightly grouped herd of cattle that signaled a Belorin homestead was nearby. Erelin had given Torrin a note that said he would be staying out in the wild and would rejoin them the next day. Saris had also arranged a more believable story – that they had been attacked by Raider mercenaries who mistook them for someone else. No sense scaring their potential host with tall tales of Seraphs and flaming swords.

As they passed the herd, another rider spotted them. Upon his approach, he recognized Saris, his demeanor relaxing considerably. They discussed a few things in Belorin.

He switched to River-Tongue to address the group. "Friends of Saris are friends of mine," the man said, doffing his cap at the other two. "Are you Karolians?"

"Yes, they are," Saris answered on their behalf. "They're making their way home and asked me to guide them as far as Takorran."

"Well we have plenty of meat in the smoke pit," the man assured them good-naturedly. "If you don't mind the smell, you're welcome to bed down in the stables. A thunderstorm is on its way, and it might break overnight, so you're lucky you came by."

The homestead was in some ways similar to Saris's, with many rooms built into the sod. This one had a small watchtower built from timber, and a modest house above-ground made of sunbaked brick. The smell of smoked beef made them all hungry.

They went to the stables and their horses were looked after well.

Dyrk had his wounds re-stitched. He was beginning to feel like his mother's pin-pillow at home, needles sticking into him again and again. His previous injury from the crash of the tarn had just scabbed over, so he had those stitches removed.

The extended family was not much smaller than Saris's. They immediately took the food into the house and arranged for them all to sit around the common room as the raindrops began to fall. Their meal was sumptuous, especially for Torrin who had not eaten so well since he was still at home. They felt snug as the rain beat heavily on the roof. Only Torrin felt a twinge of pity for Erelin, camping out in the rain.

After everyone had eaten their fill, Saris called out in Belorin, "I didn't come empty-handed, friends. One of these men can spin you a yarn from the old times in the true Karolian fashion. How about we pay for the meal with a story?"

There was thunderous agreement. Torrin leaned over to Dyrk. "Are you any good at telling? I'm not sure if she's talking about me or you."

Dyrk had not understood what Saris was saying but had already given it some thought in case he was asked. "I was thinking about telling the tale of Taerfin and the Sons of Emberg," he said, but then got a bit sheepish. "I figure you might know it better than me, though."

"We can do it together," Torrin said. "I'll wait until you pass it off."

Dyrk agreed. "Just be sure to play up Belorin's involvement. Let's not disappoint our hosts."

Dyrk began the tale. Azenvar was in chaos after the rebellion of Talfod the usurper. The Vekh of Omrid, led by the demon-chief Drumeth, had seized upon the opportunity and began the conquest of the land, capturing Delvaeth and Keor, pushing Talfod into Haned. The rightful heir to the kingdom, Taereth House Rudin, lived in exile in Dar-Amund and refused to lead the people.

Taereth's son, Taerfin, was not so cowardly. He trained with a man in the wilderness named Emberg, who wished to see the restoration of the kingdom. Emberg trained an elite cadre of warriors called the Sons of Emberg, and Taerfin was one of their number. After his training, Taerfin traveled through the towns of the realm to survey them, disguised as a story-teller. He met a woman of worth in Talfod's lands, named Nereas, and she became his wife.

Taereth continued to wait at his home near Dar-Amund for a sign from above to begin the liberation of the kingdom. The sign came through an Alwem named Ez-Unedil. This marked the only time that the Alwem concerned themselves with the doings of men since the days of Ter-Athel.

Taereth and the Sons of Emberg, numbering thirty men in all, won a great victory against the Vekh hordes of Drumeth at the Rock of Asthurel. Upon hearing of their defiance, the towns of eastern Azenvar galvanized behind him, together with horsemen from Belorin, and they liberated half the kingdom.

But tragedy struck at home. Feldariem raiders attacked Taerfin's home and captured the women and children. Taerfin returned home to rescue them and pledged never to leave his wife and son again. The remainder of the reconquest would be left to Taerfin's son, Madwin, to complete.

Dyrk glanced several times at Saris when he described the appearance of Ez-Unedil and his Alwem companions, for they appeared of the pure race of the Taurilians, long-lived and without colour in their skin. Yet one difference remained, that they were given hair as white as snow, every one of them. Saris was paying more attention to the bottle of spirits that was being passed around the adults than to the story.

The tale was told in River-Tongue. Many there could understand it well. One old woman sat in the corner and quietly interpreted for a group of young children. Torrin was telling during the battle against Drumeth, and began the song of victory and lament, as Ez-Unedil had been slain in the fighting. Dyrk joined the song in harmony with his deeper voice. The audience listened in rapt attention to the two men.

On the whole, Dyrk was struck by some differences in the way that he and Torrin told the story. Dyrk narrowed in on the personal conflict between the key adversaries, Taerfin and Drumeth. Torrin shifted the focus towards a battle for the spiritual conscience of the nation itself.

They were rewarded with applause at the conclusion of the story. Torrin decided to turn in early. Dyrk wanted some fresh air. With the rain, all he could do is sit under the awning of the house, flexing his stiff knee. Saris stayed inside.

He felt tired, but his head so full of thoughts that sleep was nowhere near. He felt homesick. Not for his family home, but for his own place in Saringon. For his job, his bondservants, and for Neriah. For his society of clear expectations and rigid rules. He was sick of the travel, of the tension, the pain of injuries, the uneasiness he felt about his companions. Saris was in her home country, among family friends, feeling safe and at ease. He was jealous. He wanted to just get on with his life. This business about the Seraphs complicated things.

When I was a child, all I wanted was to be someone special, he thought. *One of these heroic men of old, shrouded in myth and story.* The scars of the past few weeks were enough for him to question if he had the mettle for it. The loss of his regiment, the near-death experience on the tarn, and, worst of all, more blood on his hands. He could not forget the feeling of his lance piercing armour, flesh, and bone, ending the life of another human being.

The rain had slowed to a drizzle. The thunder was now rumbling well to the southeast. Lands such as this were unusual places in a thunderstorm. At first the ground eagerly gobbles up the falling water, but it was soon saturated by the deluge. Rivulets and streams arose out of dry earth, moving mud and sludge from puddle to puddle with nowhere to go. A depression near the homestead filled with water quickly, by now about knee-deep. By tomorrow the water would be gone. Dyrk was happy to be under a roof in this dark, stormy night.

The door opened. He had no idea how long he had been sitting there. Saris stepped out with the man that had taken them in. "Oh, Dyrk's here," she said in River-Tongue, then in Belorin to her friend, "I'll be okay." The friend returned inside and closed the door.

She leaned against the doorpost with her shoulder and head facing Dyrk. He could not see her face in the darkness.

"Why don't you ever have a drink?" she slurred. "It would do you good. I could get some and bring it out if you like."

Dyrk got up, wincing at the discomfort from both his legs. "What sort of good would it do?" he asked, trying to be polite.

"Helps me to forget. At least for a while."

He was about to speak but she put out a hand. "Don't wreck it," she said. She put her hand to her mouth as if she was sick, then smiled, and then giggled.

"You need to get to bed," he said.

She took a few unsteady steps towards the stable. "Walk with me," she said. With another snicker, she added, "If you can keep up."

They walked through the mud together towards the stables. Dyrk knew he should be extremely uncomfortable with this scenario but at that point he was too tired to care. Torrin was already fast asleep on the hay in one stall near the doors of the stable. Dyrk led her deeper into the stables and found another empty stall. He piled some fresh hay up for her.

"Dyrk," she caught his attention as he was finishing. She wasn't quite as bubbly as a minute ago. "Do you ever get scared? I mean, when there's nothing around you trying to kill you, but you feel that there's something out there?"

He nodded. "Yes. I used to get anxious a lot, but now it is wearing off a bit. I'm just more tired and weary now."

Her eyes remained unfocused as she stood there, back against the wall of the stall. Her hair hung limp and wet, dripping. Her shoulders were sloped down again, in a gesture of despondency. "Should I be?" Her body lurched with the question, then returned to its droopy state as if it took a lot of effort to talk.

Dyrk had trouble seeing a person behind those eyes. He had rarely dealt with drunk men, much less women. What did she need? What was he supposed to do? "Right now, you should probably get some sleep," he managed. *And I should get out of here*, he said to himself, but his legs wouldn't listen to him.

A look of frustration clouded her face. "Answer my question," she demanded, sounding more whiny than insistent in her current state. "Am I in danger? Or is this all just – just part of the glow on the horizon?"

Dyrk didn't understand her metaphor. He did, however, see a woman in need of consolation. He reached and put a hand on her elbow. "I don't really know how much danger you're in, but I do know you have friends looking after you," he said.

She collapsed in his arms, head sideways on his chest. Surprised, he moved to try to deposit her on the hay. But she grasped his waist, and with surprising strength hauled him down with her. Her breath was heavy with liquor. She pressed her body to his and moved his arm to encircle her.

The times he had been physically close with Neriah, she was stridently passive, initiating closeness but never coming in direct contact. That was for him to navigate, and he did so cautiously. The four times they had kissed – two prior to their year apart, and two after – had been tender but subdued, a brief, gentle, deliberate meeting of the lips that warmed his heart for days. As they parted, they opened their eyes and gazed at each other for a moment, which wrote that memory in his mind like a page in a book.

This was much different. Saris was demanding, controlling, insistent, and stronger than he realized. There was no connection of the eyes or souls, only bodies. Her mouth found his, probing, taking, indulging. He offered no resistance and filled every silent request. The shrill warnings of his conscience were only enough to keep him from driving things onward himself. He gave her whatever she wanted.

After a few minutes, she fell limp and began to snore. He felt relieved and disappointed at the same time. His right arm was around the small of her back, his left hand she had placed on the exposed skin below her neck. Her legs were wrapped tightly around his left thigh. He did his best to extract himself without waking her.

He found her bedroll and covered her with her blanket. Then he went off to sleep by himself. His muddled brain now had a new conundrum, even more difficult than the first. Why did he enjoy that? Shouldn't he have been disgusted by it? Shouldn't he have stopped it? Wasn't he just giving her what she needed? Why did he feel so excited by it? Why was it so hard to walk away right now?

Whatever it was, it wouldn't happen again, he resolved. He had promised to be one with Neriah, and that concerned everything about their lives. He would have to tell her about this. Wouldn't he? Would she understand that it wasn't his fault? Would she be upset with him that he didn't do more to prevent it?

The rain intensified again, but he could hardly hear it through the sod.

The next day dawned dim under hazy clouds. They were richly supplied with fresh provisions by the hosts. Saris asked that word might be sent of her planned itinerary to her relatives. Dyrk expected the plains to be sodden and muddy, but aside from the occasional sodden puddle the ground was firm. The horses perked up after a calmer night with good feed.

Erelin joined them without a word. They could see him from quite a distance, sitting on his horse stock-still upon a ridge to the northwest. Torrin had been right, Dyrk thought. He needn't question the uncanny ability of the silent Taurilian to find them in this expansive wilderness.

The country they were passing through was beautiful, but monotonous. Cacti and other thorny shrubs grew amongst a mixture of green and brown grasses. Steep ridges and rocky outcroppings loomed in the distance from time to time, but for the most part their journey took gentle rises and falls. Only where a flow of water cut through the landscape would there be a narrow valley or gully with exposed earth. Dyrk understood why the Belorin valued this region as their winter grazing grounds. The grasses volunteered their green shoots willingly, coming to life after a hot summer of hibernation.

They occasionally saw herds in the distance, mostly to the north. Never did they see another person. Once Dyrk thought he could see a watchtower, a structure similar to the one in the last homestead they stayed in. The land seemed to be in peace. Dyrk knew that war and conflict was all too close. Despite the differences, he had built a lot of respect for the Belorin peoples he had met and hoped they would, somehow, be spared the Vekh onslaught.

Dyrk struggled mightily with his emotions over the next few days. He was shocked at how the encounter with Saris had completely taken over his thoughts and feelings, while the whole business with the Seraphs had faded to the background. He tried telling himself that their brief tryst had been a one-time thing, a mistake, a rash act committed within a drunken stupor that she probably didn't even remember anyway. She was incompatible with him in so many ways, he told himself. She was twice his age, though she didn't look or act like it. She was a polar opposite from a moral and religious standpoint. Her culture was different. She wanted completely different things in life than he did.

All of the ethical equations in his head were still valid. Good things come to those who work hard and endure patiently. Stray from the rules, take shortcuts, and expect nothing but pain and brokenness. They had to be right. He had staked his life on them.

Yet he found himself unconsciously finding excuses to come closer to her, looking out for her, seeking her attention. At night, his slumbering mind became free of the self-control he was desperately clinging to. His dreams descended into depths of carnal passions that he didn't think he was capable of. Being near her electrified a part of him that Neriah never did. He couldn't identify what it was exactly. Perhaps it was Saris's drive and determination to not only live life, but to pursue and relish its excitement. The way she seized what she wanted rather than letting it come to her or pass her by.

He tried to distract himself by working out the next few weeks in his head. There were many considerations. Torrin had to be brought safely to Karolia. That was Dyrk's primary task. But what about Saris? If the Gryphon was pursuing her, might Dyrk be the only one able to protect her? Would he be able to part with her not knowing if she was safe? And then there was Erelin. What were his intentions? It seemed he was invested in the safety of both Torrin and Saris. Dyrk was, on the whole, generally happy that Erelin was with them as long as they were in the wilderness but considered him a liability should they reach civilization. Would he want to come all the way to

Karolia? That would be awkward, trying to explain to the border officials. Torrin would be difficult enough.

They had spoken little about the Seraphs since that night. Dyrk had casually checked his sword from time to time, seeing if there was anything unusual. There wasn't. He looked back often during their journey but saw no signs of pursuit. Erelin would leave every night to do some scouting, or hunting, or whatever he did. The only thing Erelin ever communicated to Dyrk was that he was not to leave Saris alone. Judging by how Torrin watched her, Dyrk was not the only one given that instruction.

Dyrk barely knew what he was looking for. If they were indeed being pursued by the same creature that Torrin saw, the Gryphon that Dyrk had seen that one night, then it should be easily visible at night with its glowing eyes.

If that sword was somehow powerful, perhaps it came to life in the presence of Seraphs, he thought. That was part of the reason he kept checking the sword. As days went by, his diligence waned. He still kept an eye on Saris, but it was more for his own benefit than for hers.

It was the eighth day since Dharbur. They were traveling north, skirting the eastern side of the Doryn mountains as they headed towards Takorran. The air had become much colder during the day. Near nightfall, they found a stream that was unusually warm and had a strange smell. They followed it downstream a short distance until it merged with a cooler flow, and there made their camp in a sheltered dell.

The horses were picketed and cared for. Three tents were put up. By that time, Erelin came into camp with several small fish he had caught from the watercourse. As Dyrk cleaned them, he noted wounds on each fish that suggested they were shot with Erelin's bow.

Torrin hadn't been feeling well for two days now. He did his best to put in a full day's travel without complaining. Yesterday he had fallen asleep before supper. By the respiratory symptoms, they all figured it was a common ailment and did not merit any worry.

The three of them had their meal of roasted fish and boiled beans. Erelin then came to the fire, scraped the remainder of fish into the pot of beans, added water, and put it back onto the fire. Dyrk had stopped wondering about Erelin's peculiar eating habits. He guessed the injury that robbed him of speech also made it difficult to eat solid food. Torrin crawled into his tent. Saris disappeared for some time.

"How many days until Takorran?" Dyrk tried to engage Erelin casually.

Erelin held up a finger. (One day.)

"Do you see signs of any Vekh?" Dyrk often asked him about potential dangers.

(No.)

"I was worried they may try to encircle Holbern," Dyrk said. "They may have sent raiding patrols this far west."

Erelin finished fixing the pot at a distance from the fire so it would stay warm but not burn. He stood up. Bow in hand, he walked downstream and out of sight.

Saris came back to the camp. She crawled into her tent to get something. Upon coming out, she mentioned to Dyrk, "There's a hot spring just up the hill. I'm going to wash up."

"Enjoy yourself," Dyrk replied.

As she was walking away, she stopped for a moment and said in a teasing voice over her shoulder, "You could join me in a bit."

Dyrk wasn't quite sure if he heard her right. His body raced ahead with the implications of what she had just said, while his mind desperately tried to slow things down. He put his head in his hands as he stared at the fire. What cruel game was she playing with him?

You are going to stay by this fire, he ordered himself. For several minutes he was winning the battle. But then his resolve began to evaporate. She had told him to come, hadn't she? Shouldn't someone be watching over her? Besides, a quick dip in the hot springs would do him good too.

He had gotten up and taken a few steps before he even realized what he was doing. Again, justifications writhed through his mind. After all, he was just doing what she wanted, seeing to her needs. He was merely an amoral agent fulfilling the decisions of another.

It was a longer distance to the hot spring than he had anticipated. He followed the warm stream through bushes and sharp rocks. He had to climb a steep, rocky slope that was slick with moisture arising from condensed steam. Once he got to the top, he could see a pool in the rock, about fifteen paces away from him. A pall of mist hung over it. Near the edge, strewn over some rocks, were articles of Saris's clothing.

His eyes would not depart from the graceful figure in the water as he approached. She was immersed to her waist, her naked back to him. Her wet hair was matted to her scalp and the back of her neck. His knees felt wobbly. His heart raced. It was like a hook was in his nose, pulling him closer, or like he was being dragged by the rope of a harpoon through his belly. He was at the rocks near her clothes.

She turned her head sideways as her hands dipped into the water. "Come on in," she said alluringly. "It's heavenly."

He suddenly froze in place. He hadn't thought things through this far. The implications of what she was telling him to do came screaming through his consciousness. His body still participated, unbuckling his sword belt. But he knew now that he had run into an immovable object.

It wasn't so much the fact that he would be physically naked, exposed to another person. It was, rather, what it represented. He could not make himself fully known to her. He could not fully expose his entire self to someone he barely knew. He would never feel safe with her. There was no mutual commitment to each other's well-being. He knew it would be fatal, that first and final disconnect between his body and his soul. His conscience had finally seized control.

He turned around, forgetting his sword. "I just came to make sure you're safe. I'll wait for you at the bottom of the slope," he said. "Don't be long."

He took several faltering steps away. He had one last temptation, just to turn his head, get one look. He fought. He heard a splash. Some footfalls. What was she doing? He did not turn his head.

He was knocked off his feet by a vicious blow to his back.

His breath caught in his throat as searing pain erupted in his back and chest. He heard the sound of blood splashing onto the ground in front of him. His own. He tried to draw breath but began to suffocate on fluids. He looked down. The point of his own sword was sticking through his chest.

"Thalnuris claims his prize," an unearthly voice hissed in his ear.

NOTES

Arren and the Seven Servants

Melandar writes of one God, Arren, who has ministering spirits called Seraphs. Some Seraphs have rebelled, opposing Arren instead of doing His will.

Seven Seraphs have revealed themselves in the early days after the Great Burning. These are known as the Servants, for they came to serve mankind at Arren's bidding.

Kemantar, Servant of Justice. Him Who Divides Good from Evil. His priests are lawyers.

Anakdatar, Servant of the Earth. Him Who Holds the Earth. His priests are engineers and surveyors.

Harophin, Servant of Growth. Him Who Plants. His priests are philosophers and teachers.

Valeron, Servant of the Skies. Him Who Restores the Sun. His priests are astronomers and cartographers.

Telmanitar, Servant of the Sea. Him Who Rises to the Heavens. His priests are chaplains and funeral directors

Taephin, Servant of Health. Him Who Cultivates Life. His priests are physicians.

Nedrin, Servant of the Spirits. Him Who Protects. Nedrin does not have a priestly order.

Though Morthuldan has never revealed himself as such, Melandar attributes the rule of all rebellious Seraphs to this one prime fallen Seraph.

Calendar

The current year is counted from the Beginning of Days, the day that Melandar attests the Twelve Fathers and Mothers stepped forth from the Pelgor Mountains.

The Karolian calendar is divided up into eight months. The first seven months are named after the seven Servants and last seven weeks of seven days, for a total of 343 days. The eighth month, the Month of Waiting, lasts for three weeks, plus the number of days until the shortest day of the year (typically one or two additional days). This creates an incomplete week of festivities, beginning on the last day of the third week, during which no work or business is done.

The days of the week also use the names of the servants. A date is therefore spoken as follows:

"Valeron, sixth week of Kemantar's month, 2796"

The above date would be written as follows:

"V 6 Kemantar 2796"

Since Taephin and Telmanitar start with the same letter, Telmanitar is abbreviated to "L".

The corresponding days with our calendar are as follows:

First day of Kemantar's Month: December 22

First day of Anakdatar's Month: February 9

First day of Harophin's Month: March 30

First day of Valeron's Month: May 18

First day of Telmanitar's Month: July 6

First day of Taephin's Month: August 24

First day of Nedrin's Month: October 12

First day of Month of Waiting: November 30

The week begins on Kemantar's Day (Sunday) which is a normal workday. Nedrin's Day (Saturday) is regarded as a day for businesses to close and life to slow down. Bondservants are released from all but the most vital obligations to their masters on that day.

There are seven festivals. Each festival falls on the equal ordinal of the day, week, and month (for example, Harophin's festival falls on the third month, third week, third day).

Kemantar's Festival (Festival of the Beginning): December 22, winter solstice, also marks the anniversary that Karolia was re-established in 2368

Anakdatar's Festival (Festival of the Resting Earth): February 17

Harophin's Festival (Festival of Planting): April 15

Valeron's Festival (Festival of Summer): June 11, close to summer solstice

Telmanitar's Festival (Festival of the Fountain): August 7

Taephin's Festival (Festival of Harvest): October 3

Nedrin's Festival (Festival of the New Earth): November 29

Length Conversions

The common unit of length in Karolia is the Pace, the average length of a full stride of an adult male. A pace is equivalent to the metric Meter. Shorter lengths use a complex system of fractions. These shorter lengths have been converted to feet in the story for ease of reading (e.g. the height of a person).

A longer measure of distance is the League, which roughly represents an easy day's travel by walking. One league equals 26,000 paces, or roughly 26 kilometers or 16 miles.

Often, shorter distances are measured by league-tenths, which are about 2.6 kilometers or 1.6 miles.

Coinage

Karolian coinage is based on the Brass Piece, which historically represents an hourly wage for an unskilled labourer.

1 Brass Piece = 5 Copper Coins

1 Silver Ring = 20 Brass Pieces

1 Gold Half-Crown = 10 Silver Rings (this exchange rate floats based on the availability of silver and gold)

1 Gold Crown = 2 Gold Half-Crowns

Currency from other nations in relation to the Karolian Silver Ring:

1 Calderan Gold Piece = 9 Silver Rings

5.5 Corsavan Silver Pieces = 1 Silver Ring

Lifespans

Most races of Rhomakhiem (Zindori, Derrekh, Warrikh, etc.) have a lifespan comparable to medieval humans. They reach puberty between the ages of 11 and 14, adulthood at 16, stop bearing children soon after 40, and their lifespan is typically 60 years.

The Belorin, Lyssians, Rynekar, Calderans, Berch, and other races with traces of Taurilian blood live only slightly longer than the Rhomakhiem.

Karolians and Veranians, who are generally about half-blood Taurilian, have approximately 25% increased lifespan. They reach puberty between the ages of 13 and 16, adulthood at 18 (for women), and 20 (for men), stop bearing children around 50, reach old age at 100. They rarely live past 120 years.

Pure Taurilians, who are very rare, have about three times the lifespan of the Rhomakhiem. They reach puberty around 20, adulthood at 30, stop bearing children at 100, and can live for more than 200 years. The Alwem have even longer lifespan than this.

Vekh have an accelerated lifespan. They reach puberty between 7 and 9 years, are judged adults at 10 for women and 12 for men. Those that live past their fighting prime retire at age 28, and rarely live past 50.

SUMMARY OF HISTORY

From Tuin to Tawkin

All people of Reldaan are descended from the first Fathers and Mothers, who were protected from the Deluge of Fire in caves within the mountains of Pelgor. The Servants of Arren were their protectors.

Within four hundred years of their emergence, as men were multiplying in the land of Tauril, a man named Tuin sought to unify all men and prevent their wanderings over the earth. He was acclaimed to be the first King of Tauril. Those who wandered from Tauril before the death of Tuin became the fathers of the races of the Rhomakhiem (i.e. Unspoiled Men): Zindori, Derrekh, Warrikh, Farrakh, and the Kalthunites.

Tuin had four sons who ruled separate parts of Tauril under him: Drukudar the eldest, Kythaldar, Melandar, and Nethudar the youngest. Tuin bore a sword that was said to flame with divine fire, called the Crillslayer. In those days, the lifespan of men that stayed in Tauril was long, about three hundred years.

Late in his reign, Tuin began to conscript labour and supplies to build his capital city. This placed the people of Tauril into hardship. His three eldest sons conspired and killed him. Drukudar took the throne. Shortly after, he invaded the lands of his youngest brother, Nethudar, killing him and driving his people out. This is known as the War of the First Sundering. A plague came upon all who remained in Tauril as divine judgment for the murders of Tuin and Nethudar. The plague turned the colour of the skin a sickly green, and the lifespan of the people began to sharply decline. They became known as the Vekh.

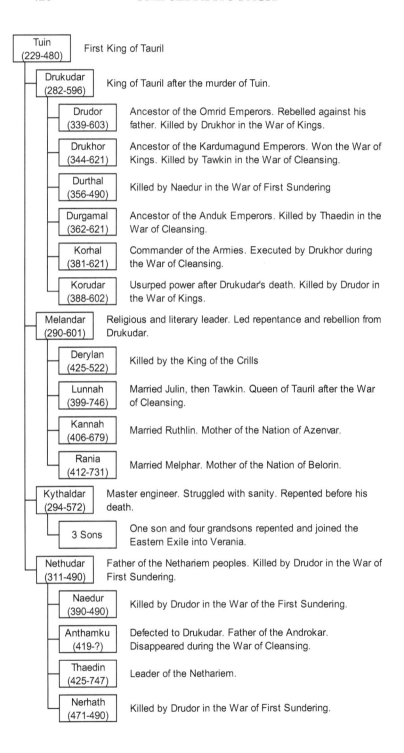

Tuin (229-480) — First King of Tauril

Drukudar (282-596) — King of Tauril after the murder of Tuin.

Drudor (339-603) — Ancestor of the Omrid Emperors. Rebelled against his father. Killed by Drukhor in the War of Kings.

Drukhor (344-621) — Ancestor of the Kardumagund Emperors. Won the War of Kings. Killed by Tawkin in the War of Cleansing.

Durthal (356-490) — Killed by Naedur in the War of First Sundering

Durgamal (362-621) — Ancestor of the Anduk Emperors. Killed by Thaedin in the War of Cleansing.

Korhal (381-621) — Commander of the Armies. Executed by Drukhor during the War of Cleansing.

Korudar (388-602) — Usurped power after Drukudar's death. Killed by Drudor in the War of Kings.

Melandar (290-601) — Religious and literary leader. Led repentance and rebellion from Drukudar.

Derylan (425-522) — Killed by the King of the Crills

Lunnah (399-746) — Married Julin, then Tawkin. Queen of Tauril after the War of Cleansing.

Kannah (406-679) — Married Ruthlin. Mother of the Nation of Azenvar.

Rania (412-731) — Married Melphar. Mother of the Nation of Belorin.

Kythaldar (294-572) — Master engineer. Struggled with sanity. Repented before his death.

3 Sons — One son and four grandsons repented and joined the Eastern Exile into Verania.

Nethudar (311-490) — Father of the Nethariem peoples. Killed by Drudor in the War of First Sundering.

Naedur (390-490) — Killed by Drudor in the War of the First Sundering.

Anthamku (419-?) — Defected to Drukudar. Father of the Androkar. Disappeared during the War of Cleansing.

Thaedin (425-747) — Leader of the Nethariem.

Nerhath (471-490) — Killed by Drudor in the War of First Sundering.

Nethudar's remaining people, the Nethariem, were blessed by the Servant Nedrin with great size and strength. Their skin turned black as night to aid their escape. They disappeared into the East and out of these tales. A few, however, turned back and entered the service of Drukudar. The plague came upon them as well, and they became known as the Androkar.

Melandar had one son, Derylan, and three daughters, Lunnah, Kannah, and Rania. His daughters married three brothers, the sons of Cormuthan: Julin, Ruthlin, and Melphar.

Julin and Ruthlin accompanied the army of Tauril in a war of conquest over a northern territory named Kalthund, inhabited by a race of Rhomakhiem, the Kalthunites. The brothers were captured by a young Kalthunite chieftain named Tawkin. Within captivity, Tawkin and the two sons of Cormuthan became close friends, and he forgave them for participating in Drukudar's belligerence.

Tawkin was captured by Drukudar's son, Drukhor, who ruled in Kardumagund. Julin and Ruthlin led a small band of Kalthunites into Kardumagund in a daring attempt to rescue Tawkin. They succeeded, but Julin was killed, and Tawkin lost his right hand and left eye. The survivors crossed the Sea-Lake of Cith and traveled back to Tauril. After meeting with Melandar and reporting Julin's death to his widow Lunnah, Tawkin did not stay but entered the hills of Anduk to begin a clandestine war of revenge against Drukhor.

In the meantime, horrible demon-possessed beasts called Crills began to ravage Tauril. None could stop them. They challenged Drukudar and his brothers to combat at Gel Aladu, a vale in western Tauril. The three brothers came, with their sons, and defeated two of the three Crills. The third withdrew after slaying Derylan, Melandar's only son, who died without heir. Melandar had given Derylan the Crillslayer, which had not saved its wielder.

A myth tells the story of Galion, who was convinced by the last Crill to bear the discarded Crillslayer into the depths of the earth before being murdered. There Tawkin would find it.

Tawkin was arrested by Ruthlin on Drukudar's orders. When Tawkin arrived at Melandar's home, Dar-Manost, the last Crill (named the King of the Crills) had also just arrived and was ravaging the town. Tawkin seized the Crillslayer being carried by Ruthlin, using it to destroy the Crill and save an orphaned infant boy who was about to be killed. The infant was raised by Lunnah, Julin's widow, and was named Atlan. Tawkin was then seized by a Servant of Arren. He delivered a condemnation on Melandar for his sins and a call to repent. Melandar, together with many of his people, heeded the call and repented. The disease was removed from their bodies, though their skin remained grey and lifeless as a perpetual reminder. These people and their descendants were initially called the Melandarim, but later were simply known as Taurilians.

Those who did not repent, and who still carried the disease, beset upon Melandar's people, led by Korhal, Drukudar's fifth son. Tawkin warned Melandar that he would not be victorious and had to lead his people into exile. Two groups of exiles left at that time. The first under Pedriath escaped to the East and founded the nation of Verania. Pedriath asked for Lunnah's hand in marriage but was refused. The eastern exiles will not come into these tales again. The second group, led by Tawkin, crossed the Istrith and settled in the land now known as Azenvar and built the fortress of Dar-Amund. Melandar himself protected their escape and was captured. This is known as the War of the Second Sundering.

During these exiles, Pedriath sent his brother to convince Lunnah to reconsider and join him in the east. When Tawkin found out, he slew Pedriath's brother in a fit of anger. Upon rebuke from Lunnah, he was overcome with remorse and sought his own death against Korhal's armies. Korhal himself challenged Tawin to fight, which neither could win as they were equally matched. Tawkin was released and rejoined the exiles to the south.

In Drukudar's captivity, Melandar was able to convince his brother Kythaldar of the need to find atonement for their sins. Kythaldar released Melandar but did not fully repent. In his final days, Kythaldar sought Melandar in the south and was given relief of the plague just before his death. Melandar also died shortly after.

Tawkin was now the leader of the Taurilians in Azenvar. He married Lunnah, the widow of Julin, and their only child was a son named Teren. They also raised Atlan as their own. Realms were established in the land of Belorin by Melphar (Belorin himself was the son of Melphar's daughter), and in the land of Azenvar by Ruthlin.

In the meantime, Drukudar had died and his six sons vied for power, slaying each other in a conflict known as the War of Kings. Finally Drukhor took the throne by force, allied with his brother Durgamal. Upon a sign given from above, Tawkin mustered his armies and allies and re-entered Tauril. Korhal pleaded with Drukhor to negotiate peace, but Drukhor ordered his execution. This caused many Vekh, led by a man named Lyrus, to defect to Tawkin's forces. Drukhor and Durgamal were defeated, the enemy Vekh were driven out, and the kingdom of Tauril was re-established with Tawkin as its reluctant king. This was known as the War of Cleansing.

From Tawkin to Eldorin

Tawkin became king and Teren after him. His line continued to the fifth generation, but the kings and the people did not wholeheartedly follow Arren. Under the rule of Talthor, Teren's grandson, Tauril allied with the powerful Vekh empire of Tunakhel. The worship of Arren was prohibited and Emperor-worship was instituted in its place. Talthor's reign was also marked by war against Azenvar and Belorin. Talthor's soldiers destroyed Azenvar and imprisoned their king, Deriak, but were defeated twice upon invading Belorin. This is known as the War of Loyalty.

Ter-Athel, another descendant of Teren, was part of a diplomatic mission to Tunakhel on behalf of Belorin, Azenvar, and Tauril, intent on finding an end to the war. They were known as The Twelve. They were betrayed by Talthor and arrested as spies by the emperor of Tunakhel, Nurag. By the power of the Servant Anakdatar, they escaped and did great harm to the Empire. They also returned to Altyren in secret and rescued Deriak. Afterwards, they had a hand in uniting Belorin with the remnants of Azenvar to restore Deriak's kingdom. Finally, Ter-Athel's people retreated into the woods of Feldar. Their descendants kept to themselves and were called the Alwem, who were thereafter known by their white hair.

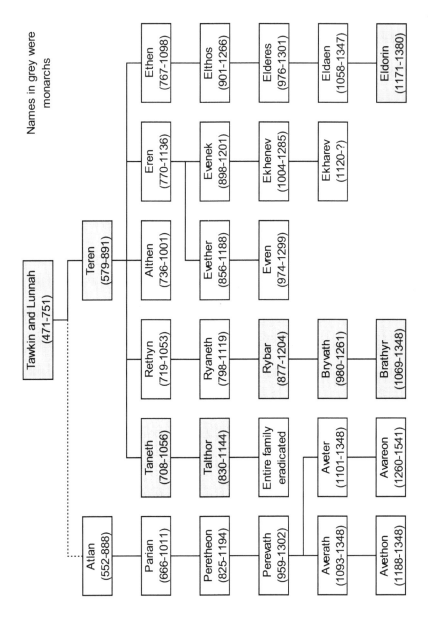

King Talthor was slain by his own general, a great-grandson of Teren. His name was Rybar, and he took the throne for himself.

During the reign of Rybar's grandson, Brathyr, Ter-Athel returned as a prophet, and came to a descendent of Teren named Eldorin. He was told to prepare for another exile, taking to himself what people would follow. Eldorin was a fisherman. He prepared three ships on the Crystolin river and waited for a prophetic sign to leave. He was branded a traitor by his king, who captured and imprisoned him. He was freed by Avareon of Atlan's house, who replaced him in his cell. Eldorin received his sign and his people departed in his ships. They sailed up the Istrith and into the Sea-Lake of Cith, pursued by the Vekh. There one ship, the Kadeth, was overtaken by the enemy, but Telmanitar the Servant bore the ship and its occupants up to heaven.

The two remaining ships, with six hundred men plus women and children, came to the land of Karolia. There Eldorin befriended the local people, the Warrikh, and established a kingdom in exile.

In the meantime, Tauril was completely overrun by the armies of Kardumagund, led by four demon-possessed captains named Vaezur, Kharon, Drumeth, and Vynek. Days after Tauril was taken, the lands were devastated by a great volcanic conflagration. Few survived, and the land was torn beyond all habitation. One who survived was Avareon of Atlan's house, still impersonating Eldorin. He salvaged many sacred scriptures written by Melandar from the libraries of Altyren. Though he was pursued by the demon-captain Vynek, he managed to find shelter in caves under the ruins of Dar-Amund. There he compiled the writings into three books that would form the basis for history, law, and prophecy for many nations to come. He finally escaped to the kingdom of Azenvar. Towards the end of his life he yearned to be reunited with Eldorin. His wish was granted, a ship was commissioned, and Avareon joined Eldorin before his death. Avareon left behind his son in Azenvar, the last heir to the house of Atlan.

From Eldorin to the Age of Turmoil

Eldorin was not a strong king, and his sons did not always follow Melandar's ways. Furthermore, they were beset upon by two of the captains of Kardumagund, Vaezur and Kharon, who mercilessly hunted the remnants of the House of Teren. Within sixty years, Vaezur had succeeded in killing Eldorin and his younger son, Esmarin.

The elder son of Eldorin, Esdarion, bravely pursued Vaezur who had taken Esmarin's wife as prisoner. Upon confrontation, Esdarion bore the Crillslayer and slew Vaezur. Esdarion then ruled for more than a hundred years, slowly expanding the fledgling state. Later in his life, Esdarion answered the plea of Azenvar's king, Anaren, and fought at his side, slaying Vynek with a flaming sword before the gates of Keor.

Over the next five generations, Kharon nearly succeeded in his quest to eradicate the House of Teren. Eldorin's kingdom was, over time, utterly destroyed. The people of Eldorin dispersed throughout that land. This was known as the Age of Turmoil.

The kingdom of Azenvar, meanwhile, slowly declined from the days of Anaren. At one point it was nearly destroyed by Drumeth and the Vekh of Kardumagund. It was again restored by two heroes of Ruthlin's line, Taerfin and his son Madwin. The kingdom lasted until the re-establishment of Karolia, whereupon it was merely a shadow of its former glory. Belorin, meanwhile was constantly harassed by the Zindori to the south and the Vekh from the north, when they were not dealing with civil wars within their borders. They maintained their own identity and their principal territories throughout the Age of Turmoil.

During this time, there is the tragic tale of Tular, last heir of Teren, who sought to save his niece from Kharon's captivity. He was eventually murdered by Kharon, but left behind an infant heir, Rulen.

In that period, the lands about the Elgolin River was contested by two rival empires: the Derrekh Himn and the Vekh of Omrid. The Himn were kinder to the remnants of Tauril than the Vekh. A tale is told of Reon, Tular's grandson, who pursued his betrothed to the very palace of the Himn. There she abandoned him for a prince of the Empire, but in recognition of Reon's bravery the Emperor granted him and the people of Tauril a small subject realm in Kaderish, which is in the south of present-day Karolia.

Five generations later, Reon's descendent Treon, together with a descendant of Avareon name Alerion, led a religious revival that galvanized the remnant of Tauril. At that time, the Vekh of Omrid occupied the heartlands of Karolia in an uneasy peace with the Himn. With secret permission from the Himn, Treon and Alerion led the people on an epic forty-year ordeal that culminated in the conquest of Karolia from the Vekh of Omrid. Treon died in the fighting, killed by a poisoned arrow. He had never taken the title of king. His son, Tuleon, became the first king of a re-established Karolia.

Modern Karolia

Successive kings of Karolia expanded its borders. Wars were fought, with the Vekh of Omrid, the Sej Zindori of the deep South, and finally with the Vekh of Kardumagund. The nation was blessed beyond the dreams of Treon and became the mightiest in the known world. However, as time went on, their prosperity began to dim the people's commitment to Arren and His worship.

Tuleon's great-great-grandson, Maneros, was a strong and militaristic king who expanded the borders of the land and begun exert the nation's influence in faraway lands. Maneros oversaw a modernization in the laws of succession, requiring kings to abdicate on their hundredth birthday, and the succeeding king be affirmed by the people.

Upon the abdication of King Tavideros, Maneros's grandson, his cousin Talidon was chosen king. He ruled for nearly fifty years and abdicated on his hundredth birthday. Older people in this book can recall the reign of Talidon, which was marked by peace, prosperity, and a decrease in religious adherence. Talidon's second son, Taristan, was chosen as the next king over his older brother Talisman, who bore a grudge.

Taristan tried to heal the rift with his older brother by making him Rector of the Eratur's College. The king abdicated after twenty-one years as he became unable to walk due to injuries sustained in battle. Upon his abdication, civil war nearly broke out as two candidates, Talisman's son Tremarin, and Dephetor, a second cousin, each sought to have the other disqualified as candidates. Taristan quelled the conflict by taking back the throne and declaring both candidates ineligible.

Five years later, the next king chosen was Taristan's younger
brother, Adareoth. The new king had sided with Tremarin in the
previous conflict, and therefore promoted Tremarin and his brother
Amarion to positions of authority. To heal wounds, he also
appointed Dephetor's brother Delmas as one of the Crown Princes.

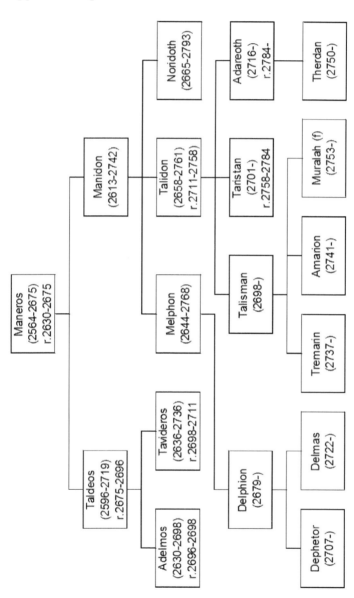

GLOSSARY

Adareoth, King (ə DAIR ee ahth): King of Karolia (born in 2716). He is of House Teren. He has one son, Therdan.

Age of Turmoil: A historical period that began with the murder of the Karolian king in 1673 and ended with the re-establishment of Karolia in 2368. During this time, the remnants of Eldorin's exiles were scattered throughout the lands of the West. Azenvar and Belorin were hard-pressed to survive. The two superpowers of this age were the Vekh Empire of Omrid and the Derrekh Empire of the Himn.

Aijen (EYE jən in Karolia, eye jen in Ancharith): Young bondservant of the Kaj Zindori race (born 2770). He is married to Careesh. He grew up in a family of farm labourers in Ancharith. He is the father of an infant boy, Mejin.

Akhiros (akh EE ros): A breed of horse from the foothills of southern Dedarrek. Its sure-footedness and aggressive temperament make it an ideal war-horse, but it lacks the brute strength of the Tevledain and the long range of the Belorin horses.

Alerion (a LAIR ee ahn): Historical figure (2281-2443). He was a Taurilian of House Atlan, a descendant of Avareon. He grew up in Azenvar, but travelled to the scattered remains of Eldorin's exiles as an adult. He led a spiritual revival, turning the people back to the Melandarim religion. He became close friends with Treon, heir to the throne of Kaderish. Alerion participated in the beginning of Treon's Sojourn, with the aim to conquer and re-establish Karolia, but died of natural causes before the quest could be completed.

almathin **(AL mə THIN)**: Melandarim for a heavily armoured warrior. In Melandar's time, it referred to a footman, but it is currently used exclusively for elite mounted warriors.

Almathin Regiment (AL mə THIN): An elite group of Karolian heavy cavalry under the authority of the Commander of the Royal Forces.

Alnarah (al NAIR a): Young Karolian woman (born 2779). She is Neriah's sister, the second living child of Vecton and Ryesse.

Altyren of Karolia (al TIRE ən): Capital city of Karolia, built upon a series of islands in the middle of the Elgolin River. It is the largest city of the known world.

Altyren of Tauril (al TIRE ən): Historical capital city of Tauril. It was named Durthonim while ruled by Drukudar and the Vekh, but it was renamed as Altyren when conquered Tawkin and the followers of Melandar.

Alwem (AL wem): A sub-race of pure Taurilian descent who removed themselves from other races millennia ago. They are best known by their tall stature and white hair. Some believe that they no longer exist, or perhaps never did. As they are pure Taurilians, Alwem live much longer than most races, with a lifespan of nearly three hundred years. They become adults at the age of fifty.

Amarion (ə MARR ee UN): Third Crown Prince and Commander of the Western Armies of Karolia (born 2745). He is of House Teren, the son of Lord Talisman, and a nephew of King Adareoth. To his armies, he is a pious leader and skilled tactician. In the king's court, he is known for his ruthlessness and ability to get difficult things done.

Anakdatar (an AK də TAR): Second Servant of the Melandarim religion. Anakdatar counseled early man on digging stone and metal from the earth, as well as the making of pottery and bricks. His priests are civil and structural engineers. His Festival of the Resting Earth is in late winter. He is the patron Servant at the dedication of public buildings and the establishment of new wards.

Ancharith (an CHARR ith): Refers to both a land and a realm south of Karolia, around the headwaters of the Elgolin River. It is a dry, upland region that is nevertheless very fertile. Vast orchards are tended there. Trade with Karolia is critical to its financial survival. Historically, Ancharith was the seat of a primitive empire of the Hajrekh peoples that stretched from Rhonaur through modern-day

Karolia all the way to Loth Tund. The present realm of Ancharith has only a minority of Hajrekh peoples; most are Kaj Zindori who migrated from the southwest.

Androkar (AN drow KAR): A race of large, black-skinned humans who reside in small enclaves amongst the Vekh. They are physically powerful and intelligent, but they lack the craftiness and ambition of the Vekh. They make effective officers and bodyguards within the Vekh armies. The Androkar are descended from an ancient people called the Nethariem, who had removed themselves from all contact with other races. The name Androkar derives from the Melandarim word for "ogre" or "giant".

Anduk (AN dook): A land forming the east shore of the Sea-Lake of Cith. In the south are several volcanoes, in which is built the Fortress of Anduk. Its central lowland regions are swampy, while its northern regions are upland plains. It is heavily populated by Vekh.

Arghand (AR KHAND): A lightly forested region north of Belorin and west of the Kullion River. There are vast swamps near the Kullion in the east. The region is sparsely populated by Derrekh, Belorin, and Pej Zindori peoples, and has no central government.

Arren (ər REN): The deity in the monotheistic religion of Melandar. Though Arren is believed to be infinitely good, infinitely powerful, and infinitely wise, various traditions differ on how close He is to the events of the world and its people. Karolians generally believe that Arren is too great and wonderful for man to directly interact with Him; they hold the Seven Servants as suitable intermediaries.

Atheron River (Adh ər on): Navigable river flowing from Halidorn to Elbing before joining with the Elgolin.

Atlan (AT lan): The name of a Karolian house, part of the Houses of Rulers grouping. Atlan was also an important historical person, according to Melandar's histories (552-888). As an infant, he was found with his dead mother by Tawkin, who saved him from the ravages of the King of the Crills. Atlan was given to Melandar's eldest daughter Lunnah, who at that time was a widow, for care. Later, Tawkin became Atlan's adopted father when Lunnah and Tawkin were married. Atlan became a prominent person in the kingdom of Tauril under kings Tawkin and Teren, making his home in Melandar's dwelling of Dar-Manost. He was credited as the religious conscience of the realm at that time. The house fell out of favour in the years to follow as the kings became annoyed by the repeated warnings from the House of Atlan.

Avareon (a VAR ee ahn): Historical person (1260-1541). He was a Taurilian of House Atlan at the time of Eldorin. He facilitated Eldorin's escape, impersonating him in prison. After his release, Avareon was permitted to take what he wanted of Melandar's writings from the royal libraries just prior to the volcanic eruption that destroyed the lands. Avareon escaped the cataclysm as the last remaining member of the house. Hidden underneath the ruins of Dar-Manost, he compiled Melandar's writings into three tomes, and later found refuge in Azenvar. Before his death, he was reunited with Eldorin, presenting Melandar's writings to guide the nation of Karolia.

Azenvar (AH zen VAR): An ancient realm that was bounded by the Istrith on the north, the Kullion River on the west, the Lorin River and Warder Mountains on the south, and the Sea of Winds on the east. It was first settled by Melandar's son-in-law Ruthlin, who was the ancestor of its continuing royal family. It survived repeated attacks by the Omrid Empire, but was finally destroyed two hundred years ago by a resurgent Vekh nation of Kardumagund. Karolia has attempted to resettle the land, but so far only a trickle of settlers has colonized the western reaches of the realm. In the east, a single settlement of Taurilians, at Dar-Amund, has never been conquered and continues its isolated existence.

Bajzin (baj ZIN): A subgroup of Roj Zindori who live in the southern reaches of Dedarrek. Like their Roj cousins, they routinely raid neighbouring peoples, including Ancharith, Rynek, and Karolia.

Battle of Rocavion: A minor conflict in 2773 between Karolia and the Vekh of Ormid. A raiding force of Vekh took advantage of the absence of Karolia's fleet, launching an invasion of mainland Karolia near Rocavion. As the coastal towns were being pillaged, a Karolian relief force set out from Geherth Altyr. The Karolians were ambushed by Vekh just north of Resgild, losing many soldiers. The

Vekh left in their ships with their booty soon after.

Bay-Tongue: A common language based on Melandarim but heavily influenced by the Daxonite languages. It is the business and casual language of the nation of Verania and many of the surrounding nations in the East. It is rarely spoken west of the Sea of Winds.

Bayern (BAY ərn): Young Karolian man of House Lyrus (born in 2774). He is the eldest son of Thur Daynen. His hometown is Doleth Sarin, the Old City.

Bellis (BEL lis): Karolian girl (born 2787). She is Neriah's sister, the fifth living child of Vecton and Ryesse.

Belorin, People of (BEL ər in): A race of semi-nomadic people who reside in the realm of the same name. The Belorin are the best-known horsemen of Reldaan. Their bloodlines can be traced back to a tribe of Rhomakhiem who lived in the north, united by Melandar's son-in-law Melphar. Belorin himself was a historical figure who was Melphar's grandson. The Belorin have a small amount of Taurilian blood, giving them slightly longer lifespan than other Rhomakhiem. They have moderate-hued skin, brown, black, or red hair, and are known for generous facial hair amongst the men.

Belorin, Realm of (BEL ər in): A long-lasting realm that extends from the Kullion River to Dharbur. It was established by a man with the same name, who was a great-grandson of Melandar. Though Belorin does not share the same traditions as Karolia, its people still follow the substance of the Melandarim religion.

Berce (BERS): A large, independent island realm near Verania in the East, marking the eastern extent of the Sea of Siven. Its people are mostly of the Veranian race. Some of the best sailors in Reldaan hail from Berce.

Berhimmon (bər HIM mon): Large Karolian town on the Elgolin River, a league south of Altyren. It is the seat of the province of Teren.

Binev, House of (BEYE nev): The name of a Karolian house, part of the Houses of Harvest grouping.

Bondservant of Karolia: A class of people in Karolia who are attached or "bonded" to citizens or the state. They include foreign-born immigrants, criminals, and the destitute. Bondservants can normally earn Freeman status after working faithfully for their master for seven years.

Braedil (BRAY ə deel): An older man of pure Taurilian descent, from House Atlan (born in 2642). He is a translator residing in Sorwail.

Caemryn Sur (CAY əm rin SUR): City along the east bank of the Elgolin two-and-a-half leagues south of Altyren. It is the provincial seat of Kurlen.

Caldera (kal DARR ah): A city-state built around a narrow isthmus separating the Sea of Winds from the Sea of Siven. Caldera is greatly enriched by taxing traffic between the two seas, which passes under a natural land-bridge. Caldera is also home to some of the best metalsmiths in Reldaan. Its people are mostly native Daxonites, but they speak Bay-Tongue.

Careesh (kair EESH in Karolia, karr eesh in Ancharith): Young woman of the Kaj Zindori race (born in 2776). She is married to Aijen. She grew up in a middle-class landowning family in Ancharith. She is the mother of a baby boy, Mejin.

Cassius (KASS ee us): A Karolian man of House Melikar (born in 2734). He is the Lord, or ruler, of the province of Saringon.

Chisim (CHIS əm): A Karolian port village on the east bank of the Elgolin, two league-tenths northeast of Altyren.

Citizen of Karolia: To be eligible for citizenship in Karolia, a man must be born in Karolia, be married, have done three years of service for the crown, be the owner of land, and have not been convicted of a crime. A man can also become a citizen if he joins a provincial or royal reserve army upon completion of three years of military service, without the other requirements. Women are also said to be citizens if they are married to a man who meets the requirements. Citizens have fewer restrictions on owning land, and can vote, hold office, and avail themselves of many public services unavailable to freemen or bondservants.

Cith, Sea-Lake of (SITH): A massive freshwater lake that is shaped roughly like an "x". Its northeast reach flows into the Kelmere, which drains into the Vruh Sea when the level of the lake is high enough. Its southeast arm separates Anduk from Azenvar, and is drained by the mighty Istrith River into the Sea of Winds. Its southwest arm extends into Karolia, fed by the Elgolin River. Its northwest arm extends into Omrid and is fed by the Kubar River.

Convent of Harophin: A complex built on an isolated mountain in the south of Karolia that is a training ground for the nation's philosophers and higher educators. It is widely seen as a source of modern thinking and heterodoxy.

Corsava (cor SA va): The name of a land south of Tirlun along the Sea of Winds. It is also the name of a vast empire with overseas holdings. The empire is made up mostly of Sej Zindori peoples.

Crill (KRIL): A mythical creature that resembles a bipedal dragon without wings. According to Melandarim legend, Crills were ancient beasts that spurned their original calling, preferring to join themselves with rebellious Seraphs to multiply their powers. When inhabited by a Seraph, a Crill was fearsome indeed, possessing supernatural powers in addition to their savage strength and towering stature. Only four of these enter the historical legends. One, who stylized himself as the King of the Crills, terrorized Melandar's house until he was slain by Tawkin. Crills have never been seen again since Tawkin's day.

Crillslayer: A sword from Melandarim legend. It was forged by a young Drukudar and given to his father Tuin at the coronation of the first king. It was said to be hallowed by the might of the Servant Telmanitar to sear and scorch the enemies of man, especially the Seraphs. After Tuin's death, Melandar gave the sword to his son Derylan who was compelled to join in a combat against three Crills. The sword did not flame for Derylan, who was killed. Melandar threw the sword into the desert in his grief. Since that time, a select few historical figures have wielded a sword that flamed. It was widely believed to be the same weapon, generating theories on how the Crillslayer could come into their possession.

Dar-Amund (DAR AY mund): Literally, "House of Refuge" in Melandarim. Dar-Amund was built as a temporary home for the exiles from Tauril under Tawkin. Later, it was an important outpost of the realm of Azenvar, and was never taken by an enemy force throughout its long history. Many of Atlan's house found refuge there as Azenvar was being destroyed by the Vekh of Kardumagund. It has maintained its self-sufficiency for the past two hundred years. Most who dwell there have never intermingled with other peoples, and it is therefore one of the few places where one might find men and women of the pure Taurilian race.

Dar-Krun (DAR KROON): Literally, "House of Stone". It was the first permanent dwelling built by Eldorin upon his settlement in Karolia. The moderately tall stone tower still stands, at the heart of the city of Altyren.

Dar-Manost (DAR MAN ost): Literally, "House of the Setting Sun" in Melandarim. Dar-Manost was a manor and small fortress on the northern slopes of the Pelgor mountains in Tauril. It was built by Melandar. After Tawkin restored the kingdom, it became the principle house of the descendants of Atlan. It had a small tower that was plated in a luminescent copper-coloured metal that shone with the light of the setting sun long after sunset. By its light, through carefully crafted fissures and crystals, the entire house would be lit up for hours. The house was destroyed during the War of Desolation.

Daxon (DAK son): A land north of Caldera. The Rhomakhiem that hail from that area are known as Daxonites, but the label has been expanded to encompass all Rhomakhiem in the East.

Daynen, Thur (DAY nən): Karolian Eratur of House Lyrus (born in 2744). He is assigned as a Headman in the Old City of Doleth Sarin. He is the father of Bayern.

Delmas (DEL məs): Second Crown Prince of Karolia and the Commander of the Royal Forces (born in 2722). His command includes the Palace Guard and the Almathin Regiment. He is a second cousin of the king.

Delvaeth (del VAY eth): Fortress in northern Azenvar, near the Istrith, that was originally built by Taurilian settlers of Azenvar. It was taken by Kharon and Drumeth shortly after the War of Desolation that destroyed Tauril. To this day, it has been a Vekh outpost and Drumeth's base of operations.

Derrekh (DAIR ekh): Literally, "Men of the Hills" in

Melandarim. The Derrekh are a race of Rhomakhiem who originally inhabited the lands of Rynek, Lyssia, Narval, and Arghand. Some groups migrated deep into the Korlani Mountains and Trobes Basin. This race founded the Himn Empire shortly after Eldorin's reign, which waned and eventually disappeared after the re-establishment of Karolia. At this time, there are many full-blooded Derrekh within the nations of Lyssia and Rynek. Some live in Karolia, either as migrant bondservants or as full citizens. The Derrekh peoples are physically smaller than Karolians and typically have black hair.

Derylan (DAIR əl ən): Historical person (425-552). He was the only son of Melandar. He was known to be wayward and promiscuous. He was killed at Gel Aladu when the sons of Tuin fought the Crills, even though he bore the Crillslayer. It was said that the fabled sword did not flame in Derylan's hand, and in fact spun from his grip when he was attacked.

Dharbur (D' ar bər): An independent city-state in the south of Belorin, within the oasis of the Red Valley. It is a multicultural enclave, populated by Pej Zindori, Roj Zindori, and Belorin peoples, plus many other racial minorities. It is currently allied with Belorin, though this has not always been so.

Doleth Sarin (DOH leth SARR in): Karolian city along the Great East Road in southern Saringon, a league and a half southeast of Altyren. It is the provincial seat of Saringon, and the fifth largest city in Karolia.

Drimugari (DRIM yoo GAR eye): A vast southern continent across the Sea of Winds, containing dark jungles, high plateaus of savannah grasslands, and a large inland salt sea within a deep depression. It is only populated along the coastlines, colonized both by Vekh and Corsavans in various places. It is joined to the northern continent only at the isthmus of Caldera.

Drudor (DROO dor): Historical person (339-603). He was the eldest son of Drukudar, but he was deposed as the crown prince after he was accused of murder. He reigned over a small subject realm while secretly building an army to take the throne by force. Finally, when his father died, he unleashed his army upon Tauril, beginning the War of Kings. He was slain by his brother Drukhor.

Drudor's descendants became the leaders of the Vekh empire of Tunakhel.

Drukhor (DROO khor): Historical person (344-621). He was the second son of Drukudar and the crown prince after his older brother Drudor was deposed. Upon his father's death, a succession crisis called the War of Kings erupted until Drukhor descended with his own armies, crushing all resistance and executing his brother Drudor. Drukhor was known to be allied with many evil Seraphs, who aided him when Tawkin invaded to reclaim Tauril in the War of Cleansing. Nevertheless, Drukhor was defeated and slain by Tawkin. His descendants formed the ruling dynasty of the realm of Kardumagund.

Drukudar (DROO kyoo dar): Historical person (282-596). He was the eldest son of the first king of Tauril, Tuin. He instigated the murder of his father and thereafter took the throne. He is widely regarded as the chief ancestor of the Vekh.

Drumeth (DROO meth): Historical person (born around 1150). One of the four demon-captains in Melandarim legend who led the armies that destroyed Tauril. Afterwards, Drumeth set his sights on the conquest of Azenvar. Upon the capture of the fortress of Delvaeth near the Istrith River, Drumeth used it as his base of operations. He nearly succeeded in the days of Taerfin, but was pushed back in a momentous campaign by Taerfin and his son Madwin called the War of Chaos. In singular combat with Madwin's champion Garon, Drumeth was driven from the cliffs of Thunya and never seen again, though the demonic fires of Delvaeth signal his continuing presence.

Duoma (doo OH ma): A parcel of land reserved for citizens of Karolia. It is typically forty acres of fertile land, but it can become much larger in less fertile areas. Ownership of one duoma of land meets the requirements for citizenship.

Dyrk (DURK): Young Karolian man of House Teren (born in 2774). He is the eldest son of Maryk and Loriah. His hometown is Tanvilon. He is a trader and trainer of horses.

Elbing (EL bing): Karolian city along the Elgolin River near its joining with the Atheron River. It is the third-largest city in Karolia.

Eldorin (EL dor in): Historical person (1171-1380). He was a Taurilian of House Teren. He was advised by the prophet Ter-Athel and the Servant Harophin to prepare a remnant for exile from Tauril prior to its destruction. He bore a sword that flamed to signify his authority. He obeyed his calling and established a small kingdom in exile named Karolia, becoming its first king. His wife was named Remah, and he had two sons, Esdarion and Esmarin. He was eventually killed by the demon-captains Kharon and Vaezur.

Elgolin River (El go lin): A sizeable river which begins in the highlands of Ancharith, flowing north into southwestern arm of the Sea-Lake of Cith. Most of the cities of Karolia are built upon its banks.

Elora (ee LOR a): Young Karolian woman (born in 2779). She is the third child of Maryk and Loriah, and is Dyrk's sister. Her name is the feminized form of Eloren, one of Karolia's kings.

Eloren (ee LOR en): Historical person of House Teren (2383-2491). He was king of Karolia after Tuleon his father. He was succeeded by his son Eletian. A bridge connecting the island of Altyren with the eastern bank of the Elgolin was named after him.

Elzabi (el ZAB ee in Karolia, əl za bee in Zindori): A young male Roj Zindori bondservant within Maryk's household.

Encarigon (ən CAIR i gahn): Philosopher and lecturer from the Convent of Harophin. Though he is accredited as a Priest of Harophin, he prefers not to use the title.

eratur **(AIR ə TOOR)**: Melandarim for "kingsman". In Karolia, aspiring men must attend at least four years of training at the College of Eraturs before entering service as an Eratur. Eraturs may be employed as officers in the army, as important royal or provincial officials, or as headmen (see Headman). If they are not working in some sort of official capacity, they cease to be Eraturs.

Erelin (formally AIR 'ul IN, usually pronounced AIR ə lin): Full-blooded Taurilian mercenary of unknown origin (born around 2725). His name is actually the combination of a truncated house name (Er) and his given name ('lin). He is mute because of a mutilation in which his tongue was torn out.

Esdarion (ez DARR ee ahn): Historical person (1317-1576).

He was of House Teren, the son of Eldorin, and the second king of Karolia. He, like his father, bore the Crillslayer that flamed. He slew the demon-captain Vaezur in revenge of his father's death, and later defeated another demon-captain, Vynek, in battle in Azenvar.

Eveth (EH veth): A young Karolian Eratur of House Eveth who manages the Royal Post headquarters at Navren Altyr.

Eveth, House of (EH veth): The name of a Karolian house, within the Houses of Stone grouping.

Farnich (FAR nich): Older Karolian man. Owner of a livery stable in Doleth Sarin. He is married to Zellna and has a bondservant named Gelda.

Farrakh (FAIR akh): A small race of Rhomakhiem who live in the Cyrani and Doryn mountains in southeastern Rynek. They are a simple but territorial people. They are the first to have domesticated tarns.

Feldar (FEL dar): A vast region between the Zelmandi Mountains and the Sea of Winds. It is mostly forested. It is moderately populated, but there is no central government. Its largest city is Sorwail, an important port along the coast of the Sea of Winds.

Freeman of Karolia: A second class of citizens who are free to seek employment or move their residence within a province, but do not have the rights, privileges, and duties of full citizenship. They may own a single property that is not classified as a *duoma*.

Gadril (GAD ril): Young Karolian man from Doleth Sarin, the son of Galmic, a jeweler. He is a recruit in the Karolian army.

Galion (GAL ee ahn): A fictional person. Often called Galion the Unfortunate, he was the protagonist in a tragic fictional epic in which the King of the Crills manipulated him into delivering the Crillslayer to the bowels of the earth. There he was murdered. The story was presented in Tauril as a fable that nonetheless illustrated the gullibility of man and the diabolical nature of the Seraphs. In later years, it was included, wrongly according to some, in the canon of Melandarim scriptures.

Gavon (GA vahn): Young Karolian man of House Teren (Born in 2776). He is the second child of Maryk and Loriah. His hometown is Tanvilon. He is a scribe in training.

Geherth Altyr (ge 'URTH al TIRE): Literally, "Within Sight of Altyren". Karolian city built on a hill a half-league north of Altyren. It is the location of the College of Eraturs. It is the provincial seat of the province of Halyron, despite being less than half the size of nearby Navren Altyr.

Gel Sonest (GEL SAHN est): Small Karolian city along the east bank of the Elgolin River. It is the provincial seat of Rianast, and boasts one of Karolia's three Scribe's Colleges.

Glannith (GLAN nith): Karolian girl (born 2790). She is Neriah's sister, the sixth living child of Vecton and Ryesse.

Grevana (gre VAN a): A region along the southern shores of the southwest arm of the Cith. This region is densely forested. It has been depopulated by continual conflict with the Vekh.

Gryphon (GRI fun): A mythological beast that has been possessed by a Seraph. For the most part, they are said to appear as large, mangy dogs with wicked-looking spines protruding from their backs, horns sprouting from their heads, and an unearthly glow emanating from their eyes and mouth.

Hajrekh ('AZH rekh): An ancient people that is argued to be a precursor of the Warrikh. They also bear some similarities to the Zindori, leading some to call them "light-skinned Zindori". They formed an empire centered on present-day Ancharith, but it was defeated and scattered by Omrid. Today, few Hajrekh are left, though they form communities in Loth Tund, northern Ancharith, and the Trobes Basin. A small but significant number have become bondservants or citizens in Karolia.

Hajwan ('AHZH wahn): An unassuming middle-aged man, appearing to be of mixed Karolian and Hajrekh blood, living in Altyren. His origin and profession are not known.

Halidorn ('AL i dorn): A large, sprawling city in southeastern Karolia, within a crescent-shaped lake that is part of the Atheron River. For hundreds of years, it was a province of the Himn Empire, and then an independent city-state upon the Empire's collapse. Only recently was it incorporated into Karolia and made its own province. As a result, the people of Halidorn have a unique culture within the kingdom, often resenting the influence of the rest of the nation.

Racially, the people are mostly Karolian, but there is much more Derrekh influence than the rest of the kingdom, which traces its ancestry through the Warrikh. Halidorn counts itself as the second largest city of Karolia, narrowly edging out Elbing for that distinction.

Hanni ('A nee): Teenage girl of Karolian descent living in Tanvilon (born in 2782). She is the fourth child of Maryk and Loriah, and the sister of Dyrk.

Harophin ('AIR u fin): Third Servant of the Karolian religion. Harophin taught early man about plant-based agriculture. The Festival of Planting dedicated to him is in mid- spring. Followers of the Melandarim religion typically address Harophin at every meal. His priests are philosophers and educators. In modern day, most priests of Harophin no longer refer to themselves as such, since they avoid the trappings of deist religion in their advancement of a humanist understanding of philosophy and society. Their base of operations is not referred to as a temple; it is called the Convent of Harophin.

Haydrest (HAYD rest): Large town on the Talvion river. It is the seat of the province of Naraven.

Headman: a Karolian political office, appointed over a "ward" of 300-600 people. They oversee all political and military affairs of the ward, and act as a mentor to the male youth. All headmen must have attained the rank of an Eratur (see Eratur).

Himn, Empire of the (HIM): The Himn refers to a political and ideological association that arose amongst the Derrekh of Hyrnistia in the mid-1600s. One of their number, named Ibavin, wrote a tract known as the Laws of Decency and Order, a set of non-religious moral principles. Ibavin became a conqueror, imposing his way of life on neighboring tribes. Successive generations expanded their conquest until it became an empire, spanning present-day Karolia, Dedarrek, Rynek, Grevana, Narval, Lyssia, and Arghand. Both Azenvar and Belorin were subject to the Himn at some point in history. The empire was contested by the Omrid Vekh, and the Himn were eventually eradicated by the Vekh in 2501. The minor realm of Lyssia was borne out of its ashes.

Though it was irreligious and often oppressive, the Himn Empire is credited by the Karolians with sheltering their ancestors from the Vekh during the Age of Turmoil.

istran (is **TRAN**): Melandarim word for "fellow soldier", good tense.

jadweir (**JAD** we **EER**): Melandarim word for an apprentice. Traditionally, it is used only for contestants at the Contest of Squires; all other apprentices would use the River-Tongue form of the word.

Januz (**JAY nuz**): Tanvilon's town drunk.

Kaderish (**ka DAIR ish**): Karolian province along the north bank of the Atheron River, east of Elbing and west of Halidorn. It is also the name of a historical realm in Treon's time, which was a province of the Himn Empire. Treon's grandfather Oreon was king of Kaderish when he began his Sojourn. Originally, the entire Atheron River valley, including the lakes to the north named Wallen Perthez, but excluding Halidorn, was part of the realm of Kaderish.

Kadeth (**KAY deth**): One of Eldorin's ships during his flight from Tauril. The Kadeth, upon being badly damaged and overtaken by the Vekh, was carried to heaven with all its occupants by Telmanitar before Eldorin's eyes.

Kaj Zindori (**KAJ**): A race of steppe-dwellers who live in the western regions of the Sea of Sand. Their easternmost realms are Ancharith and Rhonaur. Kaj Zindori are numerous but are less warlike than their Roj or Sej brethren. For the most part, they are hardy herders of the steppes, though they do tend to organize themselves into towns and cities wherever arable land can be found. They are the smallest in stature of the Zindori races, and the darkest-skinned. The inhabitants of Ancharith, while technically part of the Kaj Zindori race, regard themselves as a distinct people (see Ancharakhiem).

Kalthund (**KAL thund**): A land on the western shores of the Vruh Sea, mostly covered in boreal forests. It was the homeland of an ancient, extinct people called the Kalthunites. Today, it is sparsely colonized by the Vekh of Kardumagund.

Kardumagund (**kar DOOM a gund**): A fertile land on the north shores of the Sea-Lake of Cith. It is heavily populated by

Vekh. From time to time, Kardumagund has been the seat of a Vekh empire that has terrorized Reldaan.

Kannah (KAN na): Historical person (406-679). She was the second daughter of Melandar and the wife of Azenvar's founder, Ruthlin. She is an icon of intelligence and farsightedness among women in the Melandarim tradition.

Karam (kair AM): Elderly female bondservant of Derrekh descent, part of Maryk's household. She is married to Nabir.

Karolia, Realm of (KARR oh LEE a): A kingdom begun by Taurilian exiles in the days of Eldorin. It was destroyed several hundred years later by Omrid, led by the demon-captain Kharon. It was restored by Treon. Successive kings expanded its borders and enriched its people until it became the most prosperous and numerous kingdom in northern Reldaan, rivaling the Corsavan empire of the south. For citizenship requirements, see Citizen of Karolia.

Karolian (KARR oh LEE an): A distinct race that is an amalgamation of Taurilian and Warrikh blood. Karolians have a longer lifespan than most peoples around them, becoming adults at 20, and regularly living past 100 years. They are also taller in stature than most races. Their skin colour reflects their combined heritage, a light brownish-grey.

Kemantar (KEM ən tar): First Servant of the Karolian religion. He taught early man about morality, laws, and human rights. He is the patron Servant at any court proceeding. His festival marks the beginning of the calendar year, at the winter solstice. His priests are lawyers.

Khaldis (KHAL dis): A homeless, runaway bondservant of Hajrekh descent, living on the streets of Doleth Sarin.

Kharon (KHAIR on): Historical person (born around 1150). One of the four demon-captains in Melandarim legend who led the armies that destroyed Tauril. Kharon pursued the exiles and nearly exterminated the ruling House of Teren. After terrorizing the nascent kingdom of Karolia for nearly four hundred years, he suddenly disappeared. His demise was not recorded.

Koeric (koh err IK): Middle-aged Belorin man (born in 2744).

He is the leader of an extended household, which includes among others his wife Rothell, his nephew Orben, his son Toic, and his adopted sister Saris.

Korhal (KOR 'ahl): Historical person (381-621). The fifth son of king Drukudar, Korhal served successive kings faithfully for many years as the Commander of the Taurilian Army. He wrote the Warrior Code of Korhal which set rules for armed conflicts. He was executed by his brother Drukhor for cowardice when he counseled surrender to the armies of Tawkin. He is one of the only Vekh who is regarded as a hero in the Melandarim tradition.

Kullion (KOO lee ON): River that begins in the Hyrnistia mountains, flowing eastward along the northern border of Belorin, and then turns north into the Sea-Lake of Cith. Near its mouth, the river cuts through a deep canyon called the Thunya.

Kurlen (KUR len): Karolian province along the eastern bank of the Elgolin River, south of Saringon. It includes the lower Vestelin River and the entire Garnengen Swamps. Originally, Kurlen was the name for all the lowlands between the lower Elgolin and the Merneg Hills.

Kryna (KREE na): Woman of pure Taurilian descent, of House Atlan (born in 2729). She lives in Sorwail and works as a translator for her uncle, Braedil.

kyusi **(keye oo see)**: Roj Zindori word for "naïve child".

League: Unit of distance in Karolia, representing an easy day's travel by foot. It is equivalent to 26 kilometers or 16 miles. Shorter distances are measured in league-tenths.

Lohann (loh 'AN): Young Karolian man from the northern townships of Saringon province (born in 2776). He is an army recruit.

Loriah (lor EYE ah): Beautiful Karolian woman of House Athercen (born in 2753). Her hometown is Halidorn. She now lives in Tanvilon and is married to Maryk. She is Dyrk's mother and has four other children.

Lorin River (LOR in): A west-flowing tributary of the Kullion River with its headwaters in Feldar. The Lorin River is known to some as the "Poison River" because of the poisonous plants that grow in places along its southern banks.

Lormost (LOR most): A province of Karolia, along the south banks of the Nistellion and east banks of the Elgolin River.

Loth Bevren (LOTH BEV rən): Karolian frontier province at its northwestern extreme. Its provincial seat is a small city of the same name.

Loth Tund (LOTH TUND): An independent region on the western shores of the Sea-Lake of Cith, east of the Korlani Mountains. It is sparsely populated, mostly by Hajrekh.

Loth Torud (LOTH TOR əd): Literally, "Shores of the Void" in Melandarim. Loth Torud is the easternmost extremity of the land of Verania. It is often used in Karolian conversation as a way to say, "as far as humanly possible".

Lunnah (LOO na): Historical person (399-746). She was the eldest daughter of Melandar, and the subject of several prophecies. She originally married a son of Cormuthan named Julin, who died in an attempt to rescue Tawkin from captivity. After her father repented, and Lunnah went into exile, she married Tawkin. Later, when Tawkin became king of a re-conquered Tauril, she became its queen. She is the mother of Teren and the adoptive mother of Atlan. She is an icon of beauty and wisdom among women in the Melandarim tradition.

Lyrus, House of (LIRE us): The name of a Karolian house, part of the Houses of Rulers grouping. Lyrus was also an important historical figure (418-709). He was a lesser commander under Korhal in Drukudar's army. During the War of Cleansing, he defected to Tawkin's forces along with all of his men when Korhal was executed. Though he remained a Vekh, Lyrus became Tawkin's chief army officer after the war. His descendants married into the Taurilian peoples and were thereafter free from the plague. Lyrus is one of only five Karolian houses that are descended from Vekh. In Karolia, the head of all armed forces was traditionally selected from the House of Lyrus.

Lyssia (LIS see a): A small realm that encompasses the heart of what was the Himn empire, on the banks of the Paellion River near the Hyrnistia mountains. It is ruled by an oligarchy, a small group of wealthy merchant families. Its people are mostly Derrekh but there is a sizeable minority of Karolians. It has been allied with Karolia for its entire existence.

Madwin, Thur (MAD win): Karolian Eratur of House Ithniar (born in 2749). He is assigned as the Headman for Tanvilon. He is named after a historical person, the heir of the kingdom of Azenvar, who led a campaign to reconquer the land from the demon-captain Drumeth, but was killed in the final battle.

Mar Athel (MAR a THEL): Karolian town in the midst of the Rodakt Hills. It is the provincial seat of Rodakt.

Mar Vallin (MAR VAL lin): Port village on the west bank of the Elgolin River, a league-tenth north of Altyren.

Maryk (MAIR ik): Former Eratur of House Teren (born in 2749). He is the son of Dyareth. He now lives in Tanvilon as a breeder and trainer of war-horses. He retired from duty when his foot was maimed in the Battle of Rocavion. He is married to Loriah and is the father of Dyrk, Gavon, Elora, Hanni, and Plessa. His hometown is Caemryn Sur. Though he is a member of the ruling house, he is about as distantly related to the royal family as possible.

Melandar (ME lan dar): Historical person (290-601). He was the second son of Tuin, who was the first king of historical record in Tauril. Melandar participated in the murder of his father but later repented, beginning a religious revival. Those who followed him were healed from the disease that was turning them into Vekh, leaving them all with colourless grey skin. Melandar sent his people into exile, sacrificing himself into captivity to protect their escape. Some of the exiles traveled east and established the kingdom of Verania, while others, led by Tawkin, remained in Azenvar. Melandar was later released and rejoined Tawkin's people before his death. He was credited with the invention of writing. The written language of that period, preserved through his writing, is called the Melandarim language. He also compiled and authored many religious books that are held as sacred scriptures by the Karolians and many other societies. Melandar was the father of one son, Derylan, who died without heir, and three daughters, Lunnah, Kannah, and Rania.

Melandarim (ME lan DAIR im): The original language of Tauril that was recorded by Melandar in writing. It is still used in Karolia as a religious and official language. It is also the precursor of many other languages, including River-Tongue, Bay-Tongue, Belorin, and Vekh. It can also refer to the religion built around the writings of Melandar, which is practiced in various forms by many nations, most prominently in a strict manner in Karolia.

Melikar (MEL i KAR): The name of a Karolian house, part of the Houses of Rulers grouping. According to Melandarim history, Melikar was the son of Melphar and Rania, and a grandson of Melandar.

Melphar (MEL far): Historical person (424-736). He was a son-in-law of Melandar. He befriended the people that would later become the Belorin race. Belorin himself was his grandson. The Karolian house of Melikar descends from him.

Midrim (MID rim): Vast mountainous area north of Rasp, northeast of Tauril. It contains some of the tallest peaks in Reldaan. It is sparsely inhabited by Vekh.

Mithra (MITH ra): Karolian girl (born 2793). She is Neriah's sister, the seventh living child of Vecton and Ryesse.

Muralah (mər AL a): Historical person (714-982). She was a daughter of Teren.

Nabir (na BEER): Bondservant of Derrekh descent. He serves Maryk and lives in Tanvilon. He is married to Karam and has a son named Hagris.

Naen Ambron (NAY ən AM bron): Fortress and provincial seat in Gel Bern, along the Ulovian River.

Naen Ebrov (NAY ən EEB rov): Fortress on the west bank of the Elgolin River, a half-league north of Altyren.

Naethin (NAY ə THIN): Veteran cavalry soldier of Karolian descent, from House Kromar. He is part of the Saringon Cavalry Reserves.

Naraven (NAIR a VIN): Karolian province on the west bank of the Elgolin River, south of the province of Teren. It extends well into the Korlani Mountains along the Talvion and Rytarion rivers.

Narval (NAR val): A region of moors and sparse forest. It is bounded on the north by the Sea-Lake of Cith, on the west by the Paellion River, on the east by the Kullion River, and on the south by Arghand. It is sparsely populated by Derrekh peoples and has no central government.

Navren Altyr (NAV ren al TIRE): Literally, "Across from Altyren" in Melandarim. Karolian city on the east bank of the Elgolin River, just across from Altyren.

Nedrin (NEE drin): Seventh Servant of the Melandarim religion. Nedrin protected the first Mothers and Fathers from evil Seraphs. He instructed the early peoples on how to keep themselves safe from physical and spiritual threats. He is the patron Servant of soldiers. His Festival of the New Earth marks the closing of the calendar in late autumn, only a few weeks before the beginning of the next year. This festival is highly symbolic, giving a picture of what heaven might be like, in which people are not separated by wealth or status.

Neriah (nər EYE ah): Young Karolian woman of House Binev (born in 2775). She is the eldest living daughter of Vecton and Ryesse. Her hometown is Harwaith.

Nethariem (neth AR ee əm): A race of large, black-skinned humans in Melandar's histories. In early days, they migrated into the East and out of most tales. A few turned back into the service of the Vekh; the same discoloration came upon their bodies, and they became known as the Androkar.

Nistellion River (nis TEL ee on): Non-navigable river in central Karolia which flows westward into the Elgolin. It forms the border between Kurlen and Lormost provinces.

Obragdon (OH brah DAHN): A Seraph.

Omrid (AHM rid): A land at the northwest arm of the Sea-Lake of Cith, extending north into the plateaus and boreal forests. It is extensively colonized by Vekh. It is also the name of a historical empire that conquered much land to the south and east, including Kardumagund, Anduk, Trobes, Loth Tund, Grevana, Narval, and present-day Karolia. It had reached its zenith by the time Treon retook Karolia, and continued its decline as Karolia grew. At the present day, the empire has devolved into a loose tribal federation, though it has a combined population that nearly rivals Karolia.

Pace: Unit of length in Karolia. The pace is derived from the stride of a fully-grown Karolian man, and it is roughly equivalent to the metric meter.

Pedriath (ped REYE əth): Historical person (402-721). Pedriath was a prominent man in Melandar's court. He was assumed by all to be Melandar's successor and the logical suitor of Melandar's widowed daughter Lunnah. Upon Pedriath's appointment to lead the Eastern Exiles, Pedriath asked for Lunnah's hand in marriage, but she refused. Pedriath became the first king of Verania and the father of its royal house.

Pej Zindori (PEJ): A race of steppe-dwellers who originally inhabited the lands of Belorin and Arghand. Unlike the other Zindori, they are not adept in the ways of warfare. They were oppressed by other Zindori, and had a mixed relationship with the kingdom of Belorin. To this day, some Pej still live in isolated communities throughout Arghand, Belorin, and Feldar. The only city that can truly be said to have a sizeable proportion of Pej Zindori is Dharbur. Pej Zindori are, in general, short and squat, with dark skin and black hair. They are hardy pioneers but do not form large societies or embrace technology. Many Pej Zindori can be found as slaves among the richer Roj or Sej households.

Plessa (PLESS a): Pre-teen girl of Karolian descent (born in 2785). She is the daughter of Maryk and Loriah, the youngest sister of Dyrk.

Powerstone: A legendary artifact in the Melandarim histories that came into the possession of Kythaldar, the third son of Tuin. The artifact was said to give Kythaldar far-seeing powers, over distances and through time. Kythaldar became obsessed with the object and his sanity suffered as a result.

Raider Wars: A series of conflicts between 2706 and 2733. Roj Zindori of the Kuz Steppe attacked lands to the east and north, including Rhonaur, Ancharith, and the Bajzin of Dedarrek. After twenty-five years of continued warfare, Karolia entered the war on the side of Ancharith and brought it to a swift end, forcing the Roj to surrender all of the territory they had annexed.

Raiders: A common name for Roj Zindori warriors of the Wakin clan who come from the Kuz Steppe. Due to their warlike culture, Raiders are always fighting. If they are not raiding their neighbors, they often hire themselves out to other nations.

Rania (RAY nee a): Historical person (412-731). The youngest daughter of Melandar, Rania married Melphar and was the grandmother of Belorin. She is a symbol of carefree joy among women in the Melandarim tradition.

Rasp (RASP): A basin east of Tauril in which the Thaeron river and its many tributaries flow. It is densely forested. Though it isn't a tropical area, it is often called a jungle. It is nearly uninhabited.

Rayve (RAY vee): A teenage Karolian boy of house Melikar (born in 2782). His hometown is Altyren.

Reldaan (REL da ən): The name for the entire known world.

Remah (REE ma): Historical person (1170-1422). She was Eldorin's wife and the mother of Esdarion and Esmarin. She is credited with rebuking her husband when he despaired of his calling, threatening to take it upon herself to see that it was accomplished. Upon the murder of her husband in Karolia, she ruled the kingdom for a short time, through a male regent, until her surviving son returned. She is regarded as a symbol of assertiveness and resourcefulness among women in the Melandarim tradition. A large lake near the city of Resgild is named after her.

Reylas (RAY ə lus): Historical person (602-933). She was the wife of Teren and the mother of nine children. She is a symbol of fertility and desirability among women in the Melandarim tradition.

Rhomakhiem (rroh MA khee EM): Literally, "Unspoiled Men" in Melandarim. All men who departed from Tauril before the plague transformed them into Vekh fall into this broad category. Taurilians, Karolians, and Veranians are not classified as Rhomakhiem since they have Vekh ancestors. The Derrekh, Farrakh, Warrikh, Hajrekh, Zindori, and Daxonites are all Rhomakhiem.

Rhov-Attan (RHOWV at TAN): Literally, "Summer Festival", it is the festival dedicated to the Servant Valeron just prior to the summer solstice. Other than the New Year celebrations, it is the highlight of the Karolian calendar. Province-wide events take place in every provincial capital, including the Contest of the Squires.

Rianast (REYE a NAST): Karolian province along the east bank of the Elgolin River, just north of Altyren. Its provincial seat is Gel Sonest.

River-Tongue: A common language based on a Warrikh dialect, but with much influence from the Melandarim language. It is the language of business and conversation in Karolia and many of the surrounding nations.

Roj Zindori (ROJ): A race of desert-dwellers who originally inhabited the northern reaches of the Sea of Sand. They have spread across the eastern edges of that great desert. Though they are small in number compared to the Sej and Kaj, the Roj are well-known for their warlike nature. The Kuz Steppe, well south of Karolia, is their homeland, but they have many trading colonies in other lands. When they are not raiding for themselves, Roj warriors regularly hire themselves out to other nations. The distinctive red cloaks of their mercenary armies, connected to their habitual raiding, have earned them the common name of "Raiders". Roj Zindori are of average height, but prize slimness and agility in both men and women. They are superb bowmen and light cavalry.

Rolan (ROHL an): Most famous of Belorin kings (938-1228). He was the youngest son of Balan and not in line for the throne. Before he was of fighting age, he disguised himself and went into battle against an army of rebels. He was captured and sold as a slave. He served a Roj master faithfully for thirty years in the Kuz Steppe to gain his freedom. Upon his return to his homeland, he began a war against the rebels that his father refused to fight, liberating most of Belorin. The people forsook Balan and followed Rolan as their king, who ruled for more than two hundred years. Rolan was the only king to openly defy the Empire of Tunakhel in the War of Loyalty and defeat the invading Imperial armies.

rothai **(rah THAY 'ə)**: Melandarim word for "replacement", evil tense. It is similar to saying that something is a poor substitute.

Rothell (rah THELL): Belorin horsewoman (born in 2743), the wife of Koeric.

Rovenhall (ROW vən HAHL): Village on the Great East Road in eastern Saringon; a popular rest stop for travelers along the international road.

Ruthlin (ROOTH lin): Historical figure (405-621). He was the son-in-law of Melandar. He was one of Tawkin's closest companions. He founded the kingdom of Azenvar, and all its subsequent kings descended from him. He was slain during the War of Cleansing.

Ryesse (reye ES ə): Karolian woman (born in 2750). She is the wife of Vecton and mother of Neriah and six other children.

Rynek (REYE nek): A realm in a mountainous region southeast of Karolia and south of Lyssia. It is a loose federation of tribes and city-states. Most people who live there are either full-blooded Derrekh, or a mixture of the Derrekh and Karolian races that are usually referred to as "Rynekar".

Rytar (REYE tar): Historical figure (1220-1490). He was Eldorin's chief military strategist and naval officer. He was from House Lyrus. The greatest bridge in Karolia, connecting the island of Altyren with the western shore, was named after him.

Saris (SAIR iss): A seemingly young Belorin horsewoman (born in 2750). She was adopted into the household of Koeric and Rothell. She has unusual white hair.

Sashay (sə SHAY): Karolian girl (born 2783). She is Neriah's sister, the third living child of Vecton and Ryesse.

Sea of Sand: A wide expanse of trackless desert, beginning at the Mountains of Avrikhan and extending hundreds of leagues to the west. Only the eastern marches are truly a lifeless sea of sand dunes. As one moves west, into Kuz and Rhonaur, it turns into an arid wasteland with scattered vegetation. Nevertheless, the name is used for the entire region.

Sej Zindori (SEJ): A race of subtropical peoples who inhabit the southern edges of the Sea of Sand. "Sej Zindori" is a blanket term that northern lands give to any Zindori that comes from the other side of the Sea of Sand. In reality, the Sej are diverse and can claim to be made up of several races, numbering millions of people. The empire of Corsava comes regularly into contact with Karolians, but otherwise the Sej has little to do with the northern nations. In general, the Sej are smaller and slighter than Karolians, with moderate-colored skin and hair, but there is much variation amongst this large category.

Seraph (SAIR əf): A spiritual being from Melandarim legend. Originally, Seraphs were all ministering servants of Arren, and were able to take on their own physical form to interact with humans. This ability was lost during the Great Burning, when most Seraphs were called to heaven to minister directly to Arren, while those who rebelled were forced to forsake their earthly bodies to survive. Evil Seraphs are said to wander about the spiritual plane aimlessly, searching for a body to inhabit. Seraphs who inhabit animals grant extraordinary abilities to that animal (see Gryphon). Likewise, humans who willingly give themselves up to a Seraph gain supernatural powers but are said to be enslaved to the Seraph's will. Melandarim legend states that all evil Seraphs are loosely subordinated to a prime Seraph named Morthuldan.

Servant: In Melandarim history, seven good Seraphs identified themselves to early men and assisted them in building homes, planting fields, caring for the sick, and defending themselves. These Seraphs were called the Servants and are hallowed by the followers of Melandar's religion to this day. The seven Servants are, in order: Kemantar, Anakdatar, Harophin, Valeron, Telmanitar, Taephin, and Nedrin.

Siven, Sea of (SEYE ven): Gulf of water in the east, bordered by Caldera on the west, Verania on the north, Berce on the east, and Drimugari on the south.

Sojourn: Also "Sojourn of Treon", the Sojourn is the forty-year ordeal suffered by Treon and the remnants of Eldorin's exiles to re-establish the realm of Karolia. It began in the year 2326. Their chief opponent was the Vekh of Omrid. Treon's son Tuleon became the first king of modern-day Karolia, his coronation marking the end of the Sojourn.

Sojourn of the Ancients: An eight-day journey undertaken by military recruits of Karolia, intended to re-enact certain elements of the Sojourn of Treon. The intent of this tradition is to impress upon young men of Karolia the hardships and suffering that was necessary to establish the nation. The Sojourn begins in Mar Athel, passes through Anderrol, and ends in Perrin Ambron. Along the way are seven memorials, marking different phases of the Sojourn. Traditionally, the Sojourn was done on foot, carrying all necessary supplies for the entire journey. One phase, which passes through a swampy region, was to be done while fasting for thirty-six hours. At the present day, Sojourners typically avail themselves of inns, restaurants, and mounts, and rarely observe the fast.

tanakh **(TAN akh)**: Melandarim word for "thunder", good tense.

Taephin (TAY ə fin): The sixth Servant of the Melandarim religion. Taephin instructed the early peoples in healing, fertility, and childbirth. He is the patron Servant at weddings. Priests of Taephin in Karolia are trained as physicians. His Festival of Harvest is in mid-autumn.

Talisman (TAL iz man): Retired Eratur of Karolia (born in 2698). He was the Rector of the College of Eraturs until his retirement. Now he is an advisor to his younger brother, King Adareoth. He is the father of Prince Amarion.

Talthor (TAL THOR): Historical person (830-1144). King of Tauril and grandson of Teren. Talthor is blamed for the departure of Tauril from the laws of Melandar. He allied his nation with the Vekh and fought against Azenvar and Belorin. He was assassinated by one of his generals, Rybar, and all of his descendants were exterminated.

Tanvilon (TAN vəl ON): Unassuming village in the hills of northeastern Saringon province. It is not on any major thoroughfares, though it is close to the Great East Road.

Taristan (TAIR is tan): Emeritus Monarch of Karolia (born in 2701). He was king for nearly two decades, but he became increasingly infirm because of his war-time injuries. He abdicated the throne when he could no longer walk. His younger brother Adareoth is now king.

Tarn: A lizard-like flying creature that is about the size of a small horse. Domesticated tarns can carry riders, though riding tarns is a hazardous endeavor.

Tauril (TAY ər il): A land and historical kingdom in the east, widely believed to be the cradle of civilization. The realm was destroyed in Eldorin's day, first by the armies of Kardumagund, and then by a massive volcanic cataclysm.

Taurilian (TAY ər IL ee ahn): People descended from the followers of Melandar, who were originally Vekh but were cleansed from the discoloration. Their skin is a colourless light grey. Pure Taurilians, who are very rare at present day, have a long lifespan, in excess of two hundred years. Many races have traces of Karolian blood, which extends their lifespan according to the strength of Taurilian descent. Karolians and Veranians are regarded in particular as being nearly half-Taurilian.

Tawkin (TAW kin): Historical person (471-751). He was a foreigner in Melandar's day, one of the Rhomakhiem of the northern tundra. He won the favour of many with amazing feats of strength and fortitude, even after losing his right hand and left eye. He was the second to bear the flaming Crillslayer, and he used it to slay the King of the Crills who was ravaging Melandar's house. In doing so, he saved an infant boy, Atlan. Later, he married Melandar's widowed daughter Lunnah, and upon the reconquest of Tauril he became its king. He is the father of Teren, and the adoptive father of Atlan.

Telmanitar (TEL MAN i tar): The fifth Servant of the Melandarim religion. Telmanitar instructed the people concerning water, whether it was digging wells, constructing boats, or predicting the weather. Telmanitar was also said to be present at the death of every person who is faithful to Arren, to bear their souls to heaven. He is the patron Servant at funerals. Priests of the Order of Telmanitar comfort the grieving and dying, and are entrusted with the care of cemeteries. Telmanitar's Festival of the Fountain is towards the end of summer.

Ter-Athel (TAIR a THEL): Historical person (1004-1346). He was a great-grandson of Teren. He first rose to prominence during the War of Loyalty when he was falsely accused of treason by King Talthor, his uncle, and abandoned to the dungeons of the Vekh empire of Tunakhel. There, Ter-Athel and his companions, called the Twelve, were blessed by the Servant Anakdatar. They escaped their prison and had a hand in the rise and fall of many kings and emperors over the coming years. The Twelve were given white hair to denote their status. After their calling was complete, the Twelve retired with their families to the forests of Feldar, living apart from other races. Thereafter their descendants were known as the Alwem. Ter-Athel returned in his old age to Tauril to prophecy its destruction and instruct Eldorin to seek exile with all who would follow in Karolia.

Teren (TAIR en): Historical person (579-891). He was the only son of Tawkin and Melandar's daughter Lunnah. He was a faithful king over Tauril for many years. He is regarded by Karolian historians as the true heir of Melandar.

Teren, House of (TAIR en): The royal house of Karolia, within the Houses of Rulers grouping. All kings and Crown Princes must come from the House of Teren. The house is also the subject of many of Melandar's prophecies.

Teren, Province of (TAIR en): A province on the west bank of the Elgolin River bordering the capital city of Altyren. Its provincial seat is the riverside town of Berhimmon.

Tevledain (TEV lə dain): A war-horse of exceptional size and strength. Tevledain war-horses have excellent instincts in battle, but tire quickly, and cannot be ridden for long distances.

Thalnuris (thal NUURR is): A Seraph.

Therdan (thər dan): First Crown Prince and Lord of Altyren (born in 2750). He is of House Teren. Therdan is trained as a Priest of Kemantar and was given the honorary title of Eratur. He is the only son of King Adareoth.

Thunya (THUN ya): A canyon near Keor through which the Kullion River passes. The canyon is very deep; the bridge at Keor is the only crossing for several leagues.

thur **(thər):** Melandarim title for a representative of the king, good tense. All Eraturs in royal or provincial service inherit this title.

Torrin (TOR in): Young full-blooded Taurilian man from House Atlan, son of Paldonn (born in 2755). He ages much slower than most races (see Taurilian). He grew up in Dar-Amund. He has no defined profession, though he was trained as a mounted warrior, a scholar, and a bricklayer.

Trebier (TREB ee ər): Karolian military training base and shipyard on the southern extent of the islands upon which Altyren is built.

Treon (TREE ahn): Historical person of the House of Teren (2222-2368). He was heir to the throne of Kaderish, a small subject realm of the Himn empire. Upon a spiritual awakening cultivated by his companion Alerion, Treon negotiated a promise of non-intervention from the Himn before embarking upon an epic conquest of Karolia from the forces of the Omrid Vekh. The wars, travels, and hardships that Treon led the people through was afterwards called the Sojourn. After forty years, his people had reconquered enough territory to officially declare Karolia re-born, but Treon was mortally wounded in the final battle. He was succeeded by his son, Tuleon.

Tuin (TOO in): Historical person (229-480). He was the first king of record and reigned over the land of Tauril. He was the first to have wielded a sword that flamed, the Crillslayer, a symbol of divine authority. He was murdered by three of his sons who lusted for power, one of whom was Melandar.

Tular (TOO lar): Historical person of Karolian legend (1981-2044). He was from House Teren. According to myth, his entire family was eradicated, presumably by Kharon. Tular set out in pursuit of Kharon who had taken his young niece as captive. He stayed amongst a colony of Taurilian exiles on the shores of the lake named Wallen Gurs, just long enough to marry and father a son. He continued his pursuit but was slain by Kharon. His son, Rulen, was the last living male heir of Eldorin's line, and was eventually the great-great-grandfather of Treon.

Tuleon (TOO lee on): Historical person of the House of Teren (2295-2433). He was Treon's son and was crowned king of Karolia upon his father's death. He led Karolia through constant wars with the Omrid Vekh, steadily expanding its borders. His son Eloren reigned after him.

Tunakhel (TOO nə KHEL): Refers both to the land around

the Marolin river valley and an ancient Vekh empire that was centered on that land. The empire was destroyed by Kardumagund in the War of Desolation, the same war that eradicated Tauril. Thereafter, the land was incorporated under the authority of Anduk.

Tyrilion River (teye RIL ee on): River in southern Karolia, much of it forms the south border of the realm. The lands south of the river are known as Dedarrek. It flows from Rynek until it joins the Elgolin River.

Unspoiled Men: See Rhomakhiem.

Urdipanior (URR di PAN yor): A Seraph.

Vaezur (VAY ə ZOOR): Historical person (born around 1000, slain in 1381). He was the leader of the four demon-captains in Melandarim legend who led the armies that destroyed Tauril. Vaezur pursued Eldorin's exiles but was slain by Eldorin's son Esdarion.

Valeron (VAL ə rahn): The fourth Servant of the Melandarim religion. Valeron is known as the Wandering Servant, sweeping through the open sky and gazing at the land and seas below. He is said to guide the heavenly lights in their courses. Valeron helped the early peoples explore their lands. His Festival, the Rhov-Attan, is at the beginning of summer and is the highlight of the year. His priests are cartographers, astronomers, and official time-keepers.

Vecton (VEK tahn): Karolian wainwright of House Binev (born in 2744). He lives in Harwaith. He is married to Ryesse; they are the parents of Neriah and six other children.

Vekh (VEKH): A race of humans who are said to be descendent from the original Taurilians that did not heed Melandar's call to repent. The colour of their skin is a sickly grey-green, and birthmarks are very visible, leading many to conclude that they are diseased. They are generally stocky or wiry, but not tall. Their lifespan is short, rarely exceeding fifty years. They become adults at twelve. They speak their own language, which has some minor differences between the various tribes, nations, and federations of Vekh, but is distantly based on the Melandarim language. For the most part, they have remained at war with all other non-Vekh nations, and frequently fight amongst themselves.

Vestelin River (VES təl in): River in central Karolia, beginning at the Wallen Perthez lakes, flowing through Vestellia province and into the Garnengen swamps. The lower Vestelin, which flows from the swamps eastward to the Elgolin, is navigable.

Verania (vər AN ee a): A realm far to the east, along the shores of the Sea of Siven, that was colonized by exiles of Melandar's repentance. The kingdom has gone through several political upheavals and wars against the Vekh of Drimugari, but it has survived to this day. It is only a fraction of the size and prosperity of Karolia, but has become an important trading partner, despite the distance.

Veranian (ver AN ee an): Inhabitants of Verania, who were originally pure Taurilians but mingled over the years with native Daxonites. They have a lifespan similar to the Karolians. They speak a language called Bay-Tongue, which is a fusion of Melandarim and a native Daxonite dialect.

Verse Paper: Rough, low-quality paper cut in five-inch squares. The paper is not of sufficient quality for use with ink. Verse papers are typically used to write religious petitions in the Melandarim religion, using a black charcoal pencil. Petitions, once they are written, are folded and burned, either in a lamp or a fire, to symbolize both their spiritual recipient and the sacrificial nature of the act.

Vigheran (vigh ər un): Independent mercenary of Roj Zindori descent (born in 2758).

Vilinar (VIL i NAR): Karolian naval outpost built on an island in the southwestern arm of the Sea-Lake of Cith, just across from the city of Bevren.

Voren (VOR ən): Karolian boy (born 2785). He is Neriah's brother, the fourth living child of Vecton and Ryesse.

Vynek (VEYE nek): Historical person (born around 1050, slain in 1455). He was one of the four demon-captains in Melandarim legend who led the armies that destroyed Tauril. He personally pursued Avareon but could not overcome him. He was eventually defeated by Esdarion before the gates of Keor.

War of Chaos: Occurred between 1648 and 1731. Azenvar was occupied by an alliance of the Vekh under Drumeth and a usurper named Talfod. The rightful king, Taerfin, and his son Madwin led the resistance for nearly a hundred years, finally liberating the entire land, with the exception of the fortress of Delvaeth. Drumeth was driven off the cliffs of the Thunya and never seen again.

War of Cleansing: Occurred in 621. Tawkin and Ruthlin lead their forces in reconquest of Tauril from Drukhor. Korhal, who led Drukhor's armies, beseeched his brother the king to submit to Tawkin to avoid bloodshed. Drukhor responded by executing Korhal as a punishment for weakness. This galvanized many of Drukhor's Vekh armies to fight on Tawkin's behalf. Thaedin of the Nethariem also arrived to lend Tawkin assistance. In the end, Tawkin and his allies were victorious, and Drukhor was slain. Ruthlin, however, was killed in the fighting.

War of Desolation: Occurred in 1348. Kardumagund's four Demon-Captains led the Vekh hordes in the ravaging of Tauril. Eldorin of Teren's House escaped with several hundred survivors and founded the realm of Karolia. Shortly after the conquest was complete, Tauril was eradicated by a massive volcanic conflagration. Avareon of Atlan's House survived the cataclysm, carrying the Books of Melandar to safety in Azenvar.

War of Kalthund: The first international war of recorded history, occurring from 530 to 531. Tauril invaded the land of Kalthund to exploit its resources and enslave its people.

War of Kings: Occurred over the years of 596 to 603. Upon the death of King Drukudar, a succession crisis amongst his sons erupted in war. The youngest, Korudar, was first to set himself up as king, but was killed by Drudor. Drudor in turn was defeated and slain by Drukhor.

War of Loyalty: Occurred from 1135 to 1145. The Vekh empire of Tunakhel and its vassal Tauril invaded and conquered Azenvar, but were defeated upon invading Belorin. Ter-Athel and the fathers of the Alwem intervened to free the king of Azenvar and restore his throne. The king of Tauril, Talthor, was assassinated by his own general, Rybar, who took the throne and put an end to the war. This war solidified Tauril as an apostate nation; many prophecies warned of its eventual destruction if it did not reform.

War of Sands: Occurred from 1190 to 1198. The conflict was between Belorin and the Roj Zindori who were encroaching on Belorin's territory from the south. The war ended with Roj-occupied Dharbur being razed to the ground, and the area resettled by Pej Zindori who had allied with Belorin.

War of the First Sundering: Occurred in 490. Drukudar sent his armies to expel his youngest brother, Nethudar, and the people that followed him from Tauril. Nethudar and his sons Naedur and Nerhath died in the fighting. Nethudar's remaining people became the Nethariem, and those who turned back to join Drukudar became the Androkar. Due to his brutality in prosecuting the war, Drukudar's eldest son Drudor was deposed as crown prince.

War of the Second Sundering: Occurred in 555. Drukudar sent his armies to capture his brother Melandar and eradicate his followers, who pledged to serve Arren and rebel from Drukudar's rule. The war caused two groups of exiles to flee. The first, under Pedriath, traveled to the East and founded the nation of Verania. The second, under Tawkin and Ruthlin, crossed the Istrith, built Dar-Amund, and established the kingdom of Azenvar. Melandar was captured as he protected their escape.

Ward: A grouping of people into a political unit of about 300-600 persons. This may be a rural area, an entire village, or a part of a town or city. Each ward maintains a public tavern for religious events, civic functions, and caring for the poor.

Warrikh (war EEKH): Literally, "Men of the Forest" in Melandarim. The Warrikh are a race of Unspoiled Men who inhabited the lands about the Elgolin before the Karolians came. Most have intermingled with the Karolians over the years, but a few have kept to their own bloodlines. Their native language has nearly disappeared, swallowed up by the River-Tongue language. Warrikh differ greatly from tribe to tribe in physical appearance. Some groups such as the Naniv are small in stature and have light skin and blond hair. The Vadsen are very tall, with moderate skin and red hair. The Eynekhiem of the south are again smaller in stature, with darker skin and hair.

Winds, Sea of: An ocean between Feldar and Drimugari. It is constantly beset by violent storms for much of the year, along a north-west track that sends the storms through the Istrith River valley and into the Sea-Lake of Cith. Despite the dangers, many traders ply the Sea of Winds, carrying precious cargoes as far as Karolia, Corsava, and Verania.

Zered (ZAIR ed): The current Vekh leader of the nation of Anduk. He formed an alliance with both Kardumagund and representatives of the Omrid tribes, declaring himself the Emperor of the Vekh and launching a successful campaign of conquest against the Karolian colonists of Azenvar.

Zindori (zin DOR eye): Literally, "From the Desert" in Melandarim. The Zindori are a broad grouping of peoples that inhabit the drier lands of southern Reldaan. They originally inhabited much of what is now known as Belorin, but over the years colonized vast expanses of land to the south of the Sea of Sand. They are roughly divided into four groups, the Pej, Roj, Sej, and Kaj Zindori. The Hajrekh are also closely related.

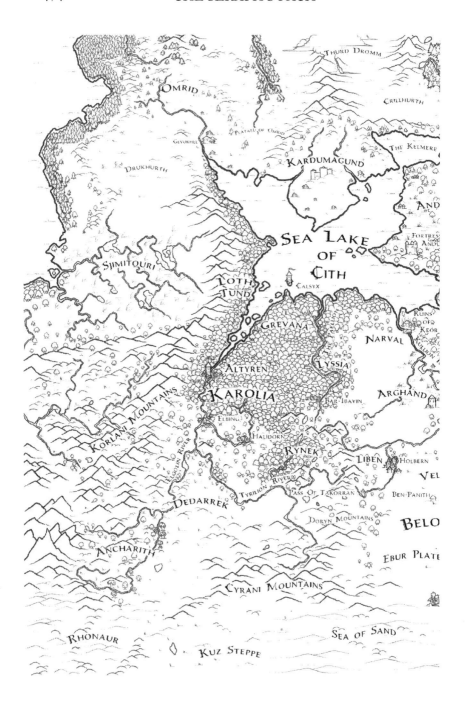

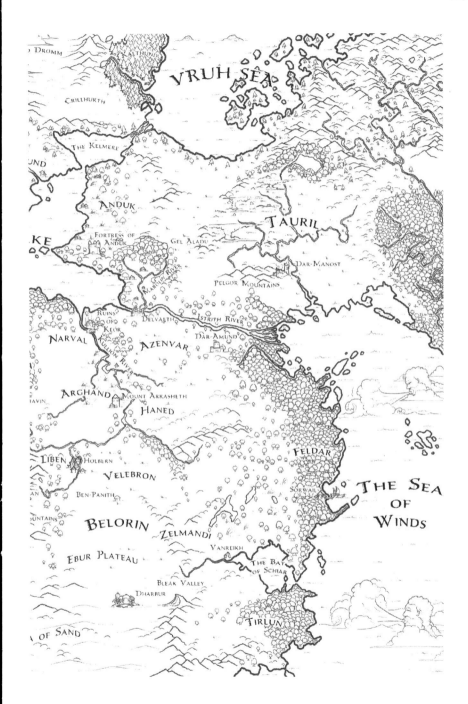

Made in the USA
San Bernardino, CA
12 January 2020

63076315R00290